Ask Me
About
My Bombshells

Also by Robert Barclay

Non-fiction

The Art of the Trumpet-maker
The Preservation and Use of Historic Musical Instruments

Fiction

Triple Take: A Museum Story
Death at the Podium

Cover art by Loose Cannon Designs

Photo of fireworks courtesy of Trelawney Fireworks, 2012

Ask Me About My Bombshells

Robert Barclay

LOOSE CANNON PRESS

LIBRARY AND ARCHIVES CANADA CATALOGUING IN PUBLICATION

Barclay, R. L. (Robert L.), author
Ask me about my bombshells / Robert Barclay.
ISBN 978-0-9936881-0-2 (pbk.)
I. Title.
PS8603.A7244A75 2014   C813'.6   C2014-900635-7

Published by
LOOSE CANNON PRESS

loosecannonpress@gmail.com
www.loosecannonpress.com

iv

Table of Contents

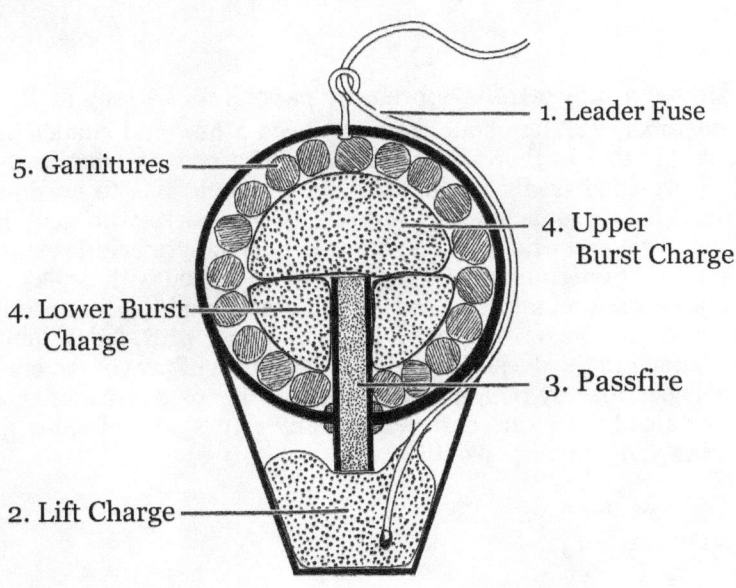

1. Leader Fuse

5. Garnitures

4. Upper Burst Charge

4. Lower Burst Charge

3. Passfire

2. Lift Charge

Note to the Reader

This is a work of fiction. The characters are all products of the author's imagination and any resemblance to real persons living or dead is not intended. Although many of the places described exist, all the incidents, actions and other aspects of the storyline are fictitious.

Acknowledgements

Although fireworks have been my passion for as long as I can remember, writing about them has been a new and challenging task. My thanks therefore go to those who read the manuscript and provided feedback. In particular, I would like to acknowledge Michael Bohonos of Garden City Fireworks who gave his time freely and who provided many details of pyrotechnic exhibition. CID Superintendent Tyrus Cameron helped with aspects of police structure, and Zac and Anna Ezekiel read the manuscript with kindly but critical eyes. My wife Janet provided valuable insights into the deeper thoughts and feelings of my characters. I apologize for any omissions. In spite of the good work of these few named reviewers and helpers, any errors or omissions are still entirely my responsibility.

Robert Barclay
Ottawa 2014

Chapter One
The Leader Fuse

The length of quick match attached to a fireworks article. The quick match is a fast-burning fuse made of black powder encased in a loose-fitting paper
Display Fireworks Manual, Natural Resources Canada (2010)

Emilio Pastorelli relaxed his old frame into his favourite chair by the record player, cup of dark Italian coffee in his hand. Eighty-two was just too goddamn old and he kind of wondered why the good God hadn't called him away yet. His sweet Alicia was... wherever we went... and Roberto too, and much too young. It's a horrible judgment to linger on this earth when your wife and your only son are both gone. All he had to live for now was his daughter-in-law Maria and the success of Pastorelli Fireworks in the hands of his grandson Rocco.

He closed his tired old eyes, recalling the stories around the kitchen table back when he was a kid. Tales of the *Risorgimento* when all Italy was on fire—the valiant struggles of Camillo Cavour and Victor Emmanuel and the great Garibaldi—but much, much more than that, the stories of the fabled fireworks. Those fabulous times when his *nonno, il patriarca*, spoke of such *fuochi d'artificio* as never seen before. Such celebrations! *Mio Dio*, it was Italians who invented fireworks! Sure there had been fireworks for centuries before that, but they were pale, *monocromatico* until Italians had invented colour! Who else in the whole world *could* invent colour? It had to be the Italians. With their supreme skill and age-old knowledge these Raphaels and Titians of the fire-craft had combined the rare earths and the burning powders to create a palette of azure, emerald, ruby, sapphire and pure, pure gold. Six generations of the Pastorellis had been mixing and forming these wonders of light and fire and magic...

But now... Here, today...

Ah, Rocco. Only 27 years old; too goddamn young to be running the whole thing. Emilio had trained him the best he could, but the age gap was so wide, and the experience so hard to gain. And at 82 the energy simply wasn't there any more. The entire

1

Pastorelli fortune in two young, untried hands. If only Roberto...

He took a long mouthful of coffee, trying to throw off the negative thoughts, but against his will he found himself remembering the bad times. The time of the *Fascisti*–Mussolini's terrible reign and the German incursion–hadn't been kind to his family, and Emilio's father hadn't been the first to realize that things would only get worse, even before *Il Duce* was just a dangling corpse and a horrible memory. There followed a terrible time for all of them during the liberation of Italy. Over the years he had locked these things away in a corner of his mind, and tried and tried to lose the key. He never spoke of those times, never would, never could. When the memories came forward, as they did more often as he got older, he pushed them relentlessly back in a kind of mental panic. But just hearing an English accent–the tones of the so-called liberators–would set him off.

Come on, Emilio told himself, concentrate on the good times. His free and open memories only resumed when he and his little family had landed in Canada, a post-war New World where fresh starts met you on every block. There wasn't a city in North America that didn't have a lively Italian community, and Toronto's was among the most active and vibrant. The little family–Alicia and the baby Roberto–soon fitted right in to the busy and prosperous 1950s, and setting up Pastorelli Fireworks had been easy and immediately successful.

A crash of the downstairs door and steps vaulting up two at a time broke the reminiscence. Rocco Pastorelli burst into the room all smiles and laughter.

"The Eighteen-twelve Nonno? Holy shit! Perfect coordination! Perfect! The music was right on! Right on! Every shot up there on cue. Christ, the software makes it so easy!"

Rocco carried all the Italian good looks of a long family legacy; tall and slim with a fine, easily-tanned skin, short black hair, and eyes of dark gold. His present effervescence masked a usually serious and business-like demeanor. He was working always to project maturity; always striving to show his grandfather that he was worthy of the role he had been thrust into. Tonight the mask slipped just a little as a childish happiness pushed through. The grandfather was bent now, and small, but the carriage of the young man showed how he must once have been.

Rocco had only had the technology for a few months, and this was the first time he had used it with live music. It was a tricky and intricate set-up to master and he was justifiably proud of the time he had spent on the computer slaving over his Timecode and FireOne software, and all the added time he had spent with the orchestra getting it all cued up. It was pure good fortune that the first real live music test of his new rig had taken place in East Gladstone, their home turf; rushing home briefly to rejoice was all part of the package.

All his labour over the screen and keyboard had culminated at dusk on this perfect Saturday in May. Surely Tchaikovsky's *1812 Overture* had never had such a rendition. With the entire orchestra seated out on the stone-flagged patio in front of the concert hall, and the fireworks launched from a barge moored in the lake, how could it have been bettered? From the opening bars, when four cellos and two violas were accompanied by soft gold, yellow and green fountains, through the folk dance for full ensemble when the lake was lit with scintillating rainbow lights and spinning multi-coloured wheels, to the cannonading blasts of five aerial shells, it was magic come alive.

The descending passage in the strings counterpointed by the yellow glare of retreat was followed by the silvery-golden clangor of tubular bells while bursting fires shot out over the water. The mighty conclusion as Moscow burns, the enemy are pursued, and eleven more thundering shots are heard on high, was all choreographed so tightly, so seamlessly that the audience were held enthralled until the last echoes were flung back from the façade of the East Gladstone Centennial Centre, and their faint reverberations had returned attenuated from the buildings of the city beyond. A pause of some few seconds—indeed, a continuation in silence of the musical score—was broken by the most thunderous applause the East Gladstone Symphony Orchestra had ever received.

A perfect spring evening! Could there possibly have been a better way to open the summer firework season? Rocco Pastorelli was ecstatic over his success and bursting to share it with the old man. He had left his two assistants at the site seconds after the last thunderclap, and had rushed home through the darkened streets to tell Nonno the good news.

If the old man was prepared to listen...

The caffeine had woken up the feistiness in Emilio, and again there was a twinkle in his eye and a lifting of the chin.

"Ah, you young bastards!" he shouted in his Italian accented English, hardly changed from the days he first learned the lingo in Toronto. "You don't know what it's like to set off a really good

3

show! With your goddam keyboards and lap-whatsits and shit. All them wires. It's bullshit I tell yer! Bullshit!"

Rocco and Emilio had been firing shows by electric ignition, or e-matches as they are also known, for years—everybody did who treasured their hearing and sanity—and the old man knew this. But the software was a whole new game; a game totally alien to him, and if it was something he couldn't understand, or didn't want to, he would quickly learn to hate it. Rocco now knew for certain what he had suspected before; that the old man had stayed home because of his disapproval. He usually showed up to gigs that were within easy distance.

"Yeah, yeah, I heard it all before Nonno," replied Rocco, his enthusiasm taking a tumble. "I know, I know, back in the day you went around with a box of matches."

"Matches? Asshole! We used portfires, and you know we did 'cos haven't I shown you how? Matches, my ass! Lighting 'em one by one, timing it you hear me? Timing it!"

"Portfires, matches, what the hell. All I'm sayin' is, we're in the modern world, and that's how it's done." Another of their futile and pointless disagreements was building with boring regularity. "You want Pastorelli Fireworks to compete, you move with the times. You wanna win jobs, you use the technology. Simple."

Emilio's face took on the faraway look of the inner eye. "Ah, in my day you had to use yer goddam head, not yer techno-whatsits. Eh, no pre-fire time written on a pissy computer screen. No way. She's gonna fly five second on the passfire. Leader fuse burn two second more, so seven second back of the climax in the music into the pipe she goes and light 'er up. God damn!" he concluded, "you keep that up for a whole show, you really know how to do yer job!"

"But you don't *need* to anymore, Nonno. That's the whole point. Just 'cos you had to do it like that 'way back in the Italian Renaissance, don't make it a virtue. We gotta be competitive!"

"Competitive? And how much it costing to keep us competitive, eh? What you pay for that box of tricks?"

Rocco wanted to stall; he was terrified of the fall-out. It had cost far more than he had imagined. He had seen the competition using the technology and knew that if Pastorelli Fireworks didn't have it they were dead in the water. But he couldn't stall; the old man had to know. Even at 82 he still descended on the office periodically and demanded to see the books. He just wished his widowed mum, Maria, were there to support him, but she must be upstairs in her bedroom.

"All in, around sixty thousand..."

"Sixty *thousand*? Sixty thousand bucks! Are you fuckin' crazy? We can't afford that! Pastorelli Fireworks is a just about goin' bust and you spending that kinda money? There isn't that much in the bank, for Christ's sakes! Where you get it?"

"Okay, so we have a liquidity issue..."

"Liquidity? Liquidity, my butt hole!" That good Italian coffee was doing its stuff. "I ask you, where you get it?"

"It's on our line of credit, of course," he sighed. "Jolly old CIBC. How else am I going to keep with the times? Keep us competitive?"

"*Jesu Cristi!* We're goin' down the pipes! Stuff I learned from *papá e nonno* back in the old country... Six generations *figlio*, and it's all goin' down the pipes. If your *papá* could see..."

"Look, look, I'm trying the best I can, but I can't work miracles!"

A short silence. The old man fixed him with his eye.

"Course, you know the real reason, doncha? Is that limey bastard Catesby. Direct competition. Every bid we make, he bid, and his bid are under ours. Why? Why? What's he doin'? He trying bust us?"

"No, Nonno, no. There's enough work for all of us..."

What was always left unsaid was the stupid war between the families. Everywhere else across the country the pyrotechnicians cooperated with each other, sharing shows, using common suppliers, organizing warehousing and distribution. But not them; not Pastorelli. His grandfather insisted on going alone, ordering only the best pyrotechnics from Italy, and paying through the nose for them. Rocco never could find out how this vendetta between him and the Catesby company had come about. Sure, they operated in the same town, but so what? And by now the dispute was irreversible.

"Well," replied the old man, "maybe he have li'l *accidente* with goddamn matches in his magazine. Izzen that a thought? Nah, too good to be true..."

The old man deflated into his chair and was silent. Rocco stood a while in the centre of the room with his head bowed, his triumph now just a spent casing. He raised his eyes slowly to fathom the reason for the continuing silence.

Holy shit, the old man was crying...

"Gotta get back," he muttered as he softly opened the door. "Help Seth and Tonio take the stuff down; site inspection…"

☆✩ ✯ ✩☆

Uncle Chuck sat in his little office in the clubhouse counting $20 bills and wrapping them with elastic bands. He was an atypical biker. Sure, he had the leathers, studs and chains, his arms sported tattoos that encompassed violence and death, and his head was clean shaven, but he was long and lean and, most surprisingly, educated and well read. Long sideburns and a small goatee framed a cold, calculating face whose features deferred to magnetic grey eyes. When he needed to—and it was infrequent—he could speak with the well modulated and schooled accent of the West Montreal Anglo ruling class. His usual mode of speech with his gang buddies and his dealers and tools was the argot of the world he was immersed in.

It was a nice clubhouse. It had a garage on one side where about eight of the gang kept their machines. They maintained a selection of tools and a few spare parts, and there was a workbench with a vise and drill press. Throughout the day there was always somebody tinkering with one of the Hogs. The Harley-Davidson was their emblem, and all the guys kept theirs in spotless condition.

The clubhouse itself was a central meeting place and storehouse for all kinds of stuff the police would be delighted to hear about… if they could only get access. The few times they had—waving their warrants in triumph and keeping their stupid grins buttoned down with an effort—word had magically preceded them, and all they found was a pool table, a dartboard, a few decks of cards and a perfectly legitimate supply of beer and little pretzels. Assholes! Uncle Chuck had a very useful girlfriend in the clerical department at cop headquarters, so any time paperwork had to be processed, who was it who had her finger right on it? Little darling was a good screw too, although he could never be sure if the attraction was his money, his good looks or just his dick. Of course, the real reason was simple: as soon as you've passed information just once you're hooked; ripe for blackmail, compliant for your personal safety.

Sort of lucky last time the cops hadn't checked the lowest cases in the pile of Molson Blue empties he'd forgotten in the garage; they were full of dynamite and detonators stolen from a

quarry. They were the leftovers of a little project he had super-
vised, where the clubhouse of a rival gang had more-or-less
ceased to exist. Not only had that scored him major points with
the honchos up the line, it also threw a little fear and uncertainty
into the motherfuckers, and that was always useful.

Ought to shift that stuff somewhere else, though; kinda dangerous...

Uncle Chuck was the chief honcho of the V-Twin Valkyries,
the town's chapter of the Angels and purveyor of all those socie-
tal delights barred to most citizens by archaic laws, rules and
regulations. The V-Twin Valkyries! What a great name for a gang
of bikers on Harleys! He'd announced his choice to his cohorts as
soon as the chapter was formed, and they'd cheered and cheered.
Even if they'd known better, not one of them would have had the
balls to tell him that Valkyries were actually women. A bit like
calling a hockey team the Senators and rigging them up with a
centurion on their shirts, or naming a team the Renegades when
that was a word for liars, cheats, finks and turncoats. He'd
missed out on Wagner, so all he knew was Valkyries were major-
league shit disturbers from ancient fuckin' mythology, and that
was good enough for him.

His prominence on the turf he had carved out was thanks to
his three years in the slammer; ooh, *pardonnez moi!* the Correctional Institute. Well, it had been correctional all right. In there
he had met some very useful people, and also 'corrected' his own
ways by seeing how stupidity gets you locked up. There was a
whole load of complete dead losses behind bars; stupid fucks
who only knew how to commit the crime, not how to get away
with it. Most of them totally fucked up on drugs anyway. He'd
never done drugs—the heavy stuff that is, 'cos who hadn't blown
grass?—but he'd sold quite a lot before he was out of his teens.
Amazing what shit high school kids will buy when they want a
good time. It didn't even start with drugs. First off it was con-
doms. He got them in bulk from a cut-price warehouse where
quality control was on the back burner—Chinese probably—
repackaged them and sold them for a huge mark-up. Rule number one: never use your own merchandise.

He was a small dope operator in those days, at the mercy of
the big kingpins who knew how to get the stuff and move it
through the system. Just a little wrench in a big workshop whose
toolkit he could only guess at. Prison had changed all that; it corrected his behaviour to the point that now he was a kingpin. He'd

learned how to acquire the shit, how to cover his tracks, how to manipulate, bribe and threaten. How to 'lose' potentially embarrassing bodies in blocks of concrete and fathoms of water, and how to set a charge of dynamite. He had officials and functionaries well in his grasp, and he sat at the nerve centre of a network of horror and violence. He was a natural.

Charles Bourassa had been raised in a nice area of Montreal, not far from West Mount where the really successful criminals like senators, politicians and mayors had their nests. Nice family; nice education. Where did we go wrong, ma? Simple; you didn't watch for the signs early enough. You raised your golden boy to be a virtuous model, but really didn't give much of a fart for what was really going on. And every time something you didn't want to know about happened you shoved it under the rug; covered up for the little bastard instead of reading the rules on actions and consequences.

Ah, nice to sit here on my throne of success and psychoanalyze the little shit I used to be, he thought as he counted out $20 bills. I was an evil little peckerhead when I was still in diapers.

And when it came to him standing there in the dock, didn't they move their goddamned asses to keep him out of the slammer? No amount of money, influence or pressure was enough to prove the innocence of their little darling. But in the end, there was the evidence, wasn't there? A prime minister might be able to buy enough lawyers to keep himself clean, but not my folks. They tried, and far's I know they're still paying off the loans. Funny, me having hundreds of thousands of readies passing through my fingers every week, yet not giving a flying fuck for them. But, jeez, you'd think Mommy and Daddy would be proud of their successful little man, but no! They'd even left the fucking country with his sisters and all, just to get away from him.

But things weren't all that great just now. The cops had busted his cocaine smuggling ring based on the Port of Montreal, and all kinds of low-level gophers had been rounded up. It was all over the six o'clock news, although of course Uncle Chuck had heard of it coming down days ago. He wasn't that stupid. So, his main route into the country was busted wide open and his supply had dried up. They'd shown it all on the box; this big table in police HQ with all those familiar little baggies stacked up, the wads of notes in elastic bands, and these smug cops with arms crossed saying how it was the biggest dragnet in years. Still, they'd been impatient. They'd jumped too soon and nabbed a whole load of small fry around the Port, while having no track whatsoever back to him. But even if they'd waited, his system was as foolproof as he could make it, and they would probably never have made any headway.

It was a bastard though. He'd gotten used to all these lovely bills passing through his fingers, and while he didn't *need* the money as such, he had become comfortable with a certain level of financial independence. It also cost lots of untraceable cash to keep all his pet officials sweet.

So, now he'd have to start from scratch; find a brand new route from Colombia for the stuff. Ah, the troubles of a busy chief executive!

✫✫☆✫✫

The early music ensemble *Tischmusik* was to perform Handel's *Musick for the Royal Fireworks*—written in 1749 to celebrate the Peace of Aix-la-Chapelle—on authentic instruments, and they had contracted Catesby & Son Pyrotechnics to accompany them with the real thing. Alfred Catesby, the son and Managing Director, always engaged with customers at first hand although it involved quite a bit of travel. This show was in an attractive limestone town at the eastern end of Lake Ontario, quite a distance from his home in East Gladstone. But it really didn't matter where you were based; the jobs could be anywhere in the eastern end of the province, while for the bigger shows across the country and around the world you flew, and either shipped the equipment or used the gear on site.

Alfred was in his early 50s and felt he could go on for ever, especially where his beloved pyrotechnics were concerned. His dad Bob still kept control of the company he had founded, and usually travelled with the team, but now in his mid-70s he was more the figurehead than an active force in the day-to-day operation.

This rendition of *The Fireworks* would not, Alfred was told, follow the original version; not only had that performance been an absolute disaster with pouring rain, overwhelming crowds, spreading fire and public panic, it had also been scored for a military wind band. King George II, it is reputed, had insisted on the martial instruments "...and we'll have none of his damned fidles". However, *Tischmusik* would perform Handel's later version, which included a full string section and fewer winds.

Setting up the whole show had required very close cooperation between the pyrotechnicans and the musicians, and there
had been long and heavy discussions with *Tischmusik's* First Vio-
lin, the leader of the orchestra. She had argued against modern
aerial pyrotechnics so as to keep the performance in keeping with
the best the imported Italian artificers of the period could con-
trive. This would mean ground-based candles, gerbs, fountains
and wheels (they had used rockets in the 18th century, but the
potential danger to modern audiences could not be considered
and, anyway, the devices were illegal). But authenticity only goes
so far, so a limited number of aerial shells was agreed upon.

Computers and electronic firing systems were an emerging
technology only a decade ago, but it was now possible to stage
shows with astonishingly accurate choreography. Potential clients could even be shown computer-generated simulations,
where choices of colour, composition and timing could be made
long in advance of inking the contract. When using recorded music such organization was now a cinch—international firework
competitions always ran that way—but live music was a whole
order of magnitude more tricky. It was hellishly difficult to coor-
dinate a real-time orchestra with the computer program, and it
demanded a lot of compromise from the huge musical egos that
routinely sat in those chairs. Alfred had slaved long and hard
with his Show Director software and was confident that he had
got it as good as it could be.

The Royal Fireworks was the climax of a Baroque Evening in
the Park that included a suite by J.S. Bach and Handel's *Water
Music*, a perennial favourite. From the opening *Ouverture* of the
five movements of the *Fireworks* and through the *Bourrée*, the
choreographers had clearly given their nod to authenticity by
keeping the fireworks at ground level. Gold, yellow, orange and
silver were the keynote colours, with more vibrant accents of
primary hues, while loud sounds such as crackles, whistles and
bangs were kept to the minimum, the better to hear the music.

The following movements, *La Paix* and *La Réjouissance*, had
demanded a deviation from authentic practice, so their huge
chords and harmonies were amply underscored with many-
coloured bursting stars, thudding detonations and softly falling
waterfalls of green, red, blue and turquoise that spread across an
entire quadrant of the sky. The first of the closing *Menuets* re-
verted to ground fire in glorious variety and colour, and then the
final homophonic punctuations of the second *Menuet* were again

underscored with crowd-pleasing star bursts and lots of thundering concussions—known in the trade as reports—roaring into a climax that quite drowned *Tischmusik*, although not one person in a hundred gave a damn. That wasn't what they were there for.

That night *Tischmusik* had probably their greatest standing ovation, although in truth most of the audience had preferred standing to sitting on grass damp from spring rain and the last remnants of the winter's snow. But the applause did continue for many minutes longer than those usually heard in the concert hall.

As the yellow/grey smoke cloud drifted leeward Bob Catesby, the patriarch, separated himself from the moving crowd where he had been standing, stepped over the yellow tape, and shook his son's hand, smiling at another job well done. After brief but heartfelt congratulations to the pyrotechnicians, the old man headed back to the hotel, leaving Alfred and their assistant Mike to oversee the basic inspection that took place 30 minutes after the show.

☆☆☆

As soon as he got back to the Comfort Inn, a short walk from the park, Bob Catesby called his granddaughter Julia, hoping his daughter-in-law Angela would there as well.

"Oh, my love, you and your Mum oughter bin here!" His accent was pure South London, scarcely modified by half a century away. "It was perfect! Perfect...! Yes, yes... no, no, not a wrong move... Of course your dad was great. He's got the software down perfect... He missed you too... Mum's there? Tell her... Yes, yes... Oh great, 'cos I so wished she could have bin here... And you too, of course... Okay, we'll talk soon. See you back home."

He flipped the phone shut and smiled. One of the best we've ever done and they had to miss it. *Les Miz* down in Toronto had been booked long before, and Julia and Angela hadn't wanted to waste their tickets. Young Julia; she was only 23 but she really looked promising. She just loved to help with the shows, and she was becoming extremely knowledgeable about all this new-fangled technical stuff. I mean, it's a new world when a young lady could be considered to run an outfit like Catesby's. Changing world... 'Cos Alfred's going to have to think about succession eventually. Son, daughter, doesn't matter a damn as long as she's good. And she is.

11

He made himself a nice cup of complimentary Comfort Inn tea and took it to the chair beside the bed. He took off his bifocals and placed them on the bedside table, then shut his eyes and re-played it all behind closed lids.

He had been fascinated with fireworks for as long as he could remember. When he was a kid his parents would start buying all sorts of fireworks long in advance of November 5th, the sacred Guy Fawkes Day trumped only by Christmas. The firework companies had quickly thrown off the restraints of the war effort and produced some lovely stuff. Weeks before the great day the corner confectionaries and toy shops would dedicate glass-faced cabinets to displays of Roman candles, penny bangers, cones and rockets.

Mum and Dad would come home with one or two selected items every few days, adding to the collection that he and his brothers would take out and arrange, anticipating the moment when the blue touchpaper would be lit. Then, at weekends when they were given their pocket money, they'd head straight for the sweetshop round the corner to buy whatever their sixpences could afford. Penny bangers were displayed in bundles held together with elastic bands, and on their coloured paper labels they carried such evocative names as *London Rouser* and *Cannon Crasher*.

The big department stores had huge displays, and it was one of his parents' treats to buy at least one enormous firework for the boys to grace the finale of their own back garden show. One year it was a Brock's *Sky Rocket* that shot out coloured stars and cost five shillings—a good bit of money in those days—and another was the *Devil Among the Tailors* made by Standard... or was it Wessex? One year a *Feu de Joie* by Pains seemed to have great promise—a huge cylindrical thing the size of a giant tin of beans with a prodigious touchpaper—but it produced the most astonishing pea-souper of yellow smoke, quite obliterating the *feu* that was probably fizzing and spluttering somewhere in its shrouded, *joie*-less interior.

His long love of fireworks, coupled with an inquisitive desire to emulate, was the reason for a long career spent in burning inorganic compounds in as many combinations and varieties as can be imagined for the awe and joy of the public. It started with 'improvements', still in his teens and long before his working life. Wouldn't it be fun to open the bottom of a *Mount Vesuvius* and mix in half a dozen 0.22 blank cartridges with the powder? Or, how about making the cone out of sheet metal instead of paper? And wouldn't it be fun to open the top of a *Sky Rocket*, empty out the stars, and fill the cavity with potassium permanganate and powdered magnesium, and then glue in a wooden stopper? All these improvements had spectacular success; the brass cartridge fragments howling about his head like demented shrapnel, the cone falling on its side and whizzing around in a dervish spiral of increasing velocity, and the rocket—somewhat top-heavy due to its added payload—soaring in a mighty arc before exploding far too close to the ground, causing a dog and its owner out for a quiet night stroll to leap howling and yelling into the air.

He'd got a great job with one of the big firework firms right out of grammar school. Low on the totem pole, shitty pay, but right where the powders and cardboard cases, the sealing wax and clay, all came together. He'd worked hard those years from the mid-50s, when things were tough for most ordinary folk like him, and he rose high in the company as a show specialist. It was on a company trip to Montreal to set up a display that he had met Carmelle, a sort of industrial spy for a chemical company that was looking to set up a fireworks business. With Carmelle the attraction was instant and lifelong. He ended up moving across the Pond, taking a job with Carmelle's firm, and eventually branching out himself. Catesby Pyrotechnics had been a small, but going concern ever since. He had begun inculcating Alfred as soon as he could toddle, and it seemed like no time before the Son was added to the title.

Dear Carmelle had passed away some years ago. Wouldn't it be nice when their granddaughter Julia took the firm to a third generation?

She looked so much like Carmelle...

Damn, tea had got cold...

☆☆☆

Emilio Pastorelli might have been less than enchanted with his grandson's latest electronic foray with *The Year 1812*, Opus 49, but the maestro of the East Gladstone Symphony Orchestra had become an unlikely fan. Initially, he had been highly skeptical and had consented only to meet with a representative from the fireworks company, nothing more. There was a good slice of chauvinism in his agreement to discuss this farce at all; of the two companies that had submitted bids, the name of Pastorelli

Fireworks had carried some old-world guarantee of quality and, an Italian himself, he considered that like souls should stick together in this cultural wasteland. Still, he was convinced the inaccurate timing and poor choreography of any firework show could only ruin the music. If only Tchaikovsky hadn't scored for artillery all this nonsense wouldn't be necessary. In the end, the Italian promise of quality and good taste swayed him, so he considered the thing might not be too far beneath his dignity.

Even so, staging the piece in the opening concert of the summer's *Pops by the Water* series had not been without its issues. The maestro considered the piece vulgar; or, at least, its popular appeal to be vulgar. Then again, pops concerts were all about appealing to the masses who would scarcely otherwise attend. Picnics by the lake were their style, with such routine classics as the overtures to *Light Cavalry* and *William Tell*, or the *Ride of the Valkyries*, playing in the background while they munched their hotdogs covered in that awful yellow pseudo-mustard. (He never could understand why the *Ride of the Valkyries* was greeted with such hooting and cheering by the masses, until someone had explained about a local bicycle club of some sort.) Whatever the case, pops concerts were part of the contract, so he would wear the mask he habitually donned for these occasions and do the job.

His work with the younger Mr Pastorelli had been something of an eye-opener. There was a professionalism about the process he had never imagined, and the young man had dealt with the preparations with skill and diplomacy. Even so, the role reversal irked him; he found wearing headphones with a click track odious. So that *he*, the *maestro*, should keep time in tandem with a computer! No, not even in tandem! The *computer* called the time! Outrageous! However, after the performance of this chemical *son et lumière*, the maestro had wallowed in the applause that he naturally assumed had been directed his way, and he did have to admit to himself that the choreography had been exemplary.

Once he had parlayed this resounding success to his favour, and sucked all the credit his way, he would at least admit the experiment had not been a complete failure. Whether he would ever again consent to lowering the tone of the East Gladstone Symphony Orchestra in this fashion was a moot point.

It all depended upon the level of applause...

☆☆☆☆☆

The Pastorelli family—grandfather, daughter-in-law and grandson—lived in a large old house east of the town centre in a predominantly Italian neighbourhood. Emilio had bought the place back in the 1960s when they had first moved here, and divided it to accommodate the family. His son Roberto and daughter-in-law Maria had the first floor, which also had common spaces of living room, dining room and kitchen. When Roberto passed away Maria kept the place for herself, glad to be within the family dwelling. Emilio and his dear Alicia had the second floor, a self-contained living space, which he now occupied alone. Once Rocco had entered his teens Emilio had a bedroom on the third floor fitted up for him. As Rocco seemed to have no desire for an independent place of his own, his floor had eventually been fitted with a small kitchen and bathroom. The reduced family generally ate together downstairs, and Maria had moved easily into the role of keeping house for the three of them.

This Monday morning his mother had made Rocco waffles for breakfast. Normally on workdays he just took a coffee and a bit of toast and headed off to the office, but today she felt she needed to feed him a little; find the way into a heart that was sometimes closed and aloof.

"Here. Eat," she urged as she placed the plate in front of him. "Give you some energy for the day."

He sat, picked up the fork and pushed a waffle to and fro on the plate.

"Tell me," she said quietly. She had heard him come in after the show, and had heard him go out again, but she had been in her bedroom and hadn't had a chance to ask him how it had gone. Emilio was still upstairs in bed.

He sighed, torn between talking and leaving so much unsaid. Lately, with Nonno in his hypercritical mood, his mother had come closer to him, trying to bridge a gap they both acknowledged within themselves. But where do you begin...? He pushed the waffle around some more, then in a low voice, "It's not like I'm not trying. I do what I can. I work and work; I work my butt off, but he just..."

"I know. I do know. But we have to remember he's eighty-two years old."

He looked up at her, meeting her eyes, giving her a small surge of joy. "Look Mama, I try to cut him some slack, I really do, but when everything I do is wrong..."

"Only in his eyes."

"I've never been able to satisfy him. From 'way back. I never could do anything right. You know that."

"Like I say, it's only in his eyes. You know as well as I do that without all you're doing we would have gone bust a long time ago."

He nodded. "I know that; you know that. But why do I always let him get under my skin? Why?"

"He's always been uncompromising. You know that. Even when your papa was working with him..." She sighed, an inward look crossing her face.

"What really worries me," and here he began to open out to her at the thought of the food she had cooked out of the goodness of her heart, "is not failure, not bankruptcy, not laying off our people. I think I could stand that. But it's the thought of it happening while he's still alive. While he *knows* that it's all a failure."

She moved over to the table and gently held his left hand. She knew, and he didn't need to express it, that if his father were still alive this huge responsibility wouldn't be his. It tore her; the lost husband, her beloved Roberto, and the too-soon-grown-up son. This knowledge remained between them, tacit, never to be expressed, but understood by both.

"See," he continued, "it's all he's ever done in life. Six generations up in smoke; how ironic!" An empty laugh. He paused and looked into her eyes again. "He was crying last night... Greatest success I've ever had with a show, and he was crying."

"Eat. We'll find a way. Eat. And then you better get going; you'll be late."

He left soon after, while Maria began to moot the structure of her day. Keeping the Pastorelli house was one small part of the devices she had conceived after Roberto had gone. During his long illness he had dominated her entire world, but once the cancer had taken him to his bitter end, Maria had forced herself to find ways of filling the searing, naked void of his loss. She volunteered at her church, finding paradoxical solace and fulfillment in counseling the bereaved and the terminally ill. But her son, who was the mirror her absent Roberto still held up to the world, she couldn't allow to come close. She saw the lost husband in the living son and was filled with dread, so rather than clinging to the life that so closely mirrored his, she withdrew. She deeply mourned those critical months when she had not been a mother to her needing son, and did as much as she was able to repair the rift that was still subtly present between them.

Even if it was only waffles and the squeezing of a hand.

Maria would not confess to being deeply religious, but she did find comfort in a belief that Robbie was... somewhere, and that this period in her life was a patient and testing pause between earth and heaven. She found it impossible to believe that what had been was all there would be. Perhaps her beliefs were simple, but there had to be a God and a life hereafter; the alternative was not to be thought about.

⋆☆ ⭐ ☆⋆

When grandfather Emilio had started Pastorelli Fireworks back in Toronto in the 1950s he had begun by manufacturing and selling consumer fireworks, the sort that could be bought in the corner store for celebrating Canada's Birthday, Victoria Day and other officially sanctioned celebrations. This was a come-down from the halcyon days back in Italy, but he knew he had to start small and grow as he felt the market move. Rules and regulations were pretty lax back in those days, and it was only later that the Federal Government applied legislation to manufacture and sales. So, from backyard products Emilio had branched out into what had been his father's and grandfather's pride and joy back in Italy, the category of pyrotechnics produced solely for public display and either ignited by the maker or by a licensed pyrotechnician. In effect, this meant dividing manufacture between two separate facilities, so when he moved the firm out of Toronto in the 1960s–where rents and accommodation were becoming exorbitant–to East Gladstone, some 100 or so kilometers north, he sold off the manufacture of domestic fireworks to a competitor, concentrating totally on the specialized facility that produced the big stuff and made all the contractual arrangements for large scale public displays.

In hindsight this sale had been a mistake, because the competition found that a line of candles, cones, burning schoolhouses, small bore mortars and the like, provided a steady income. Boxes of Catesby's assorted consumer fireworks were a feature of many stores in the lead-up to the main public holidays, but lacking this continuous money-making line of the competition, Pastorelli Fireworks had to rely purely on setting off large pyrotechnic shows. The lump sum that Emilio had received for the sale of the manufacturing plant produced interest to bolster the firm's finances–and it had been well invested–but year by year the only way to stay afloat had meant picking away at the principal. There would come a time very soon when that source of income would dry up.

Pastorelli Fireworks was on the east side of the town, surrounded by buildings still used for light industry. Unlike the gentrified ex-warehouse district Catesby occupied, this neighbourhood was still solidly working class and predominantly Italian. The factory contained offices and the workshop with a staging area and a loading bay at the rear. On the other side of the rear parking lot a second brick building had been retrofitted as a magazine.

When Rocco arrived at work he was in a sensitive and unsettled mood. The elation of last night's successful deployment of the electronic gizmos had quite evaporated, and he now knew that he would need success after success, just like last night, if the outfit was going to stay afloat. The old man was right, at least in that respect; he might spend most of his days in a chair by the fire, but he still had the pulse of the company.

Oh, the smell when he walked in that door! Each day the uniquely firework aroma would be with him for only a few minutes before the sense of smell became conditioned to it—like the delicious smell of rubber when you first step into Canadian Tire—but those few moments were always a delight. No matter how fast the 21st century pushed its innovations into every cranny of life, you still had to make firework casings out of paper, cardboard, clay and wax. At least, they did. The old man had always used hot hide glue, and as a kid he recalled the aroma from the double boiler in the corner of the workshop where all the technicians would go to dip their glue pots. Times had moved a little; they now used liquid fish glue, or hot-melt adhesive in glue guns—so, no antiquated double boiler—but the aroma was just as delicious to those used to it.

The combined smells gave him a lift. It was the redolence of things as they once were; it spoke to his senses of the normality and stability of a golden time. Unfortunately, there was less call for such old-world craft in the present tight economy, and Rocco could see a time when the workshop would sit idle. Initially, Emilio had insisted on producing in-house every single item he fired into the air. Pyrotechnics made by Italians were the best in the world, and that's all there was to it. But as the years passed, Pastorelli bought-in much more of its stock, although Emilio still insisted on buying only Italian wares. Frankly, they were much more than twice the price of the equivalent Chinese products, but Rocco agreed with him that they also happened to be at least twice as good. Nevertheless, he had tried in vain to convince the old boy that, although the two of them were fully aware of the quality difference, could the same be said of the audiences? Were they literally blowing their profits off in smoke?

So, even though that old-fashioned ambience was all around him, Rocco knew that in the modern competitive North American market no firework company could possibly survive purely by setting off its own products. Pastorelli still crafted an exclusive line of specialty items, and it had been one of Rocco's joys—and Emilio's before him—to oversee their design, then roll up his sleeves and help make them come alive. These *studadas*, as the traditional Italian products were known, were the best of the best and preferred by many firms in competitions. Little of this work was possible nowadays, and the total staff in that department was two women who spent their days making the specialty items to order with minimal supervision. Soon, Rocco knew, the next cost saving at the company would be the closing of this little enterprise. Pray God, he thought, that Nonno wouldn't be around to see that. Or the time when the equity from the manufacturing sale of years ago finally dried up.

"Snap out of it," he told himself. "Work to do."

Firework show clients were given a menu of options with an accompanying price list, and could choose from a huge variety of shows. The new software helped tremendously; you could screen a real-time rendition and make selections from a vast array of effects. Naturally, any organization that was planning to spend thousands of dollars on a show would seek competitive bids, and government departments were obliged to. Yes, Pastorelli's quality was better—Rocco believed this with all his heart—but his rock-bottom prices were still too high. In effect, this meant the competition won the plums while he was often hired as the fallback.

He sat at his desk with a sigh. The redolence of gunpowder and glue had faded into the background and the ordinary day of a busy executive loomed.

First there was a post-show review with all involved in last night's gig, then straight into the on-going planning for the rest of the year. It couldn't stop—could not be allowed to stop—because every show you bid on had a competitive edge. Every weekend throughout the entire year there multiple functions somewhere around the province and across the country. Clients had to be met, bids put forward, permits to address, and contracts signed. It was important to meet with the customers, show them what they would get on the various price scales, and pin down their desires.

So, a huge number of orders had to be processed from the manufacturers, shipments had to be met at the docks, endless paper processed, and the ever-moving stocks in the magazine inventoried, sorted into lots, moved to the loading dock, and prepared for delivery to the show sites. The bulk of their supplies were shipped in by sea, which meant that timing was critical, and keeping the magazine well supplied with lots of duplicate stock was a very good idea.

It would have been so much easier if Pastorelli could cooperate with the competition. This was Rocco's main beef. He knew that elsewhere around the country the major pyrotechnic firms pooled their resources, ordering together, warehousing together and organizing distribution. But at some time, 'way back in ancient history, his grandfather had gone alone, pissing off the competition—Catesby's in particular—and creating one hell of a lot more work. He wished he had an inside track on that ancient history but Nonno was never forthcoming.

Rocco spent the first part of the morning in the post-show review with his two assistants, the tall rangy Seth and the short Mediterranean Tonio. Then he had to go over stocks and shelving with Len, his middle-aged and stolid go-to man who kept the place running smoothly. Most of the remaining time was spent checking and firing off e-mails, and phoning agents, suppliers, shippers and clients. Then there was a little issue with their assistant Willy that had to be dealt with very diplomatically. Willy was a lovely little boy of 24; he smiled and laughed at everything, understood direct orders, and carried them out quickly and well. When his dad or mom picked him up at the end of the day, he always told them in his simple way what a great day he had had. Today there were tears because of something someone had said to him, so he had to be mollified with gentle words and a cup of good Italian coffee, which he loved.

Days like this you went home wondering what you had actually accomplished.

☆☆⭐☆☆

20

Rocco always had lunch at the same place, just round the corner from the facility, a little Italian diner in a district well known for its little Italian diners. He bought his lunch at the counter after a brief give-and-take with the owner and then sat at a corner table. A figure from a past life he would rather forget pushed into the door, spotted him at his lunch, and came over.

"Hey."

"Hey." They greeted, raised palm to raised palm. "How's it going?"

"Great, great. Haven't seen you for years," replied Rocco. And *I don't want to now*, he thought, *if the truth be known*. "I'm doing just fine."

"Yeah? You just look like the horse that walked into a bar, that's all. Business bad?"

Steve Bacon had been a friend from high school, but all the stuff they had done together ought to have been buried in the past. They had been hell-raisers, always in trouble and always just the safe side of the law. 'Way back in their teens Rocco had arranged for Steve to take a part-time job at Pastorelli's, while helping out himself between classes, but that hadn't worked out at all well. Trouble was, Steve had no sense of responsibility and not a scrap of work ethic. The job didn't last long, and the recommendation had made Rocco look bad to Emilio.

Then, having been burnt once, he had really messed up by lying to keep his friend out of jail. Bacon was accused of break-and-enter and would probably go down for a long stretch, so even though he knew it was all wrong, Rocco had perjured himself by setting up a solid alibi. So now they shared a particularly strong bond, and it was a debt Rocco continually regretted granting. Steve was always on the wrong side of things, and since then Rocco had tried to keep his distance. You heard things about the company Steve was keeping, and none of it was good.

Nevertheless, for some bizarre reason, and one that he would curse himself for, he was moved to open up. Against his better judgment, he started to talk over his problems.

"The firm would be doing just great if it wasn't for the overheads. There's enough work for two shops in this province, no question, but Catesby's usually underbid us."

Steve swung into a chair across the table and fiddled with the salt and pepper.

"I mean, it's always playing catch-up," continued Rocco, feeling comfort in unburdening himself to one who was now essentially a stranger. "The competition's doing Gwillimbury on Saturday; you know, down Newmarket way. I would love to have snagged that one, but that's how it goes."

"Gwillimbury, eh?" mused Steve with a grin. "So, sounds like one of the firms—which shall remain anonymous, but let's say just for the sake of example, Catesby's—would benefit from a little accident."

"No, no, no! Don't be so stupid!" Rocco was horrified at the speed with which a thrown-out line could take on a frightening concrete form. The old man had hinted the same thing last night, for Christ's sake! Holy shit, why didn't I keep my mouth shut? "I'm in no mood for jokes."

"Yeah, well, I *was* just kiddin'. You know me! But I do owe you a big favour, y'know."

"*You don't!* I don't want it paid back, Steve. It's in the past, forget about it, okay!"

"Sure, sure. But wouldn't it be fun..."

"Cut it out! You don't owe me nothing. I should never have mentioned it. We're doing just fine. A little rough patch right now, but nothing we can't fix." He drank some coffee and picked up his panino.

"Okay pal." Steve slapped him gently on the shoulder. "See you around."

Rocco sat nursing his coffee and mentally kicking himself for being all kinds of a fool. Steve Bacon was buried in his past—a past he preferred to forget—and he should have remained there.

What *was* he thinking?

☆✫☆

The Catesby team headed back home in the company bus to East Gladstone. The show in the limestone city had been a great success, and they chatted happily at a job well done, while Alfred sat in the driver's seat and watched the road. The bus was divided into seating at the front and equipment storage and workshop at the back. The launching structures for the mortar tubes and the majority of the pyrotechnics were carried in the rented company trucks, although fuses, igniters and other such 'apparatus of initiation' were kept in a separate locked container in the back of the vehicle. Alfred insisted on a physical separation. People thought him paranoid because he even refused to use his cellphone when travelling, convinced that the signals could affect the electronics in his cargo. No amount of persuasion could convince him otherwise. There were too many examples world-wide, he was fond of saying, of what can happen with the slightest slip in vigilance.

As Alfred drove through the flat Ontario farmland he started to chuckle at a stray thought.

"What?" asked Mike, their assistant pyrotechnician and general helper in the stores and magazine. He was a solid, square middle-aged guy they had 'stolen' some years ago from a competing firm in Montreal. He was immensely experienced and quite content with his role in East Gladstone. In fact, this family firm was very much to his liking.

"Oh, I was just laughing about the authenticity game and what Dad said to that stuffed shirt violinist."

"Oh, yeah," laughed Bob. "You don't push that authenticity in firework performance bit in my face, especially when you're using bullshit instruments that would have made Handel weep into his claret. The *balls* of these people!"

"Right. What was it you said about their trumpets? Bastard agglomerations of plumbing..."

"...invented in the nineteen-sixties," finished Bob, "to look superficially like the real thing to the unwashed masses."

Mike laughed. "Bastard agglomerations! I love it!"

"Lucky I didn't mention the violins..."

"Would have cost us the contract, you silly old fool!" replied Alfred with a frown. "And a nice boost for Pastorelli that would be!"

"Yeah, well, didn't happen," he smiled. "And then after I'd said it, d'you remember the Glacial Silence?"

All three of them laughed as the bus hummed north-east.

Alfred pondered how he had got where he was now. How many people on this planet, he mused, have a career in burning inorganic chemicals in such a variety of creative ways? He wasn't really sure why his father had moved Catesby's out of Montreal. It was a complex subject and the only time he had raised it Dad had been more than evasive. He was only a kid during the FLQ crisis, but as he watched Québec independence stagger on its weird, wonderful and doomed path over the years he thought that perhaps Dad had been uncomfortable with the politics. Also, although Dad had married a Québecoise, he could scarcely manage the lingo, and perhaps her death, far too young, had pushed him to go west. So when he moved out of Québec he initially stopped just the other side of the Ottawa River in Hawkesbury, and that's where Catesby & Son Pyrotechnics still maintained a factory for producing domestic items for the mass market. He rarely visited Hawkesbury these days, although Dad did sometimes, just to keep his hand in and to breathe in the aroma of old-fashioned firework manufacture.

The move to East Gladstone had followed in the early 1990s. From what Alfred could glean, his father had moved to East Gladstone because the city council had proved very lenient with firework manufacture, and a disused warehouse with great potential was available. Though his father didn't know it at the time, this move had really upset Emilio Pastorelli, who had set up there decades earlier. Alfred was at a loss to understand why. It was not as if the companies were infringing on each other's turf; the business was province-wide, if not country-wide, so where you were located didn't matter a damn. No, it didn't make sense. All he knew was, old man Pastorelli loathed Catesby's. And with that attitude it wasn't hard to reciprocate.

Catesby's had never manufactured the larger display fireworks, always relying on supplies from big international companies. Like all pyrotechnic outfits in the country, with the exception of Pastorelli, they pooled resources. The companies got their stocks wherever the price was right and the quality assured. A process call homologation ensured that composition and weight were regulated and that laboratory testing of the products had been conducted. China and Japan had been the chief suppliers for decades, while Italian, Spanish and Portuguese products were excellent, although more expensive.

Although Bob Catesby had mooted the idea, it would have been very difficult to establish a production line in the Canadian economy, being prohibitively expensive and mired in bureaucracy. Putting on the shows was a kind of loss-leader to the sales of the domestic product anyway, and the large firework displays were mostly used to keep the firm's profile high. It was also the most enjoyable. But Bob did have a quite extensive workshop in a corner of the facility where he made shells for his own pleasure. Alfred liked to take time off as well to tinker with new combinations of effects, but it was almost impossible these days.

East Gladstone was a nice enough place, mostly advantageous for its central position to the markets of southern and eastern Ontario. It's not as if they got much work locally anyway; their Italian competition had won the *Pops by the Water* gig, one of the few firework celebrations actually in the town. The maestro of the orchestra had pulled the old tribal card, employing Italians even though Catesby's bid had been much lower. In fact, Catesby's costs were always low due to a lucky contact at the World Symposium on Fireworks held in Malta. Alfred had been introduced through a business acquaintance to an excellent agent in Colombia who could supply a huge range of aerial shells at prices that couldn't be beaten. And the aerials were a huge part of any show; the most expensive. He'd ordered a wide selection of items and tested them rigorously for quality—just one or two failures could be a company's death knell—and they had performed flawlessly. So what if he was working outside the cooperative? Don't want everybody feeding from the same trough... Besides, most of his stuff came through the regular channels anyway.

So, Alfred's bids for shows were often lower than anything the enemy could throw in. Tough for Pastorelli, but business was business. That old bastard Emilio would do anything to get an advantage anyway, and it was a good bet that the grandson was in the same mold.

Still, plenty of other work if you kept the profile high and beat the bushes. There were the seasonal variations, of course, with the summer months being the busiest, but throughout the winter there were always gigs to be picked up: the *Skate Lake Ontario* festival, the *Northern Arts Gala*, and of course good, reliable *Winterlude* in Ottawa, which they had won just the once. God, those were bloody cold gigs! You couldn't wear gloves when handling the electric matches and firing cables, and of course the laptop and main firing console with all its switches had to be bare hands. You couldn't park the bus close enough because of regulations, so it was rarely possible to work indoors. The best you could usually do was a plywood lean-to.

All in all, though, what a life to have been born into!

He turned in his seat and smiled at Dad. Dad was just having fun at all this—all the enjoyment and little of the hard work—but he guessed he'd earned it.

★☆⭐☆★

Julia Catesby was sorry to have missed the show at the other end of Lake Ontario, but the musical in Toronto was a must. She and her mother Angela shared a great many experiences, and they were perhaps closer than many mothers and adult daughters. They had driven back from Toronto on Sunday afternoon, after a pleasant morning of strolling and shopping around Bloor and Yonge, and her mother had dropped her off at her apartment.

She was sitting at the table in her little kitchen/dining room on Monday morning, spreading orange marmalade on a croissant and taking occasional sips of her coffee. She'd got the taste for marmalade from her grandfather, and in the brief period when the Seville oranges came in, the family home would be redolent with the aroma of batches of lid-popping jars as her mother laid down the year's supply. She took a bite and smiled, the flavour and aroma taking her to thoughts of Grandpa and his little foibles.

Julia's face was regular and pleasant—certainly not beautiful, as she always told herself to her mirror—but a smile was never far away, and then the high cheekbones and blue eyes joined the upward curve of her lips and transformed her face. It is not the features of the face that dictate true attractiveness; it is how the mind behind the features chooses to approach its world.

As she worked slowly at her breakfast—perhaps a little reluctant to engage her day—she felt the need for a huge change in her private life. She had a date tonight, but she really wasn't interested. In truth, Richard, her present swain, was becoming plain boring. Straight after work at 5:00 she faced the usual routine of a meal somewhere, maybe some dancing, and then quite likely closing out the evening with the half-hour of inevitable sweaty wrestling on his couch or hers. As if this represented the high point of any relationship! It was a routine, fulfilling on one very basic level, that had lost whatever magic it had once held.

She finished her breakfast, dropped the plate and cup into the miniscule dishwasher, picked up her bag, and set out on the brief walk to work. The firm's main facility was in a converted warehouse in the old industrial part of town, now much gentrified as industrial buildings became transformed into art galleries, craft stores and eateries. The building had been fitted out with office and meeting spaces at the front, with a loading dock and staging area in the rear. Very few fireworks were kept in this building at any one time; deliveries would be processed and inventoried there before being transferred to the magazine, a secure storage area in an adjacent building. When a show was being prepared the pyrotechnics required were brought from the magazine to the staging area just prior to being packed into the trucks, along with the racks, frames and other firing equipment.

Working here in the main facility, at the heart of the enterprise, she felt completely fulfilled. Employed in the family company and knowing that one day she would be chief honcho (honcha, honchess?) gave her drive and purpose. She seldom regretted not pursuing higher education. Dad had told her there was plenty of time, and that if she wished to do a degree or to travel for a year or two he would foot the bills. But somehow work at Catesby & Son Pyrotechnics was all she had ever wanted or needed.

☆ ☆ ☆ ☆ ☆

Angela Catesby had taken off early today and was at home, doing nothing much except sitting with a cup of coffee in the kitchen and downloading from a more than usually horrible day. She could have chosen to work in the family firm—and on days like this, she wished she did—but her master's degree in social work from McGill in Montreal had been a calling. The more she had studied psychology, sociology and the human condition, the more she had been drawn into helping in the very lowest strata of society. She was employed by the city as a social worker, which entailed visiting some of the areas that an openly tourist town like East Gladstone would rather not have acknowledged. Drug addicts, safe injection sites and rehabilitation were her specialties, and it was often with some irony that she reflected on three-quarters of her family sending tens of thousands of dollars up in smoke for pure amusement, while the other quarter just squeaked by on insufficient funding for any single project she tackled.

Part of Angela's beat this morning had been at the end of Sandford Street, a disused piece of industrial land on the east end of town where alcoholics, drug addicts and the mentally ill hung out in appalling conditions of want, need and disease. The only halfway habitable structure was a filthy Airstream trailer with no wheels, although God knew who lived there. Looking at the soiled tents, the sheets of warped plywood and the plastic sheeting always sobered her, reminding her how well-off she was, and how tenuous status can be.

Angela had a loathing born of deep experience for anyone who would stoop so low as to deal in drugs. Such people were beyond her comprehension.

The Catesby home was on a couple of acres of land that sloped gently down to the lake on the nicer western edge of town. The house was one of the older ones in East Gladstone, built by a minor lumber baron when forestry was still done here. This was in the late 19th century, in the days when steam trains carried the logs away and brought back the first tourists. Not far along their road there had once been a grand hotel catering to the evacuees from Toronto who escaped every summer for a few weeks of peace and recreation. The rails had long since been pulled up, and the hotel was a sepia-postcard memory. You could still see where the railbed had skirted the lake, and it was now maintained as a bike and pedestrian path. The whole family, even old Bob, liked to get their bikes out and pedal slowly beside the water on a Sunday. They would stop frequently to admire the view while giving Bob's legs and wind a little surcease, although they never let on.

Angela and Alfred had the sprawling ground floor to themselves, while Alf's dad had an upstairs apartment. They were a close family and it had seemed quite natural that her mother- and father-in-law would occupy the same house with them when they had moved from Hawkesbury. When Carmelle had passed away it became even more important for Bob to be close, especially as he could watch over young Julia as she grew up. When Julia had moved to her own apartment at the age of 19 Bob had been dismayed, but she was just a short distance away and he would see her often.

Angela poured herself more coffee and took it out into the backyard. She strolled down to the low wooden fence that marked the bottom end of the lot, leaned over the rail and looked out over the beach. Waterfront access was lovely, and she mused upon how expensive such a view and such beach access would be today.

A nice place to be, and all was now well with her world. She heard the distinctive roar of the sports car as it drove up to the side of the house, checked her watch, and realized how quickly the afternoon had gone. She went up the lawn to greet Alf.

☆ ⭐ ☆

Julia was Alfred Catesby's son. With his only child in her 20s, and no likelihood of male offspring, she would carry the family business, Catesby & *Son*, into the third generation. Alfred was deeply conscious of family tradition and adamant that the company his father had founded would remain a family concern. He owned a Morgan sports car; had met the grandson of the founder, had ordered the car personally at the family-owned factory in England, and had visited Malvern Link in Worcestershire to watch it being built by hand. Every time he sat behind the wheel of his Plus 4 he was reminded of what it meant to be at the helm of a proud and rigorously maintained small family enterprise.

It was Alfred's father who had persuaded him to inculcate Julia into the pyrotechnical arts by having her make aerial shells from scratch. Dad had promoted this idea enthusiastically and, to his great surprise, his preteen daughter had taken to it immediately. Even then, Alfred saw it as a game with no serious long-term prospects.

But now, with Angela just touching 50, it was clear that one was the number. So Julia would take up the torch for the family (although portfire might be a better term) all in good time. He had been reluctant to see her in this role, perhaps biding his time until he could be sure no son would come his way.

Julia's serious apprenticeship to the firm began when she left high school after Grade 12. Bob and Alfred had her performing every task that any member of staff was likely to pursue, so she worked in administration, helped in the magazine and, on the best occasions of all, assisted with setting and firing the pyrotechnics.

One other job Julia really enjoyed was hosting the open house for elementary school children. The East Gladstone school board made much of their local industries, and in the absence of large museums and similar civic sites, visits to the firework factory became a grade school staple. Julia loved children and she loved to communicate to them her love for fireworks. It was a natural fit because in many ways launching fireworks into the air and being delighted and awed at their colour and noise and variety were very childish sentiments. Perhaps her whole family had never really grown up, but that was just fine with her.

This Monday morning she had moved the chairs to the sides of the reception room, set up the laptop and projector, and brought in a few dummy samples of fireworks from the store in the rear of the building. She had started her talk to about 20 Grade Threes sitting in a semicircle on the floor, by showing them a box of Catesby's consumer fireworks.

"There are two kinds of fireworks," she simplified a little.

29

"These are the ones you can buy in the drugstore for Victoria Day and Canada's birthday. And Victoria Day's coming up soon, isn't it?" There were a few nods. "These are the kind your mommy and daddy light for you." Yes, mommy as well; she was damned if she'd give dad all the fun. "And there are the big, big ones that specially trained people like me shoot off."

She picked up a couple of gerbs, cardboard cylinders with fuses at the end, and passed them to the kids at each end of the semicircle. "See, these are fountains, but we call them gerbs. Isn't that a funny word?" She turned to the whiteboard and wrote the word for them. "There," she said, "that's your first new word of the day. Gerb."

The little ones passed the gerbs from hand to hand in silence.

"Now, how many of you know," she asked the half-circle of faces, "how we make fireworks burst in the sky?"

The kids had only just arrived and were still too shy to speak up. Julia picked up two cardboard hemispheres from the table in front of her and gave one each to the students on her left and right, encouraging them to pass them along.

"Those are to make the shell." She picked up a dummy aerial shell, holding it by the leader fuse at its top. "This is a complete shell. Don't worry," she assured the frowning teacher in an aside, "this one's empty; just for show."

By this time the two shell halves had reached the middle of the semicircle and an active little tyrant with a buzz-cut was busily clip-clopping them together. Julia focused her attention on him.

"Tell me," she demanded, "how those two pieces get up into the sky."

"You send them up? With a bang?"

"Exactly! Look, see this little cup on the bottom?" She held up the dummy shell. "It's full of powder that goes with a big bang and drives the shell up into the air." She thrust the shell upwards dramatically with both hands.

The all sat in silence with big, wide eyes because now she had their attention. She clicked a hand-held remote, and on the screen behind her a video showed a shell ascending to a height and exploding in a sphere of stars. Now they were really interested.

"So, I drop the shell into this tube." She had a mortar tube on the floor in front of the table, attached to a plywood base. She showed them where the fuse passed around the shell and entered the cup from below, and the she slid the shell into the tube. "And then I light it."

Several of the children put their hands over their ears, and one little man gave a shriek.

"Don't worry! I wouldn't light a firework indoors. That would be *very* dangerous, wouldn't it?"

"My bruvver lit a fi'work in my house," observed a serious little girl with braids, "an' my dad got mad, an' there was smoke..." Julia wondered what kind of household that was, and wryly imagined it was just the sort of thing Grandpa would have done when he was a kid.

"Well, I won't do it here!" she assured them. "I think I might get in trouble with your teacher, don't you?"

Several wise little heads nodded.

"So now," she continued, "we want the shell to explode high, high in the sky, so we have a little time fuse here." She took the cup off the bottom and pointed out the end of the passfire leading into the shell.

"I seen that! I seen that!" yelled a little terror in jeans and T-shirt. "You see it going all wiggly with fire coming out. I seen that!"

"You're very observant," Julia praised him. "You saw the fuse burning on the bottom of the shell. Now, some people..." she lowered her voice confidentially. This was the bit she really enjoyed "...call it a spitool." She pronounced it slowly and carefully and wrote it on the board, scanning the little faces for any reaction. Sure enough, the little terror had a wide grin on his face and two little girls nudged each other. The teacher assumed an 'old fashioned' look.

"But we don't call it that," continued Julia. "We call it the passfire. Does anyone know why?" She wrote 'pass' and 'fire' on the board and waited for a good long time, but the silence around the circle was unbroken. "Because," she continued at length, "it passes the fire from the lift charge to the burst charge. Pass... fire. See?"

They saw, although getting most of them to say so was like pulling teeth. Ah, Monday mornings...

"Now, I wonder... what happens next?" She scanned round the semi-circle and focused on a little Muslim girl in a hijab.

"What do you think happens next?" The girl just stared with huge brown eyes.

"What do you think, Maryam?" prompted the teacher. "What

happens next?" But Maryam remained mute.

"The spit tool makes it go BANG!" yelled the little terror. "BANG! And there's all these stars and fire and there's whistles and... and stuff! I seen that!"

She praised him mightily because she knew that this was the kind of experience that would stay with him, and that he would remember and cherish it. His parents would hear all about this.

With the exception of three out of nearly 20, this bunch were quieter than usual, so Julia concluded her presentation with the rest of the video, a section from the simulation program that was shown to prospective clients. That grabbed their attention.

It was times like this that she was tempted horrify the teachers and fascinate the students by telling them that a Catherine wheel was named after the Christian saint who was martyred in a highly creative fashion, and that Roman candles were originally live Christians coated in pitch. Or that Mount Vesuvius had immolated thousands. And what about the *Boy Scout Rouser* that Grandpa had told her about? Don't even go there...

In an era when none of their fireworks carried those names, and when you couldn't even sell a Burning Schoolhouse without irate parents howling at local politicians, such a presentation would be less than politically correct.

Pity.

She remembered sitting on Grandpa's lap while he retold the story of the Gunpowder Plot; how Guido Fawkes, whose day he had celebrated as a child on November 5th, was really only the fall guy, the one who got caught with the barrels of gunpowder below King James's Parliament. "Remember, remember, the fifth of November," he had intoned to her often. "Gunpowder, treason and plot!"

When Grandpa had told her the name of the mastermind behind the plot she had laughed and laughed and laughed.

⋆☆ ☆ ☆⋆

On a disused section of land in the east end of town–all dirty slab-sided yellow brick punctuated with steel-framed, multi-pane smashed glass at the end of working class Sandford Street–was a plot of garbage-strewn scrub favoured by druggies, bums and the homeless mentally ill. This was where the War on Drugs met its nemesis; the practical, brutal reality of social injustice. The gathering place of Uncle Chuck's end users; the shareholders who

32

create millionaires. A seemingly disused Airstream trailer was parked in one corner, although 'parked' suggests a temporary arrangement. This Airstream would never move again, having cinderblocks in place of wheels, and strips of delaminating plywood jammed along its underside, the purpose of which appeared to be the provision of a safe haven for photophobic vermin. The dented vertical surfaces were smeared with gang graffiti and the windows misted over with condensation and cooking grease. Parked beside it was an ancient and rusted VW Rabbit from the pre-recall days, when if your car caught fire it was just tough shit. This one looked as if it had, but had somehow survived.

The interior of the trailer was only slightly less squalid. A woman dressed in jeans and T-shirt sat in a folding camp chair and dragged hungrily on her first cigarette of the day, a cup of instant coffee cooling on the Arborite surface beside her. She was small and scrawny with short, hacked-away brownish hair above a tired, cynical face that still showed some small spark of the shit-disturbing that had formed her life's work. Sue Tort had done nothing in all the years of her adult life except complain. Name any sit-in through the 1970s and she had been there. Name any protest in the '80s and she had been a key organizer. Through the '90s and into the new millennium she had been the prime mover of social discord, and she and her team of anarchists had brought it to a fine art.

It had become a profession.

Tort's right-hand man sprawled on a busted chesterfield across from her. The contrast could not have been greater. Terry O'Weight was huge, orange-haired and guileless. He was the multi-purpose tool she had discovered years ago, like one of those gizmos you got at Home Hardware around Christmas time, or two-for-one on rapid-fire TV ads. And this one would do anything she asked of it provided the instructions were explicit, and provided it was supplied with enough beer, cigarettes and cheap peppermint chewing gum. A cerebral *tabula rasa* upon which she had formed his script since their first acquaintance. Stupidity –pure, clean, featureless stupidity–is a wonderful gift, and he had it in fine measure. God-given bone-headedness, innocent of education, literacy and curiosity allows its lucky owner to side-step all those problems associated with working things out for yourself. He did what he was told to the letter, never really pondered deeply why, and took immense pleasure in doing it.

33

They absolutely never touched each other. Never had, never would; never even contemplated the thought of it. Sue had no idea how he got his jollies, and she didn't give a damn. His bedroom was at the other end of the trailer, and what went on in there was as interesting to her as Shakespeare's sonnets were to him. She was about as sexless as made no difference, and the occasional finger was all she ever needed. She had had a boyfriend once, back in the university days, but... ah, shit, that was ancient history. Since then, nothing.

"Now lissen Terry," she fixed him with a mad stare that made him sit up slightly. "There's two firework shows this weekend, one out Markham way tonight, and the other at Ontario Place Sunday, so tons more of this heavy metal shit and stuff is goin' into the atmosphere. We'll do Markham; it ain't too far."

Terry nodded and smiled past his cigarette. He liked the idea of fireworks; make a change from all the other crap they usually marched against. Yeah, he had always liked fireworks.

Terry had no mechanism for measuring success or failure, but if he had, in all their years together it would have been impossible for him to ascribe success to any of their ventures. Sue Tort knew this; nothing she had ever turned her hand to had resulted in even an official acknowledgement of her justification, let alone a movement towards improvement. Be it jacked-up student fees, repatriation of native artifacts, G-however-many summits, pollution or seal hunting, her input had never made a damned bit of difference. But the 'sponsors' didn't care; that wasn't why they provided the funds to keep her network going. Quite who the shadowy sponsors of her enterprises were she didn't know, and didn't really want to know. The police of many jurisdictions kept files on serial protesters, faces that kept appearing again and again all over the country, but they were hampered by a lack of both solid information and an inside track into the organization. If it was an organization; it professed to practice anarchy, and anarchy is by definition antithetical to organization.

What their true motive was she shut out of her mind. By a feat of mental legerdemain she reconciled her ideology with their sponsorship, closed a door in her mind, and took the money. She adopted cause after cause in an endless trail of shattered failure. She simply knew no other life. It was an addiction as heavy as cocaine or tobacco or gambling.

Sue had several accounts with different banks, and supplies of money always appeared in them whenever required. She could take out cash to hire condemned school buses to transport her supporters, she could pay them (miserably) for their services, and she could pull enough to keep her and Terry in food and accommodation (sort of) and still run the car and buy cigarettes. It was a pathetic life on the eroded edge of a society that didn't really give a shit, but she was now habituated to the role and she would do it until she couldn't do it any longer.

Her instructions always came in cryptic, anonymous e-mails from an address that she had tried to trace a couple of times. She was sure the instructions didn't emanate from any of the legitimate anarchist organizations, because she had checked most of them on the Web and nothing rang a bell. Besides, in her decades of protesting she had met most of them and—although she didn't admit it, even to herself, because it would be too revealing—they were mostly pathetic. Sure, they were all 'militant' in their approach, but none had that smell of evil that hung around her sponsors. Why they had chosen fireworks was anybody's guess, and she had no way of finding out anyway. The money came in; the job got done. Simple.

"Fireworks're the cause of all kindsa sicknesses and pollution in the groundwater and stuff, so we gotta get in their faces."

"Yeah," replied Terry, taking a huge drag on his cigarette. "All that fuckin' smoke goin' into people's lungs. Should be illegal."

"I'm calling up the Network." She ground out her latest cigarette and lit up another one, swallowed tepid instant coffee in quick glottal gulps, and hauled out her cellphone. "Get outside and kick some of them druggies and bums awake. We need numbers, make a good showing. Offer 'em money for their next fix or somethin'. Free transport."

'The Network' was Sue Tort's list of disaffected individuals who didn't mind taking a few bucks to show up on demand and create mayhem. Most of the big demos around the world could not take place without these creatures. Many civic-minded citizens, for whom protest is a democratic right, have had their agendas hijacked by this bunch of yahoos who, in almost all cases, know practically nothing about the issues, and care even less.

There might have been more pressing issues than pyrotechnics. The fact that Tort and O'Weight's temporary home in this run-down trailer floated in a midden of social illness, want and disadvantage, simply never entered her mind. Fireworks were the flavour of the month and the word came from on high.

☆✫⭐✫☆

A travelling midway had set up its machines, and kids and adults were still hurtling through the air as evening came, and the gaudy lights flared and the music blared. Tomorrow there would be a firework show to close out the week's festivities and to celebrate Victoria Day, the Old Queen's birthday and quite simply a springtime excuse for having fun and burning black powder. Then the carnies would unbolt all their ramshackle human-whirling devices and drive to another small town, to another fair, another pink cotton-candy, cheap teddy bear, rattling, rock-and-roll celebration in the short growing season of the Ontario farms.

This was a small show; Alf and Bob did these sometimes, more for the enjoyment of letting off fireworks than for economic reasons. Break-even at best, and almost a loss-leader providing PR for the firm. Bob didn't like to travel as much as he used to, but this show was only a couple of hours drive from home, so if he wanted to he could scoot back home each night. In practice, he liked to be close to the action, so he took a room in the only decent motel in town, along with Alfred and Julia. Mike's wife was in hospital for minor surgery, so Julia had come along instead. She was a willing substitute, sympathetic to Mike, but knowing that the more gigs she worked with, the more capable she would become.

It was Friday evening, the day before the show. The light began to fade early in late May and it wouldn't be long before they had to quit work for the day, cover the set-up with tarps and plastic bags, and hand over to the nighttime security crew.

"That's it for me today," observed Bob, completing a wiring connection. "Can't see a damned thing. I'm going over to razz the protesters."

"Ignore 'em, Dad," said Alfred, still busy. "These people thrive on attention."

"I'm not having them put off our audiences. We should call the bloody police!"

"You know you can't. They have a democratic right to protest, and as long as they're breaking no laws, we can't do a damned thing."

"I know, I know, but I'm gonna talk to them anyway."

"What for? You're not going to talk them out if it."

"Information session." Alfred looked skeptical as his father continued. "At least, find out what their beef is. What makes 'em tick."

"You know what their beef... Oh, what the heck." Alfred shrugged and got back to the e-matches he was attaching to a set-piece on a wooden frame.

The frame, a radiating curve of cardboard candle tubes and gerbs, was lying flat on the ground. Once the matches were clipped in place on the fuses, and the wiring twist-tied to the frame, the whole thing would be pulled upright and set into the ground. He had several of these to prepare, and then there were four wheels to deal with, but those would have to wait until tomorrow; too dim now.

Wheels were his favourites among the ground-based fireworks, although the ones for this show were rather simple, each consisting of a wooden cross with drivers at the ends of the arms, and a variety of other effects distributed over the structure. There was one massive one back in the store at home, called a Maltese Wheel because that was where the device had become famous. He had only used it a couple of times, but it was gorgeous. It consisted of a huge hexagonal wooden wheel with six smaller wheels at the corners. The main drivers—great big fat things with a huge force—set the main wheel in clockwise motion, while a series of quick matches fired the drivers of the smaller wheels and set them going counterclockwise. And, in addition to the drivers, there were also fountains, candles and gerbs contributing to the display. He wished he could use it more often.

Bob walked over to where the little group squatted on the grass some way from the firing ramp. There were about 20 of them, most looking as if they were there just to incite mayhem. He actually thought it was a bit sad. Yes, he loved to launch fireworks, as many as possible and, yes, he knew they were a source of pollution, but it seemed to him that the people who had the democratic right to protest his activity were being highjacked by bunches of malcontents like this lot. So, it wasn't the legitimate protesters he was interested in, because he knew their story inside-out and backwards. It was the others, the malcontents he was after. And this was fertile ground.

"So, who's the boss here?" asked Bob in a mild tone. He held a hand up, palm flat and vertical. "Take me to your leader!"

Sue Tort stared at him insolently, cigarette between her lips. "I am, but what's it to you?"

Hmm, good start, thought Bob. Still, I am the enemy. "Oh,

just wondering if you'd like to talk it through, y'know."

"If you're expecting to talk us out of it, think again."

"Far from it," continued Bob in the lightest voice he could muster. "It's just that we're going ahead anyway, and of course it's your democratic right to protest."

"So, whadda y'want then?"

"Oh, I dunno," he shrugged. "Just a sort of idea of what your beef is."

"You know what it is! Yore spreading filthy pollution all over the planet. That's what! Getting into people's lungs, messing up rivers, lakes..."

"Drove here, did you?" he asked mildly. "Big diesel bus for all your supporters?" He pointed at a decrepit yellow school bus that was almost a collector's item.

"Oh, yeah, I get it!" Tort replied in scorn. "Well, that's horse-shit 'cos travel's a necessity, whereas fireworks is just mere pleasure."

"*Mere* pleasure? Good God, pleasure is what drives us. All of us. Pleasure is what got us all conceived in the first place!" Then Bob looked at this shriveled and timeworn specimen and conceded that perhaps there was a tiny stratum of society to whom the rocketing height of sensual pleasure might be biting an out-of-season Mexican strawberry shipped in ethylene oxide. He took another tack.

"Got a cellphone, have you?"

"What's that got to do with anything? Cellphones don't pollute."

"True. But you know those great big rockets that launch the communications satellites and all the other telecommunications equipment; cellphones, GPS, TV, the Web, stuff like that?"

Dumb insolence was the only recourse because she knew exactly where he was going.

"Those solid-fuel boosters produce more pollutants than all the fireworks in the world put together."

"Yeah," she shouted. "But I just tole you, didn't I, that there's necessities and choices, and you don't give nobody a choice with your fireworks. They're breathing it in, but they don't have a choice!" She crossed her arms in triumph.

"What brand are you smoking?" he asked innocently. "Drawing pollutants into your lungs, I mean? By choice."

She turned her back on him, glowering and refusing to say another word.

"Of course, you do chose," he smiled. "But remember this; I agree with everything you say about firework pollution. Everything. You've obviously done your research—or, at least, Google and Wikipedia have—and you're perfectly correct."

She didn't want agreement; she wanted dissent, she wanted argument, she didn't want some stupid bastard nodding his head wisely at everything she said. Agreeable shithead.

But she turned to face him anyway. "Okay, you're so goddamned agreeable, why don't you stop then? Eh?"

"Oh, I'll stop. As soon as you stop driving your bus, smoking cigarettes and using your cellphone. Is it a deal?"

She turned her back again.

None of the others seemed inclined to step up to the podium, so he strolled nonchalantly back to the ramp. Well, thought Bob Catesby, did I expect anything better? No, not really. And maybe the pleasure I feel at winning something is a little bit tainted. Fish in a barrel.

But it still left unexplained why fireworks were so damned important to these people...

☆⭐☆

As dusk fell on Saturday the group of protesters, carrying their placards and banners and megaphones, marched in ragged file into the park. Sue Tort had only just raised the megaphone to her mouth as she marched along in the van, shouting, "Now lissen! Lissen!" when she was confronted by a portly, nose-veined official from the fair's organizing committee.

"You can't protest here. This is private." He placed his considerable corpus in front of her, causing her and the group to slow to a standstill.

"This," she pointed at the ground at her feet, "is a public park. We can do anything we want in a public park! Outta the way!"

"You come any further and I'll call the police!" His face belied his resolution.

"We're here t'wage war on the forces of neoliberal capitalism currently embodied under the rubric of fiscal conservatism," shouted one of the supporters. "Yore the corporeal embodiment of an unjust mercantile ruling class embroiled in a right-wing ideological conspiracy of escalating greed and self-interest!"

"I'm telling you," puffed the official. "Get back or I'm calling the police!"

A guy called Steve Bacon, one of her stalwarts from East Gladstone, pushed forward and stood directly in front of portly nose-veins. He stared at the official with crazy eyes.

"Aw right! Call 'em," he invited. "Call the newspapers. Call whoever you want. Call the fuckin' Pope. We're goin' in. C'mon guys."

The official fell back puffing as the group pushed forward.

"Thanks Steve," said Sue as she elbowed along. Steve wasn't just a hanger-on; he was there for the money. He had no idea where this skinny malcontent got her funding, and he didn't give a shit, but a wad of notes in his hand just for showing up and shoving his weight around was fine with him. Being in her network supplemented his wages, which were crap because he was never able to hold down any job for long.

"Now lissen!" boomed and howled the megaphone as the group reached the security control barriers, and Sue turned to face the crowd. "Fireworks is a massive cause of pollution and sickness and yore all breathing it in. There's carcinogenic sulphur compounds and airborne arsenic, an' cadmium an' lithium an' strontium an' lead..." Tort had done her homework, "...and potassium and stuff, all contaminating the air, an' the water supply, and even acid rain..."

Alfred Catesby, over at the control panel, gave a broad grin and a thumbs-up, and pressed a key. Protest away you buggers!

Sue Tort's final words were quite drowned out by the first of many thudding detonations at ground level as the firework show got underway, followed by earsplitting cracks above their heads as the first reports burst above the crowd. She yelled into her megaphone as loudly as she could. "Perchlorate levels thousand times higher...! Thyroid gland...! Dementia..." but it was useless.

The thunderous noise was one thing. But the firework show had stolen any attention the crowd might have given her, and fully half of her volunteers, including that lunk-head Terry, had dropped their banners and placards and were gaping skywards.

Pops, bangs and whistles sounded, glorious streamers of filthy pollution rained down from the heavens, accompanied by Oohs and Aahs, as she raged up and down the diminishing ranks of her army, exhorting them in vain.

"Thousands 'er tons 'er heavy metals! And yore *enjoying* it!" she raged. "They're killing you slow and inexecrable..."

She stormed on in a hopeless paroxysm of rage and frustration, all her past failures rising up before her like an over-toppling mound of ripe ordure.

Finally, voice ruined by yelling, message obliterated by detonations, supporters wooed away by celestial magic, she flung down her placard and stormed off the field.

Terry O'Weight stood with his neck bent skyward, a huge grin on his big silly face, and drank in the spectacle.

He really loved fireworks.

☆★ ★ ★☆

Steve Bacon so-o-o enjoyed the moniker his gang at school had given him: Bacon Enter. It was what he was good at. He'd had that tear-away attitude for ever; he felt he always had to test himself, see just where the limits were. The guys he hung around with in high school were all like that. Life was for fun; it was for finding out what your limits were, it was for testing edges and brinks and precipices. It was for showing the guys where you stood.

They all go through it, teenage boys. It's all part of the process of settling into your niche and knowing more solidly where the man will fit into his world. Steve was in his late 20s and the transition had never been made. He had become an addict for the edge. Unless he was skating a fine line between the ecstasy of escape and the fear of capture, he never felt himself alive.

Now then, he thought, that favour he owed old Rocco; shit, why not have some fun, just like he said it would be, and fix things up for him? Rocco didn't want anything done about it, but that was just bullshit. Of course he did! Anyway, even if he didn't, now the idea was planted in Steve's mind the old addiction kinda kicked in. Once you get an idea like this in your head, you gotta do it. Thing is, it wasn't the mayhem he was after. Too dangerous to arrange a huge accident—didn't want to have Rocco or one of the gang have to set up another alibi—so subtlety was in order.

No, it wasn't the mayhem; it was the Bacon Enter. Just the act of going in; it was penetration, and it was ecstatic! And no point in going solo. You might get a good charge from doing it solo, but the biggest charge was when the other guys watched you doing it! And talked about it later. It was just... wow... there's no words for it.

And that was why, on a dark Tuesday night, Steve was carefully easing himself into a hole in the screening he had cut in a window around the back of the Catesby & Son facility, with his friend Hefty Beale peering up at him from the rear parking lot. Hefty Beale was a proud member of the V-Twin Valkyries and a friend of Steve's for many years. They had met in one of Steve's short stays in prison, and rather than beating the shit out of him as the other inmates did on a fairly regular schedule, Hefty had come to his defence. And as Hefty was inside for grievous bodily harm and was hugely muscled, Steve had never been beaten again.

Neither of them worried about defining their attraction; it was friendship, sure, but it went further than that, while remaining quite nonsexual. Hefty seemed to act as the big brother Steve had never had, and perhaps as a father too. Although he never spoke of it, Hefty saw Steve as the little brother he had lost to an accident in childhood. They were close.

"Gimme the bag," Steve hissed to his friend, "then climb up. Mind the sensor wires; I cut 'em and bent 'em back."

He had rigged up a dummy alarm sensor in parallel with the working one then carefully disconnected the latter. Now the system detected the same resistance throughout its circuits, and recorded that all was well.

He slid onto the inner window sill, leaned back for the bag, then helped Hefty to slide in and down to the floor. Hefty nearly didn't make it, and the noise he made gave Steve a delicious frisson of fear. They advanced slowly into the darkened building.

"Now then, let's have a look around, see what we got. I used to work here, so I know what's up. Shine the light this way."

The powerful LED beam lit up the end of a storage rack. He eyed the ranks of fireworks in boxes, all sorted according to the show they were earmarked for. The end of the angle-iron rack carried a metal slot into which a card was slipped with the date and location. As the rack was emptied, and the contents loaded into the trucks for the next show, so the next show took its place and an appropriate label was inserted. So that stupid summer job of his years ago was finally paying off.

"Ah, ha! Gwillimbury. That's what he said. So, what have we here?"

He checked the boxes on the shelf until he located his target. "Here they are; four-inch shells. I only have to screw around with a few of them."

"Whatever! Get on with it," whispered the flashlight-holding accomplice.

"Maybe one shell out of each box. See, that'll be enough to

screw up the show, but not so much they'll make a big case of it. You want 'em to fly, but not burst, see?" He loved to boast his knowledge.

"Like I said, whatever." Hefty was getting impatient. "Get it done and we're outta here."

Steve opened the bag he had brought with him and took out a huge ear irrigation syringe and an awl. He picked up one item out of a box of ten, undid a twist tie around the fuse and slid back the plastic bag that sheathed the shell. He pierced a small hole in the top with the awl, and inserted the syringe. A quick squeeze injected enough water to ruin the burst charge, but not enough to soak down into the lift charge. He then slapped on a little rectangle of gummed tape, slid the plastic bag back up, and closed it with the twist tie. He did this with five more shells from other boxes, filling the syringe from a Running Room water bottle.

"Should do it. They'll never even suspect they bin fucked with."

"Hey, look at this," said Hefty, shining the flashlight on the side of one of the boxes. "See, these things are made in Colombia. That's where our stuff comes from."

"Your stuff? What stuff?"

"Don't be a dumb ass, man. Whadda ya think?"

Steve returned his sabotage gear to the bag and they both headed back to the open window. Passing a shelf loaded with pyrotechnics Steve paused and picked up a fat three-foot long Roman candle.

"Just imagine if we lit this! Just imagine..."

"You outta your fuckin' mind? Blow the place up! Put it down you asshole."

"No, no, I mean like point it out the window." He laughed in an unsettling way.

Hefty grabbed him by the sleeve. "C'mon. I tole you to put it down, so let's get outta here! Sometimes you are so fuckin' out of control."

Steve reluctantly replaced the firework on the shelf and followed Hefty back to the window. They exited the way they had come, carefully reconnecting the sensor wires to the live sensor on the window sill and removing the dummy. Finally they replaced the cut wire mesh in the window just so and dropped down to street level.

Steve had a huge hard on.

It was well done. There was a distinct professionalism about the whole job, and a distanced observer would have mourned a talent so wasted.

And Steve was simply dying to tell all his pals.

☆ ⭐ ☆

"You asshole! Baby Jesus in his manger! You fuckin' asshole!" Sue Tort's body was lying where she had flung it in her chair, and she was dragging hungrily from a bright-lit cigarette. "Supposed to be my right-hand man and there you are, gawpin' up at the sky and going Oooh, Oooh, Aaah! Asshole!"

"But I like fireworks..." Terry O'Weight stood in a pose that replicated mute apology.

"I don't care what you *like*! We were there to protest, and that's what we were 'sposed to do! *Shit*!"

More blazing drags of cigarette, disgusting smell of singed filter, new cancer-stick lit from butt end. Interlude of harsh, liquid coughing. Finally, she cooled down and the anger was replaced with an ominous calm. Terry liked the ominous calm much better; the anger was always fired in his direction, but when she got all cold and calculating it meant that some real shit was gonna go down. That was much more fun.

"Now, look. There's another show we gotta go to next weekend, so we gotta get our act together. Know what I'm saying?"

Terry nodded, not wishing to break the spell and thus invite vituperation, although he might not have expressed it in quite that way.

"Standing up there with banners and loudspeakers and shit doesn't cut it. Three goddamned shows we're been totally drowned out. Gotta do this more effective. Sponsors'll dry up if we don't."

She lolled in her chair, scheming out the next move. Sure, they'd do the next demo or two, but it was becoming obvious that to demonstrate in the way they were doing was totally pointless.

But, how else to get the message across? How else to disrupt and damage?

☆ ⭐ ☆

Hefty Beale couldn't wait to tell Uncle Chuck all about his lucky find in the Catesby warehouse.

"What? You did a B and E with *Steve Bacon*? Are you out of

your fuckin' mind!"

"He owed some pal of his a favour and he, like, asked me, an'..."

"Didn't I tell you to steer clear of Bacon? Didn't I?"

"No. Never told *me*."

"Bullshit! He's poison. He has no control; he's off the edge. I don't want him knowing nothing about what goes on here. He's poison. Get it?"

"Yeah, okay. I got it. What he do?"

"Just act the asshole, that's all."

"I thought I heard..."

"All right, all right. He was caught helping himself to weed in the grow-op up beyond Hearst. Selling it on, for all I know, but couldn't prove it. He knows I'll kill him if he ever gets in my way."

"Well, anyway, Steve and me broke into this fireworks store, right, and they get their stuff from Colombia, same as us."

"So? Fuckin' Starbucks get their stuff from Colombia for all I know. Far's I know they make incontinence diapers in Colombia. So what?"

"Yeah, but, I was thinking, shipments of fireworks all nicely sealed up in boxes. Are you thinking what I'm thinking?"

"Nah, never work. Stuff from Colombia gets the beady eye. Customs just open one box and we're done. Gotta find a safer route than that."

Hefty shambled out, disappointed that what he thought was a good idea... wasn't.

☆✫⭐✫☆

It was a weekend in June and Rocco had decided to take a little time out and snoop on the competition. He'd lost the contract for the Gwillimbury Elks to Catesby, so why not drop down there tonight and check them out? Funny he had never thought of doing this before but, perhaps because of Nonno's pernicious influence, he had always considered them the enemy and had avoided them. Talk about paranoia! Well, it's always good to scout the enemy's position; like reading the occasional rightwing paper, or watching Fox News.

Gwillimbury was a couple of hours south of East Gladstone, so after a quick supper at home he gave his mother a peck on the cheek and headed out. The old Toyota Corolla was getting to the end of its life, but there wasn't enough in the bank to think about replacing it. It was a question of watching the balance of the cost of servicing versus monthly payments on replacement wheels, and when the two graphs crossed, bingo! They were close to that point at the moment, but nothing he could do about it.

The Gwillimbury Elks had their annual garden party, barbecue and firework show in the David Willson Athletic Facility, and it was child's play to flash his Natural Resources Canada firework licence to gain access to the ramp inside the yellow tape. Even so, he kept himself quietly unobtrusive in the falling twilight as he checked out the rows of mortars, the cakes and candles, and the big wheels. The ramp on this site was simply an asphalt surface, which was a basketball court in the summer and doubled as a rink in the winter when wooden boards were erected around it.

Of course they had all the up-to-the-minute electronic gear; didn't expect anything else. These days it was only the smaller community association outfits that lit the stuff with portfires. These guys were professionals, of course. Might have been a waste of time coming as this was obviously going to be a well polished show with probably not much to learn.

As Rocco wandered slowly over the ramp, he spotted a nice rear end and a head of pony-tailed fair hair leaning over a rack of 4″ mortars while their owner checked ignition wires attached to a harness. As she turned towards him, away from her work, he saw a woman perhaps a few years younger than him; high cheekboned face, blue eyes with a smile in them that complemented the wide mouth, and a slim figure dressed in hugging dark tights, with a tiny skirt that scarcely reached her high thighs. She wore a low-slung black tee that exposed the tops of her tits, across which ripples passed as over a voluptuous, high-viscosity fluid. Printed across the shirt in large white letters was 'ASK ME ABOUT MY BOMBSHELLS'.

He was intrigued.

But, whoever she was, she was working for the other side, so he decided to back off. Even so, their eyes met. She saw a tall, slim man with the fashionable well-barbered shadow of a four-day beard, and one of those Mediterranean skins that would tan in no time to a gorgeous bronze. And his eyes were gold. He wore stone wash blue jeans with a loose linen jacket over a light brown roll-neck shirt. He smiled, and his whole face joined in the fun.

She was intrigued.

The light was failing, the time for the show was approaching, and before she could think of quizzing his presence here, he smiled again, turned and headed for the crowd. It would be a busman's holiday, but he would hang around anyway and watch the show.

It was beautifully choreographed but there were elements he recognized from software simulations he himself had shown to clients. Certain combinations of colours, effects of light, angles of projection, and sequences of events were familiar. Not that this detracted from the audience's enjoyment of course—this was insider information, one pro to another—but it did make him realize that his presentations were just as good, and that he could match Catesby show for show. And his Italian stuff was definitely better. He had known this before, but this experience brought it home to him and gave a positive boost to an ego that needed all the sugar it could get.

But what was this? One of the aerial shells had failed to explode! That never happened; at least, he couldn't remember an incident. As the show continued he thought perhaps he'd imagined it, but there it was again. Another one had snaked up into the air, its passfire clearly burning, and... nothing... No burst charge; no effects. Holy shit! What the hell was going on? You never saw this. *Never*.

A few minutes later there was another! At first he thought of Nonno and how delighted the old man would be with the failures. But then his heart turned as more shells failed to burst, and he began to feel really strange, almost guilty on his grandfather's behalf. He thought of that girl, and how she would feel, and it just didn't seem right for anyone to wish that on somebody else.

By the close of the show he'd counted six failed aerial shells.

He drove home with a very heavy heart, *schadenfreude* far from his mind. He'd tell Nonno about this expedition, but he wouldn't let him know about the failures. The thought of the old guy's pleasure gave him pain.

☆ ⭐ ☆

Alfred Catesby was shaken. Never had he seen one single dud aerial shell. And last night he'd had six. Six! He sat at the head of the long table in the boardroom, his father Bob and Mike, their assistant pyrotechnician, on his left with Julia further up the table on the right.

"Okay, I don't get it. Up to now those Colombian shells have been absolutely dead reliable."

"No problem in any way at all," agreed Mike, who had been responsible for firing off the show in Gwillimbury. "Never seen that before. Never."

"The guy who recommended them—guy at the international conference—swore by them. We're going to have to look long and hard at this."

"Damned right," agreed Bob. "Get a reputation for duds, you're in big trouble."

"Maybe it was one bad batch?" suggested Julia a little diffidently.

"Could be," replied her father. "But can we assume there won't be another? It's a hell of a risk."

"But what could cause it?" continued Julia asserting herself a little more, and getting a slight nod from her grandfather. "The only thing I can think of is some fool leaving out the burst charge."

"Highly unlikely," said Alfred, "but the only logical answer."

"You saw the passfires burning, right?" asked Bob.

"Sure," replied Julia. "That was the weird bit, because I just can't see how anyone could leave out the burst charge. And even if they did, you'd think once the passfire reached the inside of the shell, the garnitures would at least burn and break out. But nothing."

"Did you retrieve the duds, Mike?" asked Bob.

"Sure," Mike replied. "We found 'em all this morning and labeled them for disposal, as per regs. But I checked one of 'em out. It rained overnight so they were soaking wet, but even so, I wouldn't have thought the rain would penetrate. The powder was all there; nothing wrong inside, except wet."

"This is bizarre," observed Alfred. "Well, the only thing we can really do is keep an eye on all the Colombian shells, and if we have even one more dud we simply stop ordering."

"Sure," agreed Bob. "Too much resting on it."

"Okay," concluded Alfred, "I'll write to Francisco and tell him; threaten cancellation of our orders. Might be enough to push them to better quality control. If that's really the issue..."

☆✭ ✩ ✭☆

Rocco had to go down Main Street to pick up a package at UPS. He could have called them and had it delivered, but it was a nice sunny day in late June and a brief respite from juggling with numbers and finding out how much money the company didn't have would be welcome. Why not a coffee first? There was a new place just up here on the corner; why not give it a try?

He stepped into the coffee shop and lined up at the counter. As usual there was some idiot ordering a goddamned frappaccino, cappuccino, mochaccino what the hell, with whipped cream and sprinkles of cocoa powder and Christ knew what else shit. And it was *grande* of course. You should go to Italy, he thought, and see how far that horseshit will get you. Finally he got to the counter and ordered his plain, ordinary café Americano without any crap whatsoever, and took it over to the seating area. All the soft chairs were taken by people with laptops or tablets, all taking advantage of the free WiFi and maybe buying a coffee every couple of hours, figuring that was sufficient rent. There was only one table not fully occupied; a lone girl sat there with a cappuccino.

"Do you mind if I sit here?" he asked, then stepped back in surprise. A little coffee slopped onto his thumb, but he didn't notice. It was her! 'Ask me about my bombshells'. She looked up as he swung a chair around.

"It's you again," she said meeting his eyes. "I saw you at the gig in Gwillimbury. What are you doing here?"

"I... I live here."

"Oh." A pause while they assessed each other.

"May I...? Nowhere else to sit..." A sweep of his hand indicated the crowded room.

She nodded. "Sure."

He sat down slowly. She sipped her coffee. What was it about that quick flash of her tongue as she licked the milk foam around her mouth?

"I recognized you when I saw you at the counter," she continued. Oh, God, she thought, what a pathetic opener. "But before that..."

"Well, you've probably heard of my grandfather. My name's Pastorelli; Rocco Pastorelli."

"Oh, Jesus!" A flush rose in her cheeks. "You're the enemy! I know your name."

"Well, I don't like to think of myself in quite that way. Obviously you work for them, but even so...."

"I meant... I mean... the competition."

"Don't worry about it. My grandfather has your outfit totally in his sights." How easy she was to talk to!

"I know; I hear it too from my pa..."

"Your pa?" he interrupted. "So you're..."

"Julia."

"Julia?" He ran the name over his tongue, tasting sweet places and smelling the clear air of high fields. Julia... What *is* this? Ordinary girl; regular face, fine cheekbones sure, and blue eyes, pretty tied-up ponytail, nice smile that seems to hover all the time, even when her mouth is still. For Christ's sake get a grip!

"Julia Catesby, of course!" She smiled.

"Jeez! I really am fraternizing with the enemy!"

"But, like you said, are we really the enemy?"

"Well, if you'd heard the stories as long as I have... I mean, my Nonno..."

"Nonno?"

"Oh, sorry. Grandfather. Anyhow, he doesn't have a good word to say about your outfit. 'We was here first', 'They're undercutting us', all sorts of stuff like that."

"But that's just competition, surely? Look, you won the Tchaikovsky gig. That was huge." Another sip; another enticing lick.

"It surprised us. Couldn't figure out how..." He couldn't stop looking into her eyes. She couldn't stop looking into his. No, she thought, I don't want this. Not after the last one. Not another bullshit sexual roller-coaster. Please! But how could she not?

"Yeah, that was a big boost for us," he was saying.

She brought her wandering thoughts back. "Oh, Dad figured that one out really quick. You're Italian."

"So? Tchaikovsky was Russian." Was she messing with him?

"No, no. The maestro of the symphony is Italian too. Dad says he's a complete prick."

"Oh, I get it! He chose us instead of you 'cos he's a complete prick?"

She laughed over her cup, and my God she lit the place up. What is this, he thought, some stupid chick-lit paperback with gossamer-wisped tits on the cover? Real people don't act like this!

"Pity there aren't more Italians around then. Get a few more gigs, maybe."

She laughed again. This is nuts, he thought, all the chicks I've had over the years—and did I *ever* use these knockout Italian good looks—but none of them did this. Not one. And she's not even... what...? Beautiful...? Attractive... what?

50

Then he thought of what Nonno would do if he ever found out. It'd kill the old bugger. But maybe the old bugger would kill him first.

She caught the drift of thoughts across his face. "What?" She was smiling broadly. "What?"

"I was just thinking about family... issues..."

"You mean," she translated, "how pissed they would be if they knew you had met me... Twice!"

"My love life is absolutely none of their busi..." Oh shit! What kind of dumb ass thing to let out. She was smiling radiantly again, with laughter dancing at the corners of her lips.

"Did you know your skin looks absolutely gorgeous when you blush?"

"I was... No, I mean... Look, I gotta get going; package to collect."

"I'll be here tomorrow. Same time, same place."

"Okay. I'll... yeah..." and he was on his way to the door.

"Then that'll be three times!" she called after him with a laugh.

Chapter Two
The Lift Charge

The charge in an aerial shell that propels it into the air
Display Fireworks Manual, Natural Resources Canada (2010)

Uncle Chuck wasn't quite as dismissive of Hefty's idea as the big lug had first thought. The more he thought about fireworks from Colombia, the more he realized the subtlety of the idea. He'd seen those round shells they fired up into the sky. They were containers embedded in and surrounded by gunpowder. Surely to Christ nobody would dream of opening firework shells and checking them out one by one. And you could do one, maybe two boxes in a big shipment. Shee-it! And it would be an open, legit shipment coming in to port, right in front of their eyes from friggin' Cocaine Central. And surely, Ziploc bags, totally cleaned on the outside and packed alongside gunpowder would be undetectable. Have to do some research on how fireworks are made...

He picked up the phone. "Hey, Hefty. This asshole who wanted a favour? Steve's pal? Who was this guy...? What d'you know about him...? Oh, did he? Now ain't *that* excitin'!"

So Rocco Pastorelli was the one who kept Bacon Enter out of jail? Mister Alibi. Of course, he remembered now. Nice.

He pulled up Google on his laptop and checked for sites on making fireworks. Pay dirt within seconds; diagrams of how firework shells were made, lots of description from guys who make them, all confirming that a large and very useful cavity in aerial shells existed to be exploited.

Next, he typed in Pastorelli and got their website, complete with phone numbers. Rocco Pastorelli... chief honcho... lots of leverage...

He decided to stew over this one. No harm in waiting a few days. It looked good but it needed thinking about and sleeping over.

Then, we'll see if we can't do a little useful business in Latin America...

☆⭐☆

The Detective Inspector of CID for East Gladstone wandered to the window of his office high in the police station. He'd been transferred here from Toronto and though it looked at first like a demotion, he actually rather liked it. Unlike the job in the big city, this one gave him much more freedom to do what he enjoyed best; being a real cop. And, surprisingly for a small, ostensibly tourist-driven town, there was actually quite a lot of dangerous shit going down.

His privileged window overlooked the forests stretching north of the town. He mused upon the terrain over the horizon of his vision; millions and millions of black spruce, scarcely a road; lakes and forests and more lakes and rivers until the tundra. We all know how wide this country is—us who live and work here—but few of us realize how *tall* it is. Here I am nearly halfway to the equator and all I can see is miles and miles of virtually nothing stretching to the North Pole.

What the hell started that train of thought, he wondered. Oh yeah, the DS's friggin' fishing trip. Get a grip.

He turned from the window to face Detective Sergeant Delios patiently sitting the other side of the desk. Fred Delios was the DI's favourite cop. He had arranged for him to be transferred from Toronto, and the man had come willingly. He had a steady determination and he was smart with the intricacies of the law, but he also knew exactly when to aim a huge boot in the balls and get away with it. At least, he used to. These days every fuckwit with a cellphone can record the actual moment of contact, but ignore all the crap that leads up to it. Try wrestling down a paranoid knife-wielding drunk sometime without playing a little body music. Doesn't happen. But the media sure like to jump on the shaky out-of-focus videos and subject us to the pillory.

Damn, another train of thought that ran full steam ahead on its own rails. Come back to the real world, man!

"So, nice relaxing time out on the lake?" he asked. "Good to see you back! I'm glad you caught a few big 'uns, 'cos in this part of the world we just let 'em slip through our fingers."

"What, the drug bust?"

"Of course, the drug bust." There was little else on the DI's radar.

"Well, at least the pipeline's stopped." Delios tried a bit of optimism, but it was a clear failure.

"Yeah, great! We had this wonderful photo op with all the media. You saw it; pictures of all those little baggies, and the

RCMP, the Sûreté de Québec and the OPP all telling us what a great coup it was, but come on! They pinched a few minor players, that's it."

"Jumped too soon?"

"Of course! I'll grant it's tempting to spring the trap, catch as many as you can, but you gotta be patient with these guys. I am damned sure the stuff was coming through here, but they're just too canny. We've raided the Valkyries twice, and looked like complete idiots both times. We can *not*," and he punched his fist into his palm in emphasis, "we *can not* treat these people as if they're stupid. Cardinal mistake. Now we still don't have the kingpins, and the traffickers'll just find another route for the stuff. It's endless!"

"What evidence do we have that it's coming through our little neck of the woods, anyway?"

"That's it! There's nothing definite; it's all rumour and hearsay from our ears in the town. Had a hell of a time getting the warrants. I feel like we're on the outside looking in, but my nose is twitching, and I'm not often wrong."

"I also wondered," said Delios a little diffidently, "if there was also a coordination issue?"

"Yup. Course! Three forces, not including us–the OPP, the Mounties and the SQ–all wanting to grab a slice of the pie; get their mugs on TV. We have to do these things better!"

A small silence ensued. Delios cleared his throat.

"Sorry," said the Chief. "You wanted to see me about something?"

"Nothing too serious. I've just taken over the file of those activists; been tracking them for a while. Remember, they were based in Toronto, but they've apparently moved here. Living in a trailer down on Sandford. They'll go wherever there's shit to be stirred."

"Those bastards have surfaced again? The big lunk and the skinny one?"

"Yeah, they're the ones."

"Christ, we almost had them in Toronto, but couldn't do a damned thing. What's their latest beef?"

"Protesting fireworks of all things! Last week in Markham. Complete failure by all accounts; didn't even need to call the local cops in."

"Fireworks! Christ! They have no discrimination whatsoever. What's it to do with us anyway?"

"Well, we've kept an eye on 'em because we have two pyro-technic firms here in town, both potential targets for a protest. Probably why they moved here. We haven't been able to hang anything on them, but we figure every time they surface we monitor and keep hoping. We're certain they have a well-heeled backer."

"Yeah. Their protests are never about what's actually on the agenda, are they? Somebody's using these pathetic tools and pay-ing for mayhem. It's international. See it on the news anywhere in the world..."

"Anyway, far as we're concerned, what it means is we need a few extra people on the ground if they show up anywhere near our turf. Keeping an eye on 'em."

The Detective Inspector sighed. "You know how hard it is to justify stuff like this. Legitimate right to protest, democratic rights..."

"I know, but it's the extracurricular stuff we're after, isn't it? If we can catch 'em in something illegal it could lead into their or-ganization. It's worth the effort."

It was the same old one-note symphony, thought the DI; we need more staff, more resources, our officers are stretched to breaking, we can't do our job. He was an old fashioned sort of policeman. He still figured that it was a cop's job to arrest crimi-nals and see to it they went behind bars quickly and for as long as possible. City Hall had different ideas; their idea of a fine police force was having squad cars loafing on street corners at stop signs all day waiting to ticket rolling-stops, or sending two offi-cers on motorbikes to an antique car and motorcycle rally for a whole day. That one really got up his nose because the god-damned Valkyries also sent their guys; part of the gang's image-making for Christ's sake! Our city councilors want a 'police com-munity presence' and so they have two of our boys on bikes hob-nobbing right alongside tattooed, leather-clad criminals!

DS Delios was almost sure he could see wisps of steam rising from the Chief's ears, so he got up from his chair.

"All right. Let's see how it goes. It would give me great per-sonal satisfaction to pin something on those two. Fireworks! Christ!"

"There's one other small thing," said Delios, his hand on the door handle. "Any way we can monitor their cellphones? They're probably stupid with them; talk openly..."

The DI stared into the distance for a few moments. "Doubt it.

Don't think we'd have enough to convince anybody. Legitimate democratic right to demonstrate. Not a hope. Sorry."

"Thought not. Thanks anyway," and the door closed behind the Detective Sergeant.

☆ ☆ ☆ ☆

This was crazy. Rocco had driven right into the centre of town so he could have lunch at the same place. He couldn't wait to see her again. All morning he had been working in a distracted dream with her face always in front of him. So distracted was he by the coming liaison that he didn't even register anguish at the financial numbers that passed before his unseeing eyes. He hurried to the Main Street coffee shop, scene of their second chance encounter, far too early and was obliged to wait there until she came. His mind was tortured with the thought that she wouldn't show; that he had made it up to be bigger than it really was. That she was really just some nice girl who got a kick out of talking to guys in coffee shops. End of story.

There she was! Striding in at the door with her bag swinging off her shoulder. Lovely calf-length patterned skirt, leather belt, and loose blouse in gentle olive. The elastic on her ponytail always matched her clothes.

She pulled up a chair opposite him and looked into his eyes.

"Fancy meeting you here," she murmured.

"Staggering coincidence," he replied, not breaking the eye contact.

Her small, slim hands were on the table, loosely crossed. He took one hand in his, surprised slightly by the work-textured feel of it. She neither relinquished nor gripped, but let her hand lie passively in his. His first thought, that he had committed too familiar a gesture, was stilled by this apparent compliance.

She broke a long silence. "So, you're the chief honcho down at Pastorelli's?" Amazing, she thought, that our companies have been in this little town all these years yet we know nothing about each other. Talk about paranoia.

"Yeah. I mean, my grandfather's still the boss. He likes to keep his hand in, but mostly he lives in the good old past."

"And your father?" she asked in the guileless way only a stranger could.

"He's dead," he replied quickly. "Just me and Nonno. And Mama. He's over eighty now, Nonno."

"Over eighty!" she remarked brightly, realizing she had stepped wrong and that a conversational change of tack was in order. "He was born in Italy, then?"

"Oh yeah. He moved to Toronto in the early fifties and set up there. He was only twenty-one, twenty-two. Made all his own stuff back then, too. Italian tradition from 'way back."

"Boy, he must have some stories to tell!"

"When I was a kid I used to hear lots," he began happily, but then his face clouded. "Just recently though... he doesn't tell the old stories the way he used to..."

She had seen the wave of sadness cross his face, and felt for him; it resonated with her, but it was his alone, and not to be shared. Her hand slid away from his.

"My Grandpa," she began brightly, "has all sorts of stories too..." Then she realized that she had again opened something that ought to have remained closed.

Another silence, slightly awkward, followed as she watched the thoughts cross his face. She could *read* him.

"I would do *anything* to keep him happy," he sighed. "Anything!"

She decided a quick conversational U-turn was in order. "What an amazing couple of days! I was out on the lake wind-surfing yesterday. You ever been wind-surfing?"

It worked. The smile returned. They talked and talked the time away, face to face, and spent not one red cent on coffee, tea, muffins or doughnuts. Her hands had found their way into his.

They rose together when half an hour had passed and stepped out onto the sidewalk hand in hand. They were alone on the street.

"I go this way," she pointed up the street in the direction of Catesby & Son.

"And I go that," indicating the other way, east of town.

"Same time, same place?" she asked.

"Sure."

She walked slowly deep in thought. All her previous partners stood up one by one in her memory for comparison and appraisal. I never lost myself to any of them. Ever. Richard was just like all the rest; glad he's out of the picture, although it was tough. She felt a little guilty that perhaps Richard had been more deeply involved than her, but they had scarcely ever spoken of their feelings. Had it been too difficult for him to open himself to her; had he just kept his feelings to himself, or did he have no feelings? Was bouncing around in bed the beginning and end of it? And his reluctance to speak honestly of any feelings he may have had led to a diffidence in her. Negative feedback. Well, no way to carry on a relationship.

Now this guy, this Rocco, attracts on a totally different level. That chance meeting over the mortars; the leader fuse to this lift charge. I think I know what it is; I've just found out that there was something in me that was always intact, but now whatever it was, it's broken. And I am overflowing with the joy of its loss! When had something like this ever happened to her, she asked herself. Never. How had a first glance in the twilight from someone she didn't even know have come to this? It came to her that all her previous affairs of the heart had been merely affairs of the genitals.

Jesus, she thought, you'd think this was some stupid chick-lit paperback with open cowboy shirts and bulging bronzed pecs on the cover. Real people don't act like this!

☆ ⭐ ☆

Same old coffee shop! Rocco arriving too early and sitting in an agony stretched beyond human pitch before... There she was! Swinging down the street with a confident stride and pushing open the shop door. Then she was at his side and he had stood up and they had hugged and she smelt wonderful, and he had put his hands on her shoulders and she had put her hands on his hips and she had brought her smiling face to his and they had kissed and it was all too impossible to be true.

"I thought you wouldn't come," he told her across the table, once they had taken their seats and the smiling workmen and the astonished old couple at adjacent tables had finally removed their attention.

"And I thought you wouldn't be here," she laughed so that the sun was outdone.

He took her hands across the table, staring into those magic eyes.

"Julia." He rolled the name across his mind.

"Rocco." She relished the word in all its round, promising fullness.

They sat, eyes and hands locked, knowing that the words each spoke in their minds were perfectly audible with no sound expressed. Finally he spoke.

"This only happens to teenagers you know. I'm twenty-seven years old."

"Yes. Grownups don't do this. We should know better."

"So there is an age limit, then?"

She smiled into his eyes. "Let's bend the rules. What do you think?" He nodded.

"I have known you," he said after a long silence, "for all of maybe an hour, if that, stretched over weeks. Is it to early to tell you that I am in love with you?"

"Oh, far too early," she smiled. "I have known you for exactly the same length of time, and it is only now that I think I know what love is."

"We do sound like..."

"...a Harlequin romance?"

"Yeah, one of those purple bodice-rippers."

"How would you know?"

It was his turn to laugh, and she liked it.

"This is true love," he murmured. "Think this happens every day?"

"Thank you, Westley..."

"As you wish..."

Later, outside the coffee shop, they came together as at the beginning, although this kiss was longer and less restrained by any public magnifying glass.

"Here's my number." She showed him her phone screen. He tapped it into his. "Call me."

"I will."

He didn't want her to go. It was almost as if the mirage would vanish as she turned a corner, and dreary reality rise to take its place. Then she was gone, swinging up the street with that confident stride.

He turned, willing himself to get back to Pastorelli Fireworks' horrendous financial figures. But he went with a bouncing step, feet lifted by joy.

☆✰☆

Bob, Julia and their client carried their beers from the bar and sat on high stools round a circular table on the patio. There had been a June rainstorm earlier in the day, but it was now mercifully clearing out and the forecast looked good for the evening. Following her grandfather's tastes, Julia had developed a liking for beers from smaller breweries, something with colour and body and flavour. He referred to most North American factory beers as horse piss, and she fully agreed. There's beers to get drunk on, he would observe, and then there's beers to enjoy. They both had half pints of Alexander Keith's dark ale.

It was the day of a show in Kitchener and they had travelled down with Alfred and Mike two days previously. There were only a few of gigs in the year that all four of them attended, so this made a nice change. As there was still some work to do at the ramp, the other two had stayed back while Julia and her grandfather went for a liquid lunch. They would spell Mike and Alfred off, as they felt it wise always to have someone on site. Even if security was provided, taking breaks in relays was fairly normal.

"Just watching you guys," said the client, Brian Anscombe, a local town councilor who had invited them for the drink, "there's a hell of a lot of safety precautions."

"Sure," replied Bob. "That's why we're only having half a beer each. Steady head for this kind of work."

"And you're very closely regulated, right?"

"Absolutely. Government keeps a pretty close watch on this stuff. Rules and regulations, licences, guidelines..."

"Yes," put in Julia. "It's almost a unique occupation, really, where extremely explosive materials are being detonated right in front of crowds of spectators."

"You mean you use, like, dynamite and stuff like that?"

"No, no," replied Julia quickly, "I didn't mean high explosives. I'm talking about inorganics, but still extremely dangerous."

"See," put in Bob, "going back to your high school chemistry, you'll remember that chemicals are basically divided into organic and inorganic."

Anscombe nodded wisely, although both Julia and Bob suspected that whatever he had learned from such subjects as high school chemistry had long since been considered disposable.

"See, all our reactions," continued Bob, "are inorganic; basic oxidation/reduction. But lethal nonetheless."

"I see," said Anscombe, although he didn't. "So, lots of regulation then?"

"Very tight controls," said Bob. "You've read the manual from Natural Resources we gave the town council," (he hadn't) "and you can lose your licence for even small infractions. And it's getting more and more difficult to do this stuff."

Anscombe nodded and sipped his Coors Light. "Ever have an

accident? Just wondering."

"No," replied Bob shortly, "touch wood." He placed his palm down on the sticky acrylic-coated wood of the table... and regretted it.

"Near misses?"

"You *are* fishing, aren't you?" replied Bob, a little bit nettled and taking time over his beer before replying. "Only once. Once mind you, in all the time I've done this; I've had just one flowerpot."

"*Flowerpot?*"

Julia laughed. "I don't know why we call it that."

"Maybe it looks that way when it goes off?" suggested Bob. "I dunno."

"Yes, but what is it?"

"It's when the burst charge goes off in the tube. So you get the effect you would normally see a few hundred feet in the air, right in front of your nose."

"Holy shit! What causes it?"

"Couple of things," replied Julia before her grandfather could, although he smiled and nodded. "The powder in the passfire might have loosened, causing it to flash instead of burning slowly, or maybe there was a powder leak between the lift and the burst."

"Arcane words," complained Anscombe, "but I get the idea. So, what happened?"

"Gorgeous display of crackling stars right in me face," replied Bob. "Luckily it wasn't in the portfire days or I wouldn't be talking to you right now. The crowd thought it was quite wonderful. Applauded."

"Portfire days? Sounds like something out of a pirate movie."

"Yeah, sorry. Before the days of electric firing we used to light 'em with a flare. The sort of slow-burning thing they still sell as emergency flares for road accidents. You'd drop the shell in the hole, light the fuse, and stand back."

"Boy, the electrical set-up must be a breeze."

"Yes and no," replied Julia, again earning a nod and smile from Bob. "The set-up is very time consuming. In the average half-hour show there are hundreds of electric matches to attach, one to each firework, and an equal number of circuits to be tested. Takes ages. And then, of course, you have to run dummies on the whole lot. That's what we'll be doing when we get back."

"You see," put in Bob, "once it's all wired we have to run a small current through all the hook-ups to test for continuity. It's called the no-fire current; just enough juice to test the correct resistance in the e-matches, obviously not enough to warm 'em up."

"So that's why you guys have been here for two days."

Bob nodded and finished his beer. "Time to get back. Spell the others off."

It was another fine show that night, another appreciative audience, another small but not insignificant contribution to the 500 or so tonnes of burnt gunpowder and allied materials added yearly to the atmosphere throughout the country for no other reason than pure pleasure.

☆ ☆ ☆ ☆

It was one of those 'your place or mine' situations. Julia had got back from Kitchener the day before, and she and Rocco had now enjoyed their third date, not counting their first chance encounters. This time they had eaten a fine meal in a quiet little Italian place where Rocco was known and his privacy respected. They had dallied and talked over their cappuccinos and biscotti, holding hands like a couple who had done this for ever. Now a new intimacy was creeping up on them and there, in the near future, was the inevitability of it all. Their dalliance was lightly flavoured with shyness.

Neither needed specific words.

"I have the top floor of the family house," he told her. "On Primrose, east end of town, past the hockey arena."

"I'm near here. Little apartment on Simcoe. Would you... um... like a nightcap?"

The next hour was a segment taken out of time and space. The fulfilled promise of her breasts, his tattoo in the most unusual place, the brushing hands, the slow motion ecstasy of time almost at a standstill; her fair hair, released from the ponytail and falling in luxury about her shoulders. Small details, like the flashes of reports between periods of darkness, illuminated their movements in memory. At one flash-lit moment he remembered brushing his lips gently over the base of her belly just above the curls. At another she was crying "Oh yes oh yes oh *yes!*" Flash: her face looking up at his; flash: his shoulder outlined against the window lit by streetlight; flash: their coming together. She had already given with all her heart that tiny newly-broken inner piece, so their love-making became an ecstatic formality. As he finally entered her, his spitool fired their simultaneous burst charges, signifying the endorsement of an already prepared and witnessed document; the final seal.

And, yes, *of course* it was like fireworks.

☆✩☆

She woke slowly to find him peering into her eyes.

"Sleeping with the enemy..." she murmured.

"Call that sleeping?" He moved over her. "Some enemy."

"We'll be late for work."

"This *is* work. Here..."

Later, over coffee and a little toast in her sunlit living room she opened the subject again.

"I hate it that you're the enemy."

"Do I have to be?"

"Well, I know my dad would be so-o-o pissed off if he found out." She thought for a little. "Grandpa...? I don't know; there's some history there. And Mum; she would want what's best for me, but she always does. My dad's the one I'd worry most about. See, I don't mean to be disloyal, but he really is a hard-nosed bastard. Like, in business I mean."

"My Nonno would have a shit fit! You don't know hard-nosed!"

"So, it's a secret?"

"For now, yeah. We'll have to wait for the moment."

"Christ! You'd think we were teenagers!" she cried, dropping her toast on the floor. "If they could just meet and talk. You know, sort out differences, maybe even share gigs, or at least suppliers. I don't know!"

"Ah, they're both much too hard boiled for that." He knew Nonno far too well.

"Why are they like this?" she moaned, checking her toast for dust before biting off a corner. "Stupid vendetta!"

"You know as much as I do. Something that happened 'way back in the Stone Age."

"But you could save a deal of money if you shared shipments with the rest of us! Lower transport costs, lower brokerage, common storage."

"Nonno wouldn't hear of it. We pay a lot in shipping–it's all from Italy–and the stuff's about the most expensive you can buy.

Where's your stuff come from? Mostly?"

"All the ground stuff is Chinese, Japanese, some European–candles, wheels, cakes–but we're getting some aerial shells from Colombia now."

"Colombia! That's a new market."

"Lots of factories there–good quality and real cheap–but we don't buy them direct. We use an agent, a middle-man who buys the consignment from the makers, and then prepares them for shipping. He bills us at source for the cost of the consignment and the shipping, and charges a very reasonable fee."

"Why not buy direct from the factories? Wouldn't it save money?"

"No. You see, the agent's a local guy who knows his way around the factories, and can pick and chose the best bang for your buck from the lists we send him. Just having him do that saves us a bundle because the factories jack up the price for international sales; nearly double sometimes, which matches with international prices from China, Japan and Europe."

"So you get better prices than even the Chinese? I thought they were the most competitive."

"Oh, no. Our agent, Francisco Gonçalves, real nice guy, gets us a better deal, and even with his fee, we end up making on the whole transaction. Simple."

"I should find a way into that market. Francisco Gonçalves you say? I could save a bundle of money, but if Nonno found out..."

A sudden frown of worry crossed her face. "Oh shit, Rocco, I shouldn't have told you all this. Dad'd kill me. Why do you have to be the enemy?"

"No worries. It's an open secret anyway; word will soon get around. You know our community. Anyway, I ain't no spy. Or, if I am, I'm a lousy one."

"Yeah, the spy who loved me. Worst thing you could have done, falling for the enemy."

"Best thing. Come on, let me show you..."

"Finish your coffee and that toast and get to work, you... you Lothario!"

"As you wish..."

☆✫⭐✫☆

"Somehow," muttered Sue Tort, lounging in her busted chair in the Airstream trailer, "we have to find a way of screwing up their shows. Like I said, loud-hailers and leaflets and marching around doesn't cut it. We gotta find some way..."

"What, like we burn down the fireworks factory?" Terry's inner eye was filled with an amalgam of visions from his limited imagination combined with a scene from a *Pink Panther* movie he'd once seen.

"No, no, no, you stupid tool! I'm thinking of some way of sabotaging their shows." Her face shriveled into a frown of concentration as her cheeks sucked in smoke.

A great grin spread over Terry's silly face as he threw his chewing gum from one side of his big mouth to the other. Sue recognized that grin; it told her that the big galoot had a secret he just couldn't wait to spill.

"Aw right, what the hell's so funny? Whatcha grinning like that for, you big ape?"

"Steve broke into the firework place. He told me."

"Steve? Steve Bacon? He'd tell you his grandmother's the Queen of fucking England. He's out of control."

"Him and his pal, they broke in and pissed around with the fireworks."

"What did you say?"

"I said, him and his pal, they broke in and piss..."

"I heard you!" She hauled hard on her cigarette, evil schemes passing across her tiny eyes. She picked up her phone. "Steve, get your ass over here. Wanna run something by you."

Steve lived in one of the developments on the east end of town, so it wasn't many minutes before he showed up at the trailer.

"How do you fuck up a firework show?" She stood up to face him, coming straight to the point. She handed him a smoke and, in an unusual gesture of social intimacy, she even lit it for him.

"Well, not by marching around with banners and shit, that's for sure..."

"Don't get fuckin' smart with me! You're forgetting who's paying you. I jus' asked you, how do you fuck up a firework show?"

"You mean like sabotage?"

Steve recalled the water injections but quickly rejected that approach. Just injecting a few shells like last time wouldn't work; sure, it pisses around with the show, but it hardly ruins it, and you couldn't do enough anyway. It would be much better to try something on site, like maybe their firing gear. He didn't know a hell of a lot about it, but he did know they fired the stuff by electrical charges.

"You could pull the electric matches out of them, I s'pose, but you'd have to do it real sneaky..."

"Whadda y'mean, electric matches?"

"Wires attached to every firework. Electric current fires them. Pull 'em out just a little bit so it doesn't show..."

"All right! We sneak up the night before and pull the plug on the buggers!"

"But it can't be that simple." Steve had no idea of the testing procedures on the day of the show, but he thought they must check the set-up somehow. "I mean, you can't just..."

"Well, d'you have any better ideas? We gotta do something!"

"No, but..."

"Right! We'll try it. Nothing to lose as far as I can see." She ground her cigarette into the overflowing ashtray and flung herself back into the chair with a gesture of dismissal. Steve wanted to argue further but she clearly had her mind made up, so he turned and swung the door open.

As he stepped down from the trailer, he wondered whether he should start charging her for his advice—over and above what they were all paid to show up at the demos—and also wondered whether she actually had access to all her marbles. He'd suggested the electric matches off the top of his head, but it really couldn't be that simple; they'd be crazy not to check the set-up surely. But if Sue Tort was so damned sure, it was her problem not his. Still, from here on there would be a price on his advice, good or bad.

☆✦⭐✦☆

It was a Friday and another small town. Rocco and the boys were wiring up the fireworks, unspooling cable, attaching clips, and checking circuits in a manner that would have been totally wonderful to a pyrotechnician of even 50 years ago. They had arrived in the truck on Thursday and had spent most of the day unloading the gear, orienting the mortar racks and setting up the fixed displays on the ramp. Their ramp for this show was the parking lot of a high school, hardly ideal but you did what you could. At least there were no large trees or power cables anywhere near.

Rocco kept the Weather Network on his laptop as a boot-up

file, and was continually checking it during the day. You had to contend with rain in particular, so tarps and tents to cover the set-up were essential. Mortars and other fixtures were wrapped in cling-wrap and covered with aluminum foil. Nothing short of a severe rainstorm would prevent a show going ahead. There was no way any insurance company would offer coverage—Acts of God being what they are—and no client would foot the bill anyway. You fired the show or you ate the cost; simple. There was one summer a few years ago, when Nonno was still in charge, when practically every weekend had been rainy. He had never been so wet in all his life, but hardly any of the shows had been cancelled. The old man had really shown his grit. This summer it had been good for the first month and was looking okay in the long term.

Then there was the problem of wind. It was illegal to launch shells when the surface wind speed exceeded 40kph, and even the direction could be a problem. The mortars were angled to allow for an average wind speed and direction, so the exploded casings and other debris would not fall on the crowd, but all this assumed you knew where the wind was coming from. Usually, a prevailing wind from the west could be counted on, but it could turn with very short notice, meaning in effect that the mortar tubes might have to be reoriented at the last minute. Doable, but a bit fraught.

The other chief worry was security. You couldn't just leave the set-up overnight, or even for a lunch break, without some sort of guard. On the big shows the ramp was always patrolled by hired security personnel, but in these small towns there was none of that. They had towed a tent-trailer behind the truck and had parked it as close to the ramp as possible, in a small parking space labeled 'Principal Only'. Even so, Rocco decided that he, Seth and Tonio would take turns to guard through the night. He was not normally so paranoid, but he had heard that a bunch of protesters would be showing up and making a nuisance of themselves, and he wouldn't put it past them to try sabotage. The only disadvantage of the tent-trailer was the need to locate a washroom close enough to the site and open at all hours of the night. There was one in a public park the other side of the school; close enough but hardly convenient.

There was a little stove in the camping trailer, together with a small fridge and rudimentary utensils, so the three guys cooked a simple late supper and supplemented it with red Italian wine.

Once the sun had set no more work could be done on the site, so they sat and chatted. Seth had brought his guitar, and for a while he played some old time country stuff, singing in a clear but thin tenor. Rocco thought of the help Seth had given him when he was working on his first live music show, the *Eighteen-Twelve*, and was grateful all over again, and thankful that he had landed such a gem. Sometimes you just know when an asset is presented to you, and he hadn't been wrong about Seth, or Tonio either. They were a great team.

He joined in the old songs with a gusto far in excess of his musical ability, while Tonio sang along as best he could. Once that old *Tennessee Waltz* had swung to its conclusion, it was time to draw lots for the night shifts. Rocco got the first three hours, eleven until two, then it was Seth's turn. Tonio would greet the day.

He was sitting in a folding lawn chair beside the camper, nodding in and out of sleep, when Rocco was roused by a small noise close by. Sure enough, in the light from the far streetlights he could see a figure creeping along just the other side of the front rack of 4″ mortars. Occasional flashes from a keychain light hinted at mischief. Leaping up and shouting would have been a practical way of scaring off the intruder, but Rocco was now awake enough that subtlety became a real option. Rising slowly from the chair he tiptoed around the rack, approaching the figure from the rear. Unlike the last bum he had enjoyed seeing bending over a rack of mortars, this one was wide, clad in threadbare jeans and showing an extensive and hairy plumber's crack in the dim light.

Maybe it was the wrong approach, maybe it would lead to a civil suit for assault, but the target was irresistible. With a good swing he planted the toe of his shoe as close to the anus as makes no odds. The intruder fell forward with a shriek and rolled over, before rising and stumbling away. His feet soon became tangled in the yellow security tape that cordoned the site, so down he went again. It was with ease that Rocco caught up with him, got a knee in his back and twisted an arm. By this time Seth and Tonio had been roused by the din and ran over in their boxer shorts to see what was going on.

"Geddoff me! Geddoff me!" came the muffled voice from a face having intimate relations with a stretch of tarmac.

Rocco eased off the pressure and allowed the intruder to stand, while the two others flanked him, poised to act. Terry

O'Weight offered no resistance. The boys backed off and Seth ducked out to check the equipment on the ramp. For all his imposing size, Terry was really quite the softie and was, if anything, acutely embarrassed at having been caught so easily. He was also suffering from a royal pain in the ass.

"What the hell did you think you were doing?" yelled Rocco, leaning into Terry's face, which required quite a feat of neck craning as his eyes came well below chin level.

"I was just... she told me to..." he mumbled. "I mean, I *like* fireworks..."

"Know what?" interrupted Seth, who had just come back from checking the mortars by flashlight. "Pulled the e-matches out of three of the aerials. Shithead!"

Rocco wasn't sure what it was, but suddenly all his anger evaporated as he confronted this contrite and pathetic specimen. "Did you really think we wouldn't check the rig-up at any time tomorrow? Christ, this isn't even halfway smart. What *were* you thinking, actually?"

Terry said nothing more. He couldn't really confess to thinking at all; it wasn't something he did very well, although he was great at following explicit instructions. Sue Tort had told him to go and screw around with the set-up, and she had talked to Steve who had said what to do, and that's really all he knew about it.

"You go back to whoever sent you," Rocco was almost laughing, "and tell them we weren't born yesterday. And if you or they dare to come back here, it'll be more than a sore butt hole you'll be looking at. Get it?"

O'Weight slunk off, and the three guys went back to the camper, two to sleep and one to keep watch, because you never know...

☆✮⭐✮☆

"You got caught! Holy mother of Christ, what is *with* you, you stupid fucktard?" Sue Tort raged at her lieutenant outside their tent on the patch of parkland beyond the high school parking lot. "Simple, simple task! Creep around and pull the goddamned fuses out of the things, like Steve said, and you get caught! Shit!"

"Well, I didn't know they was posting guards," mumbled Terry in contrition, his anus beating a heartfelt tattoo.

"Didn't know they was posting guards," she mimicked. "So now the whole plan's blown. We might as well head home." She

69

simmered around her Rothman's.

"He said," he continued, "that they weren't born yesterday..."

"Aw right!"

"He said they woulda checked the whole set-up today anyway..."

"*Aw right!*"

"He said it wasn't even halfway smart..."

"*Shut up!*" she cried, as if he had accused her of gross negligence. "How was I to know? Steve just said to pull the fuses. What do I know about friggin' fireworks? Christ!"

"Well, Steve did say it wasn't easy..."

"Shut! *The fuck! UP!*"

Terry had heard the tirades many times; every time she had a failure, which was mostly all the time, she raged and fumed. He just waited stoically until the storm passed because he knew that the following calm was when she hatched up the most amazing shit. He lived for the risky, dangerous moments, and walking round with banners and a megaphone and stuff did nothing for him.

"It wasn't good enough to jus' protest," she whispered into an ominous calm. "It isn't even possible to sabotage. We gotta do more..."

This was more like it. Maybe she'd change her mind about setting fire to the factory.

"They can't have a firework show," she continued, "if they don't have any goddamned fireworks."

"So, you *do* wanna burn down the factory?" he said hopefully.

"No, no, no, you mutton head! I *do not* want to burn down any factory! We *steal* 'em. Steal. Them. See? That'll screw 'em up..." She smiled around her cigarette. "So, I gotta have another little word with Steve."

☆✫☆✫☆✫

Rocco was getting out of his car in the parking spot beside the facility, mulling over the success of the last show, when the warm *chinook* of all that was Julia blew across his mind. He recalled that first glance over the mortars, the locked eyes, her smile, their night together... Then Gwillimbury and Steve Bacon turned like polarizing filters in his mind, and a new picture became horribly clear.

No, no. Please, no. He couldn't have. Oh my Christ...

He rushed into his office and prayed to God that he still had Steve Bacon's phone number somewhere. He finally found it in the address book on his laptop.

"Steve. Hey." Please, please deny it all. Please say it never happened.

"What's up?"

"Just kinda wondering; when we last met, I mentioned the competition..."

Steve's loud laugh came tinnily to his ear and Rocco's heart sank. "Yeah, man, just a few. I knew you'd be pleased!"

"What do you mean 'just a few'?"

"Got into their place, see, shot some water into the shells. Only a few, though."

"You didn't..."

"Sure! Only a few. Didn't want to completely fuck up everything..."

"I *told* you!" Rocco yelled. "I told you not to. You idiot! *You goddamned fucking idiot...*"

"Ah, come on. You do a favour for a pal..."

"*I am not your pal!* Get it through your stupid head! You are a complete moron and I want nothing to do with you!"

"Well, screw you then. Asshole!"

"D'you have an idea how fucking dangerous..."

"It wasn't dangerous..."

"*It was!* You could have blown yourself up, and the whole fucking place with you. Did you check for magnesium? Well? Did you? Course you didn't, you fu..."

But Steve had hung up.

Rocco was sweating and shaking with fear. The stupidity! God, the stupidity! The idiot can't have even imagined the danger. Sure, water damps black powder and makes it useless, but what if one of those shells was a report, stuffed with magnesium flash powder? Whole different story. Magnesium reacts with water; it heats up as it oxidizes and then God knows what would have happened. The thought of it horrified him.

If just one of those shells had been a report.

Then he thought of Julia; his first impulse was not to tell her. What good would it do? But then, when he thought of the depth of their sharing, he knew he would have to. How could he look her in the eye from here on knowing what he knew? His knowledge, and the guilt that went with it, would be a constant barrier. That wasn't the way their future was meant be. It was enough to have secrets from others, but not between themselves.

Oh, Christ, it was time to go to confession...

Rocco took out his phone with huge reluctance and dialed Julia's number. Please pick up, please pick up, I can't stand this...

"Oh, hi. Look could we meet in the pagoda in the park?" It was the most private place he could think of, high on a knoll so you could spot if anyone was hanging around. "Yeah, right now."

The pagoda was an open-sided, vaguely Oriental hexagonal structure that might once have been a bandstand, in the days when community brass bands were more common than they are now. There were solid metal tables with synthetic stone tops and hard wrought iron chairs, all of which had one leg chained to iron loops in the concrete floor. Barn swallows nesting in the peeling roof beams used the furniture as their exclusive bathroom.

He screeched a chair into place and waited for what seemed like forever. The place was deserted. Finally, he saw her coming but sat and waited for her to sit. She immediately sensed that something was badly wrong, and her heart contracted at... she didn't know quite what.

"What's up?" she asked as lightly as she was able. Are we, she thought, this fragile?

"Look, this is really hard to say. Those duds at Gwillimbury?"

"What about them?" She was utterly mystified but somewhat relieved.

"Well, see, it was sabotage." He couldn't meet her eyes.

"Sabotage? You saying someone was deliberately trying to ruin our show?"

"Yes. And I know who did it. And I know how he did it."

"Who? How?" Outrage was coupled with incomprehension.

"No, listen. Please!" He pressed the fingers of both hands over his eyes and spoke through his palms. "He broke in; he injected a few shells with water..."

"Injected?" she interrupted, leaning forward across the table. "With water? Why, why?"

"...just enough to wet the burst charge, not enough to ruin the lift."

"How do you know this? There was no sign of a break-in. Are you sure?" She remembered Mike reporting the wetness he had seen the day after the show.

"Of course I'm sure," he replied slowly. "The guy who did it told me."

She sat back in her chair, head erect on her shoulders as anger welled up. "And did you ask him *why?*"

"Oh God, this is so hard." He sat with his face in his hands, elbows on the table. When he finally looked up there were tears on his cheeks.

"What? What is it?" Her stance had hardly softened.

"It's all my fault. See, I was just talking to this guy—he was a friend from high school—and I just *said* that we were in financial trouble. That's all I said, believe me!" Every line of his face beseeched her. He paused, trying to look into eyes that were avoiding his.

"Go on." She was looking steadfastly over his right shoulder.

"So he said 'Maybe the competition should have a little accident then'."

"*No!* No, Rocco. No!" She was suddenly near to tears.

"And I said, I said," he rushed on, "I said no way, don't even think about it!"

"But he did it anyway? This is insane! What kind of criminals are you running with? We have to call the police!"

"No, no! It's all in the past. I told you! I hadn't seen him for years. How was I to know?"

"To know? *To know?* Jesus Christ, you're talking to some *criminal* about us, *about my company*, and you ask me how you're supposed to *know?*"

"But it wasn't like that..."

A sudden horrible thought struck her. She leapt up sending her chair crashing behind her.

"You... you were checking up! When we met! Making sure they failed!"

"No, no! I wasn't... Coincidence..."

"*Coincidence!* What kind of fool do you take me for? And then you got me to talk about Colombia! *You bastard!*"

"You've got it all wrong! You've got it all wrong!"

But she didn't hear; she had burst into tears and stormed out of the pagoda and down the hill.

☆☆⭐☆☆

Julia hardly remembered getting home; she had half walked, half run to her apartment, tears streaming down her face. She got the door open, ran across the apartment, threw herself face down onto the bed—the covers aromatic in her imagination from where they had so recently lain—and gave way utterly. The following hours were brutal. She couldn't believe, just could not believe, that he could have been do duplicitous. So vile. She felt betrayed; violated. No matter how many times, round and round, her brain revisited the scene, it was fresh and horrible and pitifully devoid of comfort.

She rose at about 5:00, mentally and physically wiped out, and went through to the bathroom to clean herself up. On the shelf below the mirror was Rocco's comb that he must have forgotten, and the awful scenario threatened to spill over again. She seized the comb, snapped it in half, and flung it into the toilet bowl she had just used.

What am I to do; what *am* I to do, she asked herself as she paced the little apartment. I can't carry on like this. He's in me, but he's gone. Where do I go? What do I do? Just when a wave of hopelessness threatened to overcome her, a warm counter-wave of comfort took its place. She was back in her childhood when everything was okay. She had cried herself out now, and she was through to the other side. Now she knew where to find the comfort she needed.

She fumbled her phone out of the bag thrown down by the still-open door. "Hey Grandpa," she said as she walked slowly over to the window. "How about we make a shell tonight? A five-incher?"

"Well, sure," replied the old man, surprised out of his CBC News. "But you haven't done one for years." Bob thought back to the last time. She must have been in her teens, but he remembered braids, or was he projecting back too far? They'd done quite a few over the years, until she grew up... Whatever; it had been a long time, so why now?

"I thought you were seeing some guy pretty regular. Too busy to talk to your old granddad."

A huge stab of real pain lanced through her, threatening to throw her back. "No, no..." she tried to keep her tone light. "I'll tell him... I'll tell him I'm washing my hair tonight."

"Oh, that's right," he replied, picking up the nuance. "It's really hard to enjoy yourself if you have a headache, isn't it?"

"Exactly. Can you pick me up? About seven?"

"Sure."

"Then can we let it off at the field?"

"Naturally. I'll call Malachi, make sure it's okay tonight. See you about seven."

Catesby & Son Pyrotechnics had an agreement with a farmer

about 10 kilometers out of town who allowed them to use one of his fields for testing purposes. The field was the furthest from the barns, and his only proviso was that they phone first to make sure he had the livestock indoors, and that no overnight veterinary operations were taking place.

Bob was delighted. She worked hard at the company all day, no complaints in that department, but he sometimes wondered if she was fully... engaged, committed. Was it just a job, or did she feel a vocation? And now she wanted to sit with him and make a shell! That was positive, but it could be that she wanted to return a little to a zone of comfort; to be nurtured. Maybe she was hurting. Well, if she wants some coddling, I'm game.

She was early and waiting for him on her front steps, a fragile shell with explosive contents. She slid quickly into the passenger seat of his old Dodge pickup truck with no words; just a small peck on a stubbly cheek.

On the way, Bob looked over at the too-calm face lit intermittently by passing street lamps, and asked gently, "Bad time?"

"Yeah." Monosyllable, no more.

"Anyone I know?" He didn't want to pry but hoped in some silly way that he could help. When she hurt, he hurt.

"No, nobody you knew." The last thing she was going to do was reveal she'd been sleeping with the enemy... and had been screwed over. She pushed down a wave from within, breathing deeply.

He held his peace and she was immensely relieved.

They parked beside the building, and Bob tapped in the code, opened the door with his pass key and quickly flipped off the alarm systems.

Grandfather and granddaughter sat down on the high stools at the bench with all the materials laid out meticulously in front of them. Bob Catesby had learned himself, and never failed to inculcate in his staff and family, the importance of order and method. This business was just too damned dangerous to tolerate cluttered benches and scattered materials.

"Now, I don't know how many years it's bin, but do you remember where to start?"

Julia was breathing in the magical aromas of hot glue (Bob had just plugged the glue gun in), cardboard and gum, and the nascent smell of the powders, pellets and granules waiting in their jars. She rolled the antiquated terms across her mind; leader fuse, lift charge, passfire, burst charge, garnitures...

She had always loved the arcane language of the craft. She remembered as a child lugging down Grandpa's great big *Oxford English Dictionary* (the one that came with a magnifying glass because even young eyes needed that) and learned that the other words for the time fuse–spitool, spolette and passfire–couldn't be found. It made her feel all grown up to know such words, although to her chagrin she could find no way of introducing them into conversation to show what a sophisticated young lady she was. Spitool sounded sort of rude, although it wasn't really. Fuse was in the dictionary, of course, but that was no good.

"I think I remember. The first thing I should do is drill the hole for the passfire."

"Good girl. Off you go then."

She took one of a pair of 5″ diameter cardboard hemispheres, expertly bored a neat half-inch hole through its centre on the drill press and inserted the passfire that her grandfather passed to her, and glued it in. Then she weighed the granulated black powder of the lift charge into a paper cup placed on a scale.

Concentration on the task was a balm.

"Oh, this is great!" enthused her grandfather. "You've even remembered the weight you need to lift a five-inch shell! I *am* impressed."

She turned to face the old patriarch, paper cup in hand. "Grandpa, you have no idea how I enjoyed those sessions with you. I hung on every word, and I waited for days in agony because I thought you might change your mind. But, of course, you never did."

He was warmed and moved, but behind her eyes he saw a need, a longing, for something that had gone and would never come back.

At every stage of the construction Julia felt another little block fall into place in a line of dispassionate thought. The emotional storms of the afternoon, diametrical to reason, had given way to a gentle, rational appraisal of all the facts.

She glued the paper cup onto the underside of the shell, nosing the passfire into the powder, and inserted the leader fuse. This was length of quick match about 18 inches long that burns at 100 feet a second.

"What garnitures should I use, Grandpa?" He knew, and she knew, but there was a ritual here between them that went back years.

Garnitures was the general term for anything that could be

blown out of a shell. Modern firework people called them effects, which Julia thought rather bland. There were stars, serpents, whistles, comets, crackles, the loud explosions called reports, and many others. The variety was almost endless, and Bob must have had 20 or so jars on his shelves. He made them in batches of hundreds.

"Up to you. What sort of mood are you in?" He had often asked her this when she was a kid–this was part of the unspoken ritual–and her choice had always given him a mirror into her mood. He didn't realize how dangerous a question it was.

"Reports! I want something that makes a hell of a noise." He nodded. Yup.

He handed her a jar of little cardboard cylinders sealed with clay at each end, and having a short fuse sticking out of the side.

"Take about twenty."

"Yes, half in the bottom shell, spread out to the sides." She counted out 10 and placed them around the perimeter, and tucked in the lower burst charge; gunpowder enclosed in a small paper bag. The other 10 reports and the upper burst charge were inserted into the top cardboard hemisphere, then she ran a bead of hot glue around the rim and quickly flipped it over onto the bottom half.

"Finally," she sighed in satisfaction, "we wrap the leader fuse around the shell, and cover the whole thing with gummed tape."

She wrapped the quick match round the shell from the base to the top and secured it there with a small bridge of glued paper. A slow-burning fuse would be inserted into its end, although in their shows they used electric matches.

As she followed the old familiar stages of construction her thoughts had come full circle, nurtured in the comforting arms of pure handwork, and now she felt the coming of a resolution.

Once the shell was covered in gummed tape she held it up, appraising her work, glancing over at her grandfather for his seal of approval.

"A fine piece of work, my dear! You have just created one of the finest examples of pre-industrial chemical technology. And now, I think you've earned the right to blow it to smithereens!"

Bob had phoned Malachi earlier to forewarn the friendly farmer of the coming holocaust. They got into the pickup truck and drove a good distance out of town. Granddaughter and grandfather parked the truck beside a gate and walked carefully into the field, guided by the light of a gibbous moon floating high in the south east, until they found the embedded mortars. Bob had set several tubes into the ground for testing his 3″, 4″, 5″ and 6″ shells. He pointed out the five-inch tube with the aid of a pocket flashlight.

"All right, lower her in to make sure she slides okay." Holding the shell by the fuse she checked that it slid in well. It needed to be loose enough that there was no friction, but not so loose that the lifting force was diminished around its sides. She pulled it back out and held it at arm's length.

"All ready? I'll shine the light on the tube. Here we go!"

She lowered the shell back into the tube and he stepped forward and lit the slow fuse at the end of the leader with a cigarette lighter. As soon as it fizzed they both stepped well back. The thump of the lift charge was more visceral than sonic, as most of the sound went upwards. They watched with craned necks as the passfire traced a smooth, golden arc. There was a slight wobble to its upward motion, which increased as the shell lost speed. Right at the high point of its arc the shell burst with a satisfying thump scattering its cargo of reports widespread. You could just discern the fizzing lights of the little fuses until the reports began. Then the whole sky became splintered lightning bursts as each one, right on the heels of the other, woke the heavens to intermittent daylight. The sound followed the flashes momentarily, the crepitation battering on their eardrums.

When the last thunderous echoes had faded Bob turned to her and said, "All better now?"

"Yes, Grandpa. All better." She grabbed a hand and squeezed very hard.

As the score of tiny cumulus puffs of yellow smoke, illuminated by the moon, drifted with the breeze in the upper air and gradually dissipated, so also did some great hard fist that had squeezed her heart. She knew now that Rocco had not been duplicitous or callous or mean or underhand. He had just been plain stupid. And she was equally to blame for rushing to judgment; reacting too quickly, too harshly, and not weighing his story against an honesty which she knew was deep seated within him.

She had hurt him badly and she was equally stupid. And plain stupid on both their parts she felt she could deal with.

☆☆ ⭐ ☆☆

Rocco went right back to the bad old days; before he was a business manager, before he had started work at the company, before he was an A student in technical college, right back to high school when he had run with a criminal crowd. She was quite right there. Bang on. And what did we criminals do back then? Apart from petty robbery and graffiti and dope, we got totally blind drunk as often as we could.

And that was what he intended to do right now.

He bought the cheapest bottle of Canadian Club he could find at the Liquor Control Board of Ontario on Main Street, took it back to his top floor flat and began drinking. It was an easy, familiar route downhill; suivez la pissed.

All the years of his successful climb out of the mess he had been in were obliterated. As the level in the bottle went down he returned to the useless waster he used to be, realizing for all his little successes since then, he was still basically a failure. Factory just about bankrupt, grandfather sliding into senile bitterness... couldn't even hold onto the best thing that ever happened to me.

Why didn't I just shut up? Why did I have to tell her? What good, he thought to himself, came of being honest. Just the opposite; he had made it worse for himself. Worse for both of them.

That's where honesty gets you; a slap in the face.

He cried.

☆⋆⟡⋆☆

It was paradoxical; contacting Rocco and asking him to meet her was one of the hardest things Julia had ever done, and also the most urgently desired. She was terrified that he had been utterly repelled by her sudden stupid reaction, and that they would never find that soft, comfortable... mutual... place where they used to be. Was it always this way; when two real lovers argued did they cross a divide that could never be retraced? Did the flow of time prevent a reversal?

More to the point, would he even agree to talk to her?

Only one way to find out. She scrolled down her contacts, slipping twice and starting again. It picked up on the second ring.

"It's me. Please! Please, don't hang up!"

When he heard her voice he could have cried with relief. He couldn't dream of hanging up on her. He had woken sick and stinking in the morning, but buoyed with a weird optimism. At some point during the evening he thought he had heard fire-

works far off, and waking from his stupor he had suddenly figured out that she had got him all wrong. The only thing he had
been was completely goddamned stupid. To have opened up his
problems to Steve Bacon, for Christ's sake! For all the distance he
had travelled since those stupid days, he was still enmeshed in
them and probably could never escape.

The big question had been: Should I call her? And then: What
would it do to me if she refused to even talk? Surely, the thing
they had couldn't be that fragile? But he couldn't steel himself to
call her, so he showed up to work as usual in a daze, not knowing
what he was doing and not caring. At nearly noon of an utterly
wasted morning he had finally decided that if he didn't call her
soon he never would. And then he would never know the terrible
truth. But deciding to do it and carrying the thing through were
still poles apart when she... *called him!* The sound of her voice
pushed him over an edge; his voice broke and he couldn't speak.

"It's me!" she repeated. "Please answer!"

"Let's meet," he finally croaked out. "Same place."

She was there before him, sitting at a table. She looked gorgeous in the abstract, and he could hardly believe that he had so
recently known all there was to know about the form that stood
slowly and came towards him. He had had his lips *there...*

Their arms were around each other, face beside face, breathing into each other's ears their relief, their longing, their comfort.

"I've been so stupid." He was the first to speak. "I wasn't going to tell you, but I had to. Had to let you know. Couldn't... I
don't know how you can forgive me."

"No, it was me. One throw-away remark over lunch to a
chance acquaintance?" she whispered. "And I flew off the handle.
How could I have been so cruel to you?"

"No, you don't understand. It didn't start then. I think you
were more right than you knew."

"But that's all it was, my love; all it was. And I'm so, so sorry."
She was crying into his shoulder, mingled relief and contrition.

"No, no. You drew conclusions and I don't blame you. I've had
a bad past. I thought it had all gone away, but I don't think you
can ever get away, not really away."

They pulled apart but she kept her arms around his neck,
looking up into his eyes.

"I don't care, okay? This is now; this is us. What's done is
done."

He placed his forefingers just below her eyes and swept the

tears away across her cheeks.

"Let's see if we can leave it in the past," he murmured hopefully.

They came together again and their long kiss healed wounds, repaired hurt and damage, and sealed the future against the past. They sat down, hands together across the table, amid dried barn swallow guano and sticky crescent stains of slopped soft drinks, and stayed so for many minutes.

"It's been..." he began. "It's... it's hard to keep going straight. There's always stuff from the past... I mean, I should never have even talked to him."

"Who is he?"

"Just some shithead who never grew up," he replied, concealing from her the real bond that he and Steve Bacon shared. "He's off the map; hangs around with biker gangs, break and enter... Poison. What was I *thinking?*"

"It's done. I told you."

He nodded, distant eyes looking out over the park trees. As she looked into his face she felt she could read where he had been and what he had come to. She saw the tough handsome exterior, all business and hard work and go-getting, laid over an insecurity that went back to his formative years. Yes, the past does keep peeping through the cracks.

"When did your father die?" she asked him quietly.

The question came at him sideways. Nobody had ever asked him that before. He had never let anyone come close enough that such a question could be posed.

"I was about eight," he replied slowly. "The house, the silence, the crying... It never goes away. None of it."

"So hard for a little boy..." She thought of the little ones in her show-and-tells and realized how devastated their small lives would be.

"When he died... I thought... I thought I'd get my mother back. See, she'd nursed him all along... Then after... she still wasn't there. Little guys, they don't understand mourning; how could they? She kinda locked herself away."

"Your grandfather? He was there."

"Ah, he was always so tough. No tenderness there. I think Dad's death made him even more pig-headed. I love him and respect him, don't get me wrong, but he's not the one to give back, if you know what I mean?"

She nodded, thinking of her own father. "No one to turn to?"

He shook his head, then turned and met her eyes. "Never told anyone this before."

She squeezed his hands hard. "My love."

They sat again in silence while the barn swallows fluttered their annoyance at the intrusion, selfish in their own lovemaking.

"So now," she cried, practicality returning in a heartbeat. "There's the little matter of the duds."

"Look, I know it sounds cowardly, but what else can we do but keep it quiet? Had to tell you, but..."

"You're right of course. Dad was mad as hell; wanted to cancel the Colombia orders all together. We had a sort of post-mortem. That's what we called it. In the end we agreed to write a letter to Gonçalves complaining about it and threatening cancellation. Trouble is, the deal we get is too good to walk away from."

"So, another little secret between us and... them."

"I hate this! It's bad enough that we're... seeing each other! Sneaking around..."

"Starshell-crossed lovers, eh?"

She smiled at that.

☆ ✩ ☆

A Tim Hortons away out of town was the neutral site that Uncle Chuck had chosen for his meeting with Rocco Pastorelli. At first it had been difficult to persuade the young fireworks executive of the need for a meeting–the name Charles Bourassa meant nothing to him–but the mention of a 'fireworks promotion opportunity' had done the trick. Anything that smacked of commercial possibility was too enticing; the company was hurting and Nonno was becoming increasingly fretful and angry. When he arrived at the coffee shop at five after noon, a few minutes later than the agreed meeting time, a long, thin biker caught his eye and beckoned him over.

"Mr Pastorelli? I'm Charles, but friends call me Uncle Chuck. Bought you a coffee." He indicated the cup at the empty place. "So, sit down and enjoy. Don't doubt it comes from Colombia."

This didn't look like any kind of business deal. "Who are you, and what do you want?" Rocco felt prickles of fear, but he was goddamned if he'd let it show. He remained standing.

"Sit. C'mon, they make it fresh every twenny minutes. Seen 'em mark it with a chalk right there on the jug. Enjoy!"

He sat slowly and reluctantly. He didn't touch the coffee.

"Steve did you a big favour, did he not?"

"Steve?" Oh, shit! It was Steve Bacon and his stupid caper! Disappointment was followed by anger as he realized he had been duped. Loose mouth Steve had been blabbing to bikers, for Christ's sake. "Fucking Steve! No, he did *not* do me any favour! I didn't want it! And I told him I didn't want it. It was a shitty thing to do."

"But he did it anyway, silly feller, so now he thinks his little debt is erased. Sorta *quid pro quo* as we Latinists would put it." A long pull at his own coffee, and a grimace.

"Fine." Rocco made to stand up, leaving the coffee untouched on the table. "If that's all you wanted to tell me, I'm outta here."

"No, it isn't." Holding Rocco with his eyes. "As a matter of fact, I need your help. Please have your coffee."

"Help?" Rocco was immediately wary. He sat. He thought of slippery slopes. "Why me? What help?"

"Well now, I am led to understand that Catesby's buy their stuff from Colombia. I happen to have business interests in that fine country myself, and I think there's something we can do together to our mutual benefit."

"No, no!" This was getting really scary. "I don't want to get involved. Sorry."

"But you *are* involved Rocco, my sweet. You hang around with guys like ole Bacon Enter, you're involved whether you like it or not."

Now Rocco was becoming really frightened. "You... you can't threaten me..."

Uncle Chuck brought his eyes into play. He had always had those remarkably magnetic eyes, but he had further enhanced their power by exercising control over the reflex that makes you blink when evaporation dries your eyeballs. When you want something bad enough you work at it. He had concentrated until his eyes were red and sore, and worked and worked at it day after day, until now he could outstare anybody.

"Can't threaten you? Can. Am. There's two things that work in this world, my friend: money and violence. And I think you'd be wise to take the money..."

"Money? What money? I don't want your money, I told you. I don't want to get involved!"

Uncle Chuck's eyes paused in their appraisal. "When I think of how you're hurting for cash–goin' down the tubes, I'm told– and when I think of all that lovely folding-ready just waiting to fall into your hands... Y'know what? A guy refuses an offer like that, it's downright insulting."

"No, no, no! What do you want? What do you want?" He looked desperately around the coffee shop but the few clientele there were studiously minding their own business. There was definitely a Somebody Else's Problem field surrounding the two of them.

"Like I said," Uncle Chuck replied calmly, "I want us to do a little business together in Colombia. You get your supplies, I get mine. Shit, we even save on shipping and brokerage!"

"No, I won't do it. You can't threaten me. I'm not afraid of you." He was; absolutely petrified. "I'll go to the cops."

"Oh, re-e-ealy? I met some guy in Timmies, you tell 'em, no witnesses, and he says... and then I says... Come on, Rocco! Get with the program. And the guys you use t'run with? Getting Steve off the hook like you did? Lots of shit there my friend."

This was hellish. He couldn't think; couldn't breathe. This couldn't be happening to him. He felt dizzy, near collapsing. Sweat ran down his face, his neck, his chest.

"Tell you what," continued Uncle Chuck finishing his coffee. "I'll piss off now and let you think things through, 'cos you're probably having some trouble getting used to the idea of such a lucrative business opportunity. Bit of a shock."

His gangly length rose laconically from the chair, and as he passed Rocco he slapped him gently on the back. "I'll give you a call."

Rocco hardly heard the splattering blat of Harley exhausts pulling out onto the highway and fading into the background.

✫✫⭐✫✫

An utter and absolute shit storm.

Rocco's mind was in turmoil for the remainder of the afternoon and, once again, little if anything got accomplished. He poured himself a huge Scotch as soon as he had ascended the stairs to his apartment (this was getting to be a habit) and ran through the meeting in his mind once again. There was no doubt that he was completely and thoroughly screwed. The whole mess of the past that he had hoped and prayed was finished was actually set to overwhelm him. And when he thought of Julia and his half-promise to leave it all in the past, he threw himself down on his couch and cried in anguish.

What could he do? What could he possibly do?

The Canadian Club helped a little, and presently he got up, his head somewhat clear, and reviewed the whole stinking mess. First and foremost, he could go to the police and spill the whole sordid plot. But, no. As Uncle Chuck had said, they'd never believe him. And even if he was believed, the police would have nothing to act upon–no crime had yet been committed–and when the bikers discovered what he'd done he would be as good as dead. And he was hardly going to qualify for police protection for the rest of his stupid life.

So, go along with the scheme? Become a criminal by abetting a felony, and live with the knowledge that he had helped get people hooked on drugs. Well, he was already a criminal, having kept Steve out of jail, but here was a steeper portion of that same slippery slope. Then, wouldn't the traffickers find a route anyway whether he helped or not? And wouldn't druggies find a fix anyway, whether it came by his help or not?

One enormous advantage loomed in front of him in ugly certainty; he had tried to push it away, but it was as beguiling as it was revolting. Their money would go a long way to staving off bankruptcy. When he thought of Nonno and the pain the old guy was going through, the anguish hit him again.

In the end, the tears of his family at the prospect of his failure, imprisonment and penury weighed heavier in his decision than the moral and the criminal.

Julia's face rose in his mind's eye. She would never hear about this. Never! Another secret to gnaw away at their lives, and one that couldn't even be shared. Everything good they had found was being inevitably driven away. It couldn't hold; eventually she would find him out or he would confess, and either way their little dalliance of a few weeks would be done, finished. A dud.

So, with a wild smashing anger, followed by more tears and a deep hatred of himself and his stupidity, he concluded that he would have to go along with the scheme. One small rag of decency clung to his decision; perhaps he might still be able to go to the police at a later date, and win some kind of clemency.

It would just have to do. Life was a crock of shit, and anyone who tried to tell you otherwise...

Yes, an utter and absolute shit storm.

⋆☆★☆⋆

A horribly sleepless night resulted in a new resolve. He would not be pushed around by this bastard. He would write it all down and deposit the envelope with his bank. He would refuse point-blank to have anything to do with it. He would threaten to go to the cops. He would...

The resolve was built on cirrus, and all those things he swore he would do had begun to evaporate even before he stopped far too early for his midday meal. He got a cup of coffee and nothing else from the counter at his usual haunt, said not a word to the owner serving behind the counter, and sat on the single chair at a corner table feeling wretched. It was still only 11:30 and the place was empty. Sometime soon he would be contacted for his 'decision' and he hoped to God when the time came he'd have the guts to say no. As he took a sip of his coffee his eyes met the familiar figure striding in the door.

How did he know I always go here for lunch? What kind of spying are they doing on me? This was more than frightening.

"Hi there, Rocco," said Uncle Chuck as he swung a chair round from an adjacent table. "Time we discussed business details..."

"I'm not gonna to do it!" he blurted out even as his nerve was failing. "I'm not gonna to do it! You can't make me!"

"Rocco, Rocco, Rocco." The too-reasonable voice of Uncle Chuck failed to soothe him. "You don't want the whole world to hear us, do you?" He motioned with his head towards the serving counter. "I'm sure we can work something out, you and me."

"I don't care what you say, I'm not doing it," he replied in an undertone.

"Come on! Even with the lure of all that folding green?"

The money, the release from debt, Nonno's tears, all rose up like a wave in his mind. He faltered.

"No! No! No!" he hissed, checking the bistro owner, who was swabbing the coffee machine. "It isn't any good..."

"Well, like I said, there's money and then there's violence."

"You wouldn't dare!" A new anger flared. "You touch me and I go to the cops!"

The server behind the counter looked up from his swabbing.

"Oh Rocco, I wouldn't dream of touching you," soothed the biker lowering his leveled hands like a maestro calling for pianissimo. "You, my friend, are far too valuable, and anyway I kinda like you." There followed a long pause. "But that little chick of yours... Now that's another story."

Rocco's heart faltered. So he knew about Julia, too! He was everywhere!

Uncle Chuck's eyes bored into Rocco's face. Then, after a long hanging silence, which Rocco thought would never end, "D'you want to see her dead? Well, do you?"

His heart shrank, his chest crushed in on itself and his eyes lost their focus; his ears roared and his head swam. He shuddered as sweat broke out all over.

He was beaten. There was nothing left for him except to do exactly as he was told. Now, with Julia's life on the line, it was no longer a moral issue. And with this knowledge, buried beneath the deep bowel-grinding fear was a sense almost of relief. He was now doing this because he was absolutely compelled, and not because it was expedient or profitable.

It was life and death. Simple.

☆☆☆

In the following days Rocco began to wonder if there wasn't something in his nature that was inherently criminal, and that his life's path hadn't always been an effort to cleave a course away from it. He likened it to faulty alignment in a car's steering; you could drive in a straight line and to all external evidence everything was fine, but only the driver knows what an effort it is to compensate. This was his realization when he discovered to both his horror and his fascination that arranging to fill aerial shells with cocaine in far-off Medellín, and to ship them in secrecy, was actually quite alluring. There was some secret place within him where he was hugged by emotional glee; somewhere deep inside where a voice told him what a clever boy he was. To walk around the workshop, to sit and meet clients in his office, to give instructions to staff, and all the while carry this secret within! It was beguiling. And it was frightening.

His relationship with Julia began to prey upon his mind, because in their most ecstatic and complete lovemaking that little secret bundle of glee was always gloating there. Their ultimate sharing encapsulated an ultimately un-shareable secret, and his fulfillment at the top of their passion became the greater for it. He knew the dishonesty of this, and he knew that it could not possibly be maintained. It was as corrosive as it was beguiling.

Julia would soon become aware of the misalignment; tell-tale wear would appear on the tires of their liaison.

✫☆ ⭐ ☆✫

Uncle Chuck's communication system was elaborate and convoluted. At no point in any of his communications could a message, either phone or e-mail, be used as evidence for criminal activity. E-mails to his suppliers in Colombia were bounced through several accounts and encoded, so that by the time they were received the electronic trail was blurred to indistinction. He used pre-paid cell phones by the job lot, discarding them regularly, so when he phoned it was always on a unit that would become landfill before the possibility of analysis.

Uncle Chuck had called Rocco, dictating a meeting place and time. Rocco was to discover that their meetings would almost always be in coffee shops, and never in the same one twice. As Tim Hortons has a franchise on every major block of every city in the country—and in some cases two or more—one of its franchises was usually the venue. This one was virtually empty, which suited their needs very well.

"So. To business," said Uncle Chuck as he sipped his double-double, scanning the empty tables for eavesdroppers out of habit. "My genius in thinking of this is now gonna be combined with your technical know-how. Hmmm?"

"It's doable," replied Rocco morosely, untouched cup in front of him. "It's simply a matter of opening the shells, whipping out the contents, and substituting 'em."

"May sound simple to you. We'll deal with the nitty-gritty in a minute. Right now, here's the thing. From now on our meeting places and drop-off locations are going to be encrypted. Here's how it works."

He pulled out a propelling pencil and a notepad. "Five days of the working week." He printed them in large letters. "Now, first initial is useless 'cos it's too obvious, and the second has number problems. So we use the third initial, see?" He underlined N in Monday, E in Tuesday, D in Wednesday, U in Thursday, and I in Friday. "Now, count along the alphabet, up to ten then round again for each letter."

Rocco did as instructed on his fingers and came up with four, five, four, one and nine. "But N and D are the same number," he said. "Four. You only go round once for D, twice for N."

"Right. So assume D is three instead of four. Simple."

"Okay," replied Rocco as mystified as ever.

"Now, you phone me. One single word; don't give a shit what

it is. *One word*. Then I text you twice, each time with a string of numbers."

Rocco nodded, imagining himself back in his high school math class, and seeing Uncle Chuck at the blackboard instead of old Dr Cruickshank. He was concentrating harder now than he ever did with that old fart droning away.

"Each text'll be a long string with the GPS coordinates buried in it. First one's gonna be latitude. Here's an example." He wrote 44.576073. "So, it's Tuesday. You run along the string until you come to the first number five. Five is the E in Tuesday. Okay? So, the numbers following that number five will be the GPS; two units, a decimal and then six more units. Only we leave the decimal out, of course. See?"

"Okay, now I see where this is going..."

"Good. Smart boy. You'll go far. Next set of numbers is yer longitude. Same deal, run along 'til you come to five, 'cos it's still Tuesday. But this time you put a negative in front of the string." He wrote down -79.495354. "Leave out the minus you end up in fuckin' Kazakhstan. Got it?"

"Yeah. I just tap these into my Garmin and it takes me there."

"Right. One other thing. The first number in the *second* string will be the time. Mostly evenings between eight and twelve. The time'll be followed by a zero." He wrote 80 and 120 as examples of eight o'clock and midnight. "*Capiche?*"

Rocco nodded, imagining himself is some sort of spy novel, playing with secret rendezvous and drop-boxes and covert communications. Of course the underworld had to work this way, but who really thought about it?

"Now," continued the biker boss, "we gotta set up the deal in Colombia so your agent buys the stuff and moves it on to my guys for the switcheroo. Who do you buy from?"

"I don't... Yet." A pang of guilt shot through him. He knew the name of an agent in Medellín of course. Francisco Gonçalves. Julia had given it to him. Now he began to feel utterly dirty at another betrayal of confidence. Part of his mind asked him how he could possibly do this, while the other part told him he didn't have a choice. Not when Julia's wellbeing was in the balance. The evil eyes across the table settled the matter.

"Well, isn't this where your little chicky comes in, then?"

"No, no. Won't work." Think! Think fast; clammy sweat, heart flutter. No way he was going to involve Julia. "I... I can find an agent. No problem." He had absolutely no clue as to how he would locate Gonçalves, but he sure as hell couldn't ask Julia. Got to be a way. "No... no problem."

"Are you shitting me?"

"No, no, I know a guy there," he blurted too quickly, "'cos I want to get into that market myself."

"And he is?"

"Francisco Gonçalves," he replied reluctantly, feeling like crap.

"Okay." He wrote the name down on a scrap of paper from his wallet. "Just one small wrinkle, then; I don't know shit about fireworks, and neither do my boys in Colombia."

"Yeah, well I can fill you in on that. I'll contact Gonçalves, and you can send your... your people instructions."

"Send instructions! Are you fuckin' crazy? No way! Far too risky."

"What are you getting at?" An awful certainty was looming.

"Obvious, my friend. You gotta go meet these good people."

"No! No, sorry." Anger was trumping fear. "There's no way I'm going to Colombia. No way!"

Uncle Chuck scanned the empty tables again, lowering his voice almost to a whisper. "So, you have some sort of idea there's a choice? That it?"

"I can't! I can't just go pissing off to South America at a moment's notice..."

"You'll make an excuse. And you'll go."

"But, I couldn't even afford it! What do you take me for? Think I'm some kind of jet-setting businessman?" This was getting beyond crazy.

"Oh, if that's your only worry, I'm prepared to underwrite your jaunt as a legitimate business expense. No worries there." He leaned back in his chair, exuding largesse. Rocco shrunk under his gaze.

"Look, I can't just disappear from the company..." Those magnetic eyes focused upon him, shrinking his choices down to a close approximation of none.

"Make your bookings. Soonest. Gimme the bill. *Capiche?*"

Rocco nodded, stood up, left the table without another word and headed for the washroom. He entered the single stall, locked the door and sat on the lid of the can breathing deeply. It was like being sucked down the plughole of a sink, or swirling around this very toilet bowl with every other filthy thing that was finding its swift way to the sewers. Every time a new demand was made he reacted with fear and dread, but then every time he rose to the inevitable and did what he was told. After a few minutes of controlling breathing, drying sweat and easing shivers, he stood up and returned to the table.

Uncle Chuck remained at his coffee, weighing carefully the fragile compliance he had already achieved with the possibility of pushing too far, and decided to play soft and slow. Threats are great in their place, but sugar and cream would probably do a better job right now. Double-double on diplomacy.

"Tell you what we'll do," he said, fixing Rocco with his magical eyes. "We'll get you there and back real quick. I'll have my guy in Medellín see you around, make it as easy as we can. Three days max."

"Okay," replied Rocco, savouring the return of some of his presence of mind. "I'll do it. I can find a way of taking off for a few days. Sure."

Uncle Chuck nodded wisely. I've got a live one here, he thought. He could go a long way. "Right on. Now the nitty-gritty. How's it done?"

"There's only certain types of shells that lend themselves." Rocco had been giving this a great deal of thought. "So I'll need to tell your... your agents which kind to open. Show 'em how."

"What do you mean, which kind?"

"There's stars and comets, serpents, whistles, reports, crackles..."

"Yeah, very fuckin' pretty I'm sure. *Which* kind?"

"It would have to be ones with loose contents. Easy to tip out."

"No sweat then. You visit the agent, set up the deal, show my guys what to do, fuck off back home. Simple."

Rocco nodded, going through the processes in his mind. A sudden horrible upsurge of fear was quelled when he remembered his passport was, in fact, up to date because he had been to the US just last year.

"When you place your order for a whole mess of fireworks," continued Uncle Chuck, "some of 'em will be these... what... loose contents ones, right? So my guys will know which ones to open."

"Sure, you'd have to send a message, tell 'em which ones. Single word: serpents, whistles, or whatever. Even just alphabetical." Rocco was really getting into this! The deeper part hugged itself; the part just under the surface was appalled; on the surface all was serene, a thin skim of ice over freezing lethal drowning.

"Clever. Clever. You an' me, we'll get along fine. I figure ten shells in an order will be plenny. How many d'you order at a time?"

"Depends. Eight-inchers would be best. Might be eight boxes of four, might be a lot more."

"So, one, maybe two shells per box? Five, six boxes? Suit me just fine."

Uncle Chuck finished his coffee in several easy gulps. "Drink your Timmies for Christ's sake! You're costing me a fortune."

Rocco didn't even take a sip; it was already cold and sickly.

"Call me when you're booked. Soonest!" And he swung out of his chair and made for the door.

He had to kick-start his Hog three times before it fired.

☆ ☆ ☆

"Why so quiet?" Rocco had been more than usually silent and withdrawn over their supper and now the three of them were finishing their coffee in the living room.

"Oh, nothing serious, Mama. I have to make a business trip to the States, that's all. Three, four days."

"Business?" Nonno looked up quickly from his cup. "What business?"

Rocco had the lies all prepared and he had rehearsed his story well. Or so he thought. "I gotta visit the FireOne people down in Pennsylvania. Have to talk to them about their software..."

"Ah, it's that goddam electronic bullshit again! Thought so. And who's gonna look after the shop while you're away, then?"

"There's just the one show, fairly small affair in Barrie. Nothing that Seth and Tonio can't handle."

"Ah, no! We're not doin' a Pastorelli Fireworks show without no Pastorellis there!" Before Rocco could say a word the old man continued. "I know, I know, you're gonna make me go along, eh? Hold their hands. Izzat it?"

"No, Nonno, no. Those two guys'll do just fine, and it's just one show."

"Just one show! Then it'll be just another show. And then where will we be? And all this computer shit."

"It's just once, that's all." He was getting a little frazzled at his stretching of the lie that he thought he had practiced so well.

"Why don't you just talk to these people in Pennsylvania with that goddam Sky you're always on? That's what I wanna know.

Use yer lap-what's-it 'stead of going there."

God, thought Rocco, what a dumb-ass idea to use the software as a pretext. Talk about waving a red flare at the old bastard. Christ, what was I thinking?

"No, I can't use Skype because I have to meet with the people and go over the software. It's not something I can do remote."

"Well, *Jesu*, who's paying for this little jaunt? Eh? The company?" The old fellow was starting to get really steamed and Maria had set aside her coffee cup ready to intervene.

"I'll drive there. Stay in cheap motels, pay for my gas. And, anyway, there's going to be money saved because I won't be going to Barrie."

"*Jesu Cristi...*" began Emilio, then Maria spoke up.

"Come on, Papa, cut the boy some slack. He works hard and he deserves the chance to make the company even better..."

"Better? *Better!* What's better about leaving the show to the assistants and pissing off to America?" Emilio swallowed the last of his coffee and got up. "We're goin' bust and you pull off this kinda stunt!"

Well, if you're so worried about going bust, thought Rocco, you shouldn't have sold the manufacturing plant all those years ago. That's your missing cash cow. Except for what I'm doing now, of course...

"I'm goin' to bed," grumbled the old man. "You just do as you goddam-well please."

After the door had slammed Rocco and his mother sat in tense silence avoiding eye contact. Presently she sighed. "I know it's important to you, but I do so wish there was some way of..."

"He's getting worse. Sometimes I wonder if he doesn't *want* me to fail..."

"No, no, don't say that!" This was too close to the truth for her comfort. "But, you do have to go, eh?"

"Course I do. Do you think I would have brought it up if I wasn't sure?" But he couldn't meet her gaze, and she knew by his evasion and his earlier silence that this wasn't the whole story.

"It's just a few days," he mumbled to the hands in his lap.

Maria sighed, stood up and took their cups to the kitchen. And she cried within herself at the new void that had opened between them.

☆✩🟊✩☆

Rocco had made all the arrangements for the trip. Tonio and Seth were secretly delighted to be on their own for a show, even a small one, and they were unable to conceal their pleasure. The satisfaction of his two employees was about the only upbeat part of this whole sorry enterprise. Rocco had booked his flights on-line and packed a small overnight bag. He wouldn't be able to take it as carry-on baggage as it contained a few selected tools and materials, and a dummy bombshell with the contents emptied out. If he was going to demonstrate what to do, it had better be done right. There would be no chance of detection at airport security, and even if there was, the reason was innocent enough.

Uncle Chuck had briefed him at another rendezvous. His phone had rung and a string of numbers had appeared on the screen; the GPS coordinates for the latitude of the drop location. He had noted them down and closed the phone. Less than a minute later the time and longitude information had arrived. He had been quite tickled to be playing this cloak-and-dagger game... until the seriousness of it settled into his mind once again.

"You'll meet my guy, Ernesto," Uncle Chuck had told him, "at the airport in Medellín. He'll take you round, do what you have to do, make the arrangements. He's located your agent, Gonçalves. Tell him Ernesto's your shipper. Get the orders sorted out, then you show Ernesto and his boys what to do with the fireworks. Got it?"

It all sounded so simple, but Rocco knew he would be in high tension mode until this whole thing was finished and he was back in good old, boring East Gladstone. So, early one Friday morning, with just the slight easing of night's black backdrop in the east, he kissed his mother on the cheek at their front door, climbed into his car and set off for 'Pennsylvania'. Nonno was nowhere in sight. He headed down Highway 11, joining the 400 on the way to Pearson International Airport and his 8:30 flight to Medellín via Panama City. The flight was routine, the food at least edible and the drinks copious, but Rocco's tension refused to unwind. The long hours of the first flight and the repeated boredom of the following one tried his patience to the extreme. He had brought books with him, and his laptop and a sheaf of crosswords puzzles clipped out of the newspaper, but none of these things could provide any distraction.

True to Uncle Chuck's word, Ernesto was there at the gate to meet the Copa Airlines flight, a tall heavily bearded guy sporting a linen suit and dark glasses, and complete with a cardboard sign labeled 'Mr Roco Firewok'. He was hustled quickly to a waiting car and helped into the back seat. Ernesto climbed in beside him and waved to the driver to pull into the traffic.

"We go first to your hotel. In the morning nine o'clock we go to Gonçalves."

"You've located him?"

"Sure. *Agencia de fuegos artificiales de Medellín*. Find him easy. No problem." Ernesto remained silent for the remainder of the drive to a modern hotel near the city centre.

Since the plane had taken off in Toronto, Rocco had been continually reminding himself that this was actually real; that this was truly happening. But his sense of adventure—always so strong on family trips to Italy—was at war with a dampening sense of doom. Enjoyment of novelty kept stumbling over the reason for his presence; it was an experience he wished would end quickly. The sense of the unreal continued on the car journey. He had had no idea what to expect of Medellín and was astonished to find a go-ahead modern city nestled in a mountain valley, and rich with ancient Spanish-style buildings, modern high-rises, elevated trains, and even a cable car ascending the mountain. Shantytown shacks creeping up hillsides showed the contrasting poorer side of the population, but visit any reservation in Northern Ontario and you'd see worse. The general sense of beauty, order and peace, however, was quite at odds with the horrible traffic he was involved in. It didn't make sense.

The hotel room was adequate, the bed soft, and the water lukewarm. He stripped off his clothes, had a quick wash and wondered whether he really wanted to eat anything. By this time it was 8:00 in the evening, but his stomach said no. He opened the mini-bar and took out a bottle of Cerveza Colón Roja and found it excellent. He flipped through the TV channels, finding a great many shows in Spanish which, with his knowledge of Italian he could just about follow, and some utter rubbish from the North American continent.

He went to bed much earlier than normal, flipped on the alarm on the bedside table and nodded to sleep over the book he had brought with him.

☆★☆

Seth and Tonio had left East Gladstone on Thursday afternoon, arriving in Barrie in time to begin their set-up. The timing of

Rocco's absence couldn't have been better; Barrie was only a short drive away around the lake, and the show was not too complicated. Seth, in particular, was well acquainted with the software and was fully confident he could run the whole show from his keyboard. With only two pairs of hands it took longer to get the launching equipment set up and all the intricate connections made, but they ran into no problems. The launching ramp was at the edge of a soccer field in a pleasant park, and they had positioned their truck close by in an adjacent public parking lot.

Saturday morning dawned clear and bright, and the slight showers that had passed through overnight looked to have made their way eastward and would not be repeated. The guys finished breakfast in their hotel, returned to the site slowly and uncovered the previous day's work. They continued their set-up, and by midday they were confidently ahead of schedule for the evening's show.

An ancient Ford LTD Squire station wagon pulled into the parking lot beside their truck, and an elderly gentleman stepped out and headed towards them.

Then the shit hit the fan.

✩☆ ⭐ ☆✩

Ernesto arrived at the hotel after breakfast. Rocco had eaten some fresh fruit and yogurt and had drunk two cups of truly excellent coffee. His confidence was restored and although this was going to be a tough day, he felt energetic and positive enough to carry it through and get the hell back home. He picked up his bag as he saw the car pull up outside, and spotted Ernesto emerging.

"First to *Agencia de fuegos artificiales de Medellín*," said Ernesto through his beard and from behind his perennial dark glasses as they got into the back seats of the car. Not one further word could be extracted from him, and Rocco's observations on the scenery and culture as they drove were studiously ignored and soon petered out. The driver took them to a hilly area of crisscrossing streets mostly devoted to what looked like light industry. They pulled up in front of a nondescript concrete block building and got out of the car.

Ernesto motioned him forward to the door of the building, and Rocco suddenly suffered a knee weakening pang of fear as if expecting an ambush. The whole situation was so far outside his experience and his companion so mysterious. If asked to describe

Ernesto, Rocco realized that it would be impossible. He swung the door open and, to his relief, was greeted by a rotund, middle-aged man who could only be Francisco Gonçalves. Ernesto stood in the background near the door while the firework agent shook Rocco's hand and waved him to a seat.

"It is a great pleasure to meet another from Canada," enthused Gonçalves, still gripping Rocco's hand. "Nice to greet customers from your good country."

Gonçalves showed him catalogues and lists of products while Rocco checked the offerings and explained what pyrotechnics he wished to order. The business was concluded quite quickly as Rocco's needs were simple and explicit. Regular consignments of aerial shells, four to a box, among them hummers, whistles or reports, would do the job nicely. Rocco had decided these would be the best shells to use because the contents are packed loose; when the shell bursts, these loose garnitures are free to fly willy-nilly. Stars, on the other hand, are often packed tightly inside the case to hold them in place, so it's not as easy to quickly tip out the contents. Only the top hemisphere of the shell would need to be emptied because he figured that the only way to deal with the tampered shells was to refill them from his own stock with garnitures and an upper burst charge, thus returning them to innocence. Therefore, the passfire and lower charge should be left in place, making both his job and that of the loaders in here in Medellín quicker and easier. Also, he thought the presence of gunpowder in close proximity to the dope might confuse any sniffers. He had no evidence for this, but it seemed a safe precaution.

The Pastorelli workshop had huge stocks of garnitures and gunpowder, but Rocco would still have to replenish the stocks by making more whistles, serpents, or whichever garnitures were used. The skills that his grandfather had taught him would come into use in a horrible way. One small worry was that the garnitures he made would differ slightly from those made here, but over that he had no control. In truth, they would probably not be noticed. Although it would be a tedious business spending long evenings on the repetitive task of filling little cardboard tubes with various powders, it would turn out to be somewhat therapeutic.

The business concluded Rocco introduced Ernesto, who had remained silently at the door, as his shipper.

"No need, my friend," said Gonçalves expansively, arms out to his sides like the Jesus in Rio de Janeiro. "My shippers they do a good job."

Rocco insisted that this was the way it would be, and amid further protestations it was agreed that Ernesto would be contacted when a consignment was ready, and he would pick it up and take it to the docks at Cartagena.

Rocco bade goodbye to the proprietor of *Agencia de fuegos artificiales de Medellín* and got back into the waiting car. As soon as the car was underway Ernesto produced a black bandana from his pocket, and before Rocco could do anything more than react in surprise he bound it round his entire face, totally concealing his eyes.

"No argument. No struggle. This is the way we do it," muttered Ernesto with a grinding grip on Rocco's upper arm.

There was no point in resisting, and Rocco soon began to see the sense of this precaution; the less he saw of what was coming up, the better for all concerned. It was just a pity that Ernesto hadn't run his bandana through the washing machine first...

After perhaps half an hour of twists and turns the car came to a halt. Rocco made to remove his eye covering but was restrained. He was helped out of the car, a hand pushing down on his head, and then led across a gravel walkway and into a building. Only when he and his captor had passed down passageways and through two doors was the blindfold whipped off. He blinked in the harsh fluorescent light of a bare room; white walls and ceiling, light wood floor, no windows, nothing on the walls. The only furnishings were a bare folding table and three metal chairs. The two chairs behind the table were occupied by two figures wearing *papier maché* carnival masks, one smiling the other grimacing, the classics of Comedy and Tragedy. The third chair was for him. Ernesto stood by the door, behind Rocco, with his arms folded.

Rocco sat, pulled the chair forward and took the equipment out of his bag: lead pencil, small backsaw, box cutter, roll of gummed paper tape, and the 5" dummy shell he had prepared back at home so far away.

"This is a five-incher, but you guys'll be doing eights." The smiling mask of Comedy nodded, so at least one of them understood English.

Without the need for further words he swiftly marked the equator of the shell accurately with the pencil then gently sawed through the gummed tape covering and the cardboard right along the glued seam between the two halves. He carefully avoided sawing in the area of the leader fuse, which was wrapped around the shell, and instead used the box cutter to cut the cardboard away as closely as possible. He was then able to swing the top hemisphere off, with a small hinge of cardboard still supporting the fuse, thus exposing the dummy contents. He removed the paper bag of the upper burst charge and the empty cardboard cylinders that represented the garnitures.

"See," he said at last, showing them the opened shell. "I've kept the fuse intact and the stuff is still in the bottom half." He held it towards them. The smiling mask nodded again. "Now all you do is put your stuff in the top half and close it like this."

He clopped the two pieces together, took a long strip of gummed tape, tried to moisten it with his tongue, and found that his tongue was too dry.

"*Agua*," said Ernesto with a gesture to Tragedy. The grimacing mask returned in less than a minute with a Styrofoam cup of water. Rocco dipped his finger in the cup and moistened the tape enough to apply it round the shell. He drank the rest.

"You follow this *exactly*, so when I open the box I'll see this band of tape. Okay?" Comedy nodded again while Tragedy maintained a stoical wooden pose. "You can keep the shell. Reminder. And I'll leave you with the tools."

Ernesto stepped forward and replaced the blindfold. Rocco was again led by the arm and helped into the car. The return journey seemed shorter and it was only 15 minutes or so before the rancid bandana was removed from his face. The bright sunlight of downtown Medellín dazzled his eyes as the car pulled up in front of the hotel.

"Morning you take a taxi to the airport," said Ernesto as Rocco picked up his bag and got out of the car. The car sped off.

"Well, fuck you and the horse you rode in on!" shouted Rocco to the trunk of the retreating car as it merged into traffic and vanished. "Nothing like rolling out the fucking welcome mat. Assholes!"

He pushed through the hotel doors and headed for the bar.

After a miserable and forgettable meal and too many beers at the bar, and with absolutely no desire to play the tourist, he returned to his room. He flung his bag down on the bed and checked his watch. Nearly 7:30. The time here was the same as at home, so he decided to give Tonio and Seth a call to see how they were getting on. Cost a fortune, but well worth it for peace of mind. And a slender thread to home.

"Hey, Seth, it's Rocco. How's things?"

"Rocco...? Yeah... Where are you?" He sounded... what...? surprised, confused.

"Med... er... Pennsylvania, of course. But how's it going?"

"It's... it's just fine. Yeah, just fine."

Rocco was feeling a stab of fear. If there was some sort of fuck-up while he was away he'd never hear the last of it. And Seth sure as hell didn't sound happy.

"Okay, what's up?"

"Well, see, I can't really talk now." Seth's voice was a mumble. "See, your grampa's shown up and pretty well taken over the show."

"*What!* What in Christ does he think he's doing?"

"Wait a minute. Wait... That's better. I'm round the back of the truck. Look, he's pulled the laptop off and he's rigged up that firing board you used to use in the old days. The one in the back of the storage?"

"Oh, the senile old fuck! He'll ruin us!"

"Not so fast old buddy. He really does look like he knows what he's doing. Look, I gotta go. Skype me around eleven, okay?"

"I dunno. I don't know how good the WiFi is here..."

"What, in Pennsylvania for Christ's sake? It's not like it's the Third World. You won't have any problem. *Really* gotta go."

And he was gone.

Three hours and more to wait in suspense! As if today hadn't been full of shit already, and now this. The blued steel spring in Rocco was tight wound again. There was nothing for it but to leave the hotel and walk and walk and walk. He didn't make much of a tourist as his attention was never upon the externals; the cafés, the buildings, the bustle of people enjoying themselves, the rumble of trains, and the sexy waft of Latin music from open doors. His mind was filled with the unfolding scenario back in Barrie, Ontario. A failure and he would get almighty shit from Nonno; a success and... he would still get almighty shit from Nonno. God damn it, Rocco, you just can't win, can you?

Prompt at eleven back in the hotel he booted up Skype, thanked the gods of WiFi for a good connection, and called Seth. He positioned himself so that an anonymous hotel wall was in the background; could be anywhere in the world. Seth and Tonio appeared on the screen, faces plastered in smiles.

"It was priceless!" crowed Seth. "Oh, man, you should have

been there! It was just priceless."

"Yeah," put in Tonio. "Not a single shot wrong. It was a virtuoso performance!"

"See," laughed Seth, "I've never seen him in action. Like, before my time, eh? But, Christ, he's good!"

"Ain't no goddamn way yer firing off this show without a Pastorelli," mimicked Tonio so precisely that Rocco had to smile. "Jesus, no offence Rocco, but we have just sat at the feet of a Master!"

Rocco didn't know what to think. "Oh, shit, I haven't heard the last of this. I was so worried it'd be a complete fuck-up…"

"But, I tell you, it's lucky he showed up when he did," interrupted Tonio, "'cos we'd already cut the leaders and attached the e-matches. If he had of come earlier he would of launched the whole show with a passfire! Said he would."

"God, yeah," replied Seth, "he was psyched, man."

"Okay, thanks guys." He didn't want to hear any more. "I'll see you tomorrow night."

He shut down the computer with his thoughts in turmoil. Uppermost was relief that the show had gone well, but then there was an almost envy that the old man still had it in him, could still pull off a good show at the age of 82. This was coupled with an anger that he, Rocco, had been shown up; his dereliction had been the occasion for an uncalled-for intervention. Now he felt belittled and marginalized, less of a leading figure in his employees' eyes. This led to an unworthy thought; perhaps he would have felt better in himself if the gig had been a failure.

Then his thoughts turned to his mission here in Colombia. How many people in prison, he wondered, got there because of something they did when they were young and stupid? How many of them were sucked in bit by bit, threatened, cajoled, bribed, flattered, whatever, to the point where they couldn't get out, couldn't break away? And now I've come to Cocaine Central and dealt with the really evil ones, I'm as dirty as they are.

Guilt took over and for a long while he just lay on the bed feeling miserable and very lonely.

Rocco woke early the next morning in a surprisingly upbeat mood. The miserable thoughts of the night before were replaced with a tentative optimism. Whatever fallout there would be from the success in Barrie he would handle when it came. He got shit from Nonno anyway, so how would this be any different? And the cocaine show-and-tell simply meant he was that much further along a road that had started years ago. You can cry and complain, or you can go ahead and do what you have to do. Somehow the blazing anger that often threatened to break out was held in abeyance. The future wasn't written, and anyway it could wait.

Over his early breakfast and before taking a cab to the airport, Rocco mentally checked off his achievements of the day before, and his plans for the future. The procedure had been worked out perfectly at this end; no problems there. So when the shipments from Cartagena arrived in the Port of Montreal the Pastorelli truck would be sent to clear customs and load them for transport to East Gladstone. He would make it a rule that the shipment would always be left on the pallets in the loading dock until the following day. That way he could return later in the evening, open the boxes and remove and replace the contents of the loaded shells. Once returned to normal the whole newly-innocent shipment could be transferred to the magazine.

It was clean, it was clever, and it was foolproof.

Chapter Three
The Passfire

The fuse that burns while an aerial shell ascends, thus providing a time delay between lift and burst [also called time fuse, spolette or spitool] *Shells, an Introduction*, Ned Gorski, Skylighter.com

Hefty Beale was ignoring the boss's injunction and chatting with his friend Steve Bacon on the patio of their local Royal Oak. There were two half-full glasses in front of them, and five empties waiting to be picked up by the lovely lady in black tights with the nice boobs and plastic smile. If his boss had the slightest inkling of what Hefty was blabbing about, and who he was blabbing it to, there would be a death in the biker family. Hefty lived for the moment, so close friendship and three-and-a-half pints of Guinness tended to override strict injunctions.

"Uncle Chuck was pissed with me for doing that job with you, y'know."

"You think *he* was pissed? Rocco was fuckin' fit to be tied. Try to do a guy a favour..."

"Didn't appreciate our good deed, eh?"

"No siree. Asshole stormed on about it, gave me shit. Well, he's no pal of mine anyway. Screw him. But the job was a lot of fun, eh?"

"Yeah," replied Hefty cagily, "but I can't keep doin' that kinda thing. Big trouble."

He lit up a cigarette, defying anyone on the patio to lodge a complaint. Steve sipped at his Guinness, failing to keep pace with his huge pal's appetite. The mellowing effects of the ink-brown nectar were loosening the biker's tongue.

"So, I have this great idea, right?" Hefty took a good long drag at his cigarette and blew a cloud over his head. "Why not hide the shit from Colombia in crates of fireworks?"

"So, that's what was going through your tiny head that night?"

"Yup. Looked great to me," he replied doubtfully.

"But Uncle Chuck didn't buy it?"

"Nah, thought it was too risky, see? Least, that's what he said. Then, know what, next thing I find out is, he's got the supplier in

Colombia doing *igzakly* what I said."

"So, when Catesby's take a delivery, the shit is hidden in it?" Steve was instantly alert. Vistas of financially rewarding break-and-enters were dancing in his head.

"Nah, not Catesby's; the other outfit. Pastorelli."

"Holy shit! Pastorelli's! My ex-friend Rocco! So he's in on it?"

"Yep, taking a good roll of bills, too."

Well, that little bugger, thought Steve; gets all moral about fixing a few fireworks, then pulls a stunt like this. Just shows, he may have moved on from our crowd, but he's still right in the groove. Shit! He really is an asshole.

The second half of Hefty's Guinness went down in three swift gulps.

"How about I get you boys another?" smiled the server with her lips and teeth.

"Nah, gotta get back to work. Whadda we owe you?" Hefty pulled out a wad of notes from his leather jacket and peeled off much more than necessary. "'S all right Steve, I got these."

"Thanks, you're a pal."

The server took the money, counted it and smiled at Hefty with her whole face. Young, capable, pretty, and bringing up two pre-school kids on her own. Guys like these, you give 'em a real smile.

"Y'know," rumbled Hefty around a vast yeasty belch, "I shouldn't a mentioned that shit about the fireworks. Uncle Chuck'd kill me if he found out."

"Safe with me," assured Steve as he belatedly finished only his third Guinness. "My zips are lipped."

☆☆☆

The Detective Inspector stood with his back to the room, looking out of the window of his office. It was a common pose. He was thinking about law enforcement and the uphill battle his people always faced in simply keeping the peace. Trouble was, law enforcement was so grotesquely biased in favour of the criminals. We have to abide by such concepts as truth, honesty, fairness, integrity, justice, whereas the other side has no such restrictions. He was just about sick and tired of the V-Twin Valkyries; knowing they were dealing drugs, selling sex, laundering money and God knows what else, but doing it with such consummate skill that ordinary cops simply couldn't keep up.

He'd called Detective Sergeant Delios to his office to discuss the latest scuttlebutt that his undercover men were picking up, and here he was at the door.

"Siddown. There's more bullshit going on with the fireworks," said the DI, as he sat behind his desk and crossed his arms.

"Those protesters..."

"Well, maybe, but I think there's more. There's this guy called Steve Bacon, petty crook, B and E artist, been in for a couple of short stretches, complete loose cannon. He's been shooting his mouth off about doing, and I quote, a Main Street fireworks store. Favour for an old friend."

"Main Street? Catesby's on Upper Main. What sort of favour?" Delios was much more familiar with organizations like banks, payroll outfits, security firms; the sort of magnets that usually attracted the real crooks. "And who's the friend?"

"Good question!"

"Bacon has been seen with the fireworks bunch," observed Delios. "Him and that skinny bitch and the thick one sometimes hang out. Maybe the protesters are upping the ante, then?"

"Well, they're not getting anywhere by marching up and down, that's for sure. You really think if they're being ignored it might piss them off enough to try something dirty?"

"It's a theory..."

"Look," sighed the DI, "I dunno what it is, but my radar's showing a blip. There's something weird going on, but I can't put my finger on it."

"I see what you mean," replied Delios. "The protesters wouldn't do stuff under cover; after all, it's public recognition they're after. Doesn't add up."

"Exactly. So who else could Bacon's old friend be then? Find him and we might find a motive. Bacon also hangs around with one of the bikers. Beale. Know him?"

"Hefty Beale," replied Delios. "Yeah, he's an Uncle Chuck stalwart, but he'd be stupid to hang around with Bacon."

"Well, that's what the informant told us," answered the DI. He slapped the file on his desk. "Maybe he is that stupid."

"I wonder if there's some ancient history we need to check into?" suggested Delios. "We haven't been in this district long enough."

"Well, if it's not in the files..."

"There's this retired cop I know, Stan Howard. I curl with him Thursdays. He was with this division for Christ knows how long.

Want me to chat him up? You never know."

"Yes, why not?" The Detective Inspector got up and went to the window. "It's not just some whacko protesters complaining about pyrotechnic pollution; there's got to be a bigger picture. Got to be."

"I'll buy him a beer; let you know."

☆✦ ⭐ ✦☆

Another Timmies, another evening, another waste of coffee. Rocco never drank the coffee Uncle Chuck so generously supplied. It was a strange act of defiance against sociability. One little cup of coffee, it seemed to him, would seal a social bond that he resisted. Yet, great wads of ready cash had already been dangled, and he would have no compunction about accepting them when the first delivery was made. Yet one little cup of coffee was hugely symbolic.

"Done!" cried Uncle Chuck before Rocco had even sat down. "You clever little bastard. A sweetheart system just ready to be set in motion." He slipped Rocco a wad of bills; compensation for airfare and per diem, with a little extra on the side, just because he was such a generous bastard. All aboveboard and businesslike.

"Ready to place an order?" Rocco asked the rhetorical question as he stuffed the wad of cash into his pocket. He felt a sudden upsurge of mingled enthusiasm, excitement and fear. He had already checked the stocks in the magazine at Pastorelli, so he knew exactly what aerial shells he needed. So now it was just a question of placing an order with Francisco Gonçalves. Even so, the delay in transit by ship would mean that his regular suppliers in Italy would continue to receive orders. Besides, it would be folly to sole-source to Colombia anyway.

"You bet!" replied Uncle Chuck. "Sooner the better. But listen; we do this real slow."

"You said a batch of maybe ten shells..."

"No, not a *batch*. One single fuckin' shell, my friend. I told Ernesto, we e-e-ease into this. We just e-e-ease into it real slow."

"Playing it safe?"

"Yup. Customs opens one single shell in a whole shipment, you deny any knowledge. Just looks like some stupid cunt trying it on. One single shell. It gets through, we have a green light. Simple."

"Okay, I need eight cases of shells, and there are four in each case. A variety. Of those, one case will be eight-inch serpents. How about it's one of them?"

"Done! Eight-inch serpents? I'll tell Ernesto, send him the letter S. Course, that's not his real name."

That figured; total anonymity of dark glasses and beard, and fake name to go with it. "And I call you as soon as the shipment arrives?"

"One word. Then I send coordinates. Got it?"

He nodded. I hate you, he thought. I hate the ground you foul with your feet, I hate the air you pollute with your breath, and I'm bound to you like some fucking millstone or albatross. I would gladly kill you and enjoy doing it, if only God gave me a chance. His anger rose like a vomit and he willed his face to show no sign, his body to betray nothing.

He got up without another word and left the coffee shop.

It was another waffles morning. Maria had detected an unease in her son, rightly but not totally attributed to Nonno's success in Barrie. She knew it wasn't that Rocco resented the old guy's success as such, it was just that Nonno was making such a big deal of it.

"Here, you didn't get enough syrup," as she glugged an extra lake into the steaming, corrugated confection.

"Hey, steady, I'll be sticky all day."

"Sometimes you need sweetening up. That's my job today. Send you off to work in a sweet mood. Have some fruit." Defrosted Europe's Best berries made a beaver lodge in the middle of the lake.

Rocco had to smile. It was one of those ironies, and one that he had so accurately predicted back in Colombia when he had first heard the news. Sure enough, his grandfather's triumph with his old-fashioned electric technology had made him full of piss and vinegar. So instead of razzing his grandson about the impending failure of the business, he was now razzing him over how he had made sure a Pastorelli was at the helm in his absence, and a goddamn good one at that. Sure, the new feisty Nonno was a welcome change, but he was still just as obnoxious.

"You can't win, can you?" he observed to his mother. "I get shit for running the company into the ground, and then I get shit for abandoning the boys. On the plus side, although he's still a pain in the ass, at least he's a positive one."

"Something to take away with you," she smiled. "I must say, the new bouncy Emilio is a lot less hard to take. But, you know, for all his talk, when he came back from Barrie he was just wiped! He couldn't do that on a regular basis."

"Yeah, it'd kill him. Although he'd go out with a bang, doing something he loved."

"Well, at least, my love, his attention's off the finances."

"So, suck it up. That what you're saying?"

She shrugged and attempted to slide another waffle onto his plate. Her move was met by a flanking ploy as he slid the plate out of reach of the poised spatula. "Enough already! I have to go." He stood and headed for the door.

"Work hard. Keep those gigs rolling in."

"I think we'll get back in the black soon," he replied, sounding perhaps a little too optimistic as he noted his mother's raised eyebrows. "Anyway... I'm hoping, that's all... Hoping things will look up..."

As he drove he passed pedestrians, bus line-ups, joggers and dog walkers, wondering idly how many of them were leading duplicitous, criminal lives behind their facades of normality and social conformity. He so wanted not to be alone; he wasn't liking himself all that much, and craved the phantom company of others like him.

✩☆⟡☆✩

The weeks of waiting for his first order from Colombia were agonizing. Many times a day Rocco would feel a pang of anxiety and fear mixed with a deep hugging glee mirror-imaged with loathing. When the day finally came to collect the shipment from Montreal he was all for going along with the truck to see it through Customs; to touch the boxes and realize they were real, were really here. He resisted the temptation, but sat all day in his office fiddling with things and getting nothing accomplished. Each time the phone rang he seized it in fear, but it was always clients or suppliers, mercifully taking his attention away from a truck somewhere on the highway.

When the truck finally pulled into the loading dock near the end of the working day Rocco sauntered in from his office in studied nonchalance.

"How'd it go? No problems?"

"Nah. Why should there be?" replied Seth. "Piece o' cake. René, the guy on the desk, says there's some other outfit brings in their stuff from Colombia. So he's got the paperwork down pat."

"Great. It's late; just offload here and we'll inventory and shelve the stuff tomorrow."

He wanted so badly to tear the top off the box labeled 8″ Serpents, but he held off. It was here! It was here! That was all that mattered for the present. Time to shut down the desk and go home for supper. Maria had promised that ravioli she did so well, and I'll bet there's a couple of bottles of that nice Farnese in the rack. Mustn't make it look like a celebration, though.

Rocco had dashed away after supper, telling his mother and grandfather that he had work to do, and that they would all finish the wine when he got back. Their suspicions that something more than work was going on were amplified.

"Ah, some little piece in town," was Emilio's opinion. "Probably someone we wouldn't like, maybe?"

"He's never kept his lady friends secret, far as I know," replied Maria. "Still, his business not ours."

He got the claw end of the hammer under the lid of the box and pulled. It came off with a satisfying *screek*, the brown wrapping paper was pulled aside, and there lay four gorgeous 8″ Serpents sheathed in translucent plastic bags. One, just one, had a strip of gummed tape right round its equator! Got it! He took the shell out with shaking hands and carried it through to the workshop. He plugged in the hot glue gun and placed the shell on the workbench. He quickly undid the twist-tie around the plastic bag, slid it off and peeled away the band of tape around the shell, carefully avoiding the leader fuse that wrapped around it from top to bottom. He swung the top over, hinged on the fuse. There, exposed, was the packed white powder in its little bags. Only when he actually saw the cocaine, hefting the bags in his hands, did he realize the enormity of what he was doing. He knew now, in a way that perhaps he hadn't before, just how deeply enmeshed he really was.

Just out of interest he pulled out the small digital scale he used for weighing lift charges—a most important calculation if you wanted your shells to explode at the height they were supposed to—and piled the baggies onto it. They weighed in at about 560 grams, so deducting the approximate weight of the Ziplocs, gave him around 550 grams of coke. He grabbed a notepad and a pencil and jotted some quick calculations. He knew, through certain late-night parties he used to frequent and didn't like to talk about, that a line of coke would set you back around $40, and a line was probably much less than a quarter of a gram. So, call it $160 per gram at street value, which made nearly 90 grand in this one shell in front of him. Multiply that by the 10 shells per shipment Uncle Chuck planned, and there would be pushing a million bucks, right there on the workbench in front of him. Holy shit!

He stuffed the Ziplocs into a Loblaw's canvas shopping bag and set about refilling the shell. A quick scan of the intact bottom half of the shell revealed about two dozen serpents, so he took the same number from a glass jar on the workshop shelf, swiftly packed them into the top, and pressed a paper bag of gunpowder around them. He then ran a bead of hot glue around the edge of the hemisphere, flipped it onto its other half, pressed them together, and applied gummed tape to the seam. The tape matched the original with which the shell was covered but, even so, it looked obviously different to his eyes. But perhaps not different enough to be noticed when setting up a show, especially when the translucent plastic bag was slipped back on and twist-tied in place.

He hurried back to the loading dock with the restored shell. He tucked it safely into the box, covering it with the wrapping paper, and then he pressed the lid back on, guiding the nails into their original holes. A quick tap with the hammer round the edges of the lid and all evidence was gone.

Now came the most dangerous part of the whole caper; he had to take the cocaine to a rendezvous with one of Uncle Chuck's cohort. He passed though to his office and called the latest cell-phone number.

"Condor."

His phone rang almost immediately with the first set of coordinates. The second set also gave the time, which was within half an hour of right now.

He locked up the shop, got into his car, and tapped the coordinates into his Garmin. As he drove he imagined with horror being pulled over by the police for a routine stop; the Toyota's speedometer sank to the speed limit and his eyes scanned the road in trepidation. On a dark country side road some 10 kilometers outside East Gladstone he pulled over and handed the shopping bag through the car window to a massive biker who blotted out half the sky. A bulging envelope was shoved into his hand.

Not a word was spoken.

The Harley roared away from the rendezvous, and Rocco started his car and headed home for the rest of that Farnese.

☆✩☆

Stan Howard was a local guy and had been with the force in East Gladstone since he had graduated years ago from the police course at Algonquin College in Ottawa. He was a superb resource regarding the wrongdoers of the town, and possessed a great deal of information that could not be found in any filing cabinet or database.

The curling rink at the athletic facility had an upstairs lounge with long, low windows that looked out onto the four sheets below. Two sheets were still in use, one in the tenth and the other into an extra end. Fred and Stan's four had finished their game, so it was time for the two of them to wind down with a beer and some talk.

"What a way to pull it out, eh skip? Steal in the tenth!" crowed Delios.

"Yeah, Fred, I thought we were toast. But I laid up the guard 'cos I thought he might just go for it, and sure enough..."

"That'll larn 'im!" laughed Fred. He took a long, satisfied pull at his beer, then started to get serious. "Look Stan, I want to ask you something as one active cop to another with a lot of info."

"Shoot. If I know it, it's yours."

"Steve Bacon..." began Delios.

"Oh, little Bacon Enter is still busy, is he? Wonder when or if he'll ever realize that his kind of perversion'll come back and bite him?"

"What, he gets off on B and E?"

"Big time. Break and enter's a sexual rush for him; doing the job and boasting about it afterwards. He hasn't done much time, mostly because his stuff is regarded as mischief. He hardly ever pinches anything. Just has laundry bills."

"What a case. What makes 'em do it?"

"Ah, one of those poor buggers. Life's just dealt him a handful of turds, that's all. Crap home life, father doing time."

"He was recently doing a friend a favour by breaking into a firework factory. You any idea of the background?" Another long swig of beer and a stretch of shoulder muscles stiff from hurling granite and brushing ice.

"Ah, now you're talking! There was this one case where he bit off enough for a good long stretch in the slammer. He was the entry expert for a serious robbery. Payroll safe."

"But he didn't do time for that. Not in the files, anyway."

"Exactly. That was one of my biggest piss-offs, matter of fact." He paused for a few moments for a drink, recalling the details. "This was—what?—about ten years ago. We had the accomplice, no question, and Bacon was as guilty as hell. We had enough to put him down all right. Then, up comes an unshakeable alibi. A friend comes forward and gives him the perfect 'can't be in two places at once' deal. Case collapses, he walks."

"So, where's fireworks angle?"

"Guy who provided the boiler-plate alibi was Pastorelli! Rocco Pastorelli!"

"Shit! So, what sort of favour is Bacon doing for Pastorelli?" wondered Fred Delios. "Doesn't make a lot of sense. Sabotage?"

"There's a bit of competition between Pastorelli and Catesby," mulled Howard, "but hardly enough for open warfare surely?"

"Well, there's apparently a biker connection too."

"No way!" replied Howard. "Uncle Chuck does *not* suffer fools gladly. Bacon is poison around the clubhouse."

"We'd heard that he hung around with one of them. Beale."

"Old Hefty Beale!" reminisced Stan Howard, as if recalling a good friend. "He might be pals with him, but Uncle Chuck has better taste that that. Bacon's a loser and, as you are fully aware, he loves to shoot his mouth off. Besides, we were pretty sure that the B and E that Bacon wriggled out of had a biker angle. Nothing we could pin down for certain, but he pissed Uncle Chuck off somehow around that time. Either way, I don't see Bacon doing jobs for the V-Twin Valkyries. Like I say, they have better sense."

"I wonder if Bacon would be of any use to us? Might be an inside track..."

"Sure. You could either lean on the little jerk or offer him some cash. Never know what he might be able to give you. Like liqueur chocolates, him; soft centre."

The talk veered away from the doings of Steve Bacon and the bikers, and little new information was forthcoming. At least, at the end of the evening's discussion Sergeant Delios would be able to report to his Chief that he had found a connection, but the whole situation was still just about as obscure as before.

⋆☆⭐☆⋆

"Let me get this straight," said the Detective Inspector. "We have Steve Bacon connected to Rocco Pastorelli because of what sounds like perjury some ten years ago. And because Bacon is indebted to Pastorelli he does his pal a favour by breaking into Catesby's?"

"That's the way it appears."

"So, what in hell is so important in Catesby's that Pastorelli gets a friend to break in? What actually is the game here?"

"Sabotage, maybe?"

"Sabotage? Why sabotage?" The Chief looked totally skeptical. "I could see the protesters having him sabotage the place, but even then, you've got to ask why. Why, when everything they do is out in the open? The whole point of protesting is getting in the public's face."

"Maybe it's the competition, then? Old man Pastorelli and Alfred, the Catesby son, apparently loathe each other."

"But that doesn't mean Rocco Pastorelli is going to go as far as nobbling the opposition, surely?"

"Does sound a bit thin..."

"Look, why don't you pay a little visit to Catesby's? Just check 'em out, chat with them. See what your nose tells you."

"Should I mention the break-in rumour?"

"Sure. Sound them out. See if they have any suspicions."

DS Delios rose and made for the door.

"Hey, take Chan with you," said the boss. "She had that nasty rape in the east end to deal with. Give her something light; she needs a break."

So, acting on the information of Steve Bacon's purported break-and-enter, DS Fred Delios paid a visit to Catesby & Son on Upper Main Street accompanied by Detective Constable Lucie Chan. Alfred Catesby met them at the door, mystified as to what would bring a call from the law.

"Come though to the office please." Alfred walked ahead, held the door to the office open and ushered the police in.

"So, what can I do for you, officers?" he asked.

"We've had information that there was a break-in at these premises a few nights ago..."

"No, you must be mistaken. We didn't report anything."

"Sorry, I didn't make myself clear," continued the Detective

Sergeant, apologizing on his behalf for Alfred Catesby's interruption, "but we have a report of someone boasting about breaking in."

"Well, it's impossible. We have the best in alarm systems, and besides nothing has been reported missing."

"Well, let me suggest a possible scenario. This guy breaks in purely for mischief by temporarily disarming your alarm system. He doesn't steal anything and he doesn't leave traces."

"Whatever would be the point of breaking in then?" asked Alfred, perhaps even more mystified than when the pair had first walked in the door.

"If our suspicions are correct, this is a man who enjoys break-and-enter as an end in itself. A weird perversion, you could say."

"So, he could have entered the building and we would never have known?" asked Alfred. "That's downright creepy."

"Yes, bit nasty, isn't it?"

"Sounds as if he needs treatment."

"Or booting into the slammer," was the heartless response. "Would you mind if we take a look around, familiarize ourselves with the layout?"

"No problem at all," replied Alfred, "but we have safety systems for all sectors of both buildings, so it would be best if I escort you. This way."

As he showed the detectives around the magazine, workshop and staging area Alfred recalled the dud aerial shells, and wondered if there could be any connection between them and this suggested break-in. However, there didn't seem to be any reason to mention it as the connection appeared tenuous.

Delios found nothing that might indicate a surreptitious break-in, but he was no expert in looking for clues, and there was little need at this stage to do a deeper examination.

"Oh, I see you get your supplies from Colombia," Delios remarked as he examined a pile of boxes of aerial shells with a Medellín address. "Do they make a lot of pyrotechnics there?"

Albert was a little annoyed at this, as the fewer people who knew about this wonderful cut-price deal the better, but he figured the police would hardly count among competitors.

"They're an up-and-coming market, and we are one of the few firms patronizing them at the moment," he replied curtly.

The tour concluded at the front door of Catesby & Son.

"Anything occurs to you," suggested the DS, "don't hesitate to contact us. We'd like to put this to rest; assure all parties that everything's fine. After all, it could be just a rumour."

The proprietor shook hands with the police and returned to his office shaking his head in mystification.

Could there be a connection between those duds and this supposed break-in? If so, why?

Something to think about...

☆✩☆

Pastorelli Fireworks was prospering. As shipment after shipment of aerial pyrotechnics from Colombia were received and processed, an influx of dubious used notes stuffed in brown envelopes trickled in. However, you can't just stick great wads of used twenties and fifties into the safe in the office without many very pointed questions. When the firm's accountants did the books at the end of each fiscal year, the balance was always in small change, and every transaction had to be accounted for. Large influxes of cash would raise entire hairlines. It wasn't a huge amount of money when compared with the company's income and expenditure balances, but when you're teetering right on the red line, a push over into the black side of the ledger doesn't take much.

Rocco was pleased with his creativity. He had been taking money out of the company coffers to pay salaries for himself and Nonno, and for miscellaneous expenses associated with their household, such as mortgage payments and property maintenance. As a family business such transactions were routine. He now informed his accountants that in future, because of the firm's precarious financial situation, he would finance his household and salaries from private family money, not taking a penny from the company account. The firm's books looked the better for it, and the dirty cash ran the household.

This bounty, coupled with the firing of aerial shells at a third the price of the high-end Italian products, was making the books look pretty good to a superficial eye. Emilio was visiting the facility less and less these days, not solely through infirmity but because he believed that all was well and that his guiding presence was no longer as necessary. In truth, his exhaustion after the jaunt in Barrie had given him a stern reminder that he wasn't the figure he used to be. In the end he had to give way to Rocco's insistence that, if business dealings necessitated it, the two assistants would represent the firm in firing shows. He hated it, but he could hardly do anything about it.

Nonno's non-showing at the office was a boon to Rocco; the books would not receive the once-over that would reveal immediately the switch of suppliers but, more to the point, a cursory check of the staging area or the magazine would reveal the cheap substitutes. So far no sudden drop-ins, but Rocco did think it wise to store a pallet of Italian-made shells in the staging area, just so a surprise visit would not reveal the cheat. He was a bit leery about this; the fewer fireworks there were in the facility the safer it was. Normally, when staging a show the pyrotechnics were there just as long as the preparation was underway; a few days at most between the magazine and the shipping trucks. So, it was a risk, but a small one. Len, the facility manager, found his behaviour odd, but he was an incurious sort of guy, thank God.

The books were a worry, though. Nonno had only to read the invoices and cargo manifests to tumble to the least sordid part of the truth. Rocco had mooted the idea of creating a separate spreadsheet that could be hauled out in an emergency, but it was so damned complicated and he could hardly find the time. He just crossed his fingers instead.

Deep into that long and beautiful summer Rocco worked harder than he could have believed possible. There had been times when there was so much work to do—some legitimate, but mostly otherwise—that he had been obliged to remain in East Gladstone, letting his two assistants travel the province, running the shows by themselves. He hated to do this because the gigs themselves were his chief enjoyment in life; creating the shows was rewarding in its way, but not seeing the results was doubly frustrating. Tonio had taken him aside at one point, asking why he had to miss so many shows. What was so goddamned important, he had asked, that you have to miss the best bit? But if a shipment was due to come in from Colombia it was crucial that he be there.

The summer simply evaporated off his calendar, while his family, his colleagues and particularly his lady love continued to wonder about him.

☆⭐☆

The new prosperity of Pastorelli Fireworks resulted in contracts further afield. The latest trip, deep into the heavy early July schedule, was special for Rocco, Seth and Tonio. By the grace of

God, nothing was due into the Port of Montreal until Tuesday at the earliest, so Rocco had gladly made his travel bookings. The truck had been sent on ahead by road with Tonio in charge, while the other two pyrotechnicians had flown Westjet to Winnipeg.

This was a big firework meeting where the displays would be assessed by judges and prizes awarded. A favourable mention at one of these events was great PR for the company, and Rocco kept thanking the powers-that-be that he was able to be here, yet terrified that a single one-word phone call could derail his plans.

Set-up had been somewhat simplified by the use of common equipment supplied by the hosts, and already in place at the site. Mortar racks and frames were complemented by huge towers of speakers, the sort usually encountered in outdoor rock concerts. The volume of sound necessary to match the fireworks was prodigious. Even with all this structure already in place, the usual three days of work were needed to get all the effects located in their proper places, and all the fuses, cables and sundry hook-ups set up and tested. It was with a great deal of satisfaction that the trio looked over their work, did the final no-fire continuity tests, and agreed that it was all good.

Rocco had been getting more and more familiar with the software that was used to fire the shows and now, instead of relying on prewritten choreography, he was writing his own programs to musical scores, sitting up to all hours in his bedroom, laptop on his knees. Doing the Tchaikovsky *1812 Overture* to live music had been a baptism by fire, and he wondered now how he had ever had the balls to even attempt it. Recorded music was a heck of a lot easier, with no overweening musical egos to deal with, but even so, it was long hard work. Essentially, each firework effect had its own line of code in a database, which appeared as a spreadsheet, with such information as type of effect–candle, wheel, aerial shell, etc–timing sequence, firing time, and delay.

The timing of the aerial shells was the most complex; if you wanted an effect to appear at an exact time, you needed to backtrack the firing instructions to allow for the time delay between the electric ignition voltage reaching the leader fuse and lift charge, and the actual burst in the air. All shells came with a specific pre-fire time, graded by the size of shell and its altitude at burst. This information had to be entered in the database so the software would fire them in the correct sequence. As a typical 30 minute show had hundreds of such effects, there was a huge amount of labour involved in writing the choreography. Rocco reckoned that each minute of the show took at least half an hour of design time, and that was only after you got really good at it.

It was this creative side of the electronic revolution that Rocco most enjoyed. In a way he found it akin to the joy of putting together a shell from the raw materials, firing it and watching it fly. Here he was assembling whole shows in his mind, listening to the music and imagining the best effects, colours and timing, and then seeing it all come real in the sky. But here was the magical bit: just like in music or any of the other performing arts, there was a degree of unpredictability. It could never be the same twice, and you could never be sure that what came out of the tubes was exactly what you had seen in your mind's eye.

A mistrust of the ready-made programs that the software developers sold had grown upon him. It was easy to show clients exactly what they would get in computer graphic representations, but when it came to the real show he worried that the client might remember too much, and then complain if the show wasn't exactly as promised. This might be paranoia, he thought, but let me go with my firework-man's instinct.

The sky darkened and the firing time approached. Once all the work was done, everything was set, and the crowd was quiet in anticipation, the show became like a great steamroller whose course was utterly unchangeable. It would be what it would be.

A glance at the sky, a nod from the firing desk, the tap of a key, and they were off!

As the show rolled along in colour, sound, light and smoke Rocco followed its progress almost distractedly, playing behind his eyes the planned effects and synchronizing them with those opening in the sky before him. He was more than satisfied.

The customary battery of thunderclaps, almost intolerable in their persistent earsplitting din, and matched seamlessly with the crescendo of the music, closed the show. As the reverberations died and silence settled, so the applause began.

It was time to start packing up, while awaiting the appraisal of the performance by the panel of judges.

Most of the work would be done the following morning, once the site was completely checked and declared clean, but a few small chores could be completed by flashlight. Seth was coiling cables onto wheeled metal drums and stowing them in a truck. He turned as Rocco approached him with a coil of wire wound between thumb and armpit.

"Notice anything funny about some of them shells?" he asked.

Rocco quailed a little but kept a calm face. "Funny? Funny in what way?"

"The whistles for a start," Seth replied. "I'd swear some of them were two-tone." Seth enjoyed the shows coordinated to music; he had a fine ear, and took his guitar with him wherever he went.

"Two-tone?" Rocco was mystified.

"Yeah, there were definitely two kinds of whistles in some shells. Not only did they sound different, but the timing was off as well. The higher pitched ones died out earlier."

Oh, Christ! The Medellín originals and the Pastorelli substitutes were different enough that Seth, at least, could tell them apart. Could anybody else? Thank God Nonno didn't show up at any of the gigs any more; he sure as hell wouldn't miss it.

"Well, maybe there's a quality control issue," Rocco prevaricated. "Difference between batches..."

"Well, there's a quality control issue for the serpents as well then. D'you notice how some of them spiraled tightly while others went in gentler curves? I notice these things."

You sure do, God damn you, thought Rocco.

"Well, you know, experts like us," he flattered, "notice things that the average guy doesn't. I don't think it's a big deal that some garnitures vary slightly."

"I suppose so," agreed Seth as he started stowing his cables into the truck, which Tonio had driven closer. "And there's the economical angle, of course."

Seth was well aware of the financial state of the company, and knew Rocco was trying to cut costs, but even so his feelings for the quality of the product were upset. Seth wasn't Italian, but he might just as well have been.

"Yeah," agreed Rocco, "but we'll keep an eye on it. Don't wanna compromise too much."

"Right. Judges at competitions like this one, they see that kind of stuff."

There was absolutely nothing he could do about it, but as long as Seth's suspicions remained based in quality control all was well. But this little conversation reminded Rocco yet again of the frightening tightrope he was walking.

They completed the packing, slammed and locked the truck doors, and set off with Tonio for the short walk to the judging stand. Another successful show completed.

☆✦☆

"Here's some very interesting news." Fred Delios had just returned from his visit to Catesby's and was sitting across from the DI, bursting with his new-found information. "Catesby's order some of their fireworks from Colombia. Medellín, to be exact."

"*They do*? How very interesting." The DI's face showed an increasing comprehension as pieces of information began to fall into line.

"They do indeed," continued Delios. "Now, it's probable that the V-Twin Valkyries are looking for a new channel for dope from Medellín, and as Catesby's order their fireworks from the same place, how about if they thought of concealing coke in with shipments of fireworks?"

The Chief nodded thoughtfully. "You might have something! Their pipeline into Montreal was busted open a couple of months back, they'll be hurting financially without cocaine traffic, so yes... they could be trying to be really creative..."

"But, if this is so, why did Pastorelli have his old friend Bacon break in?" asked Delios. "Surely, Bacon would be employed by the Valkyries. I don't get that angle."

"Here's how it might work," said the Chief with his fingers laced behind his head. "Just suppose that friend Rocco has been persuaded by our biker pals to assist them in trafficking. Here's the clever bit; I'll bet Pastorelli doesn't get their fireworks from Colombia, but instead the stuff is concealed in shipments ordered by the competition. So then, how would it be if this Bacon character was employed by Rocco to break in at Catesby's and collect the cocaine? It's smart on many levels, because it takes the focus away from Pastorelli's, and leaves Catesby carrying the can if anything goes wrong."

"Sorry to disagree, but it sounds far too complex."

"Do you have a better hypothesis?"

"Well, not at the moment, no."

"All right then!" As if lack of an alternate scenario gave this one credence.

"Surely, the best way to test it is to lean on Steve Bacon," observed Delios. "Stan Howard says he's likely to squeal if suggestions about his future are put before him. Or if wads of cash are dangled."

"Okay, how about you make a little visit? Put the wind up the little bastard. Know where he lives?"

"Yeah. Apartment in one of the developments in the east end. Lives with him mum. Old man's doing a stretch."

"Okay. Pop in and see him."

"Yeah, I could try the old carrot and stick routine," the DS replied. "Any chance of a warrant to monitor his cellphone?"

"Might be able to swing it on suspicion," mused the DI. "He's got a good long string of priors. I'll check into it, let you know."

"Mind you," said Delios, "there's not much you can't get by sitting down next to him in the Royal Oak and buying him a beer. Loose mouthed as they come."

"Yeah, but *ipso facto*, of course. Pay him a visit at home. See what you can get."

☆ ⭐ ☆

As he climbed the stairs to the sixth floor with his assigned detective constable, Detective Sergeant Delios wondered why they called them 'developments' when it was the last thing they were doing. The patchy grass in front of the buildings was shot through with weeds and lethal with dog shit, the concrete walls were soiled and defaced with graffiti, the play structure was mostly broken, and over the whole building complex there settled an air of desperation and fatigue. He knocked on the apartment door with his knuckles. He and the DC had entered the building by pushing through the front door when another tenant was leaving. It was not their intention to signal their arrival; they wanted it to be a little surprise. A second more vigorous knock caused the door to open as far as the safety chain would allow, while a middle-aged female nose, connected to a face that had seen much in this world and none of it good, poked out.

"Whadda yer want?"

"We'd like to have a word with young Stephen, if we may," replied Delios in his best polite policeman voice.

"Well, he's not here so ya can't," said the nose, trying to force the door shut against the pressure of a size 11 police boot.

Having seen young Stephen enter the building just recently, and fully cognizant of the fact that there was no other way out invisible from their vantage point in the street, the lie was revealed.

"I think it would be wise if we spoke to him, if you don't mind," repeated Delios.

"I told you, you can't 'cos he's not here, so piss off!"

A voice behind the woman spoke up. "Who is it Mum? What d'they want?"

"They don't want nuthin', so shut up."

"We would actually like to talk to Steve, Mrs Bacon," continued Delios, "because it would be much more pleasant here than down at the police station."

The chain was reluctantly removed from the door and Delios and his constable stepped into the narrow hallway. Ma Bacon barred the way. "What d'you want with him? He hasn't done nothing wrong. He's a good boy."

"Ah, Steve," said the sergeant, peering around the animated blockage. "Just the person we want to talk to. Do you have a minute?"

Steve's mother stepped to one side with a scowl on her face, allowing the two policemen to follow the son into the living room. Delios sat down without being invited on a faded floral chesterfield while the constable stood at the door.

"Just 'cos his dad's doing time, doesn't mean you can come here an' hassle him," continued Ma Bacon, barging into the little room and standing four square with her arms crossed. "He hasn't done nothin'!"

She stayed a moment, staring daggers at both cops, before realizing she was wasting her breath. She disappeared into the kitchen from which emanated a clattering and thumping more evocative of her displeasure than of efforts to either tidy or cook.

Steve sat opposite the detective sergeant with a wise-ass sneer on his face.

"So, Steve," began Delios with no preamble. "Fireworks. Know anything you want to share?" Steve was silent, staring into space over the policeman's shoulder.

"Because," continued the DS, "we could so easily get a warrant for your arrest on suspicion of break-and-enter. Wouldn't want that, would you? Your mom neither. Know what I'm saying?"

"I don't know nothing about fireworks. What are you on about?"

"Let me put it this way, Steve. There are two ways of looking at this thing. Firstly, there's the dossier the police are compiling on you. Over time that could get quite nasty, if you get my drift. It's getting pretty thick already. Then, on the other hand, there's the distinct possibility that all sorts of documentation on your activities, which we at present possess, could get... ah... sort of *neglected*, if you provided us with certain information."

"You're fucking with me..." said Steve with an uncertainty in his voice. "You're just fishing."

"That's for you to decide," replied Delios extracting a card from his pocket. "But, I'll tell you what; I'll let you think about it, and if you come up with anything you want to share, just give us a call. And don't forget, there might even be a payoff for you if the info's good."

He stood up, shoved the card into Steve Bacon's unresisting hand, and turned to leave the apartment. "Like I said; anything of interest. Just once in your life, do yourself a favour for Christ's sake."

Steve stood by the open door for a while with the card in his hand. He really didn't want to go back inside again; there are some real hard cases in there, especially when they find out what you did and why you're in there. Warders can't protect you all the time... His butt muscles clenched at the memory. But the bikers would kill him if they found out. You don't just rat on those bastards. Still, if the cops got them, put them away...

☆✫ ⭐ ✫☆

On a park bench with the lake lapping crystal in the background Steve Bacon readied himself to give the police what they wanted. A plain-clothes version of Detective Sergeant Delios had sat down moments before, and both of them watched the lake play with the wind. An ancient gentleman, led resisting by an equally ancient dog, passed close by. A quick cock of the leg and a point-less piss and they passed out of earshot.

"Look, if they found out I was talking to you they'd kill me."

"If you help put them inside they can't, can they?"

"They won't be inside for ever."

"There's police protection..."

"Oh, come on!" Bacon sneered, raising his voice. "How stupid you think I am? Gonna protect little me for the rest of my life, is that it?"

"No, no, that's not what I meant. There's ways of keeping you anonymous. We can get warrants acting on information. There's an elaborate system. There has to be."

"I won't tell you a damned thing if my name comes out."

"Okay, we can work with that."

There followed a long silence as cloud shadows crossed the water and a canoe wallowed inexpertly across the small bay that the park held in its arms. Steve stared out across the water, face totally unreadable.

The DS broke the silence. "What is it with you, Steve?" he asked quietly. "You hated prison, yet you just seem to want to get back in there quick as you can."

"Dunno what you mean."

"Sure you do. It's a matter of those little B and Es, isn't it?" Silence. "Tell me, which Steve am I talking to right now? Is it the one who wants to help, wants to stay out of prison? Or is it the other one? Which is it?"

"Don't play the amateur shrink with me!" he bridled.

"Okay, okay," soothed Delios. "None of my business. You're right."

They sat again in silence. Fred Delios knew that Steve was weighing the options, knew that the fear of prison was competing with the fear of opening up. Patience was the only tactic, and he would sit here a good long time before he made another move or said another word.

"The idea," Steve murmured eventually, "is that they pack Ziplocs of cocaine into boxes of fireworks."

"Who?"

"Guys in Colombia..."

"No, no! Who at this end? Who deals with it?"

"Pastorelli. Shipment comes in, Rocco unloads it, passes it along. That's all I know."

"You mean Catesby's, of course?"

"Nah, this is nothing to do with them!" Steve was suddenly on the defensive.

"Well then, why were you breaking in there?" Silence. "You were, weren't you?"

"Look," replied Steve starting to get rattled. "That's got nothing to do with it. I dunno what you're talking about. I'm outta here..."

"Steve, Steve, Steve," soothed Delios holding on gently to his sleeve as he made to stand. Steady Fred, he thought, you nearly lost this one. Backpedal and take the pressure off.

"It's all right Steve. Don't get your knickers in a twist. Just tell me what you *want* to tell me, okay?"

The young man sat back down on the bench again and a kind of resolve or resignation returned to his features. "Shipment comes in," he repeated, "an' Rocco unloads it, passes it along. That's all I know."

Delios nodded. "Don't need more than that now. You've been very helpful, Steve."

"You just better not use my name."

"My word on it," replied Delios, eyes forward over the lake, body language revealing nothing. He stood up. "Keep you nose clean Steve. Think of your mum."

The detective strolled off in the direction of the parking lot while Steve sat for a long time in thought. That wasn't so bad; actually felt good. No mention of old Hefty. Attention deflected away from Catesby's. Shit going down for Rocco, but tough on him. Do a guy a favour and what do you get? Abuse.

⁎☆ ⭐ ☆⁎

"God, these people are so stupid!" The Detective Inspector rubbed his hands in glee. "Why would they think this would work? *Anything* from Colombia gets more than just the once-over. We'll have 'em over a barrel!"

"You'd think the stuff'd get stopped at the Port, wouldn't you? They're super vigilant since the last fiasco."

"It must be that shipments of fireworks seem so innocent. Talk about complacent."

"Yes, but even so, *anything* from Colombia..."

"Think they might have another rat embedded there?" mused the DI. "But highly unlikely, though; they're as tight as a duck's ass these days."

"So, if the buggers are using boxes of fireworks, they're sure risking it being found."

"Well, the stuff hasn't been found yet! And we can't have the Port Authority people finding it, period. We want this stuff to come right through onto our turf, otherwise we lose the king-pins."

"Again!"

"No, *not again*! I'll be able to push this information up the line," grinned the DI. "We'll get a high level meeting between our Superintendant and his counterpart at the Sûreté de Québec and the bigwigs at the RCMP. The Super'll call them off; tell them anything with fireworks is our bailiwick. He's got the clout, make 'em see reason."

"And how do we know when the shipment will show up?"

125

"Once the Sûreté de Québec are on side, they'll in turn put pressure on the Port of Montreal."

"So, all we really need to do is wait until a shipment arrives at Pastorelli's from Colombia, then we get a warrant and go visit."

"Not so fast." The DI rubbed his hands again. "We wait until the evening, out of business hours when the place is closed. That's when they'll unpack the stuff, and that's when we catch them red-handed."

"Sure. Otherwise we only catch Rocco Pastorelli, and all he needs to do is play innocent."

"Exactly. He may even be innocent for all we know, but I doubt it. He runs with some dodgy people."

"Well, did anyway," said Delios. "It's my feeling that he's been blackmailed into this. Guy's got a good career ahead of him, runs a successful business, no need to break the law."

"However it comes out, he's going to get swept up," replied the DI with callous satisfaction. "So, as soon as I hear word of a shipment, be ready. We'll need at least four cars on call, but I want it quiet and subtle."

"No kicking down doors and yelling 'come out with your hands up!' then?" smiled the DS.

"No, this is real life. Softly, softly…"

☆✩⭐✩☆

Post-mortem was perhaps a melancholy term for the analysis following every firework show, but that's what it had come to be called at Catesby's after the incident with the duds. They had completed many shows since Gwillimbury without a single hitch, but Alfred still wasn't feeling optimistic. It seemed to him that his father and his daughter could go with the flow, absorb problems like those misfires, and not be too perturbed. He wasn't like that; distractions and potential problems rankled.

"Another really good one," he said to the group at the table in front of him. He might feel edgy but it was wise to project a positive vibe. "Really good and not a hitch. Comments anyone?"

"Small thing," Mike spoke up, "but it would have been easier if the hosts had known our procedures better. Asking questions that are all covered in the book. Confusion of who does what. Bit of a distraction."

"Yep, I agree," he replied. "We sent them the manual, but I'm not sure how many of them actually read it."

"They're free of charge from Natural Resources, so maybe we should send a bunch. City councils like this lot, they probably forgot to pass it round."

"Good suggestion. Anything else? Anyone?"

"The protesters don't seem to make a damned bit of difference," observed Bob.

"Like I've always told you," replied Alfred, "they have the democratic right and, anyway, as soon as the key's tapped to start the show they are totally hosed." They all laughed a little at that. "They'll have to try another tack."

There were no further comments and it looked as if the meeting would close very quickly. Julia had been taking the minutes of the meeting on her laptop, but when she looked up she saw an expression on her father's face that meant more was coming.

"Duds," he said. "There haven't been any more. Maybe I worry too much, but it's still an issue in my mind."

"I'm absolutely sure it was a one-time thing." Julia spoke up without thinking and, too late, realized the corner she had got herself into.

"How can you be so sure," her father asked her, "about what goes on in some South American sweatshop?"

"Well... I..." she stammered, colour coming to her cheeks. "It's just that... since last time, there haven't been any more problems. So I thought..."

"I'm sorry, Julia," he interrupted rather coldly, "but I just don't share your optimism."

She subsided and turned her face studiously down to her laptop. She hoped the others couldn't pick up on her embarrassment, as her face reddened, the sweat formed on her forehead, and she felt a tiny trickle down between her breasts.

"The other thing is," continued Alfred doggedly, "I had the police around here a while back. They were suggesting that there might have been a break-in here. I pooh-poohed it at the time, but I thought I'd raise it anyway. Have any of you seen anything, anything at all, that might indicate a break-in?"

"Not a damned thing," replied Bob mystified. "Definitely not."

"Me neither," said Mike. "Why would anybody?"

"Doesn't make sense to me either, but I thought I'd throw it out." There followed a long pause. "Julia?"

"No... no, nothing," she replied in a small voice that she hoped betrayed nothing. "Nothing at all."

Another long pause.

"Anything else? No? Okay, let's all get back to work."

The Catesby daughter closed her laptop and rose thankfully from the table.

☆ ✩ ☆

It was a few demonstrations later that Sue Tort finally got Steve Bacon aside. Just before they were due to march in front of yet another utterly indifferent crowd of pyrotechnic lovers, in yet another utterly indifferent Ontario town, she pulled him away from the crowd.

"Lissen. You know what a fuck-up that sabotage attempt was..."

"You went and woke 'em up..."

"I know, I know! Don't have to tell me again, for Christ's sake! It ain't gonna work anyway, 'cos these people are too goddamned careful. Postin' guards..."

"They check the day of the show anyway. I said it wouldn't be simple..."

"You gave shit advice is what it's all about."

"I said it wouldn't be..."

"Shut the fuck up! I got a better plan."

Steve became immediately interested; there was never a dull moment with this one, but this time some money was going to change hands. Good advice, shit advice, doesn't matter; from now on you pay.

"How easy is it," she asked, "to get into a fireworks outfit and steal stuff?"

You know how easy it is, he thought, because Terry's obviously told you. Well, holy shit, here was an interesting prospect. Never imagined I'd get the opportunity twice, but this time for sure there's a humungous price tag. Then he thought of the cops and what they knew, balancing their promises on one side of the ledger with the money and the enormous charge he would get on the other. Of course, having sicced that shit-head Delios onto dear old Rocco, he was off the hook. The cops were right off the scent; they'd be looking at Pastorelli's, not Catesby's. Je-e-sus!

The two Steves faced each other, each with an argument, each with a counter argument. In the end the Steve who always did it when they urged him to do it won the contest.

"Well? Can it be done?" she urged looking into his eyes.

"How much stuff?"

"As much as possible. The whole fucking lot."

"Depends." He looked directly back into her face and saw eagerness, even passion. "Can be done. For a price, of course."

"How much?"

He thought quickly. Too much and she'd back off, but he didn't want to undervalue his obvious talent either. Turning pro was a matter of careful negotiation.

"Five hundred." That seemed about right. "Used notes."

"Five hundred bucks? You gotta be joking!"

"No way." He was continually short of cash and this would do nicely. He thought it cheap at the price considering the risks. "That's the going rate."

"Going rate? What's that s'posed to mean? You some kinda East Gladstone Chamber of Commerce or somethin'?"

"Five hundred's what I want. Take it or leave it."

She ran the sums in the various bank accounts through her mind and decided to bite, just in case the deal fell through.

"Okay. But I dunno when, okay? You gotta be on call."

"There's another thing," he replied. "You thought about transport? That's a shit-load of fireworks you're talking about. Need a truck."

"So, we rent one. No big deal."

He nodded and returned her gaze. She looked up at him standing there in the half-light, away from the rest of the mob, and wondered in one of her extremely rare horny moments what he would be like. She hadn't had any since... Christ, it was ancient history!

Steve Bacon picked up on the vibe immediately, and quickly decided that this commercial transaction would carry no fringe 'benefits'. It wasn't women that turned him on anyway, and even if they did, this one was on the very edge of eligibility in the allure department. It'd be like fucking a skeleton.

She caught the counter-vibe, chalked up another decade of finger, and turned to rejoin the marchers. "Be ready, that's all."

☆☆⭐☆☆

It was a bugger. You're tooling along on your Harley, smooth as silk, visiting East Gladstone for the first time, and the engine just conks out. Charley Soames was a bike tourist who had done tens of thousands of kilometers all over North America from his native BC, with nothing more than a tent roll and a pair of panniers.

And here he was, late in the day, with an engine that just wouldn't light up, and the bike too damned heavy to push far. Nothing open now; too late to find a repair shop. Shit! The only thing to do was park the Harley somewhere safe and go looking for help. Maybe a late night garage.

The front door of the building opposite had a CCTV camera above it, which comforted him a little. He hoped it'd be safe until he got back; it wasn't a well-populated part of town, bit rundown really, but there were a few cafés and bars. He pushed the heavy bike over the sidewalk and parked it on its stand as close to the door of the building as possible. Pastorelli Fireworks, he read; cool.

A quarter of an hour later an unmarked police car pulled up slowly in front of Pastorelli Fireworks and another turned into the driveway and stationed itself at the back of the facility. Two more cars parked quietly a little way down the street on both sides. There was only one car already in the rear parking lot, an ancient Toyota. However, DS Delios was delighted to notice a motorbike parked right next to the front door. And there was a light in a window on the side of the building. The trap was set!

Suddenly, quite out of the blue, there was a posse of the local constabulary standing outside the front door and waving a piece of frightening paper. It was enough to loosen the bowels of Michelangelo's *David*. Rocco was in the workshop preparing the tools and plugging in the glue gun prior to unloading the latest shipment, and there they were ringing the bell and waving up at the CCTV camera above the door! When he saw the image his first impulse was to hurl himself through the nearest window or book a flight to Katmandu. How they had found out he had no way of knowing, but the fact they had shown up on the very day the delivery had been made was evidence enough.

He walked down the boardwalk to the scaffold with as much *sang froid* as he could muster, sashayed into the front reception area and buzzed the door open. He motioned a sergeant and three constables into the foyer, and said in a voice that threatened to deteriorate into a strangled squeak, "Good evening, officers. How can I help you?"

"My name's Delios," replied the cop in his best police voice. "Detective Sergeant Delios of the East Gladstone police force. We have a search warrant here, sir..."

"Search? Search for what? I... I don't understand."

"We have reason to believe there are concealed illegal materials on the premises, and we require your cooperation and assistance."

"Illegal materials?" Rocco cried in mock horror, although he hardly needed to act the part. "Surely not! All our pyrotechnics meet rigorous Canadian standards."

The policeman looked around. "Are you alone in the building, sir?"

"Yes. Why?"

"Just checking," replied Delios trying to mask an irritated and disappointed expression. "Only you? No one else?"

"Nobody! Why?"

"So whose bike is that outside?"

"Bike? What bike? What are you talking about?"

The sergeant directed the three policemen with a quick turn of his head and they fanned out through the building.

"Now look, I'm sorry," continued Rocco, gaining some slight control over his nervous, digestive and endocrine systems, "but you must be mistaken."

"Nevertheless, sir, we have a warrant and we are duty-bound to execute it. Where is your latest shipment of fireworks?"

Rocco thought of waffling about dangerous materials, the restricted area, federal security guidelines, anything to stave off the horror that was about to unfold, but he realized it was useless.

They knew! Christ, they knew!

"Follow me," he muttered, and turned to the corridor leading to the staging area. He was near panicking, a small voice inside him screaming at him to run, but he held fast hoping and praying that when the discovery was made he could feign innocence and brazen it out. The three policemen met them at the loading dock shaking their heads.

"No one?"

"Nope."

DS Delios knew exactly what he was after, ignoring the boxes of decoy Italian shells and heading straight for today's shipment of Colombian shells from the Port of Montreal.

"Could you open these boxes please?" asked the detective sergeant. It wasn't a request. And to one of the constables, "Bring that table over here."

With huge reluctance and a deep sense of doom, Rocco brought a pry bar from a nearby bench and levered the lid off the first of the boxes. The nails squeaked out revealing, sure enough, the 8″ Serpent shells, four of them nestled in their brown paper.

And there was the coke-filled one with a strip of gummed tape around its middle, clearly visible through the plastic bag, just screaming for attention by its obvious dissimilarity.

Then the detective sergeant was picking up the shells! *He had the loaded one in his hand, for Christ's sake, and he was turning it over, peering closely at it from all angles!*

Rocco felt dizzy and sick; he leant back quietly against the shelf behind him to steady himself. This was it; he was dead...

Just as he was on the very verge of screaming out 'I admit it! I did it! You've got me!', to his immense surprise the sergeant put the shell down on the table, took another out of the box, and so continued one by one until all four were laid out in a row. He shook out all the paper wrapping, ensured that the box was completely empty, *then returned the shells to their places!*

"Nothing in here."

Next box, same routine. *Skreek* the lid off, remove the shells, spread out the wrapping paper, fumble through...

"No, nothing in this one."

They went through the whole consignment with Rocco leaning against his shelf with a fixed rictus on his face, knees almost too weak to support him, sweat running down his sternum, but with a gradual loosening realization that the cops had missed the obvious.

Finally, the full inspection was done.

"Thank you very much for your cooperation," said the chastened policeman, unable fully to conceal his disappointment.

"It was a pleasure," lied Rocco smoothly, maintaining his mask with supreme effort. "I can show you to the front door."

"Why were you working late, if you don't mind me asking?"

"As a matter of fact, I do," replied Rocco regaining a little confidence. "I don't know how your shifts operate, but some of us in the private sector can't just do nine-to-five jobs to earn a living."

"Sure. 'Scuse me for asking."

As soon as the police were out of sight he rushed straight to his office, flung himself into his chair, elbows on knees, head in hands, and shuddered in sweating relief. Presently he sat up, patted his face with a tissue, and noted the return to near-normal of heart rate and respiration.

Rocco knew now that he couldn't keep this going; it would definitely kill him. It was a matter of time before the whole thing collapsed, and it would be far better to fold it up preemptively before disaster overtook it. He'd have to tell Uncle Chuck that the whole scheme was rumbled and that it would have to be wound up. At this thought a sense of blissful relief flowed over him. He saw the way out, saw a future ahead where all this was just one terrible nightmare; a future where wrestling with the grim financial figures of the company would be heavenly by comparison.

He wasted no time in contacting his biker nemesis. "Uncle. Personal." Two words, but that should bring him, and not one of his tools. Once again, two texts were returned with two set of numbers for his GPS.

An hour later Rocco had driven to the site indicated by the GPS coordinates, the parking lot of a picnic spot beside the lake, some 15 kilometers from town. The Harley thundered up beside the car and the whole conversation was conducted through the rolled-down window.

"What the fuck's wrong?"

"Cops showed up. Pulled the crates apart."

"*Where's the stuff?* Where's the fuckin' stuff?"

"'S okay, they didn't find it..."

"Didn't *find* it?" Shit, close call, thought the biker boss. So what happened to my inside track at police HQ? Bitch should have known. "So, where is it then? Where?"

"Still in the crates..."

"Oh, for Christ's sake!" Relief flooded through Uncle Chuck, but he concealed it by drawing upon anger. "The cops show up and scare the shit out of you. And then you chicken out and don't even unload the stuff. Jesus!"

"Look, they're obviously onto us! We've gotta wind this up before it's too late."

"You fuckin' dummy!" growled Uncle Chuck. "You're about as safe as you could be!"

"How? How, for Christ's sake? *The boxes were open and they were holding the shells in their hands!*"

"Jesus Christ, get a grip. They've got up a search warrant, they've shown up, they have found absolutely diddly. Right?"

Rocco nodded, unable to speak.

"So the heat's off, isn't it?"

"Heat's off..." repeated Rocco with no comprehension.

"They," repeated the biker, spelling out each syllable carefully, "have not found anything and so, discovering that you are therefore clearly innocent, they will go away and look elsewhere."

"So the pressure's actually off?"

"The pressure, as you have so succinctly phrased it, is indeed actually fucking off."

"Look. I can't keep doing this. I can't!"

"Sure you can." The voice was silky, the expression more than frightening. "Listen ole buddy, don't forget you're actually being paid for the work you do. I hope I'm not hearing ingratitude on your part at my largesse. 'Cos, if I am, we may need to rearrange our business model, if you get my drift. You wanna do this with folding readies, or would you prefer to use your little piece of nookie as collateral instead?"

Rocco shrank in horror; his head swam, his throat closed and he couldn't reply.

"Weird way to do *pro bono* work in my opinion," continued Uncle Chuck, "but it's your choice. If I was you, though, I think I'd take the fuckin' money and be just a tiny little bit grateful."

"So," with a sinking heart as he swallowed and regained his voice, "business as usual?"

"Yes, indeedy. But, tell you what, my friend, we'll keep closer tabs on our valiant officers of the law, and see if we can't give you a bit of warning if they ever warm up to you again. Hate for you to be worried in any way whatsoever."

"So, you think they might show up again?" asked Rocco to the face looming above him against the sky.

"Nah, but it'll calm your nerves a little if you know we got your back." He stared at Rocco with those steely eyes. "Now go back and empty the stuff out. Call me. *One* word!"

The Harley roared into life and Uncle Chuck tooled out onto the highway and dwindled in a splatter of sound. As he rode he wondered how the cops had known about the shipment. He thought he had it completely tight, but someone must be loose mouthing. If I find him, I'll kill him, he promised. And what about his little girlfriend in the clerical department at police headquarters? She'd really dropped this one. How did she miss it? Reward or punishment? He'd have to see. Pleasure either way... But, shit, it was a little disturbing.

Rocco sat for the longest while, staring out over the water, his hopes of an easy way out utterly dashed and his fear for Julia redoubled. With a heavy weight in his chest he started the old Toyota and followed the Angel back into Hell.

It would be 'way past midnight before he got to bed.

☆★☆

"You're never here in the evenings," complained Maria over breakfast one day. The same old song and dance that Rocco was getting sick of hearing. "At the office all the time? Me and Nonno hardly see you these days."

Oh, when I'm not bouncing up and down on the granddaughter of Nonno's sworn enemy, I'm unloading bombshells full of cocaine from the cartel in Colombia.

"Oh, there's so much to do at the office, what with juggling the finances and chasing up gigs, I'm kinda run off my feet."

"You should take it easy occasionally. You work too hard." She handed him a coffee, made the way he really liked it; Nonno's traditional way.

He sipped the coffee, suddenly struck by his double life and the deceit he was putting over on these good people.

"Boy's gotta keep at it Maria," piped up Emilio from across the table. "Running the business ain't a nine-to-fiver, eh *figlio*?"

"No, it's tough, but y'know I think we're keeping it all together."

"Got a few good shows," replied Nonno. "I'll give you that."

"And there's still Montreal and Lac Leamy if we're lucky."

"Yeah, sure, but I still ain't happy about you missing some shows. Well, at least your Tonio is Italian. That's somethin'."

Emilio had made one of his rare visits to the shop the day before, demonstrating to nobody but himself, really, that he was still in command. He had been very pleased with the books, what little Rocco chose to show him. In the end, with a visit like this in mind, he had taken the time to create a simple spreadsheet, and the plus and minus columns he showed the old boy didn't need to be tweaked to keep him happy. Emilio really had no need to dig any deeper, and Rocco played on his trust. If he were to reveal how the firm showed such a reasonable profit, he thought, Nonno would probably throttle him first then fall down dead over his corpse.

"So, you're still farting around with all them lap-what's-its and gizmos," observed his Nonno, "but at least it ain't harming the business."

"Far from it!" he replied over his coffee. "I know you were pissed off at the cost, but you got to admit, we gotta keep up."

The old man grudgingly admitted it, but Rocco knew his happiness was at the mercy of the numbers. Keep in the black, keep Nonno happy. If only the old bugger didn't descend on the office every few weeks and give the accounts the third degree... But give him his due; 82 and still right on the ball.

"Yeah, you're doing okay. Your *papá* could see you now, he'd say my boy's doin' okay..."

It was the kindest thing his grandfather could have thought to say, but it tore him until he nearly cried out.

☆ ✫ ⭐ ☆ ✫

"Here Grandpa, I've brought you a present." Julia handed Bob the burnt out cardboard tube of a Roman candle.

She had just returned from doing a show in the eastern end of the province. It had been a fairly small show but, as a privilege almost unheard of, she and Mike the chief technician had done it without either her father or grandfather being present. Alfred was absent in Toronto—something had 'come up' with one of the suppliers—but Julia suspected, and the gleam in Grandpa's eye confirmed it, that she was being tested. Sure, Mike could run the thing single-handed, using her just for help in setting up, but this was the first time neither patriarch had attended. She had designed the show, she had called the shots, she had run the whole program.

It had gone off flawlessly.

"You are a very naughty girl, isn't she Angela? She knows what the smell does for me."

Julia sat herself down in the easy chair opposite her grandfather. She knew that of all the sensations that returned to him as if it was just yesterday, smell was the most powerful. He put the burnt-out shell to his nose, closed his eyes, and he was there again, in that past time that is more real because of its distance. This really is *recherche du temps perdus*, he thought, because smell is the most transporting of our senses, and takes us most swiftly back to where and when we were. Perhaps it's just me, he mused, but the smell of burnt fireworks is a most delicious sensation; it's a sense coupled with a voyage. This may be the explanation for my love of smoked fish, smoked cheese, *Rauchbier* from Bamberg and good old Lagavulin.

And fireworks, of course...

"Oh, it takes me back. You know it does, you bad girl." He sighed, eyes still closed. "Ah, saltpetre, sulphur and charcoal, they're my time travel..."

"Here, let me have a little sniff," said Angela taking the burnt cardboard from him. She sniffed. "Well, it's nice of course—

couldn't marry into a firework family without appreciating that—but it doesn't do much for me."

"Unto each his own," Bob replied. "Did I ever tell you about the time Our Nan threw the empty cases on the fire?"

"It was a Pain's *Golden Rain*, wasn't it?" put in Julia.

"*Golden Rain*? No, you must be thinking of something else. She took matters into her own hands that day, did Our Nan; just after Guy Fawkes it was. We used to collect dead cases, y'know, us lads, and she picked up the whole lot and shoved 'em into the back of the kitchen fire. But there was a live one, wasn't there?"

He recalled the Brock's *Snow Storm*—surely it wasn't a *Golden Rain*?—hurling its resurrected glory about the kitchen, endangering the rugs, the curtains, the tablecloth and anything else its twinkling meteors of precious burning metal happened upon.

"Lucky it wasn't a..."

"...Brock's *Bombshell*," completed Julia.

"Oh, I hadn't told you that one already, had I? Do stop me next time, won't you?"

Julia smiled, beginning to come down from the high of her first solo show. She looked over at her grandfather and her mother and wondered, not for the first time, whether this wouldn't be the perfect moment to raise the issue of Rocco. It hurt her that she had to keep this most wonderful experience of her life secret from them, especially from her mother with whom she shared everything. But, no, the moment passed.

There was a strangeness about Rocco these last few weeks, though. Pastorelli Fireworks was showing a small profit, and the grandfather was apparently in very good temper, but this didn't result in a happy, carefree Rocco. Quite the opposite. Even in their closest moments there was something... distant about him. She had probed a few times, usually just after sex when he appeared most approachable, but he always closed up and said that everything was just fine.

Only once, leaning on his elbow with the bedside light as a halo, raising her exposed nipple with his gently brushing fingers, had he said to her, "You're good. I mean, by nature. Do you have to make an effort to be good, or does it just happen?"

This perplexed her, but before she could frame an answer the moment had passed. She couldn't fathom what he meant, but she knew that it was connected in some way to this little absence she felt in him, even when they were closest.

☆✮⭐✮☆

Julia and Rocco often met for lunch at the same coffee shop where their romance had begun. Far from staring into each other's eyes for the whole hour, and doing the shop owner out of income from sales, they each had their bruschetti and coffee, so he smiled at them as he wiped down the counter and fiddled with the espresso machine.

"Everything Italian, eh my love?" That sweet little flip of the tongue round her lips.

"I don't always eat Italian. It's just our neighbourhood; most of the restaurants..."

"But, the way you dress, your... style maybe? I dunno, but if anybody saw you on the street they wouldn't mistake you."

"Well, we have stuck together over the years," he told her. "When my Nonno came to Toronto he settled into the biggest enclave of Italians outside of Italy."

"Thing is," she held his hand across the table, "you're about as Italian as can be, but your dad came here when he was just a kid."

"Yeah. You guys, English I mean, can blend in and become fully Canadian, whatever that is, but we'll always be Italian hyphen Canadians. I don't think the Canadian melting pot is hot enough, that's all."

"Yes. Lukewarm; we're much more likely to emphasize our distinctness than our common values."

"Sure. In the fifties in T.O. you didn't need to speak a word of English, you had your own food, newspapers, your own customs, the church you always went to..."

"So, you're Catholic, right?"

"Mumbo-jumbo. I was brought up in it, but I think Mom and Dad probably just went through the motions. It was only after Dad went..." he sighed and took a swig of coffee. "That's when I think Mom got more serious. Didn't rub off on me."

"We don't do church either. I think if Grandpa had any religion at all it would be the church of St Guy Fawkes!"

"Me? I guess St Jean-Baptiste is the closest, then."

Their conversation tripped along in a fairly trivial way, and as much as she tried to take him to a deeper level, the subtle barrier was there. So subtle that she found it hard to identify it herself, let alone raise it with him. Especially in their lovemaking there was a tiny incompleteness, an absence of that total union that she knew they had both shared. Was it, she wondered to do with his Italian background, with her being a fair-haired example of the Anglo-Saxon strain, albeit with an admixture of Québec? Was it some Alpine gap that could never be crossed? Would there always be some small corner in their lives together where his southern-ness and her northern-ness always kept their distance? It was something she was utterly unable to analyze herself, so she was clearly not equipped to discuss it with him. She could only watch and wait.

They finished their food and went back to their separate workplaces.

☆✰☆

Mama was right. Rocco seemed to be living in the workshop these quiet evenings when the place was locked down and only his bench light gave evidence of late night skulking. Every week or 10 days a new shipment would turn up, then Rocco would have to return to the facility in the evening and do the switch. Even though he was swift and skilful with his hands, it still took two or three hours to get through a complete batch of shells. Then, once that was done, he had to drive to the latest unique rendezvous to make the transfer. Those nighttime drives were filled with fear; he was now transporting large quantities of pure cocaine in canvas shopping bags, pulling up in deserted spots and shoving the stuff out of the car window to the anonymous motorcyclist. Lately, as there was so much stuff, they had been showing up on three-wheelers with a trunk on the back.

All in all, he would be out from after supper until nearly midnight. He wondered if his folks really believed his story that he had to work late just to keep up. It was hardly plausible.

This evening, seated at the bench, he had only just opened and emptied the first shell of the first box of 8″ Serpents when he heard the clicking that signified someone keying in to the building security. Shit! It could only be Len, the facility gopher, or Nonno; no one else had the code. After a few seconds, during which he was nearly overwhelmed by the rush of shit to the heart, he quickly shifted the box of shells into the corner of the workshop, and swept the baggies into a tool drawer below the bench. He had scarcely got the drawer shut, with the opened shell still on the bench in front of him, when Nonno cracked the door of the workshop and stepped in.

"Nonno!" he cried brightly, swiveling on his stool, "this *is* a surprise."

"Checking up on you, *figlio*," said his grandfather, eyes scanning the workshop. "What you up to?"

Clearly, this was a time to lay on the soap and oil and hope to God it came out sincere, so with palpitating heart and rigidly controlled tremors, he looked the patriarch in the eye.

"There's so little time to do what I really love," he improvised, maneuvering on his stool to keep the opened shell on the bench out of his grandfather's line of sight, "so I've been sneaking in and making the odd shell or two. Just to keep my hand in..." Did it sound as lame to Nonno's ears as it did to his?

But the old man was touched. Since the finances of Pastorelli Fireworks had taken a surprising upswing, he was in a more positive frame of mind; still a tough old buzzard, but more like the old self that Rocco remembered as a child.

"Well, that's great. But, you know, you don't want to burn yourself out."

"Tell you what Nonno," he cried rising from the stool and seizing the old man's elbow, "let's head off down to Mario's and have a coffee or two and just talk."

Permitting no resistance he steered the old man out of the workshop, shut off the lights, and made for the front door.

"You're right," he called over his shoulder as he rearmed the security system at the front desk, "I really should learn to chill out. Let's go."

Even though Rocco was absolutely on a knife edge of impatience, they did have a great discussion over their coffees at the Bistro Rosa, and for an hour or so they were as close as they had ever been. It was so painful that a good time like this could be bought at such a high cost, but Rocco forced his nefarious activities into another mental compartment.

Just that brief discovery in the workshop had opened the old man's memory gates, so a large part of their conversation—albeit somewhat one-sided—centred on the *studadas* he had made over the years. There were lots of retold tales, but some new material as well, which Rocco absorbed happily. It was brought home to him how important it had been to his grandfather to make his own material and to fire it off himself. Inevitably, because of the firm's continuing and incremental reliance on bought-in pyrotechnics, the old man's expertise had become marginalized and relegated. Then, the electronic revolution had left him literally out in the cold. Rocco now had a new, stabbing insight into the rows they had had over his joy with the success of FireOne, and his dereliction of duty in Barrie. These were yet more waving red flags that told Emilio he was a has-been; yet more nails driven into a tradition of six generations. If only he could find more ways of impressing the old man, he thought, prove to him that the firm was in capable hands.

A new sorrow for something that could never come back was mingled in Rocco with a deep and heartfelt contrition. He would have to find a way of biting back his too-quick responses when criticized; have to find a way of spinning positive, and involving the patriarch in areas where his vast expertise could still come into play. Perhaps with the firm's new financial optimism he could increase the paltry production of shells, and involve the old fella in design? Oh, God, he thought, imagine the irony of getting Nonno to help make all those goddamned garnitures to replace the ones tossed out by the traffickers in Medellín! That was too horrible to think about, but anyway the old boy was too sharp; he'd cotton on pretty quick. But perhaps somehow all the lies he had told earlier when caught virtually red-handed might turn to some good. With this double life he was leading, any shred of decency was to be grasped with both hands.

The level in the cups went down thrice as Rocco enjoyed the renewed warmth of his grandfather's company, while the anxiety at the postponed job still ahead and the horror of what all this was about were temporarily shelved. When these conflicting emotional threads occasionally wove briefly together it made a destructive mix for the psyche.

Finally, Mario started to turn off the lights, gently hinting that it was time to wipe the tables and count the cash, so grandfather and grandson rose from the table, paid for their coffees and stepped out onto the cool sidewalk.

"This has been great Nonno," said Rocco as they headed back to their building. "Look, I hate to say this, but I really should go back in and tidy up. Left in a bit of a rush, eh?" The lie tore at him.

"Sure. We gotta talk more often. You work too hard..." he held his hands up, palms out, "...I know, I know, I've heard it all. But your Mama is worried, okay?"

"I'll see what I can do. You got your car here?"

"Yeah, right out back. See you later." And he was off, walking with a springy stride to the lot at the back of the building where his LTD Squire station wagon was parked.

The scion of Pastorelli Fireworks let himself back into the building, wondering how in Christ's name he had got into this mess, and wondering even more pointedly how he would ever get out.

It couldn't keep going like this.

But it had to...

☆⋆⭒⭒☆⋆

Uncle Chuck loved to tinker with his bike. His was an old Hog from the '60s and now he had it parked in the clubhouse garage while he farted around with some adjustments. The ignition had good old-fashioned contact breakers and the big V-twin engine had two carbs, and wasn't it a bugger to balance the bastards. But there was a persistent problem with starting; it was so easy to flood the goddamned thing, and then the cylinders and exhaust filled with fuel vapour, so when it did kick over there was a huge backfire. He'd had the HT leads off, pissed around with the ignition coil, checked the plugs, checked the points, but it still wasn't right.

"Wassup with the thing?" asked one of the other bikers, a man who rode an immaculate late model machine heavy with chrome and black leather. "You never got it starting right."

"I don't get it. Once it starts it runs sweet, but it just takes a kick or two 'fore it fires."

"Should fire straight off. You wanna put electronic ignition in; no more fuckin' around then. Or sell it to a museum."

"No way, asshole! It stays the way Harley-Davidson made it!"

"Well, backfire's getting to be your trademark."

No way was he changing a damned thing; this baby had seen the best times and had always ridden at the head of the vanguard when the V-Twin Valkyries rode through town. No fuckin' way this baby was being messed with, let alone getting pensioned off.

But, you know what, he thought, it's a shit piece of engineering. Who the hell uses big V-twin motors in the 21st century, for Chrissakes? Harleys are so goddamned out of date. Like, everybody else went multiple piston, small capacity, high rev, but not these buggers. The only reason they don't change is they know they'll lose their market. It's all about tradition and mom and pop, good old Uncle Sam and apple fuckin' pie. But mechanically it's a friggin' dinosaur.

Still, bottom line is, the Hog is part of a biker's uniform. Goes with the leathers and tattoos and chains and shit.

He got up from messing with the bike and went over to the bench for a plug wrench; maybe the colour of the plugs would give a clue about the efficiency of ignition. He had to step around the big pile of Molson Blue empties beside the bench.

"Hey, Billy-Bob," he called to the biker with electronic ignition ideas, "d'ya wanna get rid of that dynamite? Shoulda taken care of it away back when the cops came snooping round."

But Billy-Bob had just started his machine so Uncle Chuck's voice got drowned by the 'potato-potato-potato' of a smooth-running V-twin on idle.

☆☆ ☆ ☆☆

There's a little rocky promontory along the lakeshore from East Gladstone, where the Assinipequo River enters from the north. Just beyond the rocks is a small beach, not much frequented even in summer. Rocco and Julia agreed to meet there one evening after work. Although they met frequently, talked a great deal and sometimes made love, they both knew that their relationship was coming to a point of crisis.

Julia felt only that something was absent; that in some ways he wasn't fully present with her, even at the height of their bodily pleasure. It frustrated her beyond bearing and she knew that somehow she would have to find a way through it, and that could only be done by talking, a tack that had so far failed. He held secrets from her, and to her a lover with secrets was no full partner.

Rocco was torn between his love for Julia and the dishonesty of his hidden life. He wanted so desperately to confide in her, to have some other soul share his agony, but he also knew that to do this would signify the death of their relationship. Julia would be absolutely horrified if he told her; it would hurt her more than he could bear and he must refuse to put her through it. The pain of finally finding a woman like Julia–the magic of their meeting and their instant attraction–then to have her torn away from him was ripping him apart.

Here, on the small beach beyond the rocky promontory their two lives would collide. She would beg him to open out fully to her, and he would have to balk. It could only end badly.

They sat down side by side on a sloping slab of limestone that tipped its way into the sands of the beach, and watched the waves lap gently at its base where it entered the water.

"I want to talk about us," she began. "I know you find this hard, but I want us to share everything."

"We do," he replied shortly, looking out into the lake and not meeting her eyes.

"Rocco, look at me," she pleaded. "There's something between us, and I can't..."

"There's nothing. What you see is what you get." He maintained his gaze into the distance.

"Please, *please* tell me. I want you to tell me."

"It's just... it's business and work and... stuff like that. Nothing you need to worry about."

"But if you're worried about work, you can tell me," she urged. "There's nothing there that I wouldn't gladly share. No secrets."

"There's stuff... Look, just don't push me, okay?" He hadn't meant to sound angry but he couldn't bear the pressure. "I'm sorry, but let's just drop it, okay?"

"Why? Why can't you tell me?" she begged trying to look into his eyes.

"I said to drop it! Oh shit, I didn't mean to..." She had put her head down on his shoulder and had begun to cry.

He didn't know what to do; soothe her until she began to ask again, tell her the terrible truth, or just get up and walk away. As far as he could see, whatever he did would result in cruelty. Her sobbing on his shoulder brought him to the very verge of confession; how wonderful it would feel if he unburdened himself to her utterly and completely, but then how selfish it would be because he would condemn her to misery.

"I can't tell. I just can't," he muttered to the head of fair hair crying on his shoulder. "It's nothing you need to know. Really. Let's just agree to be as we are..."

They sat for a long time without moving while her sobs abated. Presently she looked up from his shoulder and their eyes finally met. She saw that he had been crying too, and this somehow softened her.

"I love you so much," she said. "Whatever it is you're carrying, I want you to know you don't have to do it alone."

He nodded, not trusting himself to speak.

"Any time. Whenever you're ready." This was unbearable because nothing had changed. Being certain now that he had some secret he refused to share had not lessened her pain in the slightest. She could only continue to be patient, but now the agony of knowing was pulling her to pieces.

"I love you too," he finally managed to say, and then his voice broke altogether and the tears came again.

Much later, as it became dark and a chill wind picked up from the west, they separated from each other and walked slowly up the beach with their hands gently together. They reached their parked cars.

"I'll see you soon," he whispered softly, turning to her.

"Sure," she replied as she gently disengaged her hand and opened the car door.

She left first, bumping slowly up the gravel path to the road, while he stood beside his car and watched her go.

In sudden anger and bitterness he lashed out with his foot at a wooden litter bin, stoving in the slats on the side. He picked up a tree branch from beside the path and smashed it against the bin again and again until it was splinters in his hand. He turned and booted the poor old Toyota Corolla, denting a panel behind the rear wheel. Just as quickly the rage abated, and he flung himself down on the ground in misery. What kind of shit universe was he living in that allowed this to happen? Where was this God that his mother was so fucking convinced of? How could any God of love throw such a bunch of bullshit at you? He roundly cursed the God that he didn't believe in, eventually running down into a pathetic string of filthy words.

He rose slowly to his feet, got into his car, and headed back into town to resume the life of a drug smuggler and all-round piece of shit. But first a stop-off at the LCBO for another bottle of Canadian Club; strong and cheap and deadening.

☆☆☆

As that glorious August stretched ahead, Julia's days became long and pointless and a gray shadow lay over her waking. She did her work efficiently and well, although with distance and less social contact. Her father and Mike noticed no difference. Her mother caught the nuance of her disaffection but could find no way to get close to the daughter who always shared everything. Her grandfather knew there was something deeply amiss, and in his loving clumsy way he tried to help, but she didn't even want to go back to the workshop and make another shell. He saw this as a sign of deep distress, and it hurt him that she was so hurt.

Then began the destructive analysis of her love. It was like crash-testing; you had to smash the object completely in order to examine the broken pieces and find clues. The thing was already smashed irreparably, but try as she might the fragments yielded no clue to the disaster. She had failed to penetrate the distance at Rocco's core and, as close as they had been, she knew that whatever it was he was withholding was the key.

She tried to replay in her mind the point at which she had first felt the reserve in him. When, during their lovemaking, had she first felt that... absence? It must have been, she thought, a week or two after their reconciliation. Yes, a couple of weeks after that storm over the duds. Could it be another attempt at sabotage? Surely not; he was open and honest enough about that. There were tears; big macho boys don't cry, or try to fake tears. And besides, there had been no firework failures since.

No, it had to be something else. But what?

Deep below the surface was a shivering fear that he had got himself into something criminal, that somehow the incident with this Steve guy had drawn him back into that world he thought he had left behind.

Often in her lowest moments she thought of calling him, meeting him, writing to him, but she just couldn't nerve herself for the rejection she knew would face her. She began to sympathize during her long empty days with those people mired in clinical depression. She thought of some of her mother's clients and felt deeply for them, not realizing or admitting to herself that she was becoming one of their number.

☆ ⭐ ☆

The Detective Inspector's fury was getting him nowhere; you don't rage at missed opportunities, for God's sake, you learn from them and steal the advantage back. Fred Delios had stumbled on the truth after his search of Pastorelli had revealed nothing. The dope was hidden *in the firework shells*. It must be! Now he thought about it, it was so bloody obvious. Never treat the enemy like a fool—his own adage—but that's exactly what he had done. Of course they wouldn't slip baggies of coke between the items of the consignment; that would be a dead give-away, especially with everybody from the Port Authority down to Uncle Tom Cobbleigh on the high alert. And DS Delios had actually had the goods between his hands, if he'd only known it. Damn, this was infuriating! And wasn't Rocco Pastorelli the cool cucumber, standing there while they opened the boxes in front of his eyes?

So, by obvious inference, if the stuff was concealed within the casings of the aerial shells, Pastorelli had to be a willing participant. Nab him red-handed and you have the perfect pipeline to the entire gang. So, no reason to delay and give him the chance to dispose of the stuff. As soon as the consignment enters their building we get a warrant pronto and swoop down. And this time we use dogs!

"Okay, Fred," said the DI as soon as Delios had entered the office. "Here's what we do." He explained the details of his plan. "Oh, and when the call comes you should take Chan with you again. She's got promise."

This time there would be no mistakes.

☆⋆ ☆ ⋆☆

The phone rang in Rocco's pocket as he was walking back to his car after lunch at the Bistro Rosa. He hoped it wasn't Julia, but then again he hoped it was. The boys were at the port today picking up the latest shipment from Colombia, so his tension was even higher that usual. And these last few days he'd been holding the phone reluctantly to his ear anyway because it gave only bad news. This was some more of the same.

Three words, "Hockey rink. Now."

He jumped into his car and drove the 15 minutes to the recreation facility north of the city centre. Uncle Chuck met him at the back of the parking lot beside a pile of snow left by the ice-making Zamboni. He leaned into the window of the car.

"Okay, Rocco my sweet, we have an amber alert." Uncle Chuck's voice seemed ominously calm and collected, which probably meant trouble. "The cops are putting together another search warrant for your shop."

"Not again! When? When?" Oh shit, oh shit, not again! His nerves simply couldn't stand this. He felt betrayed by Uncle Chuck's previous confidence.

"Later today by the looks of it. Where's the latest shipment?"

"On its way from Montreal in the truck."

"Stop it. Divert it. Don't let it into your building. They're bringing dogs this time."

"How? How?" He asked in panic. "Where do I divert it to?"

"Just do it. It's your dick's in the vice. Deniability, that's my shtick. But we're looking at a whole lot of money, aren't we?" And

Uncle Chuck swung away and headed for his parked Hog. "Just don't lose it," he called over his shoulder. "That's all."

Rocco tried to think fast in almost total panic, counterproductive at best. As he sat in the car he tried to control his breathing and marshal his thoughts. Minutes counted, so he had to act now. Okay, the shipment cannot enter the building, but the cops must know that it's in transit; that's why they're raiding today. So, when they don't find it right there in the loading dock they'll want to know where it is. So, firstly, a decoy.

He called Len, the facility assistant. "Do me a favour, Len. Could you get ten crates of eight-inch shells off the shelves in the magazine? Colombian ones, gotta be Colombian ones, okay? A selection, doesn't matter, and put them on a pallet in the loading bay?"

"Sure, but why?" asked Len, greatly mystified.

"I might be arranging to ship them out... depends. I know, it's a royal pain in the ass, but if you could get it done pronto? Thanks a million."

Secondly, where to divert the shipment? He could phone the drivers and get them to wait at a truck stop or something, but that would stink of suspicion. Besides, the truck would have to be back when the cops came, or they would be asking some pointed questions.

The next call was difficult. He dialed the number for Catesby & Son Pyrotechnics and asked for the manager. As soon as Alfred was on the line he began his desperate spiel.

"This is Rocco Pastorelli. Look, I'm really sorry to bother you but we're having trouble with our loading bay door. It's jammed... Exactly, and I don't want to park the shipment outside the building overnight... So, could I ask you a huge favour and have it stored at your place... Oh, just until tomorrow... You are very kind. Thank you."

That was tough. He'd been given the old cold, distant voice routine, but how could the bastard refuse a reasonable request? Well, of course, he couldn't.

Then he called Seth and Tonio who were somewhere between Montreal and East Gladstone. He imagined the truck humming down the highway, bringing his doom closer by the second.

"Hey guys, it's Rocco. Where are you? Yeah..." Oh great, more than 50 K. "Look, we've got a little issue here. The loading bay door's jammed, and I don't want to have the shipment parked outside. I want you to drop it off at Catesby's on Upper Main and then bring the truck back here empty... good, soon as you can. Bye."

Now to head back to the facility pronto and find a way to bust the door. By this time he was feeling an elation fueled in equal measures by a new-found sense of control and an overworked adrenal gland.

He drove back moderately quickly, mindful of the disaster that a stop of even a few minutes for a traffic ticket might incur. There was nobody in the loading bay, but he noticed a nice wooden pallet loaded with boxes of shells. A quick check; yes, Colombian. Good old Len! He hauled out a stepladder and placed it to the side of the loading bay door, just below the motor drive near the ceiling. He climbed up quickly and hauled on the metal-clad cable that led into the motor. It came loose with a satisfying ripping noise but with no shower of sparks, so that was a relief.

As he was taking the ladder down Willy, the assistant, emerged from between the storage racks.

"Damn' loading bay door's on the fritz," Rocco told him. "Give the button a push, will you Willy?"

"Give the button a push will you Willy." He stabbed the button a few times with a wide smile and nothing, satisfyingly, happened.

"Have to get on to the company," he concluded. "Damn!"

"Have to get on to the company damn!" repeated Willy and laughed.

On his return to his office Rocco encountered Len at the front of the storage area.

"Loading bay door's on the fritz," he told him. "I'll call the company right now and divert Seth and Tonio to Catesby's until it's fixed."

"Okay," Len nodded. "Lotta shit going down today, eh?"

"Yeah. Oh, and thanks for putting that stuff on the dock for me."

"No problem. Where's it going?" With a mystified expression.

"Not sure if it's going anywhere at the moment. I'll keep you posted."

"Okay. And the Italian shells?"

Rocco still kept a pallet of Italian shells in the dock in case Nonno made a surprise visit. "Just... just shove 'em aside for now. I'll sort it all out later."

"Okay. Like I said, lotta shit going down today."

Christ, you don't know the hundredth part of it!

Len went off to do whatever he had been doing, not a little intrigued.

Less than an hour later Seth and Tonio arrived with the empty truck. It was just before 4:00 PM so Rocco thanked them and told them to take off early. He returned to his office wound up like a clock spring and utterly unable to do anything, including think coherently. It was nearly 5:00 when Len called through and told him there were some policemen at the desk who wished to speak to him. He rose slowly and walked as nonchalantly as he could to the front desk, face fixed in a benign mask that would fool nobody. DS Delios was there with a young female detective constable, while outside the door were more officers with dogs.

"Good afternoon officers. How can I help you?"

"We have a search warrant here, sir," replied DS Delios in his best police voice. "We have reason to believe..."

"Not again!" he interrupted, crying in a mock anger that was not difficult to simulate. "You came here before and found nothing! And, just like last time, you've got to be mistaken. What are you looking for anyway?"

"We have a warrant here," stated the policeman, ignoring the question, "and we intend to execute it."

"All right. Follow me."

Delios went to the door and called the two special constables from the K-9 squad, who brought their eager sniffing dogs with them on straining leashes.

The immediate target of the searchers was, of course, the shipment from Colombia sitting on its pallet on the loading dock. To the grave disappointment of the police, and Rocco's rigidly concealed delight, the shipment showed no signs of anything except gunpowder. The dogs weren't even mildly excited. Even so, the cop insisted on opening all the boxes and examining each firework in them with close attention.

"I'm sorry sir, but I'm going to have to cut some of these shells open." The packers in Colombia would have to be more than meticulous not to leave a trace of cocaine on the outsides of the fireworks—plenty enough for the dogs to detect—but even so Delios was taking no chances. "Do you have a box cutter?"

"But you can't damage my property, just like that!" This was scary; even though he knew he was safe, it was quite apparent to Rocco that this guy really knew what he was looking for. "They're expensive, those things!"

"You'll be compensated for any loss. And it's better you let us do this now before the matter escalates."

Rocco pointed out the packing/unpacking workbench and the cop brought two shells over, took the yellow-handled knife off the hook and went to work, stripping off the plastic bag and slicing into tape and cardboard.

"Careful," warned Rocco, "you'll damage the bloody leader fuse!" He bit back the knee-jerk reaction, which the policeman didn't pick up on. The leader fuse didn't matter, of course; this one wouldn't be returned to working condition anyway.

Neither shell proved to be a revelation; gunpowder and pretty effects through and through. Then, just when Rocco thought the policeman might be satisfied, he went to another of the opened crates, selected two more shells and went to work again with the box cutter.

"Sixty bucks," observed Rocco laconically. "Every time you gouge into one of those things you're costing the taxpayers sixty bucks."

This was greeted with silence as the DS concentrated on his work. While he was lifting a third pair of shells out of another crate, Rocco was seized with a pang of fear; one of them had the characteristic band of tape around its middle. It was one of the ones he had opened, emptied and refilled last week. Hacked open it revealed a mixture of garnitures—Medellín originals and the Pastorelli replacements—although the policeman was none the wiser. Rocco wondered with another surge of fear if the dogs might not pick up a trace on this one. But while this systematic examination was underway the dogs were being led up and down the loading area, sniffing like mad, but finding nothing that warranted attention. At one point there was a commotion at the end of one of the racks, and Delios sprinted over in anticipation. The dogs had discovered someone's lunch that had gone missing a few days previously. The aroma of the baloney and cheese was something only dogs could really get excited over.

It became clear to Fred Delios after the sixth excavation that this whole business wasn't going anywhere. Just as the police were about the leave in disappointment, DC Chan remembered the Pastorelli delivery truck. "Where's the company vehicle? It's not in the loading bay," she asked. Delios gave her a smile and a nod. This one will really get on quickly, he thought, mentally rubbing his hands in delight. His enthusiasm was suddenly on the upswing.

"Parked outside," replied Rocco and, high on success, he continued. "Your warrant is just for the building, though, isn't it?"

"This warrant," intoned Delios in his habitual police-ese, "is for the facilities of Pastorelli Fireworks and, as such, your vehicle can be construed as being included in its remit."

Rocco made himself look nervous, which engendered hidden glee in the policeman, then pseudo-reluctantly got the spare keys from the hook in the office, and led the team out through the side door of the loading dock and down the steel steps to road level. He didn't mention the defective loading bay door, and they didn't ask.

He unlocked and shoved up the squeaky roll-up door at the rear of the truck. His relief at seeing the completely empty space was minor compared to the crestfallen disappointment of the police, who were finally unable to conceal their chagrin. The dogs did a perfunctory sniff, but the game had obviously been played.

"Thank you very much for your cooperation," said DS Delios with as much aplomb as he could muster, disappointment threatening to break out momentarily. "You can bill us for the damaged property."

"You are very welcome," replied the newly-confident Rocco Pastorelli as the police left the building, "but we would be obliged if you could restrain what is beginning to appear like harassment. In future, might I suggest you research more deeply the grounds for issuing such warrants before executing them in this rather slipshod fashion?"

I can put on the old police voice too, so fuck you with a wire brush.

It was only later, when the euphoria of outwitting the cops had worn off, that he realized how stupid he had been to antagonize them. What happened to keeping a low profile, for Christ's sake?

Problem was, even with all the anxiety, fear and plain bowel-loosening terror, there had been moments of quite delicious pleasure...

☆✩☆✩☆✩

Another cocaine drop in the middle of nowhere. A large bag in the car trunk stuffed with goodies. Lots of fun for little girls and boys. Ho, ho, ho. And laying his finger aside of his nose, and giving a snort, up his nostril it rose!

As Rocco drove, following the verbal instructions on his GPS, he ran the various delivery scenarios over in his mind. God, he'd put a whole lot of kilometers on the old Corolla these last few months. The drop site was usually within 10 or 15 kilometers of East Gladstone, but once he'd had to drive all the way to the Horseshoe Valley ski resort. Why in the world this place had been chosen was anyone's guess and, of course, he'd never asked. Drug mules just obey orders.

"In six hundred and fifty meters tuhrn left on Cohld Water Rowd west," said the mechanical lady with the weird pronunciation. He'd tried several other voices offered on the Garmin menu but he had decided to stick with this one because the British accent was so goddamned prissy it made him laugh. He needed all the laughs he could get these days.

He swung left and continued west watching his speedometer with an almost fanatical attention while obeying the rules of the road like an automaton. Having twice dodged police raids right there at the facility, to be caught in a petty traffic violation on the highway would be just too ironic. So he drove with uncharacteristic care all the time.

Police are trained to spot drunk drivers in two ways. There are the obvious ones with clear symptoms of erratic driving—weaving, crossing lane markers, ignoring road signs and general lack of control—and then there are the ones who have had just enough to push them over the legal blood alcohol limit of 0.08. They have not yet lost control of their faculties to a measurable extent, yet they know how close they are to doing so. So they drive exactly at the speed limit, they obey all road signs to the letter, and their heads are continually swinging from side to side in painstaking vigilance.

One such motorist appeared along Cold Water Road that evening, and as he passed the unmarked police car parked at the side, the two officers were able to get a brief glance at the steady concentration and focus of the driver. They looked at each other, nodded, and prepared to intercept.

When Rocco spotted the red and blue flashing lights in his rearview mirror he was filled with such a clamping, roaring, shuddering fear that he nearly lost control of the car, within a heartbeat of turning mere suspicion into certainty. It's got to be random, he thought, it's got to be random, as his heart entered his throat and his legs turned to a thrilling quivery liquid.

He pulled over carefully, put the car in park carefully, rolled the window down and turned off the ignition, all with wooden precision.

"Stay in the car please, sir." The officer was tall in the dim glow from streetlights masked by trees. "Perhaps I could just take a look at your driver's licence, insurance and ownership?"

Rocco extracted the documents from his wallet, thanking God he'd stowed the stuff in the trunk. He was desperately trying to project an obliging and harmless image. He handed the papers over silently with hands that couldn't stop shaking. While the officer examined the documents by means of a small flashlight, the second officer peered in at the rear windows of the car and played a similar flashlight over the back seat and floor.

Rocco felt sure that the officer had caught the slight whiff of Scotch on his breath. More and more these days he was fortifying himself before starting on his clandestine duties, but it was hours ago and only a small shot. But what is it about some people in positions of power that they must play with their victims? This cop had disappointedly decided that the motorist wasn't drunk, wouldn't blow anywhere near the limit, and was doubtless innocent of any wrongdoing. So he took an inordinately long time examining the documents, turning them over repeatedly, pretending to pore over the words, and comparing Rocco's face with the unflattering facsimile on the driver's licence several times.

"So, where are you off to tonight, sir?"

Oh, just dropping off a million bucks worth of cocaine to the V-Twin Valkyries.

"Friends," he lied, to himself as much as to the cops. Friends! Shit!

The officer handed Rocco's documents to the second officer who took them back to the car, running them through the police database and taking his sweet time about it.

"Anything in the trunk?" asked the first officer, even though he knew a refusal would have to be countered with a warrant.

"Spare, toolkit, jumper cables," mumbled Rocco with a sense of doom now sitting almost tangibly on his shoulders like some leaning stone gargoyle on a crumbling cathedral.

"'Kay." The officer retrieved the papers after their database check, finally handing them in the window as if reluctant to give them up. "Have a good night sir. Sorry to have bothered you."

If there was ever a time in his entire life when Rocco would have dreamed of getting pleasure from kissing another man this was it. Instead, he started the car and drove off with mechanical exactitude, fighting down the impulse to floor the thing and get the hell away. He kept his attention on the rearview mirror just in case they were teasing him with some bullshit cat-and-mouse routine. Soon he was alone again on a quiet road, just him and Madame GPS.

Not for even the tenth time, he told himself this has got to stop, while the other, deeper part of his mind told him: You know it can't. You know it can't.

He pulled up at the rendezvous 15 minutes late, still shaking from his close call, swung out of the car and opened the trunk. Instead of the usual mute and anonymous exchange, this one was punctuated with words.

"Where the fuck you bin?"

"Stopped by the cops."

"Didn't bust you. Good. Late."

As he lugged the bag of goodies out of the trunk and shoved it into the biker's arms, all his tension and fear burst out in anger. "*Just once!*" he bellowed. "Just once will one of you *fuckers* say *THANK YOU!* I go through shit for you! Here, Medellín, every drop site, every fucking where! Thanks, that's all. How *hard* is that for fuck's sake?"

"Oh, I am so sorry your royal *fucking* highness," replied Hefty Beale. "What was I fucking thinking of? Thank you so-o-o, so-o-o much. Will that sur-fice?"

"Screw you," said Rocco, deflating as the usual stuffed envelope was shoved into his hand.

"Screw you too, Pastorelli. Know what? Steve was right; you are an asshole."

The sack was stowed in the trunk of the three-wheeler, and with no more conversational niceties Hefty took off in a clap of sound and a wave of burnt gasoline.

Rocco stuffed the blood money deep into his jacket pocket. All these wads of used notes in brown envelopes; it was sleazy. He felt like a prime minister or something...

He got back into the car, started up and headed home, tired beyond imagining.

☆☆★☆☆

Uncle Chuck had called an emergency meeting of the entire V-Twin Valkyries. He sat behind his greasy desk with an expression that would split sandstone. The whole gang knew from his face that there was some serious shit going down.

"Okay fellahs, here's the scoop. The cops have gone into the Pastorelli outfit twice. *Twice!* First time, complete goddamn surprise, but they found nothing. But, the point is, we got lucky 'cos the idiots only looked in the boxes. Then, we hear they're gonna raid again, and this time we get a warning out to little Rocco-kins just in time." Uncle Chuck's cop shop contact was known to nobody but himself; such potentially dangerous information was always compartmentalized. "But here's the shit: *How did they know?* How did they know to cut the fucking shells open? 'Cos that's what Rocco told me. Well?"

The whole gang sat around the desk in dead silence, faces revealing nothing. Even Hefty Beale managed to suppress his fear although, had Uncle Chuck looked closely in the face of one of his favourite henchmen, he might have seen terror in the eyes.

"No ideas, eh?"

Shakes of heads, slight creaking of leather and jingle of chains. Breaths exhaled.

"There's two possibilities," continued Uncle Chuck enumerating on his fingers. "One, little Rocco has flapped his mouth off to someone. Or, two, someone in this room has let it out. Ideas?"

"It wouldn't be none of us," mumbled Sludge McCracken, another of Uncle Chuck's stalwarts. "Disloyal, that would be."

"Disloyal? You forgot the fuckin' death sentence!"

"Yeah, that too..."

Another long silence, in which a sweating Beale began to realize the evils of one Guinness too many. Fuckin' Steve! Now *I* could kill the little rat. But he couldn't have squealed to the cops, could he? He just couldn't have.

"So? *So?*" The face could now cleave granite. "Hefty, you been talking to that loser Bacon." Not a question.

"Not recently," lied Hefty, speaking slowly and holding his voice in check. "Anyhow, as if I'd say anything to *him*..."

The boss nodded, not at all convinced. Beale was a stalwart, but brains hadn't been part of the one lucky sperm's information package when he was conceived.

"Rocco's a pal of Steve's, right?"

"Not anymore," said Hefty. "Worst enemies."

"How do you know if you haven't been talking to him?"

"Well, I hear things," he mumbled. "Y'know, people talk..."

"Yeah, don't they just? So, pal Rocco isn't going to shoot his mouth off in that direction. That what you're saying, eh?" Hefty nodded. "But, I tell you, if Steve fuckin' Bacon has anything to do with this, anything at all, we put out a contract on him. No question. He's implicated, he's dead."

Hefty nodded, not trusting himself to speak, realizing how his blind Guinness-driven stupidity had jeopardized his little near-brother's life. He'd have to stop seeing him for the foreseeable, but warn him first. What a screw up.

"Look," put in McCracken, "if the cops didn't find nothin' both times, maybe they think it's not true."

"Yeah, that's what I told Pastorelli when he came whining to me, but I'm not convinced they're that stupid. Even before the fireworks they raided this place twice, and we made 'em look like complete idiots both times. We can *not*," and he punched his fist into his palm in emphasis, "we *can not* treat these people as if they're stupid. Cardinal mistake."

"So," put in McCracken, "the heat ain't off?"

"No way!" I better keep close tabs on my little girl at cop headquarters, he thought. Any slightest hint of paperwork in the police department, we take measures.

In the silence that followed, his eyes raked the gang, fastening briefly on each member then passing along. If you failed to meet his eyes he would file the information for later use. Hefty Beale made a huge effort and maintained the loyalty eye contact long enough to pass the L-sat.

Right after the meeting Hefty roared off on his single-seater Heritage Softail and headed into town. He was mad at himself for being so stupid, and would be mad with Steve as well if he was sure he had blabbed. But had he? Well, even if he hadn't, there was a death watch on him. Stupid little bastard.

Steve worked as a reluctant and taciturn counterman at an east end motorbike parts store, and Hefty figured he could quickly drop in, give Steve the word, and tool out with nobody the wiser. He parked the Hog in the middle of a row of bikes, kicked out her stand and strode into the store. Steve's face lit up when he spotted his pal walking between the rows of mufflers, tailpipes and gaskets. Then he saw the dour face.

"Gotta talk. Not here. Where's the washroom?"

Steve indicated with a nod in the direction of the corner, waited until Hefty had headed that way, then flipped up the counter gate and followed him.

"What's up?" he asked as he copied Hefty by pulling it out and pretending to pee.

"I don't know what you said, or who you said it to, but the

cops are onto the gang. The fuckin' fireworks."

Steve began to protest but Hefty cut him short.

"Don't need no protests. Don't need nothing. Just wanna tell you, Uncle Chuck's on to you and you're dead meat."

"I never said anythin'..." Steve began in a whine, then realized he couldn't lie to him. He just couldn't. "It was..."

Just then one of the other employees, an older man, entered the washroom, strode up to the urinals and did his thing. The man took an inordinate amount of time, trickling for ever. Not knowing what else to do, Steve and Hefty maintained their poses. This was turning into the longest piss in history; made a prostate look like a walk in the park. Finally, the guy zipped up and left, ignoring the sign about employees washing their hands. Good; he would probably have spent his time dribbling with the taps too. And at least the merchandise was bike parts, not food.

There were tears streaming down Steve Bacon's face. "The cops... they got at me... I couldn't..."

"'S alright. Just us chickens." Hefty's anger was softening. What kind of biker am I? he asked himself.

"Not back in jail... Couldn't..." he sobbed. He turned quickly at his stall, eyes flashing. "I never mentioned your name! Never! Honest!"

"Okay, okay, I believe you, man."

"What could I do? They... they..." He began crying again.

"Okay. Like I say, I believe you bro," said Hefty quietly, finally zipping up and stepping back. "I believe you. But remember, he's on your case. Now clean up and get back to work."

Hefty flung his leg over the Hog, twitched the starter, clicked up first, and pulled out of the lot. As he rode he thought of his role in the V-Twin Valkyries. It had seemed such a great thing to be in. Like finally you were somebody and people knew it. For a stupid jailbird with no prospects, no education, no future, it was just about perfect.

But now... Shit, once you were in you could never get out. Alive.

Chapter Four
The Burst Charge

An internal charge designed to burst an aerial shell at or near the top of
its flight to disperse the visual and sound effects
Display Fireworks Manual, Natural Resources Canada (2010)

René, the stores manager at the Port of Montreal Dock Authority
bonded warehouse, grabbed the two clipboards with attached
manifests from the front counter and headed to the back of the
building. Two almost identical shipments had come in from
South America and he had to clear them through and get the papers ready for signature when the owners showed. He passed
through the keypad-guarded door to the bonded warehouse and
looked for the shipments. He was only slightly surprised to see
that Claire had got there before him. The last few days they had
kept crossing paths between the front office, the coffee room and
the storage area, but had never managed to linger for more than
a quick touch of hands or a pat on the bum. Conflicting domestic
conjugal commitments meant that liaisons had to be confined to
working hours. A whiff of her chewing gum as she passed by was
about as far as intimacy had gone. The bonded warehouse was
deserted; just the two of them.

"*Enfin!*" he cried as he laid the two clipboards aside on a convenient crate.

She flung her arms around him, and he gripped her tight.
Their mouths came together and their tongues shared her
spearmint. Her breasts were flat against his chest, her groin
grinding into his.

"We should see more of each other," she gasped as their
mouths slid briefly away.

"What, you mean like surface area?" he panted.

"Yeah. I got surfaces I only see in the shower. And some of
them you need a mirror."

Their faces came together again. His hands fumbled for her
breasts. A consummation devoutly to be wish'd might have taken
place right there among the packing crates and pallets, only a
slight sound on the other side of the door meant someone else
was keying in. They broke apart and she walked smartly to the

other end of a row of shelves, turned on her heel and came back slowly towards him, while René picked up his clipboards and resumed work with what nonchalance he could muster.

As the third person entered the bonded warehouse, Claire sauntered past René and murmured, "Here. After work. Quickie."

René pulled his brown warehouse smock close around him and buttoned the front right down. He did the paperwork for the two shipments with slightly less attention than he usually gave to this important task.

Rocco had decided that morning to take the company truck and go down to the docks himself. All the other shipments had been just fine, but he was increasingly nervous and maybe just seeing one shipment right from the docks would ease his mind. He arrived at the Port of Montreal Dock Authority around noon and soon found the building. He introduced himself to the receptionist at the front desk.

"Ah, you're Rocco Pastorelli, eh?" René turned from a filing cabinet and strode over to shake his hand. "I'm René Desjardins. We've talked a lot on the phone. What brings you here? Not a problem?"

"No, no, I just... well, nice drive, not so busy... Get out of the office for a while."

René was still feeling somewhat 'elevated' and felt he could use some air. Here was a great excuse to get out of the building for a while, cool off a bit. He glanced at his watch.

"Why don't we go have lunch together? Place just across the street. Nice to meet the face behind the voice."

"Sure, but don't I have to see the shipment loaded, fill the papers out?"

Yes, the customer should be overseeing loading the shipment, checking the manifest and signing off, but as Rocco had never been here before he didn't know what normal procedure looked like.

"No sweat. Gimme your keys and I'll get the boys to back in, load you up. Here, just put your John Henry there." He took the keys and handed Rocco the form. A quick signature and the job was done. René took the truck keys and form and was back in a few minutes with one arm already in his jacket.

As they headed out of the complex and across the road René said, "Another shipment, just like yours; guys are coming by this afternoon. Catesby. Know them?"

"Sure. Just across town." Julia's face lanced briefly though his mind, but he pushed her image away.

As it turned out, the Catesby truck would only arrive at nearly 5:00, and René's attention would again be less than stellar for the second time that day.

Over their sandwiches the conversation naturally turned to dock security.

"Yeah, we had this big bust couple of months back. You probably heard about it?"

Rocco mumbled something noncommittal around his sandwich to the effect that he did recall hearing something.

"Two of our guys! Right here in this office! They were takin' big bucks—I mean *really* big bucks—for turning a blind eye. Shipments from Colombia. Cocaine!"

"No! Is that right?" Maybe we could talk about the weather, or the Habs' chances at the Stanley Cup, or... anything...

"Yeah. *Ex*-employees now, of course. Be doing time soon. Well, the management was really embarrassed; not every day that kind of thing happens right under their noses. Couldn't happen now of course."

Rocco nearly swallowed a whole dill pickle and had to pause and take stock, chewing violently and swallowing in small doses. He took a good few swigs of coffee.

"Couldn't happen?" he asked in a still slightly strangled voice as his colour returned to normal.

"Everyone in the place, front office help right up to the top bosses, have to get a police check. Really rigorous. And they have drug tests for the employees too. Sniffer dogs even, 'specially when something suspicious comes through."

"Nothing suspicious about fireworks!" Rocco hoped his jovial laugh didn't sound as brittle and artificial as he thought it did.

"No, fireworks are just fine. No sweat."

They finished their lunch and returned to the building.

Rocco drove the shipment to East Gladstone and backed the truck into the loading bay. He called Len and asked him to get the forklift and unload the pallet of boxes onto the loading dock. He was tired and keyed up, knowing there was still a busy evening ahead of him. He went through to the front of the building, shut down his office and headed home.

✩☆✩

"Sorry Mama," Rocco said to his mother as he finished dessert. "Gotta get back to the shop, finish off a few things."

"It's so frequent these days," she complained. "Know what? Nonno thinks you're seeing somebody but we wouldn't approve."

"Well, I'm not!" His laugh was utterly empty of humour. I wish, he thought, with a horrible pang. "He knows as well as I do how much work the job takes."

"He told me when he dropped in to see you that evening, you were making a shell..."

"So?"

"Well, I mean, that's not really essential, is it? Not like going over the books, or filling orders and so on."

Rocco was flustered. He resented the probing, even though it was well meant. "Mama," he prevaricated, "just that one evening I was enjoying myself, okay? Usually it's all work. Just caught me at that moment, that's all."

She nodded, sensing in his tone some sort of concealment but not wishing to force the issue. "Sure, but just take it easy all right?"

"Course I will." And he was out of the door and round to the parking space.

My God, he thought to himself as he drove, they think I'm seeing someone. There's only one someone I'd die to see, but we never talk now, never... The memory of her; her face, her body, all their words and touches, ripped at him. Seeing someone! No, I'm not. And even if I was, you'd disapprove. What a miserable mess.

He parked his car alongside the building and keyed in the security code at the door. Once inside he went straight to the loading dock where the shipment of boxes was sitting on its wooden pallet. This was odd; he thought he'd ordered more than this, and here was a box of eight 5″ Whistles, which he knew he hadn't ordered.

Oh *shit!* Oh shit, oh shit, oh shit! Don't let this be happening. *Please!*

Okay, he told himself, keep calm. He breathed slowly and regularly for half a minute. Now, the latest shipment of nose candy was concealed in 8″ Serpent shells, and here was a box of four. He pried the lid off, pulled aside the tissue paper wrapping, and confirmed his most horrible suspicion; there were no characteristic bands of tape. The shipments had been switched in Montreal! The dope could only be in Catesby's warehouse, and they had probably all gone home.

He hurried off to his office, booted up the computer—drumming his fingers while goddamned Windows twittered and farted through its routines—and went to his address book. He checked the number, rapidly dialed Catesby's business line, and got the insincere voicemail mechanical woman who said to leave a message or call back in business hours, which were...

Shit!

He'd have to wait until the morning. He couldn't dream of calling Julia. She would suspect there's something shitty going on, probably already does, and this would for sure raise a red flag. Christ, she'd think he was messing around again! Well, dear Uncle Chuck was just going to have to wait.

Rocco knew he'd have to show up at the rendezvous, with or without the stuff, but there would be a little explaining to do. He phoned.

"Problem." One word. Hopefully, the right word. The usual strings of numbers came back. When he entered them into his Garmin he got a location on Highway 12, away out of town to the west.

Rocco closed up the building, jumped into the old Corolla and headed out to the roadside restaurant shown on the map. Uncle Chuck was already there, sipping a coffee and wincing. Rocco's face betrayed everything.

"What? You didn't get the stuff. Why?"

"It's... I've... Look, there's been a delay..."

"Delay? What sort of delay?" There was menace in the clipped words and those awful eyes.

"The... the shipments got confused at the docks. We got theirs, and they got ours."

"They? They who?"

"Catesby's. In town."

"Catesby's in town," he mimicked. "You fucking moron!"

"It wasn't my fault, for Christ's sake! That's how the shipment came in!" The last thing he was going to do was reveal that he had collected it personally. "I can get the stuff tomorrow, as soon as they're open."

"You better. I better have that stuff in my hands tomorrow. *Capiche*?"

"Of course, no problem. I'll get the stuff for you. Easy."

"'Cos you respect me far too much, right?"

"Course I respect you."

"Well, here's noos for you Rocco. I'm not looking for your respect. Okay? What I want from you is fear. So, if you're fuckin' with me..."

"I'm not! Honest! Honest!"

"Okay. Call me tomorrow. *One* fucking word, 'kay? And this time make it a happy word."

Rocco got very little sleep that night, but before he went up to his apartment he was accosted in the hall and grilled, in the gentlest possible way, by his mother, who was continually worried about his health. She was telling him (again) that he was working too hard, and he was telling her (again) that he didn't have a choice. And, no, it wasn't some woman...

All through the night Mama and an Uncle Chuck who also resembled Julia's dad nagged him incessantly in his dreams, dangling women's underclothing and Ziploc baggies full of crackling stars and whistles just out of his reach, then jerking them back teasingly when he grabbed for them. When he awoke next morning it was to the wafting smell of waffles, and it was with great effort of will that he didn't throw up prior to, during and after their unwanted presence in his life.

He kissed his mother stickily on the cheek, waved at Nonno still working on the steaming pile before him, and headed off to the facility.

"Hi. Could I speak to your manager please? It's about a shipment that's got confused. Yes. Thanks." Rocco waited tensely in his office chair with the phone on his ear, listening to the thump-bump of his own heart.

"Alfred Catesby here. What can I do for you?"

"Hi, this is Rocco Pastorelli. We've had a confusion of shipments at the docks."

"Confusion?" The tone was noticeably cooler.

"Yes, we got yours and you got ours."

"What? How did that happen? Maybe your bloody driver can't read."

"Or your driver..." put in Rocco tentatively.

"Hmm. Okay, let me check into it and I'll call you back."

Alfred was annoyed and suspicious. Sure enough, when he checked in the loading bay the consignment was not theirs but, more to the point, how the hell did Pastorelli know about the deal with Colombia? Who the hell had spilt the beans? Then again, he considered, how long could it be before the community found out anyway? The suppliers were internationally known and openly selling their wares. Well, it had been good while it lasted, but he was still peeved.

Before the brusque Mr Catesby hung up, Rocco was all for forcing the issue, and was about to say that he was willing to bring a truck round right now. The abrupt hang-up meant there was nothing for it but to wait through another agonizing morning that lasted for eternity, much of which was spent praying for the call.

He grabbed the receiver on the first ring. "Café Mocambo," and a dead line. Oh, God, another gut-dissolving meeting. The rendezvous wasn't far so he left the office immediately and walked there. Uncle Chuck was waiting outside the café and seeing Rocco approaching he motioned him over to the parking lot beside the building.

"Just kinda wondering how you're coming along with unpacking that little shipment of ours? No problems I hope." The charming, singsong voice belied the threat behind the words. He crowded Rocco against a wall, not touching him but just making the space between them uncomfortably close.

"I'm working on it," he replied in a strangled voice. "I told you. Gimme time!"

"Getting a little tight in the old time-frame department, if you get my drift." It was uncanny how that gentle, pleasant voice could exude so much menace.

"I'll call as soon as I can."

"Oh, goody."

And he walked off to his parked Harley.

⁺✩ ⭐ ✩⁺

Alfred Catesby strode into the staging area, scanned the shelves, and spotted Mike down at the far end of the row.

"Mike," he called, "there's been a mix-up with Pastorelli. Where's the shipment that came in yesterday?"

Alfred noticed the somewhat sheepish look on the man's face, and the way he dithered a little and looked anywhere but at the boss.

"What is it?"

"Well, we were in a big rush to put together the show for Sault Ste Marie. Stowed the whole lot in the truck this afternoon."

The Sault Ste Marie show was an important event at the western end of their bailiwick. There was a show there every August on the last weekend, and this year Catesby's had won the contract. Alfred was especially concerned that this gig would go well, and perhaps his concern had communicated itself to Mike.

"Yeah, sure, so what?"

"Well, I took a few boxes of eight-inch shells from yesterday's shipment to complete the order. Didn't check that it wasn't actually ours. Just assumed..."

"Damn it, man," replied Alfred in annoyance. "You should always take 'em from the stock in the magazine. Always. That way we keep the stuff moving. I know there's no shelf-life as such, but it just makes good common sense."

"I'm sorry. It's just that, here they were, and being pushed for time..."

"No problem." Alfred waved it off. "Just get over to the magazine and supplement Pastorelli's order from our stock. No need to unpack the truck. Didn't save yourself any time at all, did you, in the end?"

"True. Sorry about that. I'll get on it."

Mike called the magazine on his cellphone and asked Julia, who was working over there, to take five boxes of the correct shells from the stock in the magazine, add them to the Pastorelli order, then phone them and tell them to pick up the whole shipment. Julia got onto it right away, loading the crates into a cart and wheeling them over.

But she got Mike to call Pastorelli and tell them it was ready for collection.

☆ ☆ ★ ☆ ☆

For the second evening in a row Rocco was working late in the warehouse and opening boxes of aerial shells from Colombia. Earlier that afternoon the Pastorelli truck had been sent with the correct shipment to Catesby's, and had brought their own correct shipment back, so all was well with the world.

Now then, let's see, 8″ Serpent shells, and here was the correct box of four. His relief as he pried the lid off and pulled aside the brown paper wrapping was flung back in his face, transformed into heart-stopping horror.

No gummed tape bands! Oh... *shit*! O-o-o-oh...

He slumped down onto the floor beside the shipping pallet, his brain absolutely refusing to believe what his eyes told him.

Minutes passed before he could think clearly.

He leapt up from the floor and began ripping the tops off all the other boxes, swearing and crying as the awful truth hammered home. Then a huge wave of comprehension sent his endocrine system down yet another manic plunge to weightlessness.

That was it! *That was it*! The agent in Medellín had simply fouled up. There *was* no shipment this time. It was all a false alarm. The slamming horror in his mind was replaced with a blessed wash of relief that weakened his knees and almost cost him a taste of incontinence.

He rushed to his office as fast as he could, grabbed the phone and called Uncle Chuck.

"Okay, okay," he shouted into the phone, ignoring any kind of phone protocol. "I know exactly what's happened. The agent has fouled up ..."

The roar from the other end of the line caused more nerve impulses to fire off, so that the axons and dendrons intimately associated with the functions of sphincters again came into play with potentially embarrassing results.

"*Shut the fuck up!*" and a dead line. Minutes passed as he imagined the scene in the clubhouse; the fury, the composing of the codes, the fiddling with the GPS... The incoming text beep caused Rocco to fumble the phone.

Another goddamned Timmies on Highway 12, but this one so crowded with truckers and travelers and even a couple of cops that it was an impossible place to meet. Rocco scanned the tables in trepidation, saw no sign of his contact, and returned to his car to wait. Fear was grinding into him, and again he wondered if this continuing charade would eventually kill him long before he was either murdered by the Valkyries or caught by the police. Or before he offered himself up to the handcuffs and put an end to it all.

Uncle Chuck slid into the passenger seat wearing the most evil, furious face Rocco had ever seen. The close proximity was terrifying.

"The... the agent fouled up..." he began.

"*He told me TODAY the stuff was sent!*" He grabbed the collar of Rocco's jacket and shook him. "You are *so* fucking with me! Where is it? What have you done with it?" Anger was shredding Uncle Chuck's control.

"Maybe it's still in their magazine, and they've sent the wrong stuff. I dunno..."

"What fuckin' magazine?"

Rocco fought for breath, calming himself as best he could. "Look, what probably happened was, they took the stuff into their magazine–their storage area–and gave me the wrong stuff. So it's probably still in there. Or maybe it's still in the main building. The loading bay. They're the only places it could be..."

Where in Hell else?

"*ENOUGH! You're gonna get it right now, or you're dead! HEAR ME?*"

"But I..."

"*Dead!* One hour. That's what I'm giving you. *ONE. HOUR.*"

"But it's impossible..." Rocco's protest was cut off by another wrench at his jacket.

"Get your little chick to let you in! *Get her!* Get into that fuckin' building and *get my stuff!*"

He released his grip on the jacket, shoved Rocco from him, and swung out of the car. He leant back in, his face livid. "Meet me back here. One hour. With the stuff!"

He slammed the door, turned and strode across the parking lot to his bike.

Something finally broke in Rocco's mind. The tension of the police raids, the roadside stop, the skulking at night, the excuses, the threats, his broken love, and now the horror of the missing consignment, all came together in an overwhelming avalanche that clawed at the edges of his sanity.

The tipping point came with the knowledge that only through Julia could he get access to the shells, and that meant spilling out the whole foul tale and exposing her to terrible danger.

A horrible calmness settled over him, as if he was in an everything-absorbing bubble that insulated him from all life senses. He knew only that he had to get away.

He started the car, pulled out onto Highway 12 in a near coma, and headed north and west. He drove all night long. The bubble slowly melted as the small towns flitted by, leaving his mind in turmoil. He was miserable to the point of suicide and frightened to go home. Towards morning, somewhere along the northern shores of Georgian Bay, he was suddenly filled with an awful horror. He had driven off in a blind panic, concentrating only on his own safety, but Uncle Chuck threatened him often enough through his 'little chick', his 'little piece of nookie'. Julia *was* involved, whether he called on her help or not. What if she were in danger?

Now he was racked with guilt; he would never forgive himself if she came to harm. What a coward; oh, God what a coward! He had to call her; assure himself she was okay. Their relationship was wrecked, he knew that, and it could only end, and end painfully. But if she was safe, that's all that mattered.

He pulled in at a Tim Hortons somewhere along Highway 17, sharing the space with truckers, off-duty cops and the very few early travelers on the long drag between Ottawa and Sault Ste Marie. He asked for an English Breakfast tea; he couldn't bring himself to order a coffee.

He tapped out her number. It was just 7:00.

"Julia. Listen to me," he saw her behind his eyes, perhaps sitting up in the bed, perhaps at her breakfast table, head cocked sideways as she listened to him. "You're *safe*! Are you okay?"

"Of course I'm safe. What do you want?" She was still in bed, half asleep and somewhere between dreams and the real world.

"You're safe, you're safe! Oh, thank God! That's all that matters."

"Rocco, what the hell is this?" she asked as the world asserted itself. "Why are you calling me now? Why wouldn't I be safe? You're not... right... you're not..." Her voice broke into a sob.

"Look, look, I'll call again soon, okay?" and he hung up.

Yes, yes, she was safe! An immense relief flooded over Rocco and he slumped down in his chair, holding the edge of the table for support. As he recovered some of his composure he now began to see a way out of the mess. Julia was involved anyway, like it or not, so as a last resort, if she could get him into their magazine and help identify the shells, they might both be safe. He would persuade her to give him the shells, maybe promise to replace them with similar ones, and give them to Uncle Chuck.

She wouldn't have to know what had been going on; he sure as hell wouldn't tell her, that's for sure. Maybe he could tell her they were some kind of special shells he was developing? Thin, but maybe plausible. What's another bunch of evasions and lies and silences anyway? Their relationship was dead and she was much better off without him. Breaking with her this way felt better than spinning it out with more lies and deceit. It was not meant to be, and it had to be broken.

He would have to beg as if his life depended on it. Well, it did... And hers too...

With this new resolve, he picked up the phone again.

"Julia! You have to help me. *Please* help me."

"What have you done?" in a dull monotone. As she woke fully

she felt a sudden sinking because she knew the horrible secret that separated them was now on the cusp.

"Look, there's been some confusion and I've got the wrong aerial shells, and I'm thinking maybe they're still in your place..."

"*Are you out of your mind?* What is this?" She sat up, fully awake.

"I. Need. Those. Shells! *Please!*"

"What shells?" This was insane. What was behind all this mad raving?

"The ones," he spelled out slowly, forcing calm into every word, "that were on the pallet that came from the docks."

"We shipped them back to you."

"Not all of them! Some were missing!"

Then she remembered the ones she had brought over from the magazine. "Well, you're out of luck. They're on their way to..." No, she wasn't going to tell him; suddenly she didn't trust him. She was frightened, confused and angry, and then a wave of immense sadness crested in her heart. She flung the phone down and made to head for the bathroom, but before she had even got her legs over the edge of the bed the phone rang again.

"Please! *Please!* Where are they? Where are the shells that were in that consignment?"

Anger trumped the rest, and then she became suddenly suspicious. "What is this? Has your goddamned friend sabotaged another lot? Is that it? And you've suddenly got all moral? Or is it guilty?"

"No, no, no! It's not like that at all! Honest. You have to get those shells back. You *have* to!"

"Why then? Tell me why!"

"They're special shells I've been developing..." He knew the lie was implausible as soon as it was out of his mouth.

"Like hell they are! Think I'm a complete moron? *Tell me!*"

"I can't, I can't! Please trust me. *Please* Julia!"

She took a long deep breath, calming her nerves and trying to straighten out her mind. "Look Rocco," she told him, anger now tightly under control. "I just said, the shells are on their way to a gig, and by now Dad will have his cell turned off, so I couldn't contact him if I wanted to. Which I don't."

"*You can't call him?* Oh, Christ, why not?"

"Look," she explained tightly, "he's paranoid about electronics. Always turns off his phone. Always."

"Oh, *come on!* This isn't friggin' Afghanistan! Does he think the fucking Taliban are going to blow him up?"

"Rocco! Rocco!" she yelled into the phone, totally losing control. *"What in Christ is this all about?"*

"I've gotta see you. We've gotta talk." The line suddenly went faint and scratchy, then came back as a semi roared past on the highway outside his stopping place.

"Where are you?"

"Way the hell and gone. Near Massey, Espanola somewhere. We gotta talk."

She closed her eyes, sitting there on the side of the bed, her bladder by now pushing the agenda. Her anger melted into a salty, gravelly slush of deep sorrow.

"Okay. Let's talk." A great hole opened up in her heart and she cried inside for all they had lost; for all that seemed so perfect; for that little broken piece that would never, ever be mended again.

"You know the pavilion in the park?" he was saying.

"Of course I know the pavilion in the park!" she cried fighting tears and losing. "It's etched in my memory you insensitive bastard."

"Meet me there." He figured the driving time from where he was. "Two hours. No, no wait." He had second thoughts. "I'll pick you up at your apartment building. Stay indoors! Don't answer the door. Promise?"

"Stay in? What..."

"Don't answer the door! *Promise!*"

"Okay, okay." She shut the phone and there, on the edge of the bed, she started to cry in deep shuddering gasps, moving only when forced by hydraulic pressure to sit in the bathroom and relieve herself, sobbing still.

☆✩⭐✩☆

Uncle Chuck's anger from the night before was now thoroughly clamped down. He had been livid with rage when Rocco hadn't shown up with the goods after an hour, and furious with himself for trusting the little shit. He'd waited nearly two hours before realizing the obvious; the bastard had done a bunk. He should have thought of this, and had the boys tail him. Obvious! And now he had slipped away. Still, with little Julia available there were all kinds of pressure points, especially as the stuff was stashed in her storage.

He began right away by posting guys on Hogs all over town to keep an eye out for Rocco. And he had another gang member watch over Catesby's, reporting any kind of activity, and especially when Rocco's little piece showed up for work in the morning. Another guy was busy finding out where she lived.

Uncle Chuck was lounging in his office at nine that morning talking to two of his best henchmen, Hefty Beale and Sludge McCracken, and showing every evidence of control and *sang froid*.

"Well, the bastard can't have disappeared for good," he said. "He'll have to turn up soon, 'specially if his chick's still in town. Billy-Bob just called. She hasn't showed up for work yet."

"Found out where she lives?" asked Sludge.

"Not yet, but we're on it. But I'm betting when the little shithead shows up he'll lead us right to her."

"Bin gone all night," observed Hefty. "Probberly be back soon's he's cooled off."

"Yeah," came a rumble from Sludge's huge frame. "The boys are keeping an eye on all his hang-outs. We'll get him."

"Okay! We wait." Uncle Chuck held the latest phone in his hand. "The guys are posted, in constant contact with me, so it's just a matter of time. I want my fuckin' dope and I'll kill that little bastard and his bit of nookie as well to get it."

That stupid, useless Pastorelli was driving him nuts. What a goddamned fuck-up of a human being. Should never have used the pathetic tool. He thought again of last night and again the fury rose. But anger was Uncle Chuck's worst enemy; he had to keep it under control always, or it would swiftly derail reason. His successes had all depended upon controlling the raging demon deep inside, harnessing its awful power and turning it into a cold, clinical weapon.

☆✮⭐✮☆

Rocco turned off the phone, half finished his cold tea and made to hit Highway 17 east. The starter motor turned, but not a kick from the engine. Oh for *Christ's sake*, not now! No amount of cranking made any difference, and the battery wasn't going to take much more of it. Shit, shit, shit! He got out, opened the hood and jiggled with all those things that people jiggle with when they don't have a clue what's wrong. A huge biker approached sending a momentary shockwave of looseness to his descending colon, but the man was anonymous and benign.

"Could be yer electrics," observed Charley Soames the bike tourist. "Check yer HT leads and coil. Course, car as old as this, could be anythin', eh?"

Thanking him profusely for his help, Rocco confined his jiggling to more defined areas. The engine didn't respond, while the battery slid into senility. Oh, well, thank God for CAA. Rocco had the roadside help number of the Canadian Automobile Association on the thin plastic card they give you.

"Where?" said the human voice once he had negotiated the voicemail tree, chewing the while at his nails in frenzy. "Oh, yeah, that's a long way out of town. Be a while. Hang in there."

His two imaginary graph lines of the Corolla's upkeep and the cost of new wheels were perilously close to intersecting. He pulled out his phone again.

"Julia! My car's broken down. I'll be a while longer. I'll call. *Stay indoors!* Don't answer the door. Promise?"

"I can't stay indoors all day! *I can't!* What is this? *Please!*" But he was gone.

He pulled up alongside her building late in the afternoon, a Mopar ignition coil the only brand new component of his entire vehicle. She had been standing at her window for what seemed like hours, so when she saw his car pull up it was with mingled fear and relief. She ran down the stairs and out of the door.

"Jump in! Quick!" and he was moving before she'd pulled the door shut. "Got to get you away from here."

"What's this all about?" she yelled at him. "What the hell is this all about?"

"Look, those shells. We've got to get them back. It's our only hope. Where are they heading?" He was staring straight ahead, concentrating on the road.

"Sault Ste Marie, but *why?*"

"*The Soo!*" he yelled. "For Christ's sake! I was just goddamned there practically! I could've... What the hell's he going there for?"

He swerved momentarily as he saw a motorcycle at an intersection, rolled briefly onto the hard shoulder, then regained control.

"What do you care? Why? You *have* done something, haven't you?" She was teetering between anger, fear and incomprehension.

"No, no... yes... Oh, shit, we're dead..."

He drove fast, head swiveling, eyes scanning the road with

frequent glances in the rearview mirror.

Before she could get anything more out of him he'd pulled up in the parking lot at the base of the knoll and was hurrying up the slope to the pagoda. She caught up with him halfway, grabbed his sleeve in fury and pulled him round to face her. She was as close as she had ever been to hitting another human being, and it frightened her.

As his headlong rush was arrested, his whole demeanour changed. The tension poured almost visibly out of his body; he hung his head, shoulders slumped. "I have to tell you everything. Everything." He turned from her and walked slowly up to the pagoda. "We're done; I'm done. Sit and I'll tell you the whole thing. You deserve..." He choked up and tears appeared in his eyes.

They sat again at a chained-down cast iron table with a smeared stone top, while above them the barn swallows loved and bred and died. With his hands over his face, in a low voice, he began to tell her the whole story. While he spoke she sat in mute stillness, her eyes focused upon his hands, until a welling of horror made her leap up and cry out.

"*Cocaine!* No, no!" She stood over him yelling into the face behind the hands. "Not *coke!* How could you? *How could you?*"

"What could I do? What could I do?" he implored her.

"Go the police, of course! Are you *insane?*" She had known in her heart that he was enmeshed in something criminal, but this was more horrible than anything she had imagined. "You... you..."

"I couldn't!" he shouted standing to face her. "I couldn't! *They would have killed you!*"

The air suddenly closed down on her, squeezing her heart, the world became tiny and remote, and a rush to her head made her sit abruptly. "What... what..." she could hardly breathe. "Kill...?"

"He said," Rocco replied slowly, "that if I did anything, anything at all, he would kill you. Not me. You."

She put her hands over her face and rocked from side to side. "What did he say?" she whispered. "About me?"

"He said... he said he wouldn't dream of hurting me... I was too useful..." He looked over at her momentarily then closed his eyes, pressing his chin to his chest, shoulders raised.

"And...?"

"But that chick of yours... That's a different story."

"This is horrible. Oh, God, I can't believe this..." She looked up at him, her eyes imploring him to say it was all untrue.

"So, he threatened," he continued, looking briefly into eyes that were streaming with tears, then sat and lowered his head again, "and... I couldn't... he... I was so frightened for you."

She sat quietly for a long time, then nodded slowly. "Threats against me... money for your company... grandfather happy... Oh, shit, Rocco, I can see how it all must have hung together."

Then, in a terrible instant, she brightened far too quickly.

"So now," she cried in a high, brittle voice, "Uncle Chuck's coke is about to be blown high into the sky by my Dad? My Dad!" Suddenly she was laughing, laughing desperately, gasping for breath. "My Dad... Coke... Oh no, oh no, oh no! You don't *know* him! Oh Jesus, Jesus, *Jesus*..."

The laughter became harsher and interspersed with sobs, and soon she was weeping uncontrollably. He came round to her side of the table and pulled up a chair, taking her in his arms. He tried his best to soothe, and presently the harsh weeping passed into soft sobs, muffled against his damp shoulder. He held her so long it was almost as if she had fallen asleep.

"Oh, God, Rocco," she sighed from his shoulder, "what are we going to do? What *are* we going to do?"

"We...?"

"Yes, of course, we!" She looked up at him, her face a mess. "I love you, you stupid fool. That can't change." I love you, she thought, but I hate you too. How can that be? No, I don't hate you; maybe I hate myself for being so stupid as to fall in love with you. No, that's not it either. I love you and I'm going down into ruin and damnation because of it. But I will always love you...

"I don't deserve it. Your love... I've landed myself in the worst shit, and there's no way out. I can't drag you into it. I just can't!"

"Whether you want to or not..."

"It's out of my hands, isn't it?"

She nodded; no words. They sat, arms around each other, while the swallows in the beams plied their tiny lives.

"Look," she cried, squeezing his hands painfully. "Look, we've got to go to the police. It's the only thing left."

"No proof. Nothing to show. And I took their money. Forensic audit and I'm dead in the water."

"Surely you can get some kind of clemency. You were under threat? Blackmail?"

"It'd kill Nonno. Kill him. The shame. And Mama..."

"My Dad... Oh, shit. I can't imagine... And Mum... It's her profession; the fall-out. She deals with them every day, the addicts!" She buried her face in her hands and started to sob again.

A motorcycle blattered past on the road below, appearing to slow down as the rider approached the path leading up to the knoll.

Rocco was on his feet. "Let's go! Down the other way!"

He scouted as carefully as he could as they returned to the car. He drove circumspectly out of town, watching his mirrors repeatedly. At one point he suddenly accelerated through a changing light, turned a corner fast and doubled back a little. Eventually he pulled up outside a nondescript motel somewhere beyond the marina.

The glass door swung shut behind them.

"We hide?" she asked as they checked in as man and wife, with not a scrap of luggage between them.

"For now, yes."

"And then...?"

He had no answer, but they both knew that in the morning they would walk quietly into the East Gladstone police station hand-in hand and begin the complete dissolution of everything in their lives that was good and fine and hopeful.

✩ ✩ ⭐ ✩ ✩

Catesby & Son's gigs were mostly in Eastern Ontario, so it was great to be this far west–right on Western Ontario's turf–and, who knows, a successful show in Sault Ste Marie could lead to huge expansion. It all depended on how well the show came off. His father and Julia had stayed home, so Alfred and Mike were running the show. Alfred was unusually demanding of Mike, checking and double-checking the installations, and running and rerunning the Pyrodigital computer programs. One nagging worry he could do nothing about was the dud shells they had fired in Gwillimbury. He wondered again about Julia's insistence that this was a one-off issue, and her obvious embarrassment. Or did he imagine that? How could she, he reflected, be so damned sure? In truth, he told himself, he had been on edge during all their previous gigs, but nothing had gone wrong in any way. He hoped he wasn't just being a bit paranoid because this particular show was so critical.

Another nagging nuisance was those bloody protesters. They kept showing up with their placards and banners and bloody loudhailers, not that it made a damned bit of difference. As soon as the show started they were totally drowned out and, anyway, how could an illiterate voice on a megaphone compete with the best pyrotechnics in the province? Stupid bastards should change their tactics.

All was set, all was wired, all was well, long before the sun bit the hills in back of the St Mary's River. The time you set off the first aerial announcement was very important; too early and there would be too much light, too late and your audience would get restive. The actual launch time depended upon latitude and date, of course, but longitude as well; where you were in your particular time zone. Practically, what you did was tell the client the show would go at 'dusk', and then apply the old firework-man's wetted finger. This night Alfred was much more impatient that usual, and all the operations of the orbs seemed frozen in their tracks.

Finally, with the light fading and Venus standing low in the west, he gave Mike the nod, and they were off! A 5" report was the customary opening act, drawing attention for miles around, right into northern Michigan.

The ground fireworks were gorgeous; the wheels and fountains in gold, silver and bronze, the candles firing multicoloured stars, whistles, serpents and reports. And all flawlessly executed.

But the aerial shells outshone them all.

There were quite a number of shells that failed to produce, which had Alfred in paroxysms of anger. He and Mike knew exactly what to expect of every charge that went into the tubes, so when an 8" shell appears to fail in altitude, gives a feeble burst, and only produces a scattering of garnitures, there is something really amiss. He managed to contain his anger at the factories in Medellín, his agent Gonçalves, and his folly in using the suspect shells, and could only watch in molar-grinding fury as one shell in 10 failed to meet expectations.

Not one person in the crowd was any the wiser. In fact, quite the reverse.

The half-strength burst charges of those duds proved enough to split the shells apart, shred the Ziploc baggies and scatter their contents broadcast, but were not so hot or prolonged as to denature significantly the larger part of the active ingredient.

Happy happenstance of meteorology caused the predicted wind to shift, drifting the smoke of the shells over the craning crowd. While the smoke stayed high, floating and dissipating with currents in the higher air, the heavier particulate matter from the duds drifted down the sky and impinged upon the same air that avid lungs were absorbing with their Oohs and Aahs.

The more the aerial show continued, the more profound was the collective aesthetic experience. As shell after shell lofted before them and burst in a sky, now transformed wondrously into the very vault of pure exquisite heaven, piercing blue, stabbing gold and sapphire and ruby, azure and impossible emerald–all the colours of the ridiculously fabulous East of the Arabian Nights and all the mad mythology of sun-shot stained glass, four-colour, glossy romance–lanced into the eyes, thrashing down optic nerves, spreading over the visual cortex, gripping it like a great golden-gloved fist and lighting its synapses in won'drous array. Thudding concussions ravished the ears, shaking *malleus*, *incus* and *stapes*, spiraling mightily within semi-circular canals, and ringing bronze-gonged and tympanic messages of auditory wonder across the receptive cerebrum, surpassing and transcending music, speech and thought.

Strangers fell into embraces, friends hugged friends; uncles, cousins, brothers and maiden aunts held hands in joy; there were kisses and fumbling, dancing and singing and cheering as the beneficent manna snowed down upon them.

The battery of thunderclaps that traditionally closed the show sent waves of intolerable joy though the crowd, so that whooping and laughing and joyful weeping accompanied them home as breath by breath the world as they usually knew it imposed itself again upon their rapidly normalizing brains.

Never before in the history of pyrotechnical exposition had a single firework display been so ecstatically received, or gained such rapturous approval. It was probably one of the more costly shows in history as well.

When Alfred heard the cheering and celebration from his upwind vantage point, saw in dim penumbra across the field the universal joy and dancing ecstasy, his apoplexy turned to perplexity.

Presently, one of the show's organizers approached the launching ramp in the sort of staggering run one would see of a seasoned inebriate who so often tripped but in years of hard imbibing had developed elaborate techniques to defy gravity.

"Never... never..." panted the puffing middle-aged man, gripping Alfred's hand and pumping his arm to shoulder dislocation and beyond, "...never seen anything... anything like it! So... so...

so glad we had you come... Eastern Ontario... long way..." pump, pump, pump, followed by an all-enveloping tobacco-faced hug and thundering charlie-horse pats on the back.

Alfred finally tore his damaged body away from this gladsome assault, thanked the man profusely for his sponsorship, and returned to help Mike dismantle the equipment as the client tottered joyfully away to spread his gospel news.

As he disconnected wires, stowed electronics away and assisted with the after-show inspection, Alfred mused long and hard.

☆☆ ☆ ☆☆

Sue Tort and Terry O'Weight were trying one last demonstration here in Sault Ste Marie. Their sabotage attempt had been an utter failure, and while a bold attempt to steal some fireworks was on the cards, Sue felt that the time was not yet ripe. Steve Bacon was primed, but was Sue ready to go yet?

Here in Sault Ste Marie Sue's decision would be made.

They began their routine of marching in front of the waiting crowd with banners and megaphones, shoving into unwilling hands the illiterate leaflets that Sue had had printed on neon yellow paper back at the Staples in East Gladstone. Right from the get-go it was obviously going to be another complete frost. For sure, they had caught the crowd's interest at the beginning when there was no distraction except impatient kids asking over and over again when it was going to start. Some lively souls in the crowd started razzing the protesters, but they got as good as they gave, and for a while it looked to become ugly. Then, when the first bombshell thudded into the air and split the sky, all eyes went to the heavens and soon thereafter came the ecstatic descent of heavenly wellbeing.

The wonder in the air she breathed pushed the *Yes, Yes, Yes* button repeatedly in Sue Tort's brain. Hurling down placard and megaphone with mania in her eyes, and hugging an astonished and amazingly horny Terry O'Weight around his imposing middle, she yelled tobacco and spittle into his face.

"We'll do it! We'll do it! I'm gettin' on to Steve Bacon! We're gonna steal the show! Now! Tonight, while the silly buggers are *here!*"

She rushed off to the Rabbit, Terry trailing in wonder, and they headed back home as fast as their poor little bunny could hop. He drove, she phoned.

She called Steve's cell and got voicemail. Shit! "Steve! Call me back. Now!"

The phone rang after a few minutes. "Sorry. Was in the shitter. Whaddaya want?"

"Lissen Steve, lissen. You gotta go to that all-night truck rennal place downtown—Hertz, eh?—an' get us a one-tonner, okay? Then meet us at the corner of Main and Albert. Two hours. Got it? You know what for. Ha, ha!"

Her manic, brittle laughter drove Steve exulting to the job. He had been lying low, fearing for his life, staying at home and annoying the bejeezers out of his mother. She hated having him underfoot because it reminded her that Harry would be out soon, loafing around and energetically not looking for work. The only real talent Harry had was for moving stuff that wasn't his along to people who didn't know it wasn't his. One of them loafing around the apartment was enough.

Steve didn't know it, but he had also been pissing off the police as well, because they had finally got approval to listen in on his cell traffic, outgoing calls only, of which there had been nothing of any consequence. Tonight might be some reward for all their hitherto wasted time.

Another B and E, thought Steve. It's gotta be that fireworks place! Another big charge coming up, and money with it. And a chance to forget for a while the fear of God that Hefty had laid on him. His skin started to get that hyper tingle, and shivers of pleasure ran to the base of his belly and tightened his bag. Bring on the Baconator!

Back in the Rabbit, hurtling down Highway 17, Terry O'Weight was hunched behind the wheel and driving like Juan Manuel Fangio on crack. He couldn't believe he could love fireworks even more than before. But he did...

☆✩⭐✩☆

Safe in the Lakeside Nook, Rocco and Julia looked around at their new home in despair. How long would they have to hole up here, and what could possibly be more horrible than this enforced exile? They lay down on the hard single beds and tried to think of any way out of this mess. More and more they knew that going to the police was the only answer, although it would bring disaster to both their families. They knew they ought to talk it through, but there was a sense of timeless postponement. Until they heard definite word from Sault Ste Marie the future hung uncertain.

If Julia couldn't get to a show, she knew that either her father or grandfather would always call her and fill her in, so it was certain her father would call. But when? And until he called, the silent barrier between them would not be broken and the passage of time would assume a whole new boring meaning.

They had a half-hearted sandwich from a machine in the foyer, drank a couple of Cokes, and were halfway through their second rubbishy movie when Julia's phone rang. It was just before 11:00. She seized the phone and checked the display.

Dad. Here it comes...

"Dad! How did it go?"

"It was great. Just great..." She heard him pause as if wondering what to tell her. "Just great. Yeah... Never heard applause like it; cheering, singing, laughing. The client came up afterwards and couldn't say enough. Effusive doesn't begin to describe... But I don't know why in hell they were all so happy. Manic, they were. It was insane..."

Julia had a horrible sinking feeling. "So, they enjoyed the show and it went well?" was her lame response. This was going badly; she was fishing but scared her father would pick up on it.

"No, not well. There were some duds." Her heart contracted. "Well, not complete duds like at Gwillimbury, but half-assed, as if they hadn't put in enough charge or garnitures. I'm damned sure we're being ripped off."

"Ripped off?" she echoed, not knowing what else to say, heart a-patter.

"Yeah. And you were so sure it was a one-off, remember? Well, I've a good mind to open up a few, see just what we're getting."

"Open..." she almost squeaked.

"Or maybe the empties'll tell us something. Pick 'em up tomorrow during site check."

Oh, shit, this was getting complicated. Had all Rocco's loaded shells gone to the Soo? Or were there maybe some obviously tampered ones still in the magazine? Oh, shit...

"Anyway, we'll have to talk when I get ..."

She held the phone away from her ear and checked the screen. "Damn, lost the signal. Battery's dead. And I don't have my charger."

"Well? Well?" shouted Rocco who had only heard half the conversation. "What happened? What happened?"

"There were some duds," she said slowly, "but the crowd loved it..."

"Like *really* loved it?"

"Like totally ecstatic."

"O-o-o-oh shit..."

The news was out; now all was truly lost. The impasse that held them timeless and inert was broken. As she dropped the phone on the bed they came together in a long comforting embrace that both wished would never end. This brief time was all they had left.

✰ ✩ ✩ ✰

Back in the clubhouse that evening Uncle Chuck called an emergency meeting of all gang members except those who were still out on patrol, roaming the town looking for Rocco and Julia. The gang members he had called parked their Harleys in the garage and came through to the clubhouse rec room. The dense air had a redolence of tobacco, booze, sweat, gasoline and dirty leather.

All afternoon and into the evening Uncle Chuck had been on his phones. The watchers had drawn an absolute blank until a few hours ago when the couple were sighted leaving the pagoda in the park. Then, to his writhing, gut-twisting fury they had lost the fuckers.

He swung his chair round to face his confederates. He was in a towering rage but he tried to keep it in check, not let the gang members see below the skin, behind the eyes. Anger, his enemy, must be turned to ice.

"None of you! Not *one* of you managed to follow the little bastard! Jesus shit! What in Christ went wrong?"

"I got hit with a red light," moaned one of the bikers, a wiry little bastard with a huge scar down one cheek.

"Red light my naked ass! You spot the little shit and his chick and you stop for a goddamned red light? Are you out of your fuckin' mind?"

"I know, I shoulda..."

"Shoulda, coulda, woulda, *shit!* Where are they? Where the *fuck* are they?"

"The boys were out cruising all day..."

"I know they were out cruising all day, you fuckhead! I sent them. What kinda car's he got?"

"Beat-up Toyota Corolla," piped up a narrow-faced cock-sucker with a squint. "Dark red."

Uncle Chuck simmered down to about four on an electric stovetop and willed himself to calm and constructive thought. He had nearly had them both! The chick Julia would have been the perfect entrée to the Catesby magazine. Nothing a little simple persuasion couldn't accomplish. And she looked like a tasty little bombshell, too. But there was no question; he was running out of time. He had to find that shipment now, not when his useless Hog riders eventually ran down the runaways. Christ, they could be anywhere in the province by now!

"Where did you lose 'em?"

"Heading down Edgeware, after the stop light just before the liberry."

"Edgeware?" He quickly pulled up the street map on his tablet. "That doesn't go anywhere. Opposite way from Highway 11. You! Get the fuck out there again and check every hotel, motel, flophouse, whatever down that way. Look for the car. Go!"

The wiry little bastard strode out of the door and leaped onto his bike. He would visit every goddamned flophouse in the area—case parking lots, check registries, threaten clerks—to get himself back into the boss's good books.

Uncle Chuck made a few quick calls, concentrating his riders in the Edgeware sector and telling them what to look for.

Now, he thought, calm, clear thinking, planning...

"All right," he eyed the bikers, steepling his fingers. "The stuff got switched. Either the little bastard pulled one over on us, or he was telling the truth and just bein' stupid."

"Stupid once," observed Hefty. "But twice? That strains my credulity."

"Strains your credulity? You just read a book or something?"

"See, the stuff gets switched once," continued Hefty, not at all set back by questions of his literary prowess. "Can happen. So then he has the right stuff sent back, only it isn't. Screwed up twice. Still just stupid?"

"Yeah. Gotta be. Wherever he is, he's scared shitless. I don't think he has the balls to screw around with us, so the stuff must've got switched again, and it's still in the Catesby buildings. Can't be anywhere else. That's not 'duplicity'," he mimicked. "What I smell is fear and cock-up."

There was a long silence as Uncle Chuck eyed the room. There was no use hoping they'd find Pastorelli any time soon—dodging down Edgeware could have been a false scent—so he needed to act now. He stared at each of them in turn, assessing who of the assembled gang were his best assets. He needed quick thinking and steady nerves for what he was planning.

"I think, my friends, we gonna have to liberate the dope ourselves. It's mine and I want it back!" With the last sentence his voice rose in anger.

He was beginning to lose it again but it was mostly below the seething surface—never let your confederates read you—so he calmed the fury behind his eyes.

"Listen Hefty. That little shit Steve Bacon knows his way into their outfit. How about I grant him a reprieve from his death sentence if he does us a little favour?"

Hefty nodded, unable to speak. He had been in a dead funk about his friend, scared beyond thought that Uncle Chuck would carry through the threat. He had seen the bodies, seen the evil that stopped at nothing, seen the utter contempt for human life. There wasn't much Hefty Beale hadn't done in a long life of crime, but a line was being drawn. Enforcing was one thing; killing was another. If he could see Steve back in favour, or at least out of danger, he would be able to stomach all those other things he had been more than willing to do.

"Get him. Talk to him. Pat his fucking head. Tell him what we want. And we need it now! Here's the plan: he gets in and opens the place up. Both friggin' buildings. He rents a truck and fills it with everything that looks like our stuff. *Everything*. Then he brings it back here. Got it?"

Bacon Enter might be a complete out-of-control whacko, but right now he had a very good use for him. And, of course, he was disposable. Never did forgive him for lifting that weed in Hearst; think you can piss me off and get away with it?

Beale got his phone out, put it on speaker and dialed Bacon's cell. "Steve, man. Need your help." Uncle Chuck's eyes narrowed at the familiarity.

Hefty was halfway through explaining what they wanted when there was a sound of gargling at the other end; Steve was whooping up half the beer he had been downing before heading out to pick up the rental truck. What in Christ's name was going on here? Twice in one night? Steve thought quickly between coughs; this sounded like a reprieve. If he could pull this off he might get back in favour with the gang. Better than skulking, hiding, wondering. Better than a contract on your head.

"Hate to tell you this," he replied when he had recovered his breath, "but I'm already contracted for the same job."

"What are you talking about? You nuts?"

"Nope. Fireworks protesters are planning to steal a shit-load of fireworks so's to screw up the shows. Tonight."

Uncle Chuck leaped out of his chair in fury, strode over to Hefty, and was about to grab the phone out of his hand when he stopped, frozen. He pushed the fury down hard, thinking quickly. Bacon would have to break in, open the loading bay doors, and then close down and lock up afterwards. Perfect! Abso-fuckin'-lutely perfect!

"Okay, little Stevie Wonder," he said in his most charming voice, taking the phone off Hefty and clicking speaker off. "Here's how it goes. You listening...? Good. Where are you getting the truck from...? Okay. Slight change of plans, Hefty'll meet you there. Yeah, soon as you can... Get on it!"

Steve pocketed his phone, wiped his mouth and opened the door. Two calls in one night for the same job? What the...? He started walking the six blocks to Hertz wondering what the hell was going on. Don't get it; Rocco was moving the dope through his outfit, so how come the Valkyries were so interested in Catesby's all of a sudden? Doesn't make any sense at all...

Uncle Chuck tossed the phone back to Hefty and began pacing the room, all action and with an evil glint in his eye.

"Hefty, get your ass over to Hertz. I want all the stuff made in Colombia. All of it! Tell Bacon and those other buggers. All the stuff from Colombia. Tell 'em you're Bacon's assistant; you come with the contract. Go!"

Uncle Chuck grinned a huge grin as he ran the scenario through his mind. Anger pressed down, red rage turned to blue ice. Control! No siree, Charles 'Uncle Chuck' Bourassa does not let his anger control his reason.

☆ ✦ ☆

Sue and Terry roared through the night, east down Highway 17 in an ecstasy of haste and anticipation. As small sleeping towns flashed past the car windows, Sue's chemically induced call to action gradually metabolized into an iron certainty that this was the way it was supposed to be. As the cocaine high slid away it was replaced by a high of equal proportions; a high generated by

185

the knowledge that this was what she had been put on Earth to do. There were absolutely no second thoughts about the manic scheme she had hatched up. Once set on this course, once the machinery was in motion, to abort it for any reason would plunge her into a monumental depression. Through it and out to the other side was the only way now.

And, aside from any gratification that Sue might experience, this was as sure as hell what the sponsors wanted. They paid the bucks for mayhem, and that's exactly what they were gonna get.

In just under two hours the Rabbit hit East Gladstone. They dumped the car in the East Gladstone Public Library parking lot and waited on the corner of Main and Albert.

☆✫⭐✫☆

Hefty rode the Hog over to the downtown truck rental outfit and parked inconspicuously in the front lot between two cube vans. He'd got there early so he wandered over to the office window and peered in. The lone clerk on the night shift was lounging oblivious over the counter, reading a girlie magazine and picking his nose. Every so often, as a page turned, Hefty caught a flash of tits and pudenda. He ambled back and sat sideways on the bike, unseen through the window. After several minutes he spotted Steve hurrying along and got up to meet him 100 yards down the street.

"Hey," he greeted Steve, a little diffidently as he remembered their last meeting.

"Great. What's up?"

"Basic'ly, your lot are planning to steal a shit load of fireworks, right?" Steve nodded. "But our coke is in 'em, so Uncle Chuck wants us to go along with it."

"Holy shit! *In* the fireworks! If they only knew!"

"Yeah, and the big thing, bro, is that you're off the hook. Least, Uncle Chuck needs you, and that's all good."

"So, we go along with them. Then what?" Steve's allegiance to the firework activists had quickly crumbled under the promise of something better.

"Didn't say, but I guess they intercept the truck or somethin'."

"How do we know which ones have got the dope in 'em?"

"Simple. We liberate anything made in Colombia. The lot. It's printed on the outside of the crates, remember?"

"Don't I? That's what started this whole caper." They both

laughed, perhaps a little self-consciously.

The friends reached the truck rental office and while Steve went in to make the booking and get the key, Hefty lounged on the Hog, watching the flurry through the window as the girlie magazine vanished below the counter to be replaced by a sheaf of rental contracts.

"I'll foller yer," said Hefty as Steve emerged. "I'll need me wheels for what's next."

Steve Bacon swung into the cab, started the engine and gently backed out of the lot. He drove up Main Street in the direction of Catesby's with the Harley mumbling along behind him. At the corner of Main and Albert Steve spotted Sue Tort and Terry O'Weight and pulled over to let them in. Hefty passed the truck and continued to Upper Main Street. Terry was his usual stoic self–whatever it was in Sault Ste Marie had worn off–but Sue was about as hopped up as a human being can be, flirting just the conscious side of cardiac arrest or brain aneurism.

☆✫⭐✫☆

Earlier that evening the Detective Inspector CID for East Gladstone had been watching *Wheel of Fortune* with his wife in the den, but not really concentrating on any of the yelling inanities. They both enjoyed solving the phrases but the brainless presentation made them cringe. Why do they have to shout out the letters so loud, and what's with the clapping? And why are they all so bloody fat?

"And who's with you tonight?" burbled the box.

"My fabulous, gorgeous wife Priscilla and my two mega-genius kids Chrystl and Fargo and my ossome brother-in-law Dwane..." Click!

When not solving the phrases they muted the box and took up crossword puzzles or Sudokus, filling adverts and wasted air time with good quality mental exercise.

"What's up?" she asked, after muting the banalities on the flat screen TV yet again. "You're miles away."

"Oh, the usual bullshit," he replied, dragging his mind away from pointless speculation about clapping and shouting fat people that had briefly overlaid the continual nagging worry of his work. "I've bored you with it all before; too much red tape, too much process. The crooks always a step ahead. At least, the smart ones."

"You've got to focus more on your successes. Just count the number of times you've taken some crook out of circulation."

"But, you know what? Most of the stupid ones—the ones that get picked up dead easy—are totally addled on drugs or mentally ill. Oh, I can take 'em out of circulation with no problem. Only, the last place they should be is prison. But the smart ones, the real criminal minds, they work the system. They're the ones that slip away…"

"Tough on crime…" she said with a wry curl to her lip.

"Yup. Tough on poor bastards who can't break the cycle. More jails, punishing sentences, tighter parole. All of it guaranteed to keep them criminal for life."

"It's the cocaine thing, isn't it?"

"Course it is. Coke, meth, crack, ecstasy… We just can't keep up. And it's when you know who's running the stuff but you just can't get a handle on 'em. I don't know why it is, but they always seem to be prepared for us. One step ahead."

"How d'you mean?"

"We get up a warrant, do a surprise swoop, like on the biker clubhouse, and there they are, all goddamned smiles and clean as a whistle. I'd swear they've got an inside contact. But who?"

"Frustrating, I know, but keep positive, eh? Keep working for that big breakthrough. After all," she laughed, "we all need you happy around the house, don't we?" She patted her stomach. "Junior's going to want a nice calm daddy."

"Yeah," he smiled. "Sorry, it's just that some days you wonder…"

"Come sit beside me here." She shifted over on the chesterfield. "*Jeopardy's* on in a minute."

Both kids were out for the evening so there were no distractions and, for once, the house wasn't reverberating to electric guitar practice, vocalized pre-teen angst and the twittering and beeping of video games.

"Good idea. Nice to apply your brain to something straightforward and honest."

She clicked the sound back on as he sat beside her.

"…Thank you, Johnny, welcome everybody…"

There followed a quiet and peaceful evening… until about 10:00 when the call from Headquarters came in.

☆⋆ ☆ ⋆☆⋆

Fred Delios was watching some forgettable crap on TV with his wife when his phone rang. They were just about ready to turn the thing off and head upstairs for bed. It was the DI and he sounded wired to say the least.

"I'm heading down to the station. We've had word that the firework loonies are planning to rent a Hertz truck. Tonight!"

"Rent a truck? Why would..." The DS was mystified.

"To steal fireworks! What else would they be renting a truck for in the middle of the bloody night?"

"How do we know?" he asked. "Steve's cell?"

"Yup. Finally. After all our waiting."

"Stupid bastard. I'm almost disappointed in him."

"Save it. Okay, listen. Bacon's renting a van from Hertz. Now, we know there's a link between Bacon and the Valkyries through Beale, and there's a link between Bacon and Pastorelli. And, of course, Pastorelli is linked to the Valkyries, because you know, and I know, and we all know that the bugger's running dope. Meanwhile, Pastorelli has disappeared–didn't show for work– which means he's probably with the gang. Whether they do Catesby's or Pastorelli's is anyone's guess, but that's what's going down. So, whatever the hell is going on here, we follow them but we *do not* jump too soon! Get it?"

Holy Christ, thought Delios, how the hell can any mortal un-ravel this lot? I should be brushing my bloody teeth right now, not untangling skeins of some who-dunnit fantasy.

"Run that by me again, chief," he began, wondering if the chief had been snorting something himself, then thought better of it. "Wait, why don't I go down to Hertz and check the place out?"

"Okay, but don't be seen. That'll scare 'em off, and we need to catch them *after* they've done the job. *After*, okay? Now, those trucks have built-in GPS locators, so we can track them. But we need a warrant to get access. I'll be onto that as soon as I get to the station. Head downtown and hang around some distance away. I'll call you when we have the all-clear, then we'll meet there and shove the warrant at them. I want in on this one!"

"How long will this take?"

"How do I know? ASAP!" shouted the DI into the phone. "Unlike the bloody opposition, we have to play by the rules. Christ! How we catch *anybody*, I wanna know." The phone was dead in his hands.

"Sorry m'dear, but duty calls," said Fred as he hauled on his shoes and gave his wife a peck on the cheek. "Don't wait up."

From his vantage point across the road Delios saw Hefty Beale park and wait beside his bike. Then, to his great satisfaction, he watched Hefty go to meet Steve Bacon down the road, and walk with him back to Hertz. Bacon entered the office while Beale lounged on his bike. Links were forming in an intellectual game of cat and mouse. Bacon emerged with the keys, they exchanged a few words, and the truck and bike headed up the street.

"They've got the truck and they've headed up Main Street," reported Delios on his cellphone to the DI. "So it's gotta be Catesby's."

"Stick around. I'll be there as soon as I can," he replied. *"Don't make any moves!"*

The immense frustration of knowing that a crime was taking place at this very moment was driving the DI crazy, but he knew they absolutely must let the fish take the lure. Jump too soon and you catch the activists but miss the drug dealers. Jump too late...

He took a good deep breath as he put the phone down. We won't miss this time by God! It was time to initiate Project Bombshell.

☆ ☆ ☆

Sue Tort was displeased to see Steve's accomplice when the truck arrived at Catesby's, but there was nothing she could do about it. They parked round the back of the building; Steve slipped out to do his thing and Terry took the wheel. Steve was in heaven. It was just past 1:00 AM as Bacon Enter was once again cutting the wires to that motion detector on the Catesby window, with Hefty Beale watching him from the pavement below. It was *déjà vu.*

He finished his wiring, opened the window, wiggled in and slid down to the floor. Hefty scooted round to the loading bay to await the truck. Unlike last time, Steve would need to disarm the whole system so the loading bay door in this building could be raised without setting off the alarms. He also had to disarm the systems in the magazine. He hoped to God he could do it electronically from here, rather than doing another break-in to a building he didn't know.

Steve located the building security controls adjacent to the front desk, smiled in relief and satisfaction, and flipped the switches, rendering both buildings safe to enter. He passed quickly through the storage area to the rear loading bay and hit the button to raise the door, leaving the lights turned off. Terry beeped the truck back into the loading dock space, and Steve pressed the button to close the door. Hefty followed the truck into the loading dock as the door came down.

Steve switched on the lights as Sue and Terry jumped down from the cab. Any residual passion from Sue's apotheosis in Sault Ste Marie was now entirely replaced by pure adrenalin, endorphins and nicotine.

"Okay!" shouted Steve. "Here's the scoop. We got two buildings, but you can't take everything. Too much and it would take too long. Most stuff's too big and bulky anyhow."

He pointed to the racks containing huge wheels, sprays of candles with wooden bracing, and solid bricks of cardboard and gunpowder.

"Pick the aerial shells," he told them. "They're in boxes, easy to carry, and make the most impact in any show. Hefty and me'll show you which ones. Trust us. And remember: gloves everybody."

"Yeah," agreed Sue. "Aerial shells. Take that lot and any show is completely screwed. C'mon Terry!"

Steve's familiarity with the Catesby set-up from both his youthful employment and his previous B and E helped. There wasn't the usual stock in the staging facility as a show had just left and another was only just being assembled. There were many candles, wheels and set pieces, but few aerial fireworks. They grabbed the few Colombian shells identified by Steve. He killed the lights and hit the door button as O'Weight jumped into the truck cab.

"Okay, next building," yelled Steve at the near peak of his ecstasy. "There'll be lots more there. Leave the door, I'll get it later when I close down."

Steve sprinted across the asphalt to the magazine, pushed open the electronically-unlocked side entrance and pressed the button to raise the loading dock door, again leaving the lights off until the door was reclosed. Terry maneuvered the truck around to the door of the magazine, backed in, and the same routine followed.

This time there were many more products shipped from Cartagena, and they were all conveniently packed in boxes. With Steve and Hefty identifying, and the four of them lifting and lugging, in less than half an hour they had loaded every single aerial shell from Colombia they could find into the back of their rental truck.

Steve and Hefty both knew that hidden somewhere in this haul there was a fortune in cocaine.

Sue and Terry headed the truck out of the loading dock, while Steve closed the door from the inside and exited through the side entrance. As he was doing this, Hefty walked quickly back to the main building, stepped up to the loading bay floor and opened his phone.

"Okay," he reported on the phone to the biker clubhouse. "They're off. Heading downtown. Main Street. Want me to follow?"

By now Uncle Chuck was certain that Hefty Beale and Steve Bacon were closer friends than the big lug had let on; too close for safety. Shit, Hefty was probably the source of the leak, especially if he'd been drinking, which was always. Can't have my guys hanging around a little fink like that, not when there's so much at stake. So, Hefty's allegiance would have to be tested. Here Uncle Chuck's innate evil came searing out.

"No, Hefty, you stay back."

"What, stay here? Don't get it..." They had to lock up and get the hell out. Now! Somebody might sound the alarm; cops could show up any minute.

"You're taking care of little Steve first."

"What do you mean? Taking care..." He felt as if his heart had pushed up and was suddenly beating in his throat.

"Kill him."

"Kill...? Me?" He had beaten the living shit out of lot of people over the years. He was good at it, and that was his job. He was Uncle Chuck's favourite enforcer, and he took the job seriously. But nobody had ever *died* after his treatment. And he had never been *told* to kill... "You want me to..."

"Yup. And it's gotta look like an accident. Hit him, knock him out, make it look like he tripped off the loading dock."

"I... I... please Chuck, no! I can't do it! I can't!"

Uncle Chuck smiled. He loved to feel the fear of others, loved to feel the power; knew he had to test Beale really hard, just so he could imagine his agony with pleasure.

"Gotta make a choice. You doin' it or not?" Silence at the other end. "'Cos if you're not, it'll be your turn next. *Capiche?*" Click. Another one-use phone heading for the dump.

There are times when assets become liabilities.

Steve was stepping up into the loading dock as Hefty stuffed the phone in his pocket. His friend climbed the short ladder from road level up to the dock, and as he did so his back was turned briefly.

Hefty made his decision and moved swiftly towards him.

☆ ☆ ☆

Back at the clubhouse Uncle Chuck issued orders through yet another cellphone.

A block away from Catesby's two Hogs crackled into life, turned onto Upper Main Street and closed up on the truck. Sludge McCracken drove around the block, tooled his heavy unit out of a side street and pulled up in front of the truck. Terry slammed on the brakes while the other two Harleys swung in from either side. A passenger leapt off the rear seat of the bike on the driver's side, pulled open Terry's door and yelled, "Shove over!"

The passenger from the other flanking Hog did the same thing on the other side.

"What the fuck's going on here?" yelled Sue Tort, squashed on the bench seat between a huge death's head tattooed arm and shoulder and the sliding weight of O'Weight.

"We're taking a load off your mind," replied the fat, chain-festooned and studded specimen as he hauled the truck out onto Main Street and headed for the Valkyries' hideout. "You take the credit, we take the merchandise."

"This is our heist, not yours!" she shrieked. "Stop him Terry! Stop him!"

O'Weight wisely forbore taking any action while the truck was breaking every road ordinance in the province, and especially when he saw the roughly sawn end of what looked like a shotgun projecting from the region of Tattoo's midsection.

The truck pulled up smartly on the forecourt beside the clubhouse garage, led in echelon by three Harleys. The driver leaped out of the truck, ran round to the back and pulled on the roll-up door. The three riders ran the garage door up, parked their Hogs inside and began unloading the boxes of aerial shells.

"Quick! Quick!" yelled Uncle Chuck, emerging from the clubhouse. "Stack 'em in the back, an' you, you and you, grab tools off the bench and start tearing 'em apart. *I WANT MY DOPE!*"

Sue and Terry stayed in the truck cab, their action-high now segued into a rigid fear low, while the sawn-off piece pointed at them through the window. The bikers carried the boxes of shells into the garage, past the eight Harleys parked there, stacked them in the rear beside the workbench, and the destructive search began. As soon as the truck's cargo bay was emptied the big biker waved his hacksaw-modified firearm and yelled, "Now piss off!"

Off was the direction in which they pissed.

"Drive to our hang-out," yelled Sue as he pulled the truck off the forecourt and onto the road. "It's near here. Gotta think."

☆ ☆ ☆

"You know, tomorrow it all comes to an end?" Julia pulled away from his embrace. "You have no choice. You never did."

"I can give myself up. I can do that. They can do what they want to me, but not you. Not you..."

"You *have* to do it! You don't have a choice. And I will look after myself."

"The thought of them harming..."

"Stop it! You're trying to avoid the decision. You go, you tell them everything, and let the chips fall where they may."

"But what's gonna happen?" he cried as the tears started out. "I didn't... Why did it go this way? As if I wasn't trying all these years. It's so unfair!"

"*Que sera, sera*, sweetheart." Her heart hurt for his vulnerability. "We'll see it through." But he must see through my optimism, she thought, because here, tonight is where it all really comes to an end; the high point in both our lives, followed by years of regret and recrimination.

They came into each other's arms again and he held her as tightly, as closely as he possibly could, defying the looming certainty of the morning to tear them apart. One last tango.

They broke their embrace—their long, long hug of deep comfort—and began to undress. He saw in her the only refuge he possessed and he knew that in a few hours the best, the most wonderful thing that had ever happened to him would all be thrown away. A last time of intimate sharing, a last time of bodily and spiritual union on a level he had never before experienced, and would never again. And in this final embrace there would be no lies to come between them.

Because she knew deep in her heart this was the last time she would give herself utterly and completely in the act of love, she gave all. There could be nothing hidden between them. Her overwhelming love, her agony, her sympathy, her deep sense of complete commitment drove her, and their lovemaking carried them to where no others could ever have gone before.

The noises through the thin walls of Room 15 in the Lakeside Nook were remarked upon by none of the denizens. It was that sort of establishment.

☆☆★☆☆

Finally, as his nerves and patience were turning to shrieking red Jell-O, DS Delios saw the unmarked police car pull sharply into the truck rental parking lot. The DI emerged with a piece of paper in his hands and a thunderous expression on his face. For a second time that evening the pornography on the counter was swiftly substituted for a sheaf of forms. Waving the paper in the clerk's face the DI demanded the GPS locator details of the truck that had just been rented.

Rushing back to the car with the codes scrawled on the back of a rental form, the DI slipped into the passenger seat and tapped at the keyboard of the car's built-in laptop. The image showed a map with one small moving dot. The dot was moving into the network of streets in the east end of town where abandoned warehouses and docks had yet to yield to the developers' wrecking balls.

"They're heading down Sandford!" cried the DI. "Those disused warehouses where the druggies all hang out! Of course, of course! What better place to hide the stuff! No wonder we never found a damned thing in the clubhouse. Let's go!"

He got on the radio to set the planned raid in motion. "Project Bombshell! We are go! We are go!"

Fred Delios started the car and they drove as swiftly as they could, following the moving dot on the screen, but avoiding the use of sirens or lights.

Perhaps there's a parallel universe in which the DI got his paperwork done more expeditiously, and was able to see the little dot on the screen pause for 15 minutes or so at the clubhouse of the V-Twin Valkyries before proceeding to the east end.

But it's not this one.

☆☆★☆☆

Terry headed for their hang-out, driving in fear for the first few minutes while Sue's furious, livid face began slowly to take on a paradoxical calm. She lit two cigarettes and passed one to him, an unusual gesture in one so shy of human intercourse. She was running the whole scenario through her scheming little mind and realizing that things could actually be a lot worse.

As Terry got to the unfashionable end of Sandford and drove the truck into the entrance of the dump that was their home turf, a curious sense of wellbeing came over Sue. The adrenalin had done its stuff; she was through to the other side. They had done exactly what they wanted, *and more*; they had stolen the show, literally, and as an unlooked-for bonus there was no incriminating evidence. None. No need to dump the stuff. And they could publicize their heist to the rooftops, which she damned well would in the morning, and there would be absolutely no comeback from the law. No evidence! No need to...

In an instant the whole plot of garbage-strewn scrub was brilliantly illuminated. Sirens sounded and police cars appeared from all directions. Loudhailers called, "Come out of there with your hands up!" and police in full protective gear took kneeling poses in a circle round the truck. Druggies, bums and the homeless mentally ill sprang from bushes, out of tents and from under sheets of soggy plywood, blinking in the glare.

While Sue and Terry came gingerly out of the cab, hands above their heads, guns pointing at their chests, the roll-up door of the truck was heaved upwards to reveal...

Nothing.

Clean, Hertz-rental-vacuumed innocence.

⭐ ⭐ ⭐

He couldn't do it. Hefty just couldn't do it. It wasn't in him. All the evil he had done over the years welled up like a great threatening wall, reigniting his conscience and rekindling the tiny light deep in his brain that made him better than he was.

But his refusal to kill signed a death sentence for them both. Kill or be killed was the deal.

He swung towards Steve's back, laid his hand on the turning shoulder, and said, "Lock up this place and get outta here..." His throat tightened right up and tears—tears, for Christ's sake!—came streaming down his face, concealed from Steve in the dim light. "You gotta get... get the fuck out of here, bro. He'll... he'll kill you anyway... Meet me... meet me at the Timmie's up on Gladstone. *Get outta here!"*

He couldn't say more—his gorge had turned to stone—so he stepped away, jumped down onto the loading dock floor and ran quickly for his bike. One seat only; Steve would have to follow on foot.

Steve listened to the V-twin's diminishing roar, standing in near darkness and filled now with a new fear. The renewed threat of death battled with the ecstasy of accomplishment and the fear of discovery. Fear fed into passion, enhancing every sensation of his body and doubling, trebling his penetration high. He began spinning out the thrill of break-and-enter by fantasizing fire.

The Steve who feared incarceration was trampled down by the Steve who reveled in breaking the law, the one who loved to look down at his feet ecstatically poised on the narrow precipice.

Why not? Not like a big fire or anything. Just one of them candles, directed out the loading bay door. Then people would see it, and they'd hear it, and he'd be able to tell the guys, all non-chalant-like, 'Oh, yeah, that was me. I did that.'

Do it, Steve, do it! His whole life his pals had been pushing him—do it Steve, do it—and he always did.

And now he was at that high point, standing on the dizzy edge between discovery, escape and capture. As long as the door remained gaping open he risked being caught; at any moment someone, woken from sleep in the houses flanking the parking lot, could raise the alarm. Any minute now he might hear the wail of sirens. God, every nerve was electric; it was almost intolerably delicious!

Quickly he traversed the storage shelves, raising himself to a pitch of expectation. He found what he wanted; he seized a two-foot long Roman candle and brought it back to the loading dock. He laid it at an angle on a wooden transport pallet, pointing outwards into the night, and lit the fuse with his cigarette lighter. The first coloured star shot out of the tube and went spinning and scintillating into the night, just as he had hoped. He reached his throbbing climax as he watched the star crackle silver and gold over the houses at far end of the parking lot.

But Steve Bacon knew too little of fireworks; the recoil of the lift charge that had sent the star on its way caused the tube to slew violently around. As his attention was held over the gold and silver-lit rooftops, the next star shot directly at him from the flank, searing up his arm and the side of his face. He staggered back, beating at his sleeve, leapt down from the dock and ran screaming through the open door and out into the night, followed by the smell of over-cooked bacon.

The candle discharged its contents into the building, fizzing on the floor and swiveling with every shot. If Terry O'Weight had been there, his Inspector Clouseau movie fantasy would have come alive before his astonished eyes. But modern buildings in cities with rigorous building and safety codes have extremely efficient fire suppression systems, especially those where explosives are stored and handled. The sprinkler systems were tripped within a very short time, but not before many of the candles, wheels and cakes had begun to erupt. Thick yellow smoke mingled with steam as fire alarms howled and windows lit the length of the waking street.

☆ ✩ ⭐ ✩ ☆

Uncle Chuck had been building into a towering rage. He no longer knew if he was dealing with duplicity or stupidity, but whatever happened, if his cocaine wasn't in the boxes they had rapidly stacked in the back of the garage, Rocco and his pretty little piece of tail were dead meat, wherever the hell they were.

"Tear 'em open! Tear 'em open for Christ's sake! Here, gimme that!" He waltzed between the parked Hogs, seized a box cutter and hacked the top off yet another Starbursts with Whistles, hurling its innocent contents onto the increasing pile. As aerial shell after aerial shell was ripped apart and discarded, the pile began to overwhelm the stack of Molson Blue empties in the corner of the garage.

The phone rang in the gang leader's pocket. "What? *What?*" he yelled, furious at the interruption. "Where...? Lakeside Nook? Room fifteen? *A-a-ll right...*" Timing or what! Kee-rist!

As only one box of four shells remained it was now becoming clear to Uncle Chuck that his cocaine was somewhere else altogether. A quick ripping and tearing confirmed the worst.

"*That's it!* I'm gonna kill both those *fuckers* with my *BARE HANDS!* C'mon boys, the Lakeside Nook on Edgeware. *Let's go!*"

He hit the button to raise the garage door as all eight gang members leapt onto their Harleys and started up. A crackling roar filled the small space as the Valkyries prepared to sow vengeance to the wind. Uncle Chuck stamped down on the kick starter and his engine... coughed and died. Flooded again! Shit!

In a temper and raging to get at Rocco's throat, he couldn't wait for the gas vapour to dissipate. He stamped down again with renewed anger; the engine kicked, the vapour ignited and a great roaring backfire shot out of the twin tailpipes.

"Harley fuckin' Davidson shit!" was the last mortal thought that passed through Uncle Chuck's mind as a great blossoming chrysanthemum of super-heated gunpowder joined by detonators and dynamite—and shot through with the scintillations of serpents, whistles, crackling stars and fireflies—roared crimson out of the discarded pile behind him, lifting him and his companions up and out in a great thudding fountain of shattered beer bottles, scorched flesh, leather, chains and twisted Harleys. A poisonous yellow fungal cloud of smoke and debris vaulted upward and outward hundreds of feet into the sky from the splintered remains of the V-Twin Valkyries clubhouse.

The reverberations thrown back from the walls and windows of the city died and a silence fell, punctuated only by the splats and tinkles of biker bits and bits of bikes returning to earth.

☆✫⭐✫☆

On one of the Lakeside Nook's hard beds, in her lover's arms and utterly spent of passion, Julia Catesby stirred slightly in her sleep as a wave of deep sound rattled the thin walls, tinkled the water glass in the bathroom, and startled birds to a premature dawn.

Chapter Five
The Garnitures

Garnitures [also called effects] are what an aerial fireworks shell is all about. They are the visual and/or audible effects being carried into the air to be displayed at the perfect moment
Shells, an Introduction, Ned Gorski, Skylighter.com

Rocco woke early in the half-dark from a horrible fractured night of dreams and truths mixed in seething proportions. He gently moved Julia's lax arm from his shoulder, slid out of the bed as smoothly as possible, and slipped naked into the washroom. As he stood there over the toilet bowl the whole horrible mess of his and Julia's lives slammed down on him. He returned to the room in misery to see that, as subtle as his exit was, Julia had roused and was sitting unclothed on the edge of the bed, far from awake.

Without thinking he followed his usual morning reflex, pointing the remote at the flat-screen TV bolted to the wall.

"...second of two incidents in the early hours of the morning. The Valkyries clubhouse is completely flattened and, although unconfirmed, it appears that Charles 'Uncle Chuck' Bourassa and a number of other gang members are among the dead..."

This wasn't happening. They stared into each other's faces. The TV played on. This just wasn't happening.

"...I hear this big bang, and when I come out there's bodies everywhere, just like when they did that clubhouse in Québec..."

She rose slowly and walked across the cheap indoor/outdoor carpeting towards him.

"...a number of individuals are believed to be deceased, but until we have finished conducting our enquiries..."

They hugged, body pressed to body, as the first day of this new life of theirs woke in thin grey light behind the yellow vinyl venetian blinds.

"You know what?" he said quietly into her fair hair after many minutes of silent peace. "Sometimes I could almost believe in God."

She hugged him even closer, their bodies one along their whole length, but said nothing.

"...earlier in the night, sometime after one o'clock, the Catesby fireworks building on Upper Main Street was damaged by fire..."

They sprang apart, staring at the screen in horror as the smoking building was revealed behind the reporter with the microphone.

"Oh, no! No!" she cried. "Not our place! No! What happened?"

They seized their clothes from the floor, and while he dressed hurriedly she darted into the bathroom, leaving the door open to hear the TV.

"...damage appears to be limited to the back of the building... smoke and water... strict rules about fire prevention... older building..."

Shrugging and pulling into their clothes they headed for the front desk, leaving the TV waffling away behind them.

"...as Mayor of East Gladstone I'd like to point out the significant strides in fire safety the council have achieved..."

"Oh, God, I know it's trite to talk about roller-coasters..." As the old Corolla hurtled back to the center of town, Julia's heart and mind were ripped into shreds by joy and fear. "What happened? What happened?" she kept repeating as paradoxically coloured traffic signals succumbed to Rocco's headlong progress.

He stopped down the street from the fire scene. There was a police car angled across the road with a cop directing traffic, while beyond you could see the yellow security tape and the gathering early morning crowd. There was a drift of smoke across the strip of sky between the buildings flanking the street.

They kissed quickly and deeply.

"Call me," he said. "Soon as you can."

The door slammed and she was gone up the street. He watched as she reached the scene, talked briefly to one of the officers, and was escorted under the tape, a brief flash of her thigh as she ducked.

☆ ⭐ ☆

Angela Catesby had a horrible call from the police in the early hours of the morning. When the phone rings in the night it is never good. She put the phone down with a shaking hand, wrapped a gown around herself and went upstairs to wake her father-in-law. They phoned Alfred right away, waking him from a deep but troubled sleep in his motel in Sault Ste Marie. Angela tried Julia's phone repeatedly but got no answer. Where *was* she? Meanwhile, Alfred rented a car in the Soo and headed towards the dawn, leaving Mike to clean up and return with the truck.

While Bob and Alfred were on site looking over the mess of the facility, Julia joined them. She hugged her grandfather, trembling from shock and horror. He hugged her back distractedly and returned to his son's side. Julia's mind was in turmoil with the thought that, in some mysterious way, Rocco could be responsible. Could that stupid friend of his have broken in again? Or had the biker gang broken in to find their cocaine? Why burn the place? Why? None of it made any sense, and all she could feel was the conflict between this desperate anxiety and the relief of the morning's news.

The three stood in the rear parking lot, as close to the building as the security tape would allow, looking directly in at the open loading bay door. The building was intact, thanks to the fire prevention systems, but inside the ruin of their stocks and apparatus was clear to see.

"Not much more we can do here, really," said Alfred. "I've talked to the police and that fire superintendant over there. They wanna talk to us, but not now. They'll call."

They returned home to sit quietly with Angela around the kitchen table. Angela couldn't bring herself to go; the scenes on the morning news channel were quite bad enough.

"Arson," Alfred told her, recalling his first shocked appraisal of the building. "The loading bay door was wide open. No other explanation."

"*Arson?* Who?" cried Angela. "Who could have done this?"

Alfred had long thought about the strange visit of that detective sergeant, but he kept his suspicions to himself. Plenty of time after the investigators had done their stuff, and no sense in alarming anyone any more than necessary.

"What's the building like?" asked Angela following Alfred's silence. "How much damage?"

"The place isn't quite a write-off," muttered Alfred. "But we'll have to start almost from scratch. Some smoke and fire damage, but mostly water. Thank God we're fully insured."

"And thank God all our electronics and firing equipment were up in the Soo," said Julia. "Can you imagine where we'd be without that?"

"Damn right," agreed Bob. "So, it's a setback, that's all. But there's going to be a big hole in our gigs unless we act quickly."

"Sure will," replied Alfred. "Cops won't give us access to the office until the investigation's done."

"Can't. Damp fireworks are damned dangerous. Magnesium particularly..."

"I know, I know. We'll just have to wait. So, no access, no paperwork."

"Buggers won't even let us into the magazine," observed the older man. "No idea why, 'cos it didn't look touched."

"And they won't even tell us why either," continued Alfred. He stood up quickly, decisively, rubbing his hands together. "Anyway, let's see what's in the works."

"Chatham and Burlington," replied Bob. "It's all on our laptops, so we'll have access to all the electronic files right here. First off, let's copy the files to USB keys. Just to be sure."

"Okay, we've got to make arrangements really quick to get back on track. So it's Chatham on Saturday and Burlington Sunday. First off, I'll get Mike to locate a temporary space—a warehouse, garage or something—where we can set up shop. As far as stock goes, if we can't get into the magazine it'll mean calling on a few favours, so I'd better start working the phone."

"Why not borrow from Pastorelli?" asked Julia innocently. "They've probably got enough stock. And they're right here."

Her father frowned at her. "No, we do not cooperate with the competition."

"But Dad, if we don't, you know what'll happen?" She paused to see if he would rise to the rhetorical question. "Chatham and Burlington will have seen the news too, and before you know it they'll be making other arrangements."

"I'm phoning them today, this morning, to tell them we're going ahead," he answered impatiently.

"But are we? Can we?" replied Julia. "Do you have time to call in all the stuff we need from elsewhere round the country?" There's no point in getting cross with me she thought, seeing his irritated expression, since you're the one who's training me to take over. "I think it's a huge risk."

"Besides," put in Bob, "as soon as they hear of this, who d'ye think they'll contact? Pastorelli, of course. Then we'll really be hosed."

Before Alfred could snap out a reply his cellphone rang. He listened, nodded, and said he would be there as soon as possible. An expression of vacillation briefly passed over his face, and then he came to a decision.

"Look, I've got to go down to City Hall. Sounds shitty. Tell you what Dad, can you contact Pastorelli and ask if we can borrow some stuff?"

"Sure can!" he said as he pushed away from the table. He hoped the old man, Emilio, wasn't there because that would be impossible. Perhaps the son would be easier to deal with. Julia seemed to think so.

Julia tried to hide her relief.

"Only *borrow*, okay?" pointing a long finger at both of them. "I'm damned if I'll be beholden to them." He whipped his jacket off the back of his chair and made for the door. "Take Julia with you; I want her in on this." And he was gone.

☆ ⭐ ☆

"Hello, my name's Julia Catesby, and this is my grandfather, Bob. Thank you so much for agreeing to meet with us." Only by reminding herself of the tragedy of the situation did she stop herself from cracking up with laughter. "And you're Mr Pastorelli?"

"Yes, I am. Rocco. I'm sure we've met before..." A subtle narrowing of the eyes.

"Oh, probably. It's a small town."

"Please come in."

Julia gave Grandpa a sidelong glance and was almost sure he knew more than he was letting on. He was just relieved that it was Rocco Pastorelli he was dealing with, not the old man. Didn't particularly want to see him again. Ever. Not after last time.

"It's really kind of you to help us like this," said Bob. "We know there's some... competition..."

"No, really," replied Rocco, "you guys were very helpful when I had a problem with my loading bay door. Time to pay you back, that's all." Christ, he thought, if he only knew!

Grandfather and granddaughter were shown to a side table in Mr Pastorelli's office and while they opened folders and spread out papers, he disappeared for a few minutes, returning with cups of excellent coffee. Julia's was made just the way she liked it, but she didn't think Grandpa had noticed. Discussion centred on what was needed immediately. Rocco opened the inventory on his computer and compared their requirements with his stock.

"We have almost all this on hand," he observed, looking over the orders for the two shows, "but you may have to vary it a bit. See here..." and he leant over to point out some items on the list, giving Julia and exquisite illicit thrill "...you'll have to replace serpents for whistles, and we don't have enough three-inch reports. And these shells; we've got 'em but they're earmarked for this weekend."

"That's okay," she replied. "We can improvise. We'll have to! Fortunately our Pyrodigital and all the hook-ups were out of town when the fire happened."

"That's lucky. We use FireOne, but even if it wasn't fully occupied, you'd never get the hang of it time."

"Damn it all girl!" rumbled Bob, quite forgetting where he was. "Even if the whole lot had been torched, if you and me and your dad couldn't fire a show or two without recourse to electronic gizmos we should retire right now and grow root vegetables!"

Rocco laughed outright and clapped his hands. "Just like me! My grandfather *made* me learn how to do it all with a portfire! All you need is earplugs."

"And a steady nerve."

They shook hands and agreed to prepare the paperwork to cover a loan. Mr Pastorelli was quite content to have Catesby's simply return the items without interest or other payment. Julia was sure this gesture would soften her father's attitude.

☆✩☆

Alfred Catesby entered the kitchen, now transformed to the Catesby & Son Pyrotechnics operations centre, and sat down slowly. He had been down at City Hall for most of the morning. Angela poured him a mug of tea, pushing it across the table to him. Julia and Bob had paused from their laptops, but were clearly not expecting this dour arrival.

"I'm sorry Dad, but it's about as bad as it could be." Alfred Catesby looked old. While he and Bob, with Julia's help, were sorting out the future and hatching contingency plans he had been in his element, but now he looked just plain defeated. All the energy he had so recently shown had evaporated into despondency.

"What?" asked Bob. "What can be so bad?"

"City Hall," he said in slow, measured tones, "has, in its wisdom, decided that our building permit will not be renewed."

"They're joking! They can't just do that..." spluttered Bob. "You can't shut down one of the mainstays of the town!"

"They can, and they will," he sighed. "Truth of the matter is, their hands are tied. The zoning was apparently upgraded years ago, with our building and some others grandfathered in."

"Why? Why?" Bob was totally disbelieving.

"It was industrial land when we built there," he replied. "Once the Canadian Pacific rails were torn up it became gentrified. No more big industrial, especially explosives storage and manufacture. I should have known; I *did* know..."

"Well, shit! We'll just move out of town and build where it's safer." Bob applied verbal quotation marks to 'safer'.

"Dad," Alfred sighed, "the insurance covers the building, no problem, but remember we only lease the land. We simply can't afford to buy land *and* raise a building."

"Alf! You're not folding up the shop! We've got to keep going!" Bob's voice had taken on a sharp edge.

"We can't Dad. We can't. Even if we had the money, have you any idea of how the legislation on explosives manufacture and handling has changed since we started? Remember all that bureaucratic bullshit they gave us about the magazine? Earthwork berms and brickwork and Christ knows what else."

"So, what then?" Bob asked in puzzlement, a hint of moisture in his eye.

"We fall back on the Hawkesbury outfit, which is a money-making concern, and get out of the shows."

"Oh, come on, Alf! That's not *us!*" cried Bob. "That's not what *we do!* Pimping boxes of harmless squibs dictated by the politically correct mafia."

"I can't see any other..."

But the old man had got up from the table and left the room.

☆ ⭐ ☆

The Detective Inspector of CID for East Gladstone stood in the centre of his office. The view out of the window was spectacularly green as far as the eye could see, although all too soon he would see the splendour of autumn red, brown and gold. He didn't give a good God damn.

"Not a trace of cocaine, a bunch of burnt fireworks and a whole passel of shredded bikers," he observed to Detective Sergeant Fred Delios, sitting in the guest chair. The DI had passed quickly through disbelief, incomprehension, fury, and resignation while still on site in the dark of that long night and now, back in headquarters days later, he was still deeply into the phase of plain puzzlement. "Any suggestions?"

"I've been over it again and again," said the red-eyed and un-shaven DS. "Makes no sense from any angle whatsoever. There is one unifying theme, though."

"Oh, there is?" replied the DI with a tiny seed of interest in his tone. "Reveal."

"Yeah. It's that we've been completely and comprehensively taken to the cleaners."

A long sigh came from deep within the soul of the standing policeman, and a stretched silence ensued.

"So, Tort and O'Weight?" asked the DI eventually, although it was hardly a question.

"Driven snow. Quote-unquote: They rented the truck 'cos O'Weight likes driving trucks."

"Prints?"

"None. Gloves all round probably."

"And the lovely couple's Airstream trailer?"

"Clean except for a world-class collection of pornography."

"Huh! No idea where their funding comes from either, and not a clue as to motive. Why fireworks, for Christ's sake?"

"Best I can come up with," replied Delios, "is that their 'spon-sors' cherry-pick issues. Doesn't matter what the issue is, the ob-jective is sowing social unrest. Waste everybody's time and re-sources. Look at their past history; wide range of causes, all of 'em a flash in the pan."

"That's right. Do your shit-disturbing, then move on. Zero attention span."

"Yup. Wonder what it'll be next...?"

There was silence for a minute or so while the two policemen contemplated the deeper meaning of futility.

"What about Bacon, then?" asked the DI, again knowing the answer.

"Cellphone evidence was a bust. All we have is her telling him to rent the truck. Big whoop! Circumstantial at best. Burned himself on a barbecue apparently. His pal Hefty Beale picked him up at the hospital and took him home."

"Oh, how very touching. Pastorelli?"

"Disappearance was a dirty weekend with his girlfriend in a cheap motel. Found the motel; checked with the clerk. Signed in as Ron and Kate Pastor; not even clever. Interesting though, the clerk did say there was somebody else looking for them. We chased it up, but it was a dead end."

"So, the activists steal the fireworks from Catesby's, even though we were told by Bacon the coke was going through the Pastorelli outfit, then the bikers steal the fireworks from the activists even though they, the bikers, were dealing with Pastorelli not Catesby in the first place, but Bacon has broken into Catesby's before, apparently as a favour to Pastorelli, who had a vendetta with Catesby, so working for the activists he breaks in again, but when the bikers open the fireworks that he's helped the activists to steal, because the activists suspect the coke is hidden in them, there's nothing in them after all according to our air quality tests of the whole neighbourhood, because we know, and the bikers ought to have known, that if the dope's anywhere it's in Pastorelli's not Catesby's, but then Bacon, probably, sets fire to the building where there are hardly any fireworks anyway for some totally unaccountable reason..." The clockwork ran down and stopped as it had so often these last few days.

"My thoughts have been running in similar channels," observed the DS, thinking of silted-up and weed-choked waterways, coherent thought clogged by mental zebra mussels.

Another silence. Ticking of the presentation clock on the desk, whisper of wind around the building, low roar of traffic in the street below, clatter of a keyboard in an adjacent office.

"Y'know," the DI finally observed, "I was thinking of quitting the police force and embarking on a life of crime."

"Me too. It's so much more rewarding and fulfilling, isn't it?"

"Yup. Plenty of untraceable money, lots of thrills, no consequences..."

"Big thing is," mused Delios, "there's no rule book."

"Ah, the rule book. Where would life be without rule books?"

A further long silence followed while each man pondered parallel universes; careers where they had decided that satisfaction in life and service to humanity would revolve around bagging groceries at Loblaw's or flogging Billy shelving units at IKEA.

"Solved the V-Twin Valkyrie issue, though," observed the DS. "They had to pour them into the coffins. What bits they could find."

"Yes, one of East Gladstone's more notable funerals, wasn't it? Didn't know they had so many friends."

"Just shows you what overt expressions of civic goodwill do for you. Attending town functions, fund-raising for kiddies, that sort of thing. But at least they're off our books."

"Yes, there are some instances where the universe unfolds just as it should, I suppose. But I would just love to have us take the credit for it..."

The Detective Inspector of CID suddenly stood tall, slapped his hands together and instantly regained a good measure of his old feisty spirit.

"So, what do we have on the cards?"

"Well, there's that embezzlement at the Final Harbour nursing home. Fifty-seven dollars gone missing from the recreation kitty."

"Think we can handle that...?"

☆ ☆ ☆

"I won't be sorry to see the last of this fuckin' place," grumbled Sue Tort around her cigarette as she threw the remaining clothes into a cheap fiber suitcase with a busted latch.

"Where we goin', then?" called Terry from the other end of the trailer, stuffing piles of sticky, dog-eared magazines into a black garbage bag.

"Back to Toronto. Stephan's gonna let us use the place on Bathurst."

"More fireworks?" he asked hopefully. He liked fireworks...

"No more goddamned fireworks! Fuck's sake! We're off that case. Job done."

Sue had received the cryptic word; a summer's-worth of disruption and annoyance, police resources and time wasted, and a firework outfit burned as a bonus. Time to focus elsewhere, just to keep them hopping, keep them guessing, keep them spinning their wheels. In country after country useless, rudderless human beings just like Sue and Terry were systematically bribed and coerced with money and a pitiable place to stand in an increasingly anonymous world. Legitimate protest was highjacked again and again by these pliable disaffected, who had no cause beyond their own miserable wellbeing.

And the organization that underwrote their activities wasn't an organization at all, and its agenda was simply that there was no agenda.

"So, what now?"

"City's hosting some international athletic thing an' there's thousands a homeless people on the streets. We gotta do something about it."

Terry sighed, pausing in his packing with two pairs of shredded, yellowed underwear in his hand. He'd had a good time with the firework shows, but now it was back to just marching up and down with banners and leaflets and shit. Ah well, you never knew when the chance to do a bit of real crap-disturbing would show up again. And there was always beer and cigarettes and peppermint chewing gum. Could be worse.

Sue stepped out of their run-down Airstream home for the last time, opened the rear door of the Rabbit and slung her meager belongings onto the back seat. The trunk had been jammed shut for years. While she did this she was rewriting herself, shoving the past into some rotting cerebral filing cabinet with a broken lock, and focusing on the immediate present and the ductile future.

She had no thought of retirement; there had never been anything else. Never would be.

☆⭐☆

Alfred Catesby was sitting at a desk in the corner of a disused garage in the east end of town that Catesby & Son Pyrotechnics had rented while the firm still staggered on. They had set up storage racks to contain their borrowed pyrotechnics, rescued a great deal of the smoke-damaged launching and firing apparatus from the fire site, and had somehow given clients the impression of business as usual. Mike had done wonders, rising to the occasion, having found the whole adventure quite stimulating. With jokes and willing hard work he had warmed the hearts of the whole outfit, and they had all pitched in.

Chatham and Burlington had gone surprisingly well. Alfred had never been so keyed up, what with scrambling around for borrowed pyrotechnics and equipment, and negotiating last-minute changes of program with the clients. He was exhausted now, but it was well earned. Dad and Julia had performed feats of endurance along with Mike, but the season wasn't at an end and he couldn't afford to even think of resting.

Alfred and Bob had visited City Hall the week before to make a case for temporary accommodations until they could get back on track, although both knew that building a new facility outside of the built-up area would be impossible. At best, the 30-day extension the bureaucrats had reluctantly granted would see them through September. Beyond that, it was out of their hands.

In the interim, though, one really damaging problem was the absence of quite a number of aerial shells. Once they had been granted access to the magazine, they discovered a robbery had apparently taken place. At least, that was the only possible explanation for the losses, although it remained a deep mystery because only their Colombian stock was missing. This lack made their shoestring outfit even more so, although by now the assistance of the so-called competition was actually keeping them afloat. Just.

Alfred leaned back from his desk, hands behind his head, and thought of the loans from Pastorelli. He had done the son, Rocco, a favour 'way back when their loading bay door had jammed, and had thought nothing of it. Sure, they were the competition, but that's what you do. You don't refuse; apart from anything else, it's plain bad business practice. Then, when it came to their own crunch, Pastorelli had helped them out. *Quid pro quo* for sure, but even so there was a debt of gratitude there. Alfred had called in favours from around the country in replenishing his stocks, but the loans from Pastorelli had prevented immediate disaster.

Alfred wondered, for no reason he could at first fathom, why he shouldn't visit Rocco Pastorelli himself. Sure, there were some arrangements to be made regarding further loans and paybacks, but they could easily be done by phone, of course. But Julia and Dad had made all the personal visits so far, so why not him? It was becoming clear to him that the turf war that the older generation was waging had little relevance to the here-and-now. He had no idea how it had all started, but it was obvious that the younger Pastorelli hadn't bought into it, and now Dad might be softening too. So why shouldn't the not-so-younger Catesby reciprocate? This was an erosion of the persona of Mr A. Catesby the hard-shelled businessman who, for the first time in his life, was seeing what failure might look like. Success had made him ironclad; failure had proved him... vulnerable. But there was still a great deal of pride at stake.

He made his decision, left the building quickly and drove to the east end. The nearer he got to the Pastorelli facility the more he questioned his decision. But he was committed now.

Rocco greeted Alfred at the front door. "Nice to meet you... voice on the phone..."

Alfred was equally diffident. "Just thought I'd drop by, discuss the loans..." He didn't do the social stuff very well, and it was clear that Mr Pastorelli wasn't prepared to do more than skim the surface of a new and equivocal relationship.

They passed through to the office keeping their interactions business-like and neutral. Once their negotiations were done they met each other's eyes for the first time over a closing handshake.

"Good of you to help us out."

"Think nothing of it," replied Rocco, knowing his grandfather would be fit to be tied if he ever found out, and mentally plotting the legerdemain necessary to keep him in the dark. "Maybe if we're in trouble we can call on you?"

"Hope that never happens. We'll talk again."

They released hands and Rocco showed Alfred to the door, waving to him as he turned the corner to the parking lot.

Alfred sat in the car for a moment before starting up. He seems to be a nice, regular sort of guy, he thought, polite, cooperative and reasonable. Kind of aloof, but so was I. Well, barring a miracle this would be the end of the relationship, not the beginning.

Rocco returned to his office. His daughter doesn't look anything like him, he thought, although I can see a little of her in her grandfather. Didn't appear to be such a hard-nosed bastard really; kind of mellow. 'Maybe if we're in trouble...' My trouble Mr Catesby is your daughter. It was kind of tough, only just getting to know the guy after all this time. How the hell would all this fall out? One thing he was sure of: the Julia holding pattern was running out of gas. If it didn't touch down soon it would crash.

☆ ⭐ ☆

"Hey Julia. I'd like to take you out for dinner. Are you free?"

Alfred was closing down his laptop in the corner of their retooled garage while calling Julia across the echoing space.

"Ooh, dinner! Tonight? Sure. What time?" replied Julia.

"Pick you up at six?"

"Mum and Grandpa coming too?"

"No, no, just the two of us."

"Sure," she replied, realizing something much more than a meal was afoot. "Where we going?"

"I like Maxi's. It's nice and quiet, especially the booths along the back wall."

Nice and quiet...

Maximillian's was Hungarian and did a great line in goulash, borscht and other typically Magyar dishes, although the owner was third generation at best and went by the name of Rogers. The mention of quiet booths at the back gave Julia to understand that this might be a tough little evening.

Just before 6:00 Julia heard the unmistakable exhaust note of Dad's Morgan Plus 4. She hurried down to her front door before he could get even halfway up the path. They drove to the restaurant with the top down, the wind ruffling their hair.

While they ate their meal and drank the good part of a carafe of red wine—Alfred taking much more than her—they talked in inconsequentialities. Julia received sage advice on the wiring in her kitchen, strategies on approaching her landlord about the loose paving stones on the entry way, and tips on automotive maintenance. As the second carafe arrived Alfred observed that this was Turkish wine, not Hungarian, and he had ordered it specially. The Buzbağ grapes grew on the slopes of Mount Ararat, he told her, and it was therefore incontrovertibly the oldest wine in the world, because Noah had planted the vines there when the Ark came to rest. Julia laughed but she saw that his ploy was to lighten things up, show another side of the Dad Figure. It worked, and the wine wasn't as bad as its unfortunate name suggested. Even so, she only sipped a little while her dad fortified himself for what she knew was to come.

It wasn't until after dessert, and with the tide on the ebb in the second carafe, that her father began to dig a little deeper.

"You'll be twenty-four soon," he began, fiddling with a spoon then folding and refolding his napkin. "Look, it's... it's time we thought about your future."

She nodded, seeing silence as her best option.

"Travel, university... You see, while you were working at the firm you were, well, content with your high school diploma. But now, it's all changed..."

He took a deep breath and started on a completely different tack.

"Honestly," he continued, "I... we... no, me really. I always wanted a son; you know that. Continuing the tradition, me taking over from Dad you know, then..." The poor guy was floundering and Julia felt both sorry for him and a little embarrassed. He had been there all her life yet there was a stranger sitting across the table from her. How well did she really know him; how close had she ever really come?

"You don't need to..." She put her fingers just gently on the hand that was agitatedly turning the spoon over and over, and realized that they hardly ever touched. Her hand on his seemed to calm him.

"I do need to, sweetheart. I do need to. It's not so long ago I truly realized that you could run the firm. I admit it; I'm old fashioned, and you probably think me totally sexist."

"Don't be silly Dad." She squeezed the hand and was happy to feel a corresponding pressure. "You've given me all you could in encouragement and confidence."

"It's not so simple." He remembered his wine and took a slow sip, keeping his eyes down at the table. "It was your grandfather's insistence that persuaded me, and I feel that I had failed you by not seeing sooner..."

"Dad, listen to me! There was no failing going on. You took your time in coming round to accepting me as a successor, but that's fine. Fine! Jeez, I'm only twenty-three!"

He smiled wistfully then and looked into her eyes, and her dad became a little less than a stranger. "So then," he continued doggedly, "just when your succession to the job seemed assured here we are, dead in the water."

She was holding both her father's hands now. The aloof figure she had known all her life seemed to be melting into a troubled but lovable man who needed her assurance, perhaps in some ways her affirmation. She had never been this close to him; success had held him away from her, but now failure was showing the more human side in him, and she loved him the more for it.

"Dad, I want to tell you something. I know that all this is totally horrible and it seems like the end of the world, but I'm not just going gallivanting away and leaving you. Yes, I want to travel, yes I would love to go back to school, but it can all wait."

"You, of all of us, are the most hurt," he replied slowly. "The beginning of a career, the future all waiting for you, then everything falls apart. And if I had've planned better..."

"No, Dad. I refuse to let you take the blame for the present, let alone the unforeseeable future. We'll stick with it, we'll see it through, and *que sera, sera*." The words spoken in Italian gave her a secret stab of mingled pleasure and guilt.

He squeezed her hands and smiled. "It's just..."

"No. We can't do the coulda, shoulda, woulda. Can we?"

"No, of course we can't. Doesn't stop the mind from replaying the tape, though."

For a while they were silent, he twirling the stem of his glass, she resting one hand in his, the cool lump of his wedding band under her fingers.

"Your grandfather is near the end of things," he continued. "He's looking at a bleak future, and his... view of things mostly centered on your role in taking us forward. But, now that's all gone, he's sort of lost."

"I know what you mean, Dad. He really lives through me, doesn't he?"

"He loves you dearly. You look so much like your grandmère, you know. I often see Carmelle in you; just the odd lift of your lips, a turn of your shoulder, a little look... Your happiness is his happiness."

Suddenly she wanted with all her heart to come clean. She wanted to be totally honest with him, to tell him she was in love with the most wonderful man, and that whenever she was with him and wherever they went, her future would be golden. She wanted Grandpa to know; she wanted Mom to know; she wanted to shout and shout about it, and it hurt that she couldn't. This closeness with her father—so unlooked-for and so long in coming—was far too fragile; he was so near to her now that the slightest perturbation might send him crashing back into aloofness and austerity.

And if he were to discover the true identity of her lover they would never, ever be close again. This she thought, although in truth her newly mellowed father might not have reacted in the way she imagined.

The thought of her secret love led to the image of Rocco's grandfather watching failure in his old age. Just like her grandfather, miserable at the close of life when there should be satisfaction and comfort, and vision of a secure future neither would see. Two old men with their lives in ruins.

Then, as she looked fully into her father's eyes for perhaps the first conscious time, the congruence of the patriarchs' common misery fed into the germ of an idea.

"We'll go ahead, Dad!" she cried. "We're not done yet, by God!"

They rose from the table and he put his arm about her shoulder as they left the restaurant. She stopped beside the car on the driver's side.

"Gimme the keys Dad," she demanded, holding out her hand. "You know I love to drive this baby, and you've had a drop or two too much to even think about it."

She had driven the Plus 4 on a couple of previous occasions when she had caught her father in just the right mood. It was almost like his attitude to the company; he was reluctant to let her sit behind the wheel and just drive. Tonight was different though; he had opened out to her in a way he had never done before, and her piloting the Morgan was an extension of what had happened at the dinner table. Perhaps she drove faster than she should have done, perhaps her father was over tense, huddled low in his unfamiliar passenger seat, but she got them home swiftly and parked the car neatly in the driveway.

"I can walk home from here." She leaned up and kissed him on the cheek, pressing the keys into his hand. "Love you, Dad. See you tomorrow."

"Be careful!"

"Don't worry, I've got my glue." Julia carried a small aerosol can of model-maker's contact cement in her purse, a fabulous deterrent and much more memorable to the would-be assailant than mere pepper spray. That and a huge kick in the balls while he was trying to claw the goop out of his eyes. So far, no takers.

He watched her swinging down the street in the alternating light and dark of the streetlamps, the little place on his cheek where she had placed her lips still radiating pleasure.

☆ ✩ ☆

They loved to meet at the coffee shop where they had first sat together accidentally all those months ago. Rain wetted the window facing Main Street, but inside all was warm bustle and clatter. They had their coffees in front of them, not yet touched, and sat in a cone of silence. He had a sadness behind his eyes, but perhaps Julia was carrying a little optimism into their tryst. But her great idea would need to be approached circumspectly.

"Back to normal, eh?" she asked.

"Yeah. Watching the numbers go back into the red. I can't help laughing at a crime spree that made everybody happy, and a return to the straight and narrow that's pissing everybody off."

"Crime *does* pay?" she smiled weakly. "Sure did with you, you stupid bastard."

The barb died with the gentle lift of her mouth and the softness in her eyes.

He looked quickly around the coffee shop and saw they were

relatively private. "There's something I have to tell you, and it can't wait."

His expression was so somber that Julia felt a little frightened.

"What? What is it?"

"When I was doing all that stuff... moving the cocaine through the system, meeting with the bikers..." he paused and closed his eyes. "Julia, I *enjoyed* it! I mean, part of me. A little tiny part. I mean, I felt terrible... like I was betraying and lying and so on, but underneath all that it was..."

"Yes...?" she squeezed his hand.

"I can't really explain. But imagine deep inside you this little demon rubbing his hands in glee."

She nodded, saying nothing at the moment, only gripping his hand more tightly.

"When you told me once," she began tentatively, "that I was naturally good, did you mean that for you it was an effort?"

He returned the hand squeeze hard, and she saw a moistness about his eyes.

"No problem," she said quietly. "There's the two of us now, not just you."

"Yeah, I have you. More than I ever deserved. I'm a hell of a package to deal with, you know!" He laughed without humour.

"Don't sell yourself short. We'll keep you straight. Bet on it."

He nodded and they were quiet for a long time. "Then, there's the small matter of us and them. Our secret life."

"Oh, Roh-cco, dahling!" she cried, playing the coquette of 1940s Hollywood with a huge grin. "We cahn't keep on me-e-ting like this!"

"No, seriously Julia." He was irritated. "What kinda stupid mood are you in? We gotta make some kind of decision."

"I know we do..." she sighed, returning to seriousness. She was on the verge of revealing the great idea bubbling within her when he interrupted.

"See, I can't imagine the shit storm if I told Nonno about you. He's right down in the dumps now, on my back for everything..."

"What, like you said, watching the numbers go back into the red?"

"Exactly. He's watching like a hawk, so now we're back to using the Italian shells at three, four times the cost." He smiled crookedly. "My supplier in Colombia is slightly unreliable."

"Those ones we borrowed..."

"No," he finished for her, "they didn't affect the bottom line. No worries there."

"And now your grandfather's probably as sad as mine." Here, surely, was the opening she was looking for.

"Now, he is, yes. But can you imagine when he heard about your fire? Bugger was dancing with joy. Li'l *accidente* he kept saying. Li'l *accidente*. He thought it would solve all our problems."

"Yeah," she observed. "He never did understand that being in the same town is not the issue."

"And now, of course, he's got wind of the true financial scene," he moaned. "That little ode to joy didn't last worth a damn. He's back in the dumps again. Ragging me about how we were doing fine, then all of a sudden we're on the ropes. And why aren't we getting all Catesby's gigs? Hard to live with..."

"My Grandpa's the same. Ever since the fire he's been so sad it makes me want to cry." Her face belied her words. "They–him and my Dad–they just don't know what they're going to do."

"There's your commercial outfit in Hawkesbury, I guess."

"Yeah, but that's just a factory," she replied. "Sure, we can live off the profits, maybe even expand it, but it just isn't the same. Grandpa, and Dad too, are just devastated. Dad seems at least resigned to it, but the company was Grandpa's whole life, really. He's not my Grandpa anymore."

He expected to see tears, or at least sadness, but saw instead a set of the mouth and some sort of resolution.

"Two miserable grandfathers..." he began.

"There is a way out of all this," she interrupted. Now was the moment! She had no idea how he would take what she had been thinking, but you never know until you try. Now *was* the moment. "Look. Since we've been borrowing stuff from you, just to keep ourselves afloat, I wonder if the same great idea has come to you?"

"Great idea?" he asked in bafflement.

"Yes. *Think!*"

"I'm not doing great ideas these days. Sorry."

"Oh, come on! Don't make me spell it out."

"Join forces?" he asked tentatively after a long pause. She hadn't needed to say it.

She nodded, lips clenched between her teeth.

"Christ! My nonno and your grandpa? That's gunpowder and matches, no mistake!"

"But think of the advantages..."

"Yeah, yeah," he interrupted, "I get it. But Nonno would never agree. Never. "

"But surely, if it meant keeping the firm afloat?" she pleaded.

"I dunno," he replied doubtfully. "But it sure needs thinking about."

He paused for a long time, sipping his drink, a far distance in his eyes. "How the hell could I convince him? After all, you're still the enemy, aren't you?"

"I've been thinking hard about this. It has to be subtle and gentle."

"Damn right. And what about your father? You said it yourself; he's one hard-nosed bastard. And, if anything, he's the more antagonistic of the two."

"Yes, but I think if Grandpa could be made to see the sense of it, Dad'd come along." Yes, she thought, I know Dad will follow his father. And he'll follow me. "Don't forget, both of them are hurting at the thought of ending their careers. My Grandpa would rather die than end his days as a salesman of harmless backyard squibs."

She seized his hands across the table. For a while they were in deep thought, hearts and minds on parallel lines.

"Ultimately," he said finally, "the old buggers just like letting off big fireworks."

"So," she cried, breaking out into practicality, "I think the way to their hearts is through my mom and Maria."

"My mom and yours? Hmm..." He was feeling an uplift of spirit as her ideas settled into his mind. "I agree. Damn sure if I suggested this to Nonno he'd tear me to shreds. He's not listening to anything I say these days. But Mama..."

"I could probably soft-soap Grandpa, but I think Mom would do it better."

"So, bring on the daughters-in-law!"

☆☆ ⭐ ☆☆

Julia and Angela were at the sink in the kitchen; she was washing pans and Julia was drying and putting away. Bob and Alfred had gone through to the living room, continuing a silence that had lasted through dinner.

"He's so sad," sighed Angela as the kitchen door closed. "It's as if his whole life is finished. Remember how... vital he used to be? He should still be going around lighting things."

"There is a way out of this Mom," whispered Julia, seizing the moment. "There really is!"

"Well, I don't see it."

"Amalgamation with Pastorelli." There, it was out! And it hung there in space between them for what seemed an age, like a poltergeist's brick.

"*What?* What are you *talking* about, girl?" Julia tried to hush her with her hands. "Join the enemy?"

"But, *are they* the enemy?" asked Julia is a lower voice. "Are they really?"

"We've been in competition with them ever since we got here," hissed Angela as she passed Julia the last saucepan.

"Competition, yes. But that's not warfare for God's sake."

"I can't imagine your grandfather would even think of it." She squeezed out the sponge, swiftly swiped it across the counter and made to leave the kitchen. "Let alone your dad!"

Julia seized her arm gently causing her to pause and turn slightly.

"Think of the advantages, Mom! One dedicated facility for making and selling the domestics; one dedicated facility for the shows. We couldn't spend the insurance money on rebuilding, even if it was possible, but we *could* pour money into upgrading and expanding Pastorelli's site. And then Grandpa could fire off shells again!"

"You've got a point," Angela paused a moment in thought. "But Pastorelli wouldn't even consider it anyway."

Here was Julia's treacherous ground, but she had thought this through with some care.

"I have heard," she said slowly, "that Pastorelli are hurting financially, and are contemplating bankruptcy."

"*Where* have you heard?" asked Angela intrigued.

"Since dealing with them, I've... picked up things..."

Angela looked at her daughter long and hard, but saw only an enthusiastic innocence.

"Well," she concluded. "I *can* see the advantages... It needs thinking about."

"No, Mom," Julia cried, then quickly glanced at the closed door. "It needs *doing!*"

"You are serious about this, aren't you?" Angela was intrigued.

"Look Mom, I don't mean to be disloyal, but I don't think Dad would give this the time of day. But Grandpa... he might. I think he and Emilio Pastorelli should meet and talk. I know he'd like him if he got to know him better."

"How ever would you know who he would like or dislike?"

"I hear things... You know, what people say... Anyway, what harm is there in at least having them meet and talk?"

"You know, Julia," said Angela slowly, "I think you are a very clever girl."

☆ ⭐ ☆

Nonno had gone up to his room and Rocco and Maria were sitting in the living room after supper. She was knitting something, a craft she performed almost without conscious thought, the finished work extending in steady increments while she talked or watched the TV.

"I know what you're thinking, my boy," said Maria quietly. "It's hard to handle when he's like this, isn't it? He's coming on eighty-three..."

"Mama, we're going bust and he knows it. There's no way I can say it clearer. And it breaks my heart that he's gonna see it happen, because he's still sharp as a tack."

"Well," she sighed, "unless an angel comes down from on high, that's the reality of it."

"There is one sure-fire way out of the hole." Here it comes, he thought, here's where the match hits the leader fuse. "Amalgamate with Catesby."

"*What!* Join the enemy?" She couldn't believe what she was hearing.

"Hush," he warned. "His hearing's shot, but you never know. See, they're not really the enemy, are they? Nonno has set it up that way, but right now we're cooperating, aren't we?"

"Oh, yes, and wasn't your Nonno mighty pissed that you didn't consult with him first?"

"He would've refused, you know that," replied Rocco dully. "And I was kinda touched when they asked us."

"Ye-e-s, 'they' being the daughter, I would guess? What's her name; yes, Julia."

"And the old guy. He was there as well!" he replied, hardly convincing her at all. "But when you look at it," he continued, "right now they're hurting."

"So what? We join them and we all go down together?"

"No, no. Look, they're not allowed to rebuild because of city zoning regulations, okay, but they have oodles of insurance money. So why not have them pour their cash into our facility? It's win-win Mama!"

Her initial skepticism was turning. "That's right, they can't rebuild. So, all they're left with is their domestic facility in Hawkesbury. So we would get all their show business, wouldn't we? What's wrong with simply taking over all their contracts?"

"Yeah, Nonno would love it. But we don't have the capacity—couldn't do it if we wanted to—and the way our accounts look right now, there's no way in hell the bank would underwrite us. But with the Catesby money..."

"We could expand," she finished, "more staff, more production capability..."

"Exactly!" he cried. "And here's the kicker; we could start to make and fire *all our own stuff* again. Wouldn't that give Nonno a boost?"

"You know, Rocco," said Maria slowly, "I think you are a very clever boy."

☆ ☆ ☆

Angela pondered Julia's great idea for some time, but she was reluctant to open the subject with Bob. She just didn't know enough about whatever had caused the vendetta between the families in the first place. Whatever it was, she knew it was far from trivial. Perhaps, she thought, I could first approach Emilo's daughter. Angela was owed some time from work, so why not take a day off next week; sort of scout out the territory?

Maria heard the phone from the backyard; she rose from pulling the last beans of the year, went quickly through to the kitchen and picked it up on the fourth ring.

"Hi, it's Angela Catesby. I know this comes sort of out of the blue, but would you like to meet for a coffee... or... or something..."

Maria was mystified. Why would the enemy want to meet and be sociable? No, she must stop that. It wasn't right to call them that, and she often wished Emilio wouldn't. In truth, she knew nothing about them, and they were very likely to be just... well... people.

"I... I'd like that very much," she replied, still recovering a little from the surprise. "When?"

"Well, I don't know how you're fixed. How about early next week?"

"Well... sure. Anywhere you fancy?"

"How about the Casa Capri, on Beech?"

"Yes, there's a terrace. If it's a nice day," she replied, sounding she thought slightly inane.

"Around eleven on Monday?"

"Sure, see you there," and she hung up the phone, not quite so mystified now. Things were clicking together...

The Casa Capri was only about a five minute walk away, so on the appointed day Maria finished her gardening, then washed and went upstairs to put on something a little dressier. Jeans and T-shirt wouldn't do.

There was only one single, middle-aged lady sitting out on the terrace, and even if it was a little before 11:00, Maria approached the table with a smile. Angela rose and came forward, and the two women appraised each other, slightly warily.

"It's very nice to finally meet you," said Angela as they sat down on each side of a wood-topped bistro table shaded by a large Martini & Rossi umbrella.

"And you too." Maria's wariness was dissolving into curiosity. Rocco had been urging her to consider an amalgamation, and here was Angela Catesby obviously on the same mission. Her daughter Julia must have got at her as well. She smiled broadly, recognizing a put-up job. It was some sort of telepathy that told Angela what was going through Maria's mind, and she laughed out loud. Maria joined in, and for a while it was all chuckles and smiles while the waiter stood patiently beside the table awaiting their pleasure.

"Oh, what a pair of monkeys," smiled Maria after the waiter finally left with their orders. "I feel totally manipulated!"

"Me too!" laughed Angela.

Maria and Angela took to each other very easily. They had common backgrounds, both having wedded firework nuts, and it turned out that any differences of ethnicity and upbringing were trivial. They were two women speaking the same bodily and cultural language, and also sharing the same problem.

"Let's have them do what we're doing right now," suggested Angela. "Let's get the two old guys together and watch the chemistry."

"Risky, I'd say," replied Maria doubtfully. "The antagonism goes real deep, and it's long-standing. Talk about chemistry;

that's fire and flash powder, that is."

"Tell me," entreated Angela. "What's at the root of it? How did all this happen?"

The other woman sighed deeply, and it appeared as if she was about to launch into a speech when their cappuccinos arrived. Some minutes were spent in stirring in sugar, spooning off foam and sipping the results. Angela was all too aware that the delay was not unwelcome, as Maria appeared reluctant to continue.

"Well?" prompted Angela, licking the foam from her lips in a way that would have had Rocco marveling at the ramifications of genetics and nurture.

"It's stupid really. But then again, these things usually are, aren't they?"

Angela nodded and waited.

"When you first came to East Gladstone," Maria resumed, "in the early nineties, Emilio thought right away that it was a deliberate move to put him out of business..."

"But it doesn't matter where you are..."

"No, wait, please let me finish. You see, from what I can glean, his family had some sort of terrible incident at the end of the war, and it was to do with English soldiers. We don't know any more than that, and we probably never will. So, when Mr Catesby met Emilio, not long after you had moved here, there was an immediate dislike. Competition firstly, then the English accent tipped the balance. That's all. Irrational, I know, but it escalated..."

"He's never talked about it. Bob. Always evades the issue. But Alfred's fully wedded to the idea; you as the enemy."

"And that's the way it developed, year after year. And it's so senseless..."

"Well, we can end it right here. It's trickling down; our kids have obviously built a bridge, and now we're building another. One more to go!"

"A bridge too far?" asked Maria doubtfully.

"No," was the forceful reply. "We'll do this!"

"So!" Maria rubbed her hands together. "How do we do it?"

"Well," replied Angela slowly, "from what you say, I think if we were to persuade Emilio to mend fences, Bob would probably go along. And if Bob went along, I know my husband would."

"But I can't see just sitting down with Nonno and putting it on the line," replied Maria. "No way he'd go along with it. He's such an intractable old bastard. Oops, sorry, but you know what I mean."

"I know what we'll do," cried Angela. "We'll organize a garden party. Just tell both families we're getting together. That's all. He'd hardly baulk at a garden party if he doesn't know the hidden agenda. What do you think?"

"I think that might just work. Let's have another cappuccino."

☆ ⭐ ☆

Angela had decided to jump the gun and get her father-in-law on side right away. Bob Catesby immediately saw the sense of an amalgamation when Angela had raised the idea out in the back garden on a sunny Saturday morning. She was surprised at how quickly he took to the suggestion, although she had centered her disquisition on a future scenario wherein he was again launching fireworks; his own fireworks. She had watched him, there under the apple tree, change from a sad, morose old man to one with spring in his whole body, and a twinkle in his eye.

"I think it'll work, sweetheart," Bob nodded. "Yup. It's a winner. You're a genius."

"Oh, it's not me! God forbid. It's that manipulating granddaughter of yours and her new friend Rocco Pastorelli."

"Re-a-ally? Well, well, well. As Our Nan used to say, 'ooder fought it'?"

Bob was sold, but she figured that was the easy bit. Alfred was next.

"Hey, you two!" she shouted into the house. "Come out into the garden. There's something we have to talk about."

Julia had come over for breakfast—although she hadn't eaten any—and knew that something was afoot as soon as Mom invited her. She emerged from the house first, and seeing her mother and a newly sprightly Grandpa, realized that some magic had already been done. She smiled at him and he rose from the chair, enfolding her in his arms. Alfred came through the back door just as this scene was playing out, a wondering look on his face.

"Alfred, sit down," Angela commanded. "Now, Julia has had a great idea, and Bob agrees, and we know you will too." His face took on a deeper level of puzzlement and he remained standing.

"Dad," cried Julia. "We want to amalgamate with Pastorelli!" There, it was out of the pipe and in the air. Lift charge blown, passfire burning, burst charge seconds away.

Four, three, two, one... Alfred slumped down into the remaining chair his face a study in surprise. He said nothing, but all three present could see the wheels turning. Finally, after an elastic minute that stretched for ever, he nodded very slightly.

"Well, what d'you think, Alf?" asked Bob as he saw the gears cease their grinding.

Alfred shook his head slowly, reluctant to come to the same conclusion but clearly seeing the way it must inevitably go.

"Backed into a corner, really, aren't we?"

"No, Dad," cried Julia. "No! It's not like that. It's good for all of us." She looked him right in the eye and, since their little dinner together, he was able to reciprocate, meeting her level gaze. One serving of Hungarian goulash and two carafes of Buzbağ had done what years of close family contact had failed to do. Now, just like Dad, he was soft on her, and he liked it. Here was salvation for his pride; amalgamation meant equal partnership and it staved off the humbling horror of failure. And he even forgave his daughter and the other two for ganging up on him.

"Yeah," he sighed as their eye contact broke. "It'll work, and you're right; it's good for all of us."

"Oh, Dad, I'm so glad you agree," cried Julia kneeling beside the chair and hugging him. "It couldn't work if you weren't happy with it."

"I'm happy with it if you are." And his gaze encompassed all three of them. Yes, he was happy. He had met the Pastorelli boy and had approved in his own way.

"The remaining hill to climb is Emilio Pastorelli, of course," observed Angela bringing the party back to earth.

"You don't know the background, any of you, do you?" asked Bob into a contemplative silence. Now was the time to unburden himself; it had been long in coming.

"All I know is," replied Alfred, "that the guy goes out of his way to be unpleasant."

"Some of that may be me..." Bob began. "No, no, wait. Hear me through. It was when we first got here. I mean, the reason we came to East Gladstone in the first place was because of the by-laws. You remember how we looked around, eh Alf?"

"Sure. The town council here were easy with the move. Well, Pastorelli had got here first of course, so they had precedent. It was very easy to set up, and the business development office were all for it. Of course, that's all water under the bridge now."

"No need to dwell on it. Thing is, there we were, all set up and a going concern, and I finally run into Emilio Pastorelli; some swah-ray for the city's business folk. He's over in a corner by himself, so I go over and I introduce myself, all innocent like. And he turns on me. Just turns on me. Should ha' seen the look on his face! He says to me–I can remember it exactly–'You limey bastard, why don't you fuck off back where you came from?' Sorry, Julia, but that's exactly what he said."

"Oh, come on Grandpa!" she cried. "Think I've never hear the word fuck before? It's used in every single part of speech in the English language, for fuck's sake."

He smiled, slightly deflected from his track, while the other two chuckled. "Then there was some stuff about English soldiers, and the war, and I don't know what. Raving, he was, but in a whisper. See, it was obviously something he'd been carrying around for years, and our outfit moving into town must have set him off."

"So, his antagonism goes 'way back," observed Alfred, "and is clearly nothing to do with you in particular."

"Well, not to begin with. See, I should have just shut up and walked away, or maybe even tried to reason with him. Apologized maybe. Instead, I made it worse. P'raps it was the shock, maybe all the free booze... whatever. Anyway, I started slagging him off, telling him what an arsehole he was, and then he takes a swing at me!"

"What, he hit you?" asked Angela aghast. "In a party with all those people?"

"Yup. Glancing blow 'cos I saw it coming. Couldn't believe it. By this time there's all sorts of people staring at us, so I did an end run into the toilet."

"So you still think," said Angela slowly, "that you can patch things up? After that?"

He nodded. "There's stuff on both sides. If I were to go up to him, right off the bat, and say I was sorry I'd insulted him, we might just pull it off."

"Worth a try," observed Alfred. "Pride's the thing at stake. When and where to do it?"

"Here's an idea," began Angela as if the great idea had just arrived new-formed. "We have a nice garden party and we invite the Pastorellis. How could they refuse?"

She knew Maria wouldn't, Julia new Rocco wouldn't, and all three knew that Emilio would be obliged to toe the line.

☆⋆ ⭐ ☆⋆

Keyed-up didn't come close to the feeling among all members of the fireworks garden party klatch. It was the following Saturday, a late September mercy where the sun scintillated on the lake and the leaves celebrated in emerald, gold and crimson. Six of the party were keyed-up because they were all *au courant* and knew that the whole thing hinged on the seventh. And the seventh was all keyed-up because the last thing he wanted to do was sit down and eat and drink and talk with the fucking limey Catesby bastards. He had been brought reluctantly, swearing that he would sample no food and speak no words, but if they wanted him along, those were the terms. In truth, he had sussed out exactly what was going on, but he was goddamned if he'd make it easy for them.

No sooner had the Pastorelli family station wagon pulled into the drive, than Bob Catesby was there helping them out of the car, detaching Emilio and ushering him away. It was very clear to the witnesses of this abduction that the elder Pastorelli went with great reluctance, and that only the insistence of the elder Catesby propelled him along. They went together down to the end of the yard where it met the fence and the beach, and were seen engaged in lively conversation. The party standing around the barbecue at the top end of the garden made studious attempts to ignore them; a bit like turning your eyes away when elephants are mating.

The barbecue was sizzling, hot dogs and hamburgers were well underway, and a folding side table offered paper plates, silverware and a range of fixings. A cooler chest was filled with beer, wine and soft drinks, while a lonely but forlornly hopeful magnum of Champagne was wrapped in a tea towel as if embarrassed to be seen undressed. There were beer, wine and soft drink glasses on the table, but the Champagne flutes were notably absent, still in their box, skulking under the folds of the tablecloth.

Rocco took Julia's hand in a nonchalant gesture that all the others picked up on, and she smiled up into his face, tightness in her eyes. Amalgamation on several levels hung in the balance of the next few minutes, and the tension was becoming unbearable. Conversation petered out. Even the hotdogs and hamburgers appeared to have paused in their sizzling, waiting with bated fat as if in anticipation of the outcome.

The young couple moved slowly away from the group, Julia leading, both feeling the need to be alone. When they were at the far side of the garden, almost hidden by fruit bushes, she turned to him and held him as tightly as she could. He wrapped his arms around her, feeling her shaking, trembling with tension and nearly in tears.

"I can't stand this," she whispered. "I just can't stand it. Why did I think this was such a good idea? What if they don't...? You shouldn't have let me..."

"Stop! Enough! It's in the lap of the gods. You can't do a damned thing, so just stop." And, he thought, holding her tightly, if my mother's God shows even a shred of compassion or moral decency He'll intervene.

Down at the end of the garden there was a heated exchange taking place. Nobody watched, but everybody saw. There was much head shaking and hand waving; there were wide gestures of the arms, back-turning, more words and shrugs. At one point the disputants—as they appeared to be—walked away from each with gestures of dismissal. Then some words crossed the gap, heads turned, and again they were face to face. More words, more gestures. Time stretched in painful tension while the entire worlds of Pastorelli and Catesby stood poised in abeyance.

Nobody ever discovered what Bob Catesby had said to Emilio Pastorelli, or what Emilio had said in return. It really wasn't important. What was important was the vision of the two patriarchs—brilliant water behind them, trees in riotous colour above them—walking slowly back up the garden and laughing at some joke or comment.

The tension relaxed as if some mighty cosmic cord, wound to impossible tension, had suddenly snapped in the firmament.

"Oh, my God!" cried Julia, pushing away from Rocco and tilting her tear-stained face up to his. "It worked! It worked! Oh, my God, it worked!" He clasped her closely again, his face creased and grooved in smiles. While they hurried across the grass to join the others Julia quickly wiped her face, a huge grin chasing away the tears.

Angela quickly whipped the tea towel off the magnum, and Alfred hauled out the flutes. To six smiles, he popped the cork and poured. It was to everyone's surprise that Emilio himself proposed the first toast.

"Here's to a fuckin' limey bastard who's gonna warm my old age!" They all drank.

Bob followed swiftly with his own toast. "Here's to a crusty old curmudgeon who can't even swing a punch, but we're gonna make great fireworks together!"

Everybody laughed and drank again, although Julia just sipped hers. Then it was Alfred's turn.

"I'd like to toast the new company, so, here's to Catesby and Pastorelli!"

Emilio wasn't having any of that; he'd bent over enough already today, goddamn it. Hardly pausing to drink he cried, "Wait a minute! That's Pastorelli and Catesby to you!"

A little silence descended; it seemed as if the birds had stopped calling, no waves lapped on the lake, and the wind had found an ominous calm. Again, the hotdogs and burgers withheld their sizzle. The stillness dragged out.

"Fine!" cried Bob Catesby, breaking into the silence. "Here's to P and C!"

"To P and C!" they all echoed gladly.

"But," replied Alfred before they could raise their glasses again, "Catesby's in Hawkesbury remains Catesby and Son! It's our brand."

Another silence was broken, this time by Emilio. "Ah, what the hell, I'm too old to piss around. Long as I can make my own *studadas* and light up the *cielo* with 'em I'm happy. Goddamn backyard family Roman candle bullshit! You can keep it!"

So the little impasse was mercifully circumvented and Alfred chalked up a victory. They all laughed except Emilio who just cracked a sly smile. The food was ready, so Alfred served while they all got plates and drinks and spent some time in dressing their burgers and hotdogs, all of them rattling with conversation and release.

Emilio sat in the centre of the half circle of chairs, next to Bob, and ate and drank with an easing in his soul. Finally, in the extra innings of his life, some huge, lumpy wound-up thing inside him was letting go. His father being made a prisoner of war by the so-called liberators, separated from his wife and 15-year-old son, degraded and humiliated because he was caught jealously guarding a cache of explosives. Fireworks for celebration, for Christ's sake! The useless arguments, the months of misery, and all this at the hands of the people who are supposed to be on your side. Papa was never the same once they'd let him out of the camp; Emilio, the teenaged scion of the family tradition, absorbed as much as he possibly could of the firework lore before his father and then his mother slipped away.

But now, having unloaded all this travel-worn old luggage to his sworn enemy, the immutable past was giving way to a mutable and steerable future, and with it a new contentment was settling on him. In his mind's eye he could see his own handmade *studadas* lighting up the night sky of his life's end. It was good.

Bob, too, felt a sort of gentleness; an easing of a tension he never even knew he had possessed. And he, too, thought of explosion and fire and coloured light, and all the joys of creation he would share with his granddaughter.

And Alfred saw the road ahead, saw the two contented old guys and the happy younger generation, and concluded that it wasn't bad at all.

Eating caused a brief lull, then lively conversation sprang up again, to which Emilio contributed greatly. Rocco was delighted to hear some of the old stories, ones he hadn't heard for years. He sat next to Julia and she openly held his hand when it wasn't occupied with food or drink.

Alfred returned to the barbecue, flipping more burgers and peeling off waxed paper. "Come on, my love," he called to Julia, "you're falling behind. Have another burger." He held the smoking meat out on the end of the spatula, open bun in the other hand.

"No thanks, Dad," she replied. "Had enough for now."

"Here, Rocco! I bet you're game for another." It was wonderful how easily he could slip into informality. Rocco! Enemy? Hah! He slid the burger onto the bun with a smile, and slipped it onto Rocco's waiting plate. The young man ate and drank in contentment while the old stories rolled around him.

In response to another tale of Emilio's, Bob embarked on one of his own. "I should tell you about the time Our Nan threw the empty cases on the fire. See, us kids, we used to collect dead cases, y'know, after Guy Fawkes, and she picked up the whole lot..."

By this time Julia and Rocco had begun to stroll hand-in-hand to the end of the garden, where they leant on the fence that looked out over the water. In the near distance a large pleasure yacht moved slowly out into the lake, a slight whisper of Dixieland jazz drifting across the water to them.

"It was a Brock's *Snowstorm*," she whispered to him.

"What? What are you talking about?"

"It's okay," she replied softly. "You'll hear it all soon enough anyway, but he'll swear it was a Pain's *Golden Rain*."

He shook his head in mute incomprehension. She looked up

into his eyes.

"Oh, thank God this whole crazy idea worked out." She put her arm around his waist while his arm circled her shoulder. "Somebody up there's looking out for us." She was going to say more but a kiss intervened.

"Look at those two," observed Maria from her chair near the barbecue. "The way they behave you wouldn't know they'd only met such a short while ago."

"Yes," agreed Angela. "It's surprising, isn't it? They're so *comfortable* with each other, aren't they?"

"What a lucky chance," observed Maria, "that she persuaded your husband to borrow from us. Otherwise they'd never have met."

Bob Catesby briefly halted his tale of Our Nan and peered down the garden, a huge grin occupying the greater part of his face, but he didn't say a word.

Angela smiled at the happiness of her daughter; Maria smiled for the contentment of her son; Bob smiled just because life was such a complete friggin' hoot.

The young couple leant on the fence, lost in their long kiss, arms around each other, and quite oblivious of the barbecue observers up near the house, who were pointedly not watching.

Finally, she pushed back from him a little and was on the verge of telling him her little secret, when he forestalled her.

"Julia," he murmured, "this is the way it was meant to be. For us, I mean..."

"And...?" she asked, with a lift of an eyebrow, the corner of her mouth curved in a tiny smile.

His answer waited nascent in the wind and the water and the trees. They leant on the fence, heads together, while the light danced on the lake as the sun began its drop to the west.

"Will you... will you marry me?"

"Is it me you want, or just my bombshells?" she teased.

"I never did ask you about those, did I?" he smiled. "Well, will you?"

"With all my heart!"

"And the past stays past," he murmured.

"As I've told you," she replied quietly. "There's the two of us now, not just you."

Then she reached her lips up to his ear and whispered.

"Well, three really..."